THE FINE ART OF FAKING IT

BLUE MOON #6

LUCY SCORE

The Fine Art of Faking It

The book is a work of fiction. The characters and events in this book are fictitious. Any similarity to real persons, living or dead, is purely coincidental and not intended by the author.

Cover by Kari March

ISBN: 978-1-945631-24-5 (ebook)
ISBN: 978-1-7282-8267-1 (paperback)

Published by Bloom Books, an imprint of Sourcebooks
P.O. Box 4410, Naperville, Illinois 60567-4410
(630) 961-3900
sourcebooks.com

lucyscore.com

111021

DEDICATION

To Aunt Laurie and Uncle Jerry for never missing a book.

1

FIFTEEN YEARS AGO

The halls of Blue Moon High School were crowded with a sea of patchouli scented tie-dye. Long haired teens rocking Woodstock-reminiscent fashions meandered from class to class. The administration didn't like to rush anyone and provided a full ten minutes for students to find their way to their next educational obligation.

Eden Moody stood out from the retro crowd with her purple highlighted pixie cut, vegan leather pants, and a flannel tied carefully around her waist. It had taken her four tries to get it just right. Her cousin Moon Beam yammered away in her ear about how by next year she'd have boobs *and* Beckett Pierce. Eden was newly seventeen and already had what boobs Mother Nature had been generous enough to bestow on her.

She popped her locker open and checked to make sure her eye liner wasn't too smudged. Her eye makeup proudly skated the line between goth teen and grunge rock star. Her parents' tolerance of it was annoying.

"So, it's Beckett now?" Eden asked, only half-listening. Moon Beam Parker came from a long line of boy crazy women. Eden had a feeling her cousin would give Elizabeth Taylor a run for her money in the marriage department.

She traded her geometry book for a notebook and binder before slamming her locker door.

"He's sooo sexy," Moon Beam purred. At two days shy of sixteen and the freedom a learner's permit would provide, Moon Beam was a danger to herself. Eden hoped that her cousin's mother, Laura Beth, would make sure her daughter was immediately put on birth control.

Speaking of reasons for birth control, Eden's focus narrowed to one figure strolling down the hall. He was tall and lean, with a shock of chestnut hair that always fell across his forehead. His eyes were the same warm brown as his hair. Davis Gates, in his vintage bell bottom jeans and handwoven hooded tunic, was walking in slow motion toward her.

It probably wasn't *actual* slow motion, but that's just how he moved, like he was the star of a coming of age movie. Girls swooned and guys followed in his wake eager to learn the secret to being cool. Davis Gates ruled Blue Moon High School. He was the nice guy, the good guy. His haikus made even their poetry teacher Mrs. Letchworth sigh. He was the guy who set school records for the 100-yard dash *and* gentle sheep shearing. And in art class? *Gah.* The man was a teenage DaVinci. While ninety percent of the class was smearing finger paints on canvas, Davis was creating masterpieces in non-GMO acrylics.

He was perfect in every way.

And Eden's parents hated him.

"Hey there, Moody," Davis said, lifting his dimpled chin in her direction. He had stubble, baby fine, patchy stubble on his sharp jaw. He was basically a man, Eden decided.

He stopped in front of her, those warm brown eyes

studying her as if she were the only teenage girl in the hall. A thrill prickled the hair on her arms to standing.

"Gates," she said, her tone blasé even though she could feel her heartbeat in her head.

He gave her that kinda shy, kinda sexy grin. "I saw that spin move you pulled on Birkbeck in gym this morning. Pretty awesome."

Blue Moon High School spent nine weeks of the school year on ballroom and line dancing and two weeks on self-defense.

Eden felt a little thrill roll through her at the thought of Davis watching her during gym class. "He told me I hit like a girl."

"So you kicked him in the chest." Davis nodded his approval. "You're pretty badass."

Eden's heart soared into the atmosphere. *The cute guy she liked thought she was badass.* This was better than getting her drivers license.

"Thanks," her voice squeaked and she coughed to cover it up.

"I don't want you to think that your bad-assedness wasn't enough. But a couple of us wanted to make sure he learned his lesson. So we hid his clothes and replaced them with something a little more fitting."

Just then Pond Birbeck, wearing a purple leotard with butterfly wings sewn to the back, stormed by. Apparently, the "something more fitting" was the school's mascot costume.

"How's it going, Birkbeck?" Davis asked slyly.

"Fuck you, Davis." The Blue Moon Butterfly shot his middle finger into the air.

Eden and Moon Beam collapsed against her locker in a fit of laughter.

"Guess I better go apologize," Davis said with a wink. "See you in class."

"Cool." Eden choked the word out on a laugh.

She and Moon Beam enjoyed the view as he walked away.

"Oh, my God," Moon Beam purred. "He's *so* into you! 'See you in class,'" she said, mimicking Davis's post-puberty baritone.

Eden tucked her hair behind her ear. "Do you think?" She needed a second opinion. All signs were pointing to Davis flirting with her. But there was always the possibility that her hormones were scrambling her brain. She'd had a front row seat to her sister's high school hormonal parade.

"Totally." Moon Beam's sigh filled the emptying hallway with a cloud of longing. "I wish Beckett would look at me that way. So, when are you going to break the news to your parents that you are going to have ten thousand babies with Davis Gates, thereby destroying their souls?"

Eden had two excellent reasons for being attracted to Davis. The obvious: smart, sexy, funny, really, really, really good-looking.

But the bonus—the whipped cream, cherry, and sprinkles on top—was the fact that her parents enthusiastically detested his entire family. The Moodys and the Nuswings—now Gateses—had been feuding for approximately a million years over something stupid that none of them could remember correctly. Her parents took the feud so seriously, the only thing she'd ever been forbidden from doing was befriending Davis "Demon Spawn" Gates.

Her parents should have known better. Eden was a rebel starved for a cause. She now knew exactly how many seconds it would take her to climb from her bedroom window and shimmy down the birch tree to freedom despite the fact that she had no actual reasons for sneaking out... yet. But it couldn't hurt to have a plan in place should an opportunity worth sneaking out ever present itself.

In Blue Moon, it was nearly impossible to rebel. Everyone was annoyingly accepting. Davis was the only forbidden fruit Eden had encountered. Her first recollection of him was their parents arguing over who got to the kindergarten registration table first. While her mother called his mother a sell-out yuppie and his father poked hers in the chest with an index finger, Eden had smiled shyly at Davis who, even at five, seemed immune to the drama.

"I have to get him to go out with me first. If I'm going to get in trouble, it's going to be for something that I did, not just *hoped* to do," Eden reminded Moon Beam.

"You're so wise," Moon Beam sighed.

"I'd better get to class." Eden was in a hurry to slide into the seat next to Davis. When serendipity—and Ms. Charisma Champion—had assigned her to the stool at the beginning of the year, she knew it was a sign. Eden waved a cheerful goodbye to her cousin and clomped down the hallway, slipping through the classroom door a second before the chimes sounded.

Serendipity had not only put her on the stool next to Davis in Household Management and Partnerships it had magically paired them to be pretend life partners for a class project. Ms. Champion walked students through the boring everyday pieces and parts that made up an adult life in an attempt to teach teenagers how to navigate relationships. Unit chapters included: Developing a fifty-fifty division of household responsibilities, crafting budgets, strategizing conflict resolution scenarios, and creating "bucket filling" lists for both couples and the individual members of said couples.

It would have been a total snoozefest, except for the fact that she was in a fake domestic partnership with Davis Gates.

On paper, Eden and Davis were an unmarried—Eden approved the unconventional approach to a relationship—winemaker (Davis) and indie rock music marketing executive (Eden) who lived frugally, traveled extensively, and budgeted $65 a month for movie and concert dates. Eden liked that pretend grown-up partner Davis didn't try to convince her to get a more realistic job or do the laundry. She felt it boded well for their future, real-life relationship.

Sure. Real life Eden would have preferred to find a smoky-eyed guitarist or a pierced-eyebrowed delinquent. But it was good-guy, do-right Davis who made her heart flip-flop in her chest.

Now, she just needed to convince him to ask her out.

2

"Now, if everyone will take a look at the scenario sheets I just handed out," Ms. Champion droned from the front of the classroom. Her frizzy dark hair hung like the heavy velour parlor curtains in Aunt Nell's dusty mansion on the outskirts of town.

Davis's shoulder brushed Eden's as he leaned in to read the handout. Eden's body was already in overdrive, as was usual for the forty minutes they spent together in class. She could smell his deodorant, the yummy, store-bought kind.

"Hmm," he said, skimming the paper. "It says here, we're supposed to 'enter into a conflict about one of us siding with their family and the other one holding grudges and refusing to communicate.'"

Eden wiggled a little closer to him at the lab table until her knee pressed against his.

"Sorry," she said, pretending she'd invaded his space accidentally.

He looked at her, their faces so close she could have rubbed the tip of his nose with her own.

"It's okay," he said with that shy smile.

Eden cleared her throat. It wouldn't be a good idea to throw herself into his arms and kiss the crap out of him in front of their entire class. Her parents would definitely hear about it and ship her off to Aunt Martha's commune. "Uh, so which one of us is the grudge-holder and which one is the family pleaser?" Staring into those caramelly depths, she couldn't imagine ever holding a grudge against Davis Gates, or choosing her family over him.

"Let's flip for it," he decided.

The quarter Davis fished out of his pocket determined that she was the grudge-holding poor communicator while he was the spineless mama's boy.

They bickered and bantered, crafting their argument script—Ms. Champion was big on role-playing—and within thirty minutes Eden was satisfied that they'd created a believable argument.

"Sometimes I think freedom is wasted on adults." Eden shook her head. "I mean, can you imagine us being together and actually having arguments like this instead of going to piano bars and taking spontaneous trips to the beach?" she scoffed.

Davis flipped his hair off his forehead. "If we were together, I doubt I'd be trying to convince you to not put up a fight when my mother refuses to let you be in the family Christmas picture." His voice was husky and low.

Eden's heart took flight in a triple axel in her chest. "And I definitely wouldn't be giving you the silent treatment and slamming doors."

Their bodies were aligned to each other, heads cocking, knees brushing, eye contact holding. She held her breath.

"Maybe we know more than the adults?" Davis breathed.

"Seriously." Eden nodded. "Look at us. We're the only members of both families mature enough to not feud."

She watched his Adam's apple work. Eden turned back to her notebook. "So, uh. Are you going to the HeHa dance Saturday?" she asked as casually as the adrenaline exploding in her veins would allow.

What she really wanted to know was: *Do you have a date for the HeHa Dance?*

"I'm planning on it," he said. "You?"

She gave a little shrug of the shoulder closest to him. "Yeah. Probably." Eden bit her lip, closed her eyes, and took the plunge. "Maybe we should go together?"

He rubbed his palms on his thighs. "That would really freak our parents out," he hedged.

Eden rested her chin on her hand coyly. "Only if they knew."

He nodded and stared at the lab table for nearly a full minute, during which Eden didn't draw a breath. "You know I like you, right?" Davis blurted the words out.

Eden wasn't sure which reaction to go with, the one where the doors to her vulnerable heart exploded open to reveal a heavenly choir singing, or the one that was skirting the edge of supreme disappointment and humiliation. He liked her. *Yay!* But he sounded like he was gearing up to let her down gently. *Agony.*

"I hope so, seeing as how we're in a committed domestic partnership," Eden joked, drumming her pencil on their role-playing script.

He gave a choked laugh. "I'm serious. I really like you. I just don't want to piss off my parents. They still pay for my car insurance and the roof over my head. And they're thinking about letting me apply to some East Coast schools instead of just West Coast wine country colleges..."

Eden let the words settle. West Coast colleges? She hadn't factored that into her Eden and Davis Fall in Love plan. Him migrating the whole way across the country could be a problem. That wasn't in her family's budget. Heck, if she didn't get her shit together in the math and science areas she was going to have to cook up a miracle to pay for a state school.

How were they going to start their life-long love affair on opposite ends of the country?

It was a problem she'd solve later. First, she had to convince him to be in a relationship with her right now.

"Do you *want* to go to the dance with me?" she asked finally.

Davis reached over to where her pencil had left a staccato splatter of lead dots and covered her hand with his. "I really do."

Zing! "Then maybe no one has to know. My parents never go to the dance and neither do yours. We could show up separately, dance in the corner, maybe throw in a dance or two with other partners so no one's any the wiser... It would be like a secret date."

The only thing better than a relationship with Davis was a secret relationship with Davis. They would be like a modern-day version of Romeo and Juliet. Only smarter and with better communication skills... and fewer suicides.

"You'd be willing to do that?" he asked, perking up.

"Yes!" She said it a little too loudly and the neighboring lab table partners turned to stare at them.

He nodded slowly. "Yeah. Okay. Let's do this. I'll meet you there."

"I'll be your secret date," Eden whispered. She was so excited she was surprised that she didn't rocket right off her lab stool and into the stratosphere.

She was going out on a secret date with Davis Gates. Her dream was coming true.

All they had to do was make sure their parents never found out.

3

"I see you making those eyes!" Eden's mother snapped, elbowing her in the ribs.

"What eyes?" Eden asked innocently, breaking Davis's gaze from across the sidewalk. They were in One Love Park, Blue Moon's center, mere hours away from her first dance with her one true major crush. She and her parents were manning the coat donation booth in the freezing December weather while Davis was bundled up, volunteering at the book donation tent twenty feet away.

Her mother shoved a garbage bag of winter wear into her arms.

"You stay away from the Gates family. And that includes their demon spawn," her mother said, pointing a finger in Eden's face. Lilly Ann Moody was a kind, generous spirit in all areas of her life except one. As far as she was concerned, the Gates family could rot in hell. The decades-old feud that began who knows when over who knows what had only escalated in recent years with each generation committing to public hatred. "That boy's mother sabotaged my entry in last year's casserole contest!" Lilly Ann announced.

Eden and her sister had had to listen to the story on a daily repeat since then.

"Mom, maybe the judges just weren't a fan of your Tuna Surprise It's Tofu Casserole," Eden suggested.

Lilly Ann's gasp nearly leveled her.

"I'm not getting peaceful vibes from you two," Eden's father, Ned, called in a sing-song tone from the opposite side of the tent. He lifted one of the ear flaps on his furry hat. "Do we need to hug it out?"

"Your daughter is mooning over that Gates ruffian," Lilly Ann announced, neatly tossing Eden under the bus even as she accepted a pink parka from Mrs. Nordemann with a sweet smile.

Eden winced at her father's shrill, "Over my deceased corpse!"

"I've been watching them all afternoon," Lilly Ann said. "Eden, sweetie, dating that boy is literally the only thing in the world you could do to hurt your family."

Mrs. Nordemann looked as though she were taking notes.

"Lilly Ann," Atlantis, Eden's older sister, cautioned. Atlantis was a cool adult who had called their parents by their first names since preschool. She wore her baby in a paisley sling tied around her chest. "Telling Eden not to do something is basically like begging her to do it under penalty of death."

"What do you expect me to do?" Lilly Ann demanded, dropping dramatically into the folding metal chair behind the coat collection table, her overstuffed down coat letting out a whoosh of air. "You want me to sit back and just ignore the fact that my own daughter is willing to accept decades of abuse, years of terror?"

Abuse was a bit of a strong word. Sure, the Gates family stole parking spaces right out from under the Moodys, didn't hold doors for them, and had once even flipped Eden's parents the middle finger at a junior high band concert. But, to be fair, that was after Lilly Ann had slapped the video camera out of Tilly Nuswing-Gates's hand during Davis's bongo solo. Eden's parents were not innocent victims. They'd done their share of bad things to the Gates family. Eden's father had stolen the Sunday newspaper off of the Gateses' front porch for an entire year before he was caught in his pajama pants in their front yard at 4 a.m.

Sheriff Hazel Cardona had been nice enough to give him a warning and a ride home.

While her mother and sister argued their points, Eden's gaze slid back to the book donation stand. Davis was hefting two reusable totes full of paperbacks, and she wished he wasn't wearing the heavy gray winter coat so she could admire his biceps as they strained under the load.

"Look at her! She's practically salivating," Lilly Ann shrieked.

Her father grabbed her mother's hands. "We'll send her away to live with Aunt Martha on the commune," he suggested. "They'll labor the Gates out of her there."

Eden rolled her eyes. Her mother's sister lived on a commune in Michigan that raised goats and sheep. If she were sent there, there was no hope that she'd turn out remotely normal.

Movement at the book stand caught her attention. Ferguson and Tilly Gates had arrived. Tilly had dirty blonde hair cut in a stylish pixie look. She had tattoos on both wrists and ankles and a degree in environmental conservation. Her husband Ferguson was a handsome man with monogrammed sweaters and a trust fund from a winery family in California. They'd met when Tilly was hitchhiking cross country the summer after she graduated. Together, they'd started the Blue Moon Winery, the first organic winery in upstate New York.

Eden felt the Gateses' success only added fuel to the feud. Especially after her mother's garage-based custom incense business failed. While the Gateses wore organic cashmere coats, the Moody family bundled into hand-me-down puffy coats and hand-knit caps.

Eden tried to catch Davis's eye, wanting to share a secret wink over the ridiculousness of their parents, but he was talking to his father.

Tilly on the other hand was staring her down like she was a wild animal charging down the woman's family. Her expression was clear: *Stay. Away.*

Eden raised a hand and waved awkwardly. "What are you doing?" Lilly Ann hissed. She shoved Eden's hand down and positioned herself between her daughter and her mortal enemy's scowl.

"Why don't you mind your own business, Tilly?" Lilly Ann called across the wide sidewalk.

"Why don't you keep your daughter from staring at my son like he's a piece of tofu casserole," Tilly suggested with a frosty tone.

"As if our Eden would be even remotely interested in your offspring." Eden's mother said "offspring" like it was a dirty, four-letter word. "Do you see what she did? She admitted to ruining my casserole!" Lily Ann hissed to her daughters.

"If your daughter knows what's good for her, she'll keep her eyes to herself," Tilly shrilled back.

Mr. Oakleigh, the town busybody and sweater vest connoisseur, bustled up with his wife Amethyst on his heels. They were each lugging bags. "Amethyst, my pearl, why don't you drop the coats off here with the Moodys while I hand over the Bobbsey Twins collection?" Mr. Oakleigh announced loudly to cover up the yelled insults flying between Eden's mother and Davis's.

"Helloooooo," Amethyst shouted as she dumped her two garbage bags on the table in front of Eden. "It's so lovely to see you all again!"

Lily Ann bobbed left and right trying to peer around Amethyst's slim shoulders, but the woman blocked her view. "Isn't it a wonderful day for HeHa?" Amethyst yelled.

It was twenty-seven degrees, and the freezing rain had just started again.

"Just wonderful," Atlantis agreed.

Eden heard Bruce commenting on the park's holiday decorations at full volume to the Gateses.

"Well, look at this collection of coats!" Phoebe Pierce towing her husband, John, wandered up to the coat stand. "We'll be keeping the whole town warm this year, won't we?" she asked with a pretty smile.

John was warm and farmerly in a worn flannel coat. He had his arm anchored around Phoebe's waist. None of the couple's sons were nearby. "How's everything going, Ned?" John asked. John Pierce was a calming influence, and Eden hoped he'd be able to squelch the argument before it came to blows... like at last year's Sit-In reenactment.

Eden's father quit his attempt to moon the Gateses—saving half the town from a view of his practically albino ass cheeks—and shook John's hand. "Great, John. Real great. How are your boys?"

"Mom! Can I borrow ten bucks?" Jax, the youngest Pierce boy, barreled up. He paused long enough to give Eden a flirtatious wink. He was a few years behind her in school, but the Pierce brothers were a danger to women of all ages.

"What did your father just tell you six minutes ago?" Phoebe sighed.

"He said no," Jax answered cheerfully.

Phoebe rolled her eyes heavenward. "Why did we have three boys again?" she sighed.

"Because you asked for girls," John grinned.

Lilly Ann's forced laughter was too loud. "Oh, John and Phoebe! You're *so funny*! No wonder you're *such good friends of ours*!"

To Eden's recollection, John and Phoebe Pierce had never once set foot in the Moody house.

"We'd *love* to come to dinner next week, Bruce!" Ferguson bellowed at full volume from across the way.

"We're *so* honored you would invite us!" Tilly chimed in.

Judging from Mr. Oakleigh's confused expression, no such invitation had been extended. In feuds as in war, gathering allies was an important part of the battle.

Eden felt a hot rush over her half-frozen skin and realized Davis was finally looking in her direction. She gave him a playful "aren't they insane" shrug. But he didn't smile, didn't acknowledge the family crazy that was spilling over into the HeHa festivities.

Nerves settled like an entire carton of ice cream in Eden's stomach.

4

"Damnit," Donovan Cardona, track star, son of Blue Moon's sheriff, and one of Davis's best friends, scowled at his lopsided bowtie in the bathroom mirror.

Davis snorted at his friend's disastrous attempt at neckwear as he carefully adjusted his own borrowed tie. He had a knack for it, he realized, straightening the knot. Though he doubted that skill would ever come in handy.

"Maybe just lose the bowtie?" Davis suggested.

"No." Donovan was adamant. He'd bet Carter Pierce ten bucks that he could show up to the HeHa dance in a nerdy bowtie and still score a dance with Llewellyn Chang, a notoriously high-maintenance, un-gettable senior, and he was determined to collect. Davis respected that.

He took pity on Donovan and made quick work of the bowtie.

"Thanks, man. So, you finally gonna put the moves on Moody?" Donovan asked, sliding a comb through his blond hair.

Davis skated a guilty glance at the still closed bathroom

door. Donovan and their friend Carter Pierce were the only people who knew about his feelings for Eden. And even they didn't know just how serious his crush was. "Don't say that name too loud. My parents will have a cow."

"You're eighteen. A man," Donovan insisted. "What are they going to do about it?"

Donovan's parents didn't have the golden guilt trip that Davis's did. His father's heart attack when he was a kid—a terrifying time for their family—still loomed like an ugly, dark cloud.

When he was being too enthusiastic with his bongo playing. *Don't upset your father.*

Every day of his learner's permit. *Are you trying to kill me?*

And, of course, after his mother's fender bender with a lamp post on Patchouli Street. *Let's just not tell your father about this. He doesn't need any more stress in his life.*

"It's complicated," Davis sighed.

"I'm just putting it out there. If you let your parents call the shots now, they'll be calling 'em for the rest of your life."

Davis really hoped his friend was full of shit.

"All I'm saying's you've been into this girl for freaking ever," Donovan continued, slapping on a healthy dose of Old Spice. Anything longer than a semester of school constituted forever at eighteen.

Davis had been peripherally aware of Eden since kindergarten. They'd once eaten an entire glue stick together before the teacher discovered them hidden away in the classroom's bean bag corner.

In junior high band, he'd been stationed behind the bongos when Eden had saved her friend from dreaded "fart mouth" after Pond Birkbeck had desecrated Layla's unattended trumpet mouthpiece. He'd applauded her bravery, along with the rest of the band, when Eden and Layla had pummeled Pond to the floor.

But he'd never forget the moment that he became aware aware of Eden Moody.

It was the end of the first day of school his junior year, her sophomore year. Davis had been behind the wheel of his third-hand El Camino fiddling with a Phish CD when he'd heard laughter through his open windows.

Fran, the mohawked bass player for any number of high school garage bands, gripped the armrests of her wheelchair and cackled with glee as Eden Moody gave her an enthusiastic push down the slight hill to the parking lot. Eden hopped on the back of the chair, her magenta highlights glimmering in the afternoon light, a smile brighter than the sun on her face. It wasn't some major aha moment like his mother was always talking about. It was more of a "yeah, that's the one" acceptance.

Eden had this sexy rebellious vibe going that the straight and narrow Davis found both terrifying and appealing. She wasn't worried about fitting in and doing what everyone expected of her. She was strong, exciting, and very, very pretty.

Eden wasn't like the other girls who were usually more than willing to flirt or date or hit a few bases in the back of his El Camino. Eden was different.

And then he'd remembered who her parents were. And who his parents were.

He hadn't been able to help himself, talking to her, flirting with her over the past few semesters. He liked her. She was funny and sarcastic and filled with this buzzing energy. He just wanted to be around her.

In deference to his parents, Davis had casually dated other girls. But his heart belonged to Eden. And now, he had this bright sliver of hope that he could both date her and not piss off his parents.

The bathroom door burst open, bouncing off of Donovan's shoulder. "Are you trying to give your father another heart attack?" Tilly Nuswing-Gates demanded, her mouth painted in an unforgiving frown.

"Geez, Mom!"

Donovan looked left and right for an escape route.

Davis lamented not locking the door. Sometimes he wondered if his father's heart attack all those years ago had been caused by Tilly scaring the ever-living crap out of him with one of her dramatic entrances. "What seems to be the latest crisis?" he asked, knowing exactly what it was.

She crossed her arms, blocking his escape. "I knew it! I just knew it the way you two were mooning over each other in the park today!"

Guilt settled like a bowling ball in his stomach.

"I think I'll head over early." Donovan the Coward squeezed past Tilly and ran for the hills in his perfectly straight bowtie.

"I know that you're planning to take that... that... that Moody girl to the dance," his mother sputtered with rage. "And I am telling you that you will do so over your father's corpse. You will literally kill him."

"Mom, aren't you being a little bit dramatic?" His father's heart attack had happened years ago. Since then, Tilly had badgered him into better health. Maybe it was time they stop tip-toeing and started being honest with each other.

"'A little bit dramatic'? Your father almost died and you insist on doing the *one* thing that will put him in his grave."

Tilly should have been a soap opera star. Her dramatic timing was magnificent. "Fine," Davis conceded. "Then let's not tell him. Hasn't this feud gone on long enough? She's a great girl. She's smart, she's funny."

"I can't believe you'd even consider going anywhere with her kind. Her parents are hoodlums. Her grandparents are practically circus freaks."

"Mom!"

"Davis!" His father bellowed from downstairs and Davis winced. News traveled fast in Blue Moon.

"What do you expect?" his mother hissed. "No one keeps secrets here."

"Davis!" His father sounded like a wounded animal ready to rampage.

"Shit." Davis followed his mother downstairs and prepared to face the music. He was a pretty low-maintenance son. He didn't bicker with his parents. There were no real power struggles. He was respectful, courteous. He kept his room clean. Paid for his own gas. He helped out at the winery every weekend without complaint. Maybe they could give him this one thing?

Ferguson's face was the color of the Harvard beets he was so fond of.

"I just got off of the phone with Enid Macklemore. You know what she told me?"

Davis rocked back on his heels. "I'm guessing it has something to do with the HeHa Dance," he hedged.

"She said that that mousy little Moody girl *asked you to the dance.*"

"Ferguson, your blood pressure," Tilly reminded him.

"Dad, it's not that big of a deal."

"*Not a big deal?* She's planning to humiliate you. It's all a joke. Even her parents are in on it," Ferguson shouted.

"Which is why, I've arranged for Davis to escort Taneisha

next-door," Tilly said, smoothly inserting herself into the conversation.

Davis whirled around. "Wait. What? And you did what?"

Tilly glanced at the clock on the wall. "You're picking her up in fifteen minutes."

"No. I'm not." It was the first time he'd defied his parents. They both looked at him with open mouths.

"What did you say?" His dad was working himself up to a full on hollering fit.

"Taneisha doesn't have a date and your date was an abomination," Davis's mother said primly. "She was just doing it to hurt you!"

Eden wouldn't do that. He knew she wouldn't. He'd spent the last year and a half getting to know her between classes. She might be gothy, but she was nice. Sincere. Cool. And he'd never once seen her go out of her way to hurt anyone... except for Pond Birkbeck.

"Davis, have your mother or I ever lied to you?"

He rocked back on his heels. "What about Santa Claus?"

"Oh, for the love of God," Ferguson exploded. "We said we were sorry about that."

"I was *nine* when Beckett Pierce finally told me the truth."

"Eden was going to humiliate you tonight," Tilly insisted. "We're doing this because we love you. I'm not letting that family play with your feelings like that!"

"She's not like that. I really like her, Mom." It was the wrong thing to say. His parents launched into a litany of complaints that spanned a good forty years. All the wrongs the Moodys had committed against their family.

While they one upped each other with allegations, Davis ducked into the kitchen and dialed Eden's number. He'd memorized it from a Business Club phone tree his junior year but had never had an excuse to call her before.

"Moody residence," a man chirped on the other end. "Ned speaking."

Davis plugged a finger into his ear to block out his parents. "May I speak to Eden, please... sir?"

"She's unavailable right now. She's getting ready for her date with... Buttercup, who did Eden say she's going to the dance with?"

"Jordan Catalano."

"Right. That Catalano boy."

Davis didn't know anyone in school by that name. All he knew was that was not his name. Had she given her parents a decoy date? Or was his mother right? Was Eden planning some kind of spectacular humiliation for him? His stomach dropped. He needed to find out.

"If you could just tell her Davis is on the phone—"

"Davis? As in Davis Gates the demon spawn of Ferguson and Tilly Nuswing-Gates?" Ned Moody shrieked.

"What does he want?" Buttercup—presumably Eden's mother, Lily Ann—shrilled in the background.

"Never call here again!" Ned snapped. "And if you so much as look at my daughter Atlantis—"

"Actually, it's Eden, sir."

"Either one of them!" Ned screamed and hung up without finishing his threat.

Davis stared down at the phone in his hand. He was a low-key kind of guy and in the last ten minutes, he'd had four adults scream him into submission. This did not bode well for his evening.

"Davis! Hurry up! You're going to be late picking up Taneisha," his mother called from the living room.

Shit. He'd give Taneisha a ride and then catch Eden at the dance and clear this whole thing up, Davis decided.

5

Eden snuck the small mirror out of her clutch and checked her lipstick in the blue and purple strobe lights of the high school gymnasium. She'd locked herself into her house's only bathroom for so long, her father threatened to climb in through the window to evict her.

But even rushed, she was satisfied with the end result. She looked good enough to be on Davis's arm tonight.

With as much of an outcast as she'd tried to make herself at school, there was still a part of Eden that was desperate for a *real* boyfriend who made her feel special and interesting and smart and fun no matter how rebellious or boring or unspecial she was. And that's exactly how Davis made her feel.

She just hoped the family drama from the afternoon hadn't scared him off. Davis hadn't been born with a desire to be contrary. Which meant, if he didn't like her enough to defy his parents, she could get hurt. Badly. She swallowed the lump of fear that closed off her throat.

But he *did* like her. She knew he did. And Davis was the ultimate good guy. She steadied herself with that thought. He wouldn't hurt her on purpose. Davis wasn't like the rest of his family.

Eden took a deep breath and smoothed her hands over the black lace of her dress. Everyone else was decked out in reds and greens and golds for the holiday season. But Eden liked the mystery of black, the sexiness of the short skirt. She'd see how tonight went. Maybe Davis Gates would be the one to finally relieve her of her virginity. In a few months, of course. Once she made sure he was worthy of it. Not that she was particularly attached to it. She just didn't want to give it away to any dumbass who wouldn't know what to do with it.

"Is he here yet?" Moon Beam hissed, shoving a cup of punch into Eden's nervous hands. Her cousin craned her neck to scan the gymnasium. Half of Blue Moon had turned out for the dance. The junior high schoolers stood in a line, swaying awkwardly to the music. There was a rowdy crowd of senior citizens dominating the center of the dance floor performing an enthusiastic group swing dance. Peppered in between were high school students and parents dancing, talking, and socializing.

"Not yet," Eden said, burying her nerves under a false bravado of confidence. "But he will be."

Moon Beam cracked her gum, eyes scanning the crowd for her next dance victim. "You don't think his parents grounded him for life after seeing you two making smoochy faces at each other in the park?"

Eden shrugged as her cousin voiced her worst fear. "Nah. I'm sure he just got hung up somewhere. He'll be here." Davis wasn't the kind of guy who lied or broke promises. He said he'd be here, so he'd be here.

"There he is!" Moon Beam pointed triumphantly toward the entrance to the gym.

And there he was. Tall and lean in an ill-fitting suit. His

red and green Santa tie stood out starkly from the white button down beneath, and that shock of hair that never behaved lay across his forehead just the way Eden liked it best. She felt her dopey smile start to spread. And then it froze.

"Is that Taneisha?" Moon Beam hissed, clamping down on Eden's arm.

Taneisha the willow-thin, model-like star of the girls track team was dressed in a green velvet dress. Her black hair was styled in dozens of tiny braids that coiled in a bun at the base of her neck. She was one of the nicest people in the entire school. And in Blue Moon, that was saying something.

But right now, Taneisha's hand was tucked under Davis's arm. And Eden was going to throw up.

"You should confront him," Moon Beam decided. "Maybe do one of those really dramatic slaps across the face."

It wouldn't be the last time Eden had listened to her instincts, or her cousin's bad ideas. She steamed across the rainbow- and paisley-painted gym floor fueled by rage and fear and the sliver of hope that there'd been some kind of stupid misunderstanding.

"Well, hello, Taneisha. Gates." She said their names like they tasted badly.

"Eden, I can explain," Davis said softly, putting himself between Eden and Taneisha.

"I'm going to go grab some punch," Taneisha decided wisely.

Eden took one slow breath, felt her nostrils flaring. "Explain what? That my parents are right and you're *demon spawn*?" People were looking at them and she didn't care.

He winced and shoved his hands into the pockets of his dress pants. His shoulders hunched at her outburst. "I know how this looks—"

"This looks like you said you'd be my date and showed up

to the dance with freaking Taneisha!" That beautiful unicorn of a girl who had unfairly escaped any of the awkwardness of puberty. Everyone around them had given up the pretense of dancing or talking and was watching with rapt attention.

"I'm sorry. I didn't want to hurt anyone. Especially not you, Eden," Davis started again, but Eden wasn't interested in apologies or excuses.

"And yet here we are. I'm alone and humiliated and you brought a teenage super model as your date."

"It's not what it looks like. My parents made me—"

"You know what. You're eighteen. No one made you do anything."

"Eden, it's not what you think. I tried to—"

"Whatever. At least I figured out that you're just like the rest of your family before I did something stupid. The jackass gene must be dominant in your family tree."

"Can't we talk about this?"

"I don't have anything more to say to you." There were tears clogging her throat. She liked him so damn much and she'd been so damn wrong. Eden brushed past him, pushed her way through the crowd that had gathered around them, and grabbed the first guy she recognized. Ramesh Goldschmidt was junior class president and had won an award for his hand-lettered protest signs.

"Let's dance, Ramesh," she said with feigned brightness.

Astute for a seventeen-year-old, Ramesh wisely shut his mouth and put his sweaty hands on her hips.

And while a glum-looking Davis stepped onto the dance floor with Taneisha, Eden plotted her revenge.

~

She lasted all of four minutes on the dance floor with Ramesh—a guy whose only crime was being not Davis—before excusing herself to the shadowy hallway outside the gym next to the janitor's closet.

Tears were hot on her cheeks. Her chest squeezed tight, a physical manifestation of emotional pain—as Blue Moon's guidance counselor liked to explain it with puppets.

The gym door opened. Holiday lights and upbeat music spilling out into her little dungeon of heartbreak, taunting her.

"Eden?"

Moon Beam spotted her and stepped into the dungeon-like hallway. Eden hastily wiped her eyes.

"Oh, man. I didn't know you like *liked him* liked him." Moon Beam slid down the wall and sat next to Eden.

Eden blew her nose in the punch napkin she'd snagged from the refreshment table for just such a purpose. She was crying over a boy. Just like her older sister Atlantis had sixteen thousand times between the ages of fourteen to nineteen.

She was supposed to be smarter than that. And Davis was supposed to be a nice guy.

"I *really* liked him. I thought he was smart and funny and nice and interested."

She didn't want to ask the question. Because she wasn't sure if she could handle the answer. Why would he do this to her? Was it because she wasn't special enough? Attractive enough? Had he just been messing with her with their little hallway flirts? Taneisha was beautiful and tall and curvy in all the best places. She was also smart—damn her—and really, really confident.

In a side-by-side comparison, could Eden blame anyone for choosing Taneisha?

"He's a dick, Ede." Moon Beam patted her on the shoulder. "That's all the explanation you need."

"You're sure it's not me?"

"You could be a straight-up asshole and him treating you like this would still make him a dick," Moon Beam insisted.

It didn't take away the awful ache in her chest, knowing that the boy of her dreams was currently wrapped up in the slim arms and abnormally large teenage breasts of Taneisha Duval. But it was something to cling to.

"He *is* a dick, isn't he?" Eden sniffled.

"Yeah. And you know what you're going to do?"

"What?" Eden asked, her voice watery.

"You're going to march back in there and dance every dance with Ramesh with a big, fat smile on your face. And then when this is all over, you're meeting me at my house and we're going to get revenge on Davis "The Dick" Gates.

6

THIRTEEN YEARS LATER

Righteous Subs smelled of onions and bread, the fresh-baked every morning kind that had diners composing sonnets to carbs. Eden swooned over her turkey sub loaded with pickles, onions, and sweet peppers in the orange basket that matched the wild walls of the crowded shop.

She was treating herself—and BFF Sammy—today. Her meeting with the Beautification Committee for hosting their annual reunion luncheon at the Lunar Inn had been a success. She was marching down the path of established, successful business owner, taking no prisoners along the way. Four years into the inn's ownership, Eden finally felt like she was swimming instead of just treading water.

The inn had been at seventy-five percent occupancy for the entire month, her best yet. And she was feeling good. Gone—mostly—were the days of her wayward youth. She'd left her rebellious ways in the dust. Blue Moon was finally starting to recognize her as an established, successful business owner. A credit to the community. Here she was in a smart pencil skirt and sleeveless blouse celebrating a professional success. Yes, things were finally turning in the direction she wanted.

Sammy, in her day-off uniform of gym shorts, tank, and ponytail, snagged a table as it was vacated by Wilson and Penny Abramovich. Customers had to move quickly if they wanted a seat with their subs during the lunch rush. There were seven tables, in eye-searing canary yellow with red vinyl cushioned chairs, and usually triple that many customers vying for them.

Eden executed a spin to head toward the napkin dispenser and soda fountain and smacked face first into a wall of solid flesh.

"Oh, God." Her basket flipped up against her chest in the collision spreading onions and mayo across her business-appropriate cleavage.

"I'm so sorry! I didn't see— oh, hell." That voice. Dear God.

Eden looked up from her hoagie-dosed breasts and into familiar chestnut brown eyes. Her world narrowed in one slow motion tunnel of focus. The din of the sub shop disappeared into a low buzzing in her ears.

He seemed taller than she remembered. Even in heels she still had to tilt to see that damn perfect face. He was definitely broader in the shoulders than he had been over a decade ago. Gone was the wispy facial hair. Nothing adorned that stern jaw line. And his hair. The floppy mop was missing and in its place was a sexy, tousled designer cut.

He was wearing a suit, sans tie. One that fit him like his tailor had intimate knowledge of every inch of his body.

The same blade-straight nose and those perfect cheekbones had her heart leaping into her throat and her nipples tightening to sharp points. *Traitors.*

She'd enjoyed thirteen blissful Davis-free years. In that

time, she'd dated when she felt like it. But put her focus almost entirely into building her business and carefully correcting her sullied reputation. Gone was the heartbroken teen and her quest for vengeance that was mentioned only rarely now. In her place was a strong, confident business owner.

She'd practically convinced herself that he'd never existed. But Mr. West Coast was standing in front of her, picking sweet peppers out of her cleavage with long fingers. Long, ringless fingers.

Awareness rushed through her like a fist to the gut as his finger tip grazed the upper curve of her breast.

"I'm so sorry," He was still apologizing. Didn't he know who she was? Didn't he know he wasn't allowed to speak to her?

"My first day back and I practically run you over and destroy your lunch."

"Back?" Eden's power of speech finally reemerged from the cloud of anger, shock, and unexpected lust. Just because her enemy had turned into a spectacular male specimen did *not* mean she was going to dissolve into a puddle at his feet. If anything, his physical appeal was just another mark against him.

She grabbed his hand as he went in to fish out a particularly long piece of onion.

His eyes met hers and she reconsidered her stance on dissolving... for a second. She was Eden Freaking Moody. She had three generations of pissed-offness behind her.

Davis gave her a crooked grin, one thing that hadn't changed since high school. Eden hated the sugary warmth she felt in her stomach. Her body was operating on autopilot as if it had forgotten how he'd hurt her.

"First day back in Blue Moon," he told her. "I'm excited to

finally be home. I'll be honest. I was hoping to run into you. Though obviously not like this." He gestured at the mess on her shirt.

"You're home." She repeated it carefully. For the first time since mayonnaise had met skin, Eden became aware that every single pair of eyes in the sub shop were on them. Mouths open, cellphones recording, hoagies ignored.

Eden Moody and Davis Gates in the same room. Something terrible was guaranteed to happen.

That whooshing sound she heard was all her years of hard work making Blue Moon forget The Incident collapsing in on themselves. Destroyed in one fell swoop by a sex god in a suit. A suited sex god who, upon closer inspection, had neatly escaped any sub shrapnel.

Of course, nothing ever stuck to Davis. He was the good guy, the golden boy, the nice one. Except when it came to her. Not only had he crushed her, but one tiny, little, juicy, accidental moment of revenge had propelled her into the role of the permanent villain.

"Don't piss off Eden. The fire department's response time is too slow! Ha! Ha!"

"You wanted to run into me?" Eden felt like a damn parrot.

He nodded. "I wanted to apologize. For before. The HeHa dance. I know it's water under the bridge and you probably haven't given it a second thought, but I still feel bad—"

She held up her hand, the one not clutching the remains of her sub. She worked her mouth into a strained, phony smile. "Let's not talk about the dance. In fact, let's not talk. Ever."

Davis's smile dropped as he took in her words.

He sighed, accepted, because of course he was the freaking good guy. "For what it's worth, you're even prettier now than high school."

"And I'm even less forgiving," she snapped. She wanted to take her hoagie corpse and shove it into his chest, ruining that crisp white Oxford. But she was a fucking grown-up. "Welcome home," she said loud enough for everyone within earshot to hear. Without waiting for a response, she stomped back to the table where Sammy—eyes wide, mouth gaping—waited.

"Everything okay?" Sammy asked.

"Peachy." Eden sat down, back to Davis Gates, and ate her mangled turkey with restrained fury.

SHE RAN her errands in a fog, pretending that she wasn't hearing Davis's name whispered everywhere she went. The grocery store, the drug store, the post office. She could do this. Blue Moon Bend was a small town. But it wasn't like she was going to see the man *every day*. She never went to the winery—rumor had it Davis's parents had hung her school photo like a mug shot in the tasting room with instructions never to serve her should she darken their door. Sure, she shared a property line with the winery, but with her acreage and theirs she could probably pretend that he didn't exist just as she had with his parents.

She nodded. Yeah, she could do this. She'd worked so hard. She wasn't going to let one unfortunate, handsome, sexy, *jerk* of a man derail her.

Eden signaled and turned into her tree-lined drive. She was deep in thought and had to slam on the brakes when she came around the bend. There was a moving van stuck in the middle of the lane with flares behind it. The driver gave the offending flat tire a good kick.

Eden eased into the grass and pulled alongside the truck.

Another figure tucked a phone into his pocket and leaned through her open car window.

Davis Asshat Gates gave her an apologetic grin. "Hi, neighbor."

Oh, no.

7

PRESENT DAY

He was going to drown in acrid smoke.

He'd been upstairs in the tiny spare room he used as a makeshift studio working up a palette of acrylic paints when he'd heard the thud in the kitchen. By the time Davis had made it downstairs, the first floor of his house was engulfed in yellow smoke that smelled as if an entire junior high basketball team had sweated to death in a dumpster without ever learning what deodorant was for.

He gasped in a breath. "God! What is that smell?"

He'd made it into the kitchen, but the smoke was too thick to see the walls. Or the chair he'd neglected to push in after breakfast. Davis pitched forward, meeting the cold metal of his refrigerator with his face. "Son of a bitch!" He clutched at his temple, feeling dizzy and sick. He slid the rest of the way to the floor and lay there for a minute trying to remember where the door was.

It smelled a little less bad on the floor. Through swimming vision, Davis noticed flames licking at the wall in the far corner of the kitchen. With an aching head and burning lungs, Davis belly crawled in the direction of his back door.

He miscalculated and smacked the other side of his head off of the sharp edge of a cabinet. "Mother—" his rant was cut off by a choking fit. Dazed and gasping, his searching hands finally found the wood of the door.

He felt like he was swimming through the innards of a volcano. Davis reached up and gripped the knob. His lungs were turning to ash in his chest, his cells recoiling from the smell and the smoke. The fetid scent was smothering him from the inside out.

On his second desperate try, the knob twisted in his hand and he collapsed on the threshold as the door flew open giving the smoke an escape route into the chilly November air. Weak and dizzy, he dragged himself out onto the back porch by his elbows. He collapsed on the wooden planks and coughed until his eyes watered.

His head felt wet and when his fingers came away from his forehead, they were red with blood. "Well, hell," he rasped. His phone rang in his jeans. With the last of his strength, he wrestled it from his paint splattered pocket. He rolled over onto his back.

"Yeah?" he wheezed.

"Boss, there's a lot of smoke coming from your house," his vintner, Anastasia, blandly stated the obvious.

He lifted his head and watched flames licking up the inside of the kitchen windows. "I think my house is on fire." One more thing that would piss off his next-door neighbor.

DAVIS HUDDLED under the alpaca wool safety blanket one of the firefighters had draped over his shoulders before attacking his kitchen with axes and hoses. He clutched the cup of warm liquid between his hands, not sure if it was hot chocolate or coffee or just hot water. His head ached, his vision was iffy, and he smelled like a parking lot portable toilet after the Super Bowl. And the ambulance tailgate felt like a frozen pond under his ass.

"Davis, are you okay?"

He lifted his head and through blurry eyes spotted Ellery Cozumopolaus-Smith and Bruce Oakleigh jumping out of a jacked-up black SUV. It looked like a hearse with a lift kit.

"'Zat a hearse? Am I dead?" he slurred.

"You're bleeding," Ellery said, rushing to his side in her midnight black wool coat. "Bruce, he's bleeding," she said again.

Bruce bumbled over, looking nervous.

"Just a bump," Davis said, weaving away from Ellery's gloved fingers.

Ellery leaned down and peered into his eyes. "His eyes look funny. Does he have a concussion?" she asked, grabbing an EMT who hurried past with an oxygen mask.

The EMT gave Davis the eye. "He slapped the flashlight out of my hand before I could check his pupils, called me Sally, and told me to get out of his face."

"I thought you were going to give me a shot," Davis mumbled.

"With a flashlight?"

"It looked sharp!" His head hurt. His body was cold. And his house was on fire. And it wasn't quite noon. This was not a great start to the day.

"How bad's the damage?" Ellery asked, chewing on her purple painted lip and scanning the scene. There were four fire trucks, a police cruiser, and two ambulances in the winery's drive. More than a dozen people in uniform were running all over the property.

"Why's it smell *so* bad here?" Davis wondered. "It's like a dog barfed up roadkill that died eating garbage."

Ellery cut a hard look at Bruce who squinted up at the sky. "I don't smell anything," Bruce insisted.

"Sweet Jesus. I've never smelled anything that bad in my life," a firefighter said, removing his mask to throw up in the flowerbed.

Bruce began to whistle tunelessly. Ellery pulled out a dainty handkerchief embroidered with skulls and snakes and held it over her nose.

"What are you guys doing here?" Davis asked, curling up on the floor of the ambulance. He wasn't sure what a goth princess paralegal and the town real estate agent/resident gossip were doing in his front yard on a Sunday morning while part of his home burnt to a smelly crisp behind him.

Ellery and Bruce shared another long look.

"Oh, well. We heard that there was trouble out here, and we wanted to see if we could help," Ellery said.

Davis's head hurt too much for him to further question their presence.

"Yes! Neighbors helping neighbors," Bruce agreed. "We're here to take you some place warm."

"Oh. That sounds kind of good."

"Davis!" Anastasia, the winery's vintner and resident pain-in-the-ass, crossed the driveway. "The winery is fine," she announced running a hand through her short shock of gray hair. "Looks like it's just your house." She was sixty-two and had worked in the wine industry for almost forty years. His parents had hijacked her from a Napa Valley winery on one of their last trips west. They'd convinced her to give up the California climate for New York's frigid winters and Blue Moon's quirky weirdness.

"Winery good," Davis summarized. "That's good."

"I think he's got a concussion," Anastasia said in a stage whisper to Ellery and Bruce.

But Davis didn't care. A kitchen he could rebuild, but burning his family's winery to the ground only two years after he took over managing operations? That would have been significantly more painful.

"Anastasia, we're going to take Davis somewhere to get warm and..." she sniffed Davis's general direction and winced, "maybe a shower."

Anastasia's nose crinkled as she caught a whiff of him. "I've literally never smelled anything this bad in my entire life, and my dad used to clean septic tanks for a living," she told them.

Bruce shoved his hands in his pockets. "I still don't smell a thing," he insisted.

"Uh-huh," Anastasia grunted. "Well, get him someplace warm and not smelly. I'll call when the fire crews have any news."

"Will do," Bruce said, springing into action. He pulled Davis into a sitting position and grabbed him by the elbow. "Let's get him to the car."

Ellery tugged at Davis's other arm and together they got him to his feet. "I think the smell is hurting my head," Davis mumbled.

"He's going to make my car smell like baby puke and Brussels sprouts," Ellery hissed at Bruce.

"A small price to pay to help our neighbors," Bruce said cheerfully, half-towing, half-pushing Davis toward Ellery's funeral mobile.

"Where are your shoes?" Ellery asked in horror.

Davis looked down at his feet. There was a blue drip of paint across the top of his bare foot. He shrugged. "In there?" He pointed at the small, two-story farmhouse with black smoke pouring from the gaping hole.

Davis leaned against Ellery while Bruce wrestled the rear door open. The SUV was even taller than it had looked at a distance. Davis eyed the distance between the ground and the running board.

He closed one eye as his vision swam and picked up his foot. "Am I close?" he asked, feeling blindly with his foot.

"You might need another inch or twelve," Ellery said.

"Let's give him a boost," Bruce suggested. Together, they interlaced their fingers and made a foothold for him. "Now just put your foot in here, and we'll gently toss you onto the seat."

Davis did as he was told and found himself hurtling through the air. He landed face-down on the black vinyl seat. "Ooof." He thought about sitting up and then decided he was just better off here. He pulled the blanket over his head and closed his eyes and pretended that he was safely tucked into his own bed and this whole thing had been a terrible dream.

The roar of the engine cut off a minute later. "Where are we? Did I fall asleep?" he asked sitting up and peering through the window. Fanciful turrets in navy blue and purple rose toward the smoky sky. The front doors were painted canary yellow. It was three-stories of color and whimsy topped with a crescent moon weather vane.

"Oh, hell no," he muttered. Even concussed and confused, Davis Gates knew he couldn't cross that threshold.

8

The commotion from the lobby cut through Bruno Mars crooning in Eden's earbuds. She plucked them out of her ears and covered the pie crust she'd been working with a tea towel. Wiping her hands on her apron, she headed in the direction of the noise. She wondered if it had anything to do with the weird jets of yellow smoke that were wafting over her backyard. Probably that pain in the ass at the winery trying to annoy her. She felt like Davis Gates went out of his way to ruffle her feathers just so she was forced to send him frosty, professional emails.

By the time she got to the lobby, her dogs—the big, fluffy monstrosities, Vader and Chewy—were alternately barking and hiding behind the settee near the Lunar Inn's front desk.

Ellery Cozumopolaus-Smith and Bruce Oakleigh were holding up a third barefoot person wearing a blanket between them. "Eden!" Ellery said, with a big smile that immediately made Eden suspicious.

"What's going on?"

"Is the smell following me?" the blanket asked.

Something was rotten in Blue Moon, and it was standing in her lobby. Eden put her hands on her hips. "Who is that?"

Ellery and Bruce were members of Blue Moon's infamous Beautification Committee, a not-so-secret matchmaking society that tortured couples into falling in love. If they were both standing here in her lobby, someone was in a lot of trouble.

"We're happy to announce that you have the golden opportunity to fulfill your civic duty as a Mooner," Bruce announced grandly. He opened his arms with a flourish a beat too late.

The blanket-clad figure swayed, and Bruce steadied it.

"My what?" Eden asked. There was a smell in the lobby. One that was systematically strangling out the lovely scents of coffee and fresh biscuits she'd served only a few hours before.

"Your civic duty," Bruce repeated. "It seems that one of our dear Blue Moon neighbors has suffered a small, insignificant mishap that requires a place to rest for a few hours until things are sorted out."

"Uh-huh." Eden didn't like where this was going. Yes, she was the proprietress of an inn. Hospitality went bone deep in her. But she had a very bad feeling about this particular human blanket.

The blanket stumbled forward, and when it righted itself, Eden got her first good look at the face beneath it. A dazed Davis Gates squinted at her from beneath a layer of drying blood.

"Oh, hell no!" Eden shook her head so vehemently it made her dizzy. Blue Moon had just survived an astrological apocalypse during which nearly everyone had lost their damn minds. She, in the throes of said astrological insanity, had chopped off her long hair into a spunky, chin-length bob. Thankfully, she liked the look. The fallout was supposed to be over and done with as of yesterday, but with the Gates she despised more than pumpkin-flavored everything showing up in her sanctuary, she could only assume this was the result of apocalyptic machinations.

Vader barked at her human mommy's reaction. Meanwhile, Chewy buried his nose in Davis's crotch.

Bruce held up his hands. "Now, Eden, I know that you and Davis here have had a rocky relationship, but he *is* your neighbor, and he *did* suffer a small accidental fire."

"A fire?" she repeated. "Is everything okay?"

"It's fine. Everything is just fine," Bruce crooned. Eden didn't believe him for a minute. He sounded as if he were calming a nervous crowd before an asteroid hit the earth.

Davis tottered over to her glass display case of made-in-Blue Moon products. He rested his forehead against the glass, smearing blood and face across the freshly cleaned glass.

"Oh, come on!" Eden grabbed his arm and shoved him down into one of the upholstered chairs under the bay window. "Why is he bleeding, and *why* does he smell so bad?"

"I don't smell anything," Bruce insisted.

Eden glared at Ellery, her *friend* who should have known better than to show up with a Gates in tow. Maybe Bruce and Ellery had suffered head injuries, too.

Eden grabbed the first aid kit from behind the front desk and returned to Davis.

"My house is burning down," he announced cocking his head so far to the side that his ear rested on his shoulder. Eden held him by the chin and swiped alcohol over the cut on his forehead.

"He's mildly concussed," Ellery reported. "There was a fire in his kitchen, and he fell and hit his head escaping." She said all of that while staring holes in Bruce who didn't seem the least bit perturbed.

The front door opened, and the chime tinkled announcing Deputy Layla's arrival. The dogs, ardent fans of Layla, made a mad dash to welcome her. She strolled inside in uniform. Her blonde hair was pulled back in a severe bun under her hat. Swiping her sunglasses off her pretty face, she surveyed the lobby.

"Crap. It even smells in here," she said, wrinkling her nose.

Eden slapped a patch of gauze on Davis's forehead and ripped the tape with her teeth. "Can I help you, deputy?" Friends since junior high, they were both respectful of each other's careers. Eden called Layla deputy around the guests, and Layla never mentioned their sleepover shenanigans from junior high where they practiced kissing pillows that they pretended were boy band members.

"You're really pretty," Davis whispered, making puppy dog eyes at Eden.

"And you smell like a urinal that someone vomited burritos into," Eden shot back.

"Isn't she pretty, guys?" Davis said flopping to the side of the chair to stare blearily at Ellery and Layla.

"Beautiful."

"Gorgeous."

"She has a very symmetrical face," Bruce agreed.

"So, what's the situation?" Ellery asked Layla.

Layla consulted her notebook. "Well, Davis, I'm sorry to tell you that the kitchen's a total loss. The fire crew was able to confine the blaze to just that section of your house, but you're looking at forty-some thousand in damages."

Bruce went pale and swallowed hard. "Forty-thousand *dollars*?"

"Bruce, can I see you outside?" Ellery hissed, dragging the older man out the front door by his sweater vest.

Davis closed his eyes and nuzzled his cheek against Eden's

hand. She snatched it away. Not only did she not want to touch Davis, but she didn't want that smell rubbing off on her. She was already going to have to torch the chair he was sitting on.

"When can he go home?" Eden asked Layla.

Layla pursed her lips, knowing exactly how her friend felt about said stinking mess of a man. "Not anytime soon. The inspector's gotta check the rest of the house for damage. And Davis isn't going to like this, but it looks suspicious at this point."

A trio of female guests wandered into the lobby. They were part of the Frances party of six, in town to do some holiday shopping and relaxing sans husbands and children. Eden flashed them a strained smile and gave a little wave. She was propping up a bloody man who smelled worse than asparagus pee while a deputy discussed the possibility of arson. This wasn't the kind of hospitality her five-star Travel Diary-rated hospitality business provided.

"Who in the hell would set his house on fire?" she asked, dropping her voice to a low whisper. As far as she knew, she—and her parents—was Davis's only enemy.

Layla cleared her throat. "About that—and I hate to do this, Eden—but what were you doing about an hour ago?"

Eden's outraged gasp nearly took her knees out. "I beg your pardon?"

"Look, with your history with Gates here—The Incident and all that—I have to ask."

Davis opened his eyes again and stared up at Eden like a baby deer in headlights.

"I was here making breakfast, cleaning up from breakfast, and baking," Eden said in a chilly voice. "I have about a dozen witnesses that can place me here all morning." Vader plopped down at her feet and leaned heavily against her leg for moral support.

"That's good enough for me, for now," Layla said, all business. She flipped her notebook closed. "But you might want to compile a list of your guests and a way to contact them... just in case."

Eden's fingernails worked their way into her palm. "I'll be right with you," she said pleasantly to her curious guests, pretending that she wasn't ready to give Layla a real reason to arrest her.

"I'm gonna go talk to the fire inspector," Layla began, jerking her thumb toward the door. "See what she's got for us."

"Where's Donovan?" Eden asked. The sheriff of Blue Moon wasn't investigating the only potential arson in the history of the town. That in itself was weird.

Layla cracked a grin. "Would you believe me if I told you Cardona got married about two hours ago?"

"What? Eva and Donovan?" Eden blinked. Astrological forces were definitely still in play. Eva and Donovan had been dating for barely a month, and Blue Moon's sheriff wasn't exactly known for being rash. A movement on the front porch caught her eyes. Ellery was waving her arms wildly as Bruce grabbed at the tufts of hair behind his ears. *The apocalypse was definitely still in play.*

"Yeah," Layla continued. "He and Eva tied the knot in a spontaneous little ceremony this morning. They're either still locked in their bathroom having newlywed sex, or they're out to brunch with the family."

Eden rubbed a hand over her forehead. Davis gave a little snore from the chair. His face was stained with blood and soot. But damn if he still wasn't painfully, stupidly attractive.

She hated that about him.

"Is he allowed to sleep while he has a concussion?" Eden asked.

Layla shrugged. The radio on her belt chirped. "Deputy, you got things under control out there at the winery?" Minnie Murkle's voice crackled. She was Blue Moon's dispatcher, police station office manager, and in the running for town's busiest busybody.

"I gotta take this," Layla said, pointing toward the door. "Good luck with him. He's gonna need a place to stay for the next few weeks." She jutted her chin toward Davis and gave Eden a little salute before vanishing through the front door.

"What do you mean 'good luck with him'?" Eden called after her.

Bruce and Ellery returned, both of them beaming at her. "So, we're going to go," Ellery said, clasping her hands in front of her black cat skeleton turtleneck.

"What about him?" Eden asked, pointing at Davis.

"Well, he's going to need a place to stay," Ellery said, sliding closer to the front door.

"And what does that have to do with me?" Eden demanded. More guests were clustering around the desk, whispering. She took a deep breath to control her panic.

"You know, Eden. Voting on Blue Moon Business of the Year is happening next month," Bruce said, rubbing a hand over his rotund belly. "I imagine a lot of Mooners would be very impressed that you opened your inn to your neighbor in need."

Those sneaky, manipulative tricksters. Dangling the carrot she most wanted right in front of her. She'd been gunning for Blue Moon Business of the Year—a prize that the winery snatched up year after year—for the last six years. She was the Susan Lucci of Blue Moon's chamber of commerce, and this year was going to be her year.

"So, we're gonna take off," Ellery said again, pointing both index fingers in the direction of the front door. She slid one Frankenstein boot toward the door and then the other. Eden was powerless to stop them. She watched them scurry out the door like the sneaks they were. Davis made a sad little whimper noise next to her as he tried to curl his six-foot-plus frame into the chair.

"Everything all right?" one of the guests asked. Melissa from Missouri on the upstate New York leg of her Girlfriends Tour, Eden recalled.

"Everything's great, Melissa," Eden assured her with a confident smile she didn't feel.

Everything was horrible.

9

Eden prodded Davis into the cramped bathroom. She'd reluctantly given him the small suite next to her living quarters so his smell wouldn't upset the rest of the guests. Sunny, her part-time front desk help who also waited tables at John Pierce Brews, had arrived in the nick of time distracting the guests that lingered with Eden's charmingly cartoonish maps of Blue Moon and chocolates while she hauled the smelly mess away. She would manage the situation. It was what she did best.

Eden reached around him and twisted the knobs in the skinny shower. "Get in there and don't come out until you don't smell."

"'K," he said and shucked his jeans right there in front of her.

"Holy hell," Eden stammered and clapped a hand over her eyes. Davis Gates apparently didn't bother with things like underwear. "Jesus, Gates! Wait until I leave the room."

"My head doesn't feel good," he announced with a little pout as he swayed backwards, pressing his bare ass cheeks against the glass door.

"I'm sure it doesn't," Eden sighed, peeking between her fingers despite her best efforts. She didn't want to be sympathetic. Not to him. Not after the years of judgment she'd endured because of him. It was his fault that Layla even had to ask about The Incident.

Yet here he was, naked from the waist down—an obvious shower, not a grower—and looking needy. She cursed that stupid Blue Moon Business of the Year award.

Steam billowed out of the shower. "Go on," Eden said, more gently this time. "Get in and I'll be back with fresh clothes."

She watched as Davis stepped into the shower with his shirt still on.

"Shirt, Davis!"

"Oh. Right." The sopping wet, stinking mess hit her squarely in the face. She would have gagged from the smell, but Davis's naked silhouette was eating up all her senses at the moment.

She stripped the trash bag from the can next to the sink and stuffed his clothing in it. She'd give her industrial-sized washer and dryer a crack at the smell, but if they failed she'd be burning his clothes along with the chair in the lobby.

"Try not to drown," Eden called, backing out of the room.

She slipped downstairs into the utility room that housed her gleaming laundry components and said a little prayer as she set the washer on "disaster" mode. Back upstairs she surveyed her options for clothing the naked Davis.

He had butt dimples. Cute ones. *Oh, God. Where had that thought come from?*

She mentally ran through her current guests. There were a handful of men, but none in quite the right size or quite the right character that she would feel comfortable asking them to borrow some spare clothes.

With a huff, she marched into her living quarters and dug through her dresser. Davis was going to spend the rest of his day in a pair of her yoga pants and a V-neck t-shirt. She grabbed a pair of fuzzy knee socks and added them to the pile.

It was the best she could do for now. Besides, it was only for a few hours until someone found him a more permanent place to stay.

Eden debated leaving the clothes on the bed in his room but heard a squeaky thump from the bathroom.

"Now what?" she muttered under her breath. Eden opened the door to find Davis sprawled on the floor of the shower, eyes closed, water pouring over his head in a steady river. He was going to drown in her guest room, and then the cops would really be asking questions.

"Davis," she snapped. Eden reached inside the shower and turned off the water. "Hey!"

He opened one eye and then the other. "You're really pretty," he slurred again.

"We've already established that," she said, stepping into the shower stall and doing her best to wrestle his wet, naked body into a standing position.

"You don't like me, right?" Davis asked, reaching out to touch her nose in slow motion. "Booooop."

"Are you kidding me right now?" Eden yanked a towel off the bar and shoved it into his hands. "Dry off and put those clothes on," she said, pointing to the decidedly feminine wardrobe she'd provided.

She left him alone in the bathroom to wrestle his way into her clothing. Her watch vibrated indicating a new text message.

Layla: Sorry about before. Just doing my job.

Eden and Layla had been friends since junior high when an eighth-grade boy had farted into Layla's trumpet's mouthpiece while she was getting a drink from the water fountain. Eden had saved Layla from impending fart mouth, and together the two of them had pummeled Pond Birkbeck into submission. Now, her so-called-friend was questioning whether Eden had it in her to burn down a house in front of her guests.

She tucked her phone away again, deciding to deal with Layla later and instead focused on taking inventory of the room. Pillows? Check. Quilt? Check. TV remote? Check. Dish of candy? Check.

The bathroom door opened and Davis shuffled into the bedroom. Eden bit the inside of her cheek to keep from laughing. The yoga pants were stretched to capacity to accommodate Davis's package.

"Now I get why women wear these so often. I've never been more comfortable," Davis announced stretching from side to side.

"Okay, let's not overdo it on the motion," Eden said.

"I threw up in your shower," he said.

"Is this Ruin Eden's Life Day?"

"It was eggs," he said dreamily. Davis looked beyond her to the full-sized bed dressed in a frilly duvet and tasseled pillows. "I think I'll go to sleep," he decided. With two long strides, he face-planted onto the mattress.

"Shit," Eden muttered. "Are you allowed to sleep when you're concussed?"

He didn't answer, just burrowed further under the mound of pillows. Eden swallowed hard and tried to ignore the perfect ass that was currently filling out her yoga pants better than her own ever had.

The Davis Gates that had returned to Blue Moon after

college and several years on the West Coast was still the town golden boy. Only he'd traded his hand-woven ponchos for tailored suits, and his hair no longer did the adorable flip of his high school days. He was friendly, organized, and incredibly professional. Essentially, he was obnoxiously perfect.

It annoyed the living crap out of Eden.

Seeing him like this? Disheveled and confused? Well, it was the tiniest bit entertaining.

With a sigh, Eden pulled her phone from her apron pocket and dialed.

"'Lo?" Sammy Ames, Blue Moon's large animal vet, and Eden's best friend answered.

"Sammy, I know you're probably elbow-deep in a cow vagina right now, but I need medical advice." Sammy and Eden had been best friends since the third grade when they were both put in charge of the class hamster for the week. Mr. Flufferbottom hadn't survived the week, but their friendship had endured.

There was a weird slooshing noise on Sammy's end, and Eden had no desire to know exactly what she was interrupting. "The dogs okay?" her friend asked.

"They're fine. It's a human patient. A concussion."

"You know I'm a vet, right?" Sammy quipped dryly.

"Medicine is medicine. Can he sleep with a concussion?"

She could hear Sammy's wheels turning. "Can he carry on a conversation?"

Eden stared at Davis's prone form. "Yeah, he's talking."

"How long ago did it happen?"

"I'm not sure. About two hours?"

"The sleeping thing is basically a myth when it comes to concussions. You want to keep him awake for four-ish hours after the trauma just to make sure symptoms aren't worsening.

You'll want to watch for vomiting, the inability to recognize familiar people or places, seizures, and weak limbs."

"Holy crap. Well, he already barfed in my shower."

"In your shower?" Sammy repeated. "Who is this concussed Lothario?"

Eden paused, wrinkling her nose. "Davis Gates," she sighed.

"WHAT?" Sammy's shout had Eden yanking the phone away from her ear.

"Keep it down, will you?" Davis mumbled through his mound of pillows.

"Stay focused for a second. Do I need to take him to the hospital?" Eden asked Sammy.

"Puking is normal after a concussion. Just watch for excessive puking."

"Why is this happening to me?" Eden lamented. "I was having a nice day. I was going to bake a pie."

"Ooh! What kind? Also, why is Davis Gates puking in your shower?"

"Rhubarb. And at this point, I'm not really sure. I think the universe is punking me. His house caught fire, and Bruce Oakleigh and Ellery show up with him wrapped in a blanket smelling horrible. And then they were talking about Business of the Year award. And now I'm stuck with my mortal enemy who's wearing my yoga pants and trying to build himself a pillow igloo in my guest room."

"Oh, babe," Sammy said sympathetically.

Eden shoved a hand into her hair. "They played me like a damn banjo."

"They sure did." There was a high-pitched whinny on Sammy's end. "Shit. I gotta go vaccinate this Adonis of horseflesh before he kicks me in the chest. I'll call you later okay?"

"Yeah, later," Eden said flatly. She disconnected the call

and studied Davis. She had to keep him awake for two more hours. And hopefully by then another Blue Moon Samaritan would open up their home to the guy who'd broken her heart and turned her into a small time criminal.

It took every trick in the book, but Eden got Davis back onto his feet and into her office. It was the promise of a sticky bun that did it. When he winced at the sunlight streaming through from the window overlooking the front porch, Eden adjusted the blinds. He sat in the upholstered chair in front of her desk with his long legs stretched out, his socked feet touching her desk. The sticky bun disappeared in slow, measured bites.

"Why can't I sleep?" he asked again mournfully.

"Because you might die, and then no one will ever want to stay here again with you haunting them," Eden said, scanning the search results for concussion symptoms and treatments. "Does your head hurt?"

"Do goats hate Jax Pierce?" Davis grumbled.

At least he was stringing more words together and no longer booping her.

"This says you can have acetaminophen for the pain," Eden said, skimming the article. She pushed her intercom button. "Hey, Sunny, can you grab some Tylenol and water from the kitchen and bring it to my office?"

"Totally," Sunny answered from the front desk.

"Totally," Davis parroted.

"She's a third-generation hippie, Gates. What do you expect?" Eden snapped.

"Don't yell at me, please," he begged, rubbing his hand over his temples. The gauze she'd hastily slapped on his forehead was soggy and drooping over his eyebrow.

Why was she suddenly charged with supervising Davis Gates? Why was the universe torturing her? She was a good person, damn it. She donated to charity. She never was anything but kind and helpful to the very few rude visitors to her B&B. She rescued dogs. She supported her community in weird and wonderful ways. She tried her hardest to make sure that every guest left feeling like they had a magical experience in Blue Moon. So, why was she stuck with the one man on the entire planet that she despised with the fire of a thousand pottery kilns?

Eden dug through her desk drawer for her emergency back-up first aid kit, used primarily to treat paper cuts. She yanked out a bandage and shoved the kit back in the desk drawer with a slam.

She came around the desk tearing the wrapper open. "Hold still," she commanded, ripping the soggy gauze from his forehead.

"Ow! Why are you so mean?" Davis hissed.

"Stop being a baby," Eden said, though she gentled her touch. She pressed the fresh bandage to his cut.

"Hey, boss," Sunny sang out her greeting as she swept through the door smelling like a scented candle store.

Eden coughed. "Jeez, Sun. Go a little heavy on the perfume today?"

"Have you smelled it outside?" She rolled her eyes to the ceiling. "It's like an outhouse convention exploded. It reeks. Hey, Davis." The lanky blonde turned her attention to Eden's unwanted guest.

"Hey, Sunny. How's your day so far?" Davis asked weakly.

At least he recognized her part-time help, Eden thought. Cross that symptom off the list.

"Better than yours. Heard about the fire. Rumor has it, it was either a gas leak or your septic tank spontaneously imploded," Sunny said, cheerfully sliding onto the corner of Eden's desk and swinging her feet back and forth.

Eden's office was getting crowded.

A movement on the small security monitor caught Eden's eye. "Fire chief," Sunny said.

"Keep an eye on him and don't let him fall asleep or throw up on anything," Eden ordered.

She found Fire Chief Eloisa MacDougal sniffing the collar of her jacket and wincing at the front desk.

"Hi, chief," Eden greeted her.

"Sorry for the smell, Eden. I won't stay long. How's Davis?"

"Concussed and confused. When can I send him home?" Eden asked, covering her nose and mouth. If the entire inn didn't end up smelling, it would be a miracle.

"Not any time soon," Eloisa said, cracking her gum. She was a lean black woman in her early fifties who was more than capable of hauling a two-hundred-pound victim out of a window if necessary. She lifted weights religiously and fueled her muscles with a bowl of Rocky Road every night. "Structure's not safe with the whole end of the house wide open. I've got Calvin Finestra's card in here if Davis is looking for a contractor. It's gonna be a lot of work."

Eden paced in front of the front desk, her suede boot-clad feet scuffing at the thick rug.

"So, what do I do with him? Where do I send him? Where's he staying?"

Eloisa frowned and heaved a tired sigh. "You mind if I sit down?" she asked, gesturing at the chair Davis had stunk up earlier.

"Have at it. I'm burning it anyway."

Eloisa flopped down with a relieved sigh. "I'm gonna need some serious reiki after traipsing around in that stench. Smells like cat litter and sauerkraut."

"Chief, about Davis?" Eden said, trying to get the woman to focus.

"Excuse me, Eden do you have any extra pillows we could have for our room?" Thomas Springer was tall and so thin he looked like he'd disappear if he turned sideways. He and his wife were escaping a house full of children with a long weekend getaway. Last night, they'd crawled back from the brewery drunk as two skunks and waving to their Lyft driver like he was a rock star. Eden adored them, and that was before they extended their stay by an extra night.

"Absolutely, Thomas," Eden promised with a quick smile. "I can actually let you pick the ones you like from our stash." She had an entire walk-in closet on the second floor stocked with pillows of all sizes and smush-factors.

The front door bell tinkled and in strolled a grinning Bruce Oakleigh hefting two garbage bags.

"Bruce, I'll be with you in a minute," Eden said, turning back to Thomas.

"What's the damage, chief?" Davis shuffled out into the lobby.

Everyone stopped and stared at the man bulging out of yoga pants. Eden's t-shirt fit him like a second skin and showed a dusting of chest hair at the apex of the deep V. The socks only came up to his mid-shin.

Even dressed like a tall, built woman, the man had undeniable sex appeal. It pissed Eden off that she noticed.

"Thomas, did you get the pillows?" Letiticia, Thomas's wife, shrilled from the stairway like an opera diva drawing everyone's attention away from Davis and his pants-enhanced penis.

"Getting them now, sweet pea," Thomas hollered back.

Sunny skipped into the lobby and ducked behind the front

desk. She rested her elbows on the desk as if she were enjoying the show.

"Sunny, can you please show Thomas to the pillow collection?" Eden asked sweetly.

"Oh, sure! Right this way! You're going to love our down alternative blends," Sunny predicted.

"Thomas!"

"Coming, sweet pea!"

Eden turned back to the remaining bodies in her lobby. The chief hauled herself out of the chair. Eden could have sworn she saw a puff of yellow smoke rise with her. "Well, Davis. It's not good news. A lot of damage. And worse, it looks suspicious."

"Suspicious, like arson?" Davis asked and winced at the volume of his own words.

Bruce dropped his bags on the floor with a muffled thud. "I'm sure it wasn't an *intentional* fire," he insisted.

Eloisa rolled her shoulders. "That's usually what 'arson' means. We found some kind of device in the corner of your kitchen. Looks like it fell into the trashcan. As far as I can tell, that's where the fire originated."

"What kind of device?" Davis leaned his weight on the desk and rubbed his forehead.

"Near as I can tell, it was some kind of mutant stink bomb," Eloisa announced. "A deadly one."

Bruce sputtered. "Well, if it *was* a stink bomb, obviously no one meant any harm! Maybe it was just a small, harmless accident?"

"Well, that small, harmless accident is gonna cost almost fifty grand in repairs," Eloisa said, unimpressed with Bruce's theories.

Davis looked pale.

"We can talk numbers later," Eden cut in, hoping he

wouldn't pass out or throw up in her lobby. "Let's talk about where he's going to stay."

Bruce slapped himself in the forehead and hefted the bags. "Of course! The whole reason I came here. Here you go, Davis. Mayva at Second Chances was happy to provide you a small wardrobe from the thrift store as your clothes are..."

"Disgusting fabric containers of stench?" Eloisa suggested.

"So, I can't go home?" Davis reiterated. His fingers brushed over the bandage she'd stuck to his forehead. Eden felt a pang of sympathy for him. The man was essentially homeless.

"Not any time soon," Eloisa said, zipping up her fleece jacket.

"But not to worry!" Bruce patted him on the arm and then dumped the garbage bags at Davis's feet. "Eden generously offered to let you stay here. Isn't that wonderful?"

"That's not what I—"

"Oh, wonderful." Eloisa perked up. "Listen, I'm going to go home and shower for about four hours. But I'll be back tomorrow, Davis. We'll talk more then. And Eden, I may need to ask you a few questions, too."

Eden clenched her jaw so hard she thought it might shatter.

"It's all routine. But given your history..." Eloisa let her thought trail off.

Their history. Would she never escape those five, fateful minutes fifteen years ago?

"Well, I'll leave you in Eden's hospitable hands," Eloisa said, shuffling toward the door.

"Enjoy your time together," Bruce said cheerfully, following the fire chief outside. "Is there such a thing as accidental arson?" he asked on their way out.

Silence descended as Eden and Davis eyed each other.

10

"It was that little firebug next door, wasn't it?" Ferguson Gates shouted in his son's ear from three-thousand miles away.

"Dad, calm down," Davis cautioned his father and pulled another suit from the back of his closet. It was still in the dry cleaning bag. He gave it a cursory sniff and tossed it on the bed behind him in the Maybe pile.

"I *am* calm," Ferguson yelled.

Two years ago, Ferguson Gates suffered a second heart attack and was ordered to cut out stress. Davis was called home from the west coast to finally take over winery operations while his father took a more "relaxed" role in the company. The "retirement" word was never uttered in Ferguson's presence.

"I doubt very much that Eden had anything to do with this, Dad." The woman was a saint as far as he was concerned. First, he'd stood her up, humiliating her in front of most of the town. Then she'd suffered the years-long fallout—gleefully fueled by his own parents—from an unfortunate accident.

Despite all that, she'd stepped up, patched up his wounds, and given him a room at her inn when he needed a place to stay.

"How many times have I warned you?" Ferguson continued his rant. "The Moodys are our enemies. I knew it was only a matter of time before she sashayed across the property line to destroy everything we've built."

Eden wasn't the type to sashay, but he held back that comment. His father wasn't exactly known for being levelheaded when it came to the feud.

Davis heard a commotion on his father's end while he pawed through his sock drawer. Salvaging clothing had become a top priority when he'd gone through the bags of second- and, in some cases, fourth-hand clothing Bruce delivered. Today, he was wearing an orange and red paisley button down and a pair of baby blue jeans that flared out over a pair of platform boots that were a size too small. Eden had spit her coffee out on the lace tablecloth when he'd shown his face at breakfast this morning.

The hideous outfit had been worth the reaction. Laughing adult Eden was even more compelling than he remembered the teenage version to be.

"Remember, Davis, I've entrusted the business to you. I'm counting on you to follow in my footsteps," Ferguson said in his movie trailer guy voice.

"Oh, for Pete's sake! Give me that phone, Ferguson, before you end up in the ER again," came Bryson's frustrated bellow on the other end. "Hi, honey," his father's husband said after wrestling the phone from Ferguson.

"Hey, Brys."

"How are you feeling? How's your head?"

Davis's father had forgotten to ask about his health, his rage too focused on the Moody family to remember his son's injury. But Bryson was the thoughtful, kind soul he'd been since joining the Gates family five years ago. They hadn't managed to ruin him yet.

"Getting better," Davis said. It still hurt like hell, but at least now he could look at his phone screen without getting dizzy. "Is Mom with you guys?"

"She took a little side trip to a winery in Washington State," Bryson told him. Davis's parents' divorce had been so amicable that when his father came out and introduced them to Bryson, Tilly had claimed him for a friend. The three of them spent the better part of the year traveling wine country together.

"I'm calling Sheriff Cardona as soon as you hang up," Ferguson yelled in the background.

His family could forgive his father for leaving, accept the fact that he was gay, and welcome his boyfriend into the family with open arms. But they could hold a grudge against the Moodys for generations of perceived slights.

In Davis's rarely voiced opinion on the matter, the Gates family had behaved worse than the Moodys over the years. For ten years, his mother had walked their dog seven blocks every night just to leave piles of dog shit in the Moodys' front yard. The Gates's side was not blameless.

"You take care of yourself," Bryson ordered, ignoring Ferguson's bellows in the background. "Where are you staying?"

Davis bagged the clothes he'd laid out on the bed. "I'm staying with... a friend. Just until I can come up with a more permanent solution," he lied. There was no way he was telling his family that he'd spent the last two nights under Eden Moody's roof.

"Mm-hmm," Bryson hummed. "I hope your *friend* is a knockout."

"You have no idea," Davis grinned. He'd dutifully kept his

distance from Eden in the two years since he'd returned to Blue Moon. She'd made it clear on his first day back that there would be no reconciliation or second chance to pick up where high school had left off. So he'd been left to admire her from afar.

"Tell him we can't evict the tenants at the house," Ferguson yelled. Davis's parents rented out the house—that the three of them shared—in Blue Moon for the six or so months of the year they spent traveling.

"Of course not. That would ruin his rating," Davis said, hitting on one of his father's sore spots. Once, a guest had ranked his stay in the home a paltry four stars because he didn't care for the special water metering shower faucet. Ferguson had banned the man from ever staying in another Gateses' property... as if they had more than one.

"We can be on a plane in the next two hours," Bryson reminded him.

"I'm fine, Brys. I can handle this. You guys enjoy your trip and I'll keep you updated on the repairs."

"Okay." The way Bryson drew out the word, Davis knew his stepfather didn't believe him that everything was fine.

"Listen, Brys. Don't share anything you might see on Facebook with Mom and Dad. I didn't get into details about the damage, and I don't want them worrying over something they can't do anything about." He'd flat out lied to his father about the fire. *A little smoke damage. Might need to replace some appliances...* He didn't need to add any more stress to the man who was already a ticking time bomb. Fortunately, in addition to being anti-Moody, Davis's parents were also anti-social media, refusing to join the rest of the world online.

Bryson's voice dropped. "I'll do it if you send me pics."

"Deal. Don't freak out."

"Honey, I'm not your parents. And I also want pics of your 'friend.'"

"I'll send them, but you have to swear to delete them. Both topics will probably push Mom and Dad headlong into a psychotic break."

"Now, I definitely need pics."

They both laughed. Ferguson and Tilly might be divorced, but they still shared a commitment to drama.

"Just keep them busy, okay? I've got to figure out a few things before I'm ready to tell them anything."

"Fine by me. See you at Christmas. Make good choices!"

"I'll do my best," Davis chuckled and hung up. He hauled the pitiful pile of not-quite-destroyed clothing out into the narrow hallway. Poking his head into the tiny second bedroom, he sighed. His closet-sized man cave/art studio had sustained some smoke damage. He had a desk shoved into one corner where he worked on his father-not-approved winery plans. The rest of the room was dedicated to his painting hobby.

His barely begun canvas, an abstract in colors of the vineyard before harvest—greens, purples, browns—stared back at him.

Painting wasn't exactly a secret. He just didn't share it with anyone. Swirling acrylics across a canvas was how he relaxed, how he unwound at night or on his rare days off. Davis was well aware that too much of his time was spent on winery business, leaving him with precious few hours for anything but work. However, that was to be expected when charged with carrying on the family legacy.

He considered packing up some supplies and decided to stick with a sketchbook and charcoals. He'd love to coax Eden into posing for him. Not that she'd let him anywhere near her with a canvas and brush or charcoals. But still, the idea was worth fantasizing about.

How would he capture her forced scowl that was softened by blue eyes that were never quite cold? Eden was distractingly beautiful and painfully prickly. They'd spent an hour "negotiating" his room rate. She had stubbornly refused to take his "dirty Gates money" while he wasn't interested in her "sanctimonious Moody charity."

It was the most fun he'd had in months. He could have blamed the concussion, but Davis was smart enough to realize that that high school crush had never completely faded.

Davis sighed and gathered what he needed. Another distraction.

"We're a family of entrepreneurs," his father had reminded him a thousand times. Gateses didn't do anything at the hobby level. They were too busy being successful.

Personally, Davis thought his father had committed too much of his life to proving his success to his own parents. They'd cut Ferguson off without a dime—besides the modest trust fund from his grandparents—when he'd announced he was opening a winery in New York with a wandering hippie he'd met hitchhiking, so the story went.

Every dollar they made, his father treated as a "fuck you" to his father. Nothing came between Ferguson Gates and his success. Especially not family.

He'd put that hard-headed, single-mindedness to work in other areas. Ferguson had embraced Blue Moon and Tilly's family feud with the Moodys as if both had always been his own. The man was fiercely loyal and excessively stubborn. It was an occasionally obnoxious combination.

Davis lugged his loot downstairs to the breezy first floor. The place was certainly well-ventilated with the gaping hole where the kitchen used to be.

His phone rang in his pocket. And he lost his grip on the dry-cleaning bag followed by everything else in his arms. It all landed unceremoniously on the floor just inside the front door.

"This is Davis," he answered.

"Mr. Gates, this is Lionel from the Bouffet Insurance Agency." The man sounded as if he were pinching his nose shut while speaking.

"Ah, yes," Davis said, wrestling his load back into his arms and sandwiching the phone between his shoulder and ear. "Thank you for returning my call."

"I'm sorry to inform you that while the fire is still under investigation, we are exercising our right to withhold payment."

This time when the suits and pants and shirts fell from his hand, Davis did nothing to stop them. "I'm sorry. I have a concussion. Could you repeat that? It sounded like you were saying you aren't going to pay."

Lionel was unfazed by Davis's sarcasm. "Mr. Gates, it is Bouffet policy to withhold payment until a cause has been determined. Frankly, we have to make sure this isn't some kind of insurance fraud attempt. As a business owner, I'm sure you understand."

"You want me to prove that I didn't set my own home on fire?"

"Precisely."

"What do I do with the gaping hole in my house until then?" Davis demanded. Yelling made his head hurt.

"That's up to you, Mr. Gates. Best of luck." And with that meaningless platitude, Lionel of the Bouffet Insurance Agency hung up on him. Davis briefly considered hurling his phone into the stone fireplace in his currently unlivable living room. But he'd endured enough destruction in the last two days.

Hands on his hips, he stood knee deep in laundry and surveyed his home. It had originally housed a farmer and his family of five back when the land was all pastures and fields. The two floors were chopped up into little box-like rooms. When he'd returned to Blue Moon after his years in California wine country, he'd done a little work here and there to make it more livable. Of course it had been the kitchen addition that had been destroyed. It couldn't have been the too-small master bedroom upstairs or the odd-shaped den that wasn't quite wide enough for a chair.

He had to admit, having the space at the inn to rattle around in had been an unexpected pleasure. As was the chance to see Eden up close in her home and at work. She'd remained an enigma since that unfortunate night in history. After he'd escorted Taneisha to the dance, Eden had shut herself off from him for the remainder of his senior year, even going so far as to file for a separation in Household Management and Partnerships class.

And he couldn't blame her for it. He'd caved under pressure. Something he'd become more and more familiar with doing. And that wasn't the kind of man Eden Moody was interested in. But that didn't do anything to alleviate the guilt he felt for hurting her.

They'd never spoken a word to each other in all the years since. He had, however, found small ways of pushing her buttons, forcing her into the occasional email correspondence. Discussing the paving of their shared drive, the trimming of trees that straddled the property line. She was always coldly polite. But every time he was lucky enough to be in the same room with her, well, there was nothing chilly about their shared glances.

It was interesting that they both preferred to live where they worked. He'd seen her in action these past forty-eight hours. The consummate hostess, the focused entrepreneur. She made her guests—himself included—feel as welcomed as if the inn were their home. He admired that.

He'd never imagined teenage rebel Eden Moody would settle down to a career like innkeeping. No, he would have pictured her as a tattoo artist or some other creative, adventurous profession like the folk rock marketing exec. But somehow this suited her, too. And she was damn good at it. Not that she'd let him tell her.

Davis felt rather than heard the knock at the front door in the base of his skull where the dull throb of trauma still radiated.

Stepping over suits and socks, Davis opened the front door to Calvin Finestra, Blue Moon's resident contractor. "It had to be the kitchen, didn't it?" the man in coveralls sighed. Calvin and his crew had spent a very pleasant six weeks last spring building the addition. And now it was blackened rubble.

"What's that smell?" Calvin asked.

"Stink bomb we think."

"Who'd stink bomb you?"

Davis shrugged and held the door for the builder. "Your guess is as good as mine at this point. At least the smell is better today."

The winery had been closed for two days due to the smell, and though he'd been holed up in his comfy guest bed next door to Eden, he'd seen the complaints on Facebook and knew the winds had carried the scent into town.

Calvin, his hands stuffed in his pockets and his white hair poking out from under his worn ball cap, surveyed the blackened hull of what had been a very nice kitchen. "Well, at least we didn't build anything above it," he said optimistically gazing up at the charred holes in the roof.

"I've got more bad news for you," Davis told him.

"What's that?"

"Insurance company isn't going to pay out until I can prove that I didn't set the fire."

Calvin grimaced. "Can't leave it like this. You'll end up with a wildlife refuge movin' on in."

"Maybe I can tarp it off?" Davis wondered, rubbing his forehead. He should have been meeting with the chamber of commerce right now to flesh out the details of their Christmas party at the winery next month. Not contemplating how to keep bears and squirrels out of his house.

"Me and my crew will take care of sealing it off," Calvin told him.

"Calvin, I'm not going to be able to pay you for a while," Davis told him. The winery did well, and Davis was paid a fair salary for his work, but he didn't have nearly fifty-thousand dollars lying around in a savings account just waiting for an emergency. And asking his parents for help was *not* an option.

Calvin waved his concern away. "Wouldn't be neighborly to leave it like this. I'll pull a crew together tomorrow to get started. We'll get it sealed up so you can at least turn on the heat and save your pipes. Then we'll figure out the rest."

Davis was humbled. Not only had his sworn enemy opened her home to him, his neighbors were stepping up for him without even being asked.

Davis shoved his hands in his pockets so he didn't let his emotional state run wild and hug the man. "I don't know what to say."

"I'll be by tomorrow. I'd ask for the key, but I think we can let ourselves in," Calvin grinned, eyeing the six-foot hole in the front of the house.

11

Eden hauled ass into Villa Harvest, the charming and deliciously scented Italian restaurant in town. She spotted her friends in the corner shoving breadsticks into their faces as if their lives depended on it. Layla was the tall, blonde bombshell to Sammy's petite frame and no-nonsense stubby ponytail that her honey-colored curls kept trying to escape. Lunch hours for cops and large animal vets went quickly… and in this case started at three o'clock in the afternoon.

Eden took the chair next to Sammy and picked up her menu, pointedly ignoring Layla.

"Is that smell you?" Sammy asked, leaning in to sniff Eden's shirt.

Eden swore and tugged at the collar of her olive-green tunic. "I think the smell is seeping into my wallpaper," she moaned.

"Who would set fire to the winery?" Sammy wondered.

"It was Davis's house. More personal than going after the business," Layla said through a mouthful of parmesan and carbs.

"Layla thinks I did it," Eden said, perusing the menu.

Layla kicked her under the table. "I do *not*. I was just doing my job."

"You asked me if I set the fire!"

"Doing. My. Job. You know I don't think you had anything to do with it. And no one else is going to think it either since you gave that smelly hot guy a place to stay," Layla insisted. It was as good of an apology as Eden was going to get.

And grunting at Layla was the only apology acceptance she'd give. The three of them, friends forever, took two things in life seriously: work and friendship... also food.

"I just hate that once again, everyone thinks I'm the bad guy," Eden grumbled.

"No one likes a whiner." Sammy pointed at her with a breadstick. "You've spent your entire adulthood trying to make up for being seventeen. And it's not necessary. This is Blue Moon. There are no outcasts."

It was true. Eden had spent her teenage years trying to be the rebel, and when she'd finally—accidentally—earned that status, all she wanted to do was take it back. She wasn't mean-spirited. She wasn't vindictive or wild or reactive. But The Incident had certainly painted her in that light. She still wished she could take it all back. And as part of her penance, Eden had patently refused to say anything negative about Davis to anyone for the last fifteen years. She just thought plenty of negative things.

"I get that I'm accepted," Eden sighed. "But no matter what I do, everyone always sees me as the girl who got revenge on Davis by—"

"Ladies! What a pleasant surprise." Eden was interrupted by Franklin Merrill, the jolly owner and sometimes waiter at Villa Harvest, appeared tableside, notebook at the ready. "I don't suppose I can offer any of you a margarita in the middle of the day?"

"Not today, Franklin," Layla said, batting her lashes at the man. "But you can tell us what the lunch specials are."

He ran through the specials adding in his personal recommendations, and they ordered with a healthy side of flirting. Franklin was a lovable bear of a man who turned out to be Phoebe Pierce's second chance at happiness after her first husband, John, passed away. Phoebe's sons had varying reactions to her newfound happiness. But no heart could stay hardened against Franklin. He was irresistible.

"Are you ladies trying to catch my husband's eye?" Phoebe teased, slipping her arm around her husband's waist. She was sixty, but her happy glow made her look a decade younger.

"Can't help it, Phoebe," Eden confessed. "Franklin is irresistible."

"Women throw themselves at me," Franklin confirmed with a chuckle.

"Well, as long as you don't throw yourself back," Phoebe winked up at him. "I hear there was some excitement out your way this week, Eden. We could smell it all the way out at the farm."

"You should smell the inn," Eden told them. "It's lucky the damage wasn't worse."

"I heard Davis was injured," Franklin added. The man served half the town their lunch and would have all the details by now.

"A bump on the head and a mild concussion," Eden said, trying to evict the image of Davis stripping in front of her from her mind. It wasn't working.

"And you're putting him up. That's very generous of you," Phoebe said, laying a motherly hand on Eden's shoulder. Phoebe was too nice to point out that it was surprising that

Eden would be willing to lend a helping hand to a man she disliked.

"It's just temporary," Eden reiterated. "I'm sure he'll be back in his house soon." *Please, God.*

"Well, we're all proud of you for stepping up for him. I know you two don't have the smoothest history," Phoebe said.

"Thanks," Eden mumbled.

The Merrills left them to their breadsticks and conversation.

Sammy wiggled her eyebrows at Eden. "So?"

"So, what?"

"What's it like having your sworn enemy living under your roof?"

"Do we have to talk about this?" Eden sighed.

"Is he doing okay? That was quite the head wound," Layla said.

Eden's lips quirked before she could stop them. *God, he'd been cute. All disoriented, vulnerable. Naked.*

"What's that?" Sammy demanded leaning in.

"What's what?"

"Your face, Eden. What's it doing? You look like you just thought of a yummy secret."

Eden ran her tongue over her teeth debating keeping her little tidbit to herself. But this was why she had these women in her life. "Okay, but this is Fort Knox-level stuff here."

Layla scooted her chair closer. "I love Fort Knox shit."

"Let me just make it very clear that I still intensely dislike the man," Eden prefaced.

Sammy nodded with enthusiasm. "So noted."

"And this doesn't change those feelings at all."

Layla leaned forward. "If you don't spill it now, I'm going to get my Taser out."

"So, he might have been a little confused by the head

wound thing," Eden began. "And he might have stripped naked in front of me."

Sammy's jaw hit the table, and Layla slapped an open palm down next to the basket of breadsticks. "No friggin' way," she hissed.

"Details. Let's talk measurements," Sammy insisted, snatching a breadstick out of the basket and waving it in front of Eden's face.

"Would you stop it?" Eden hissed.

"Look, the closest I've been to a cock lately is wading through the flock of chickens on Old Man Carson's farm last week," Sammy sighed. "Humor me."

Eden reluctantly took the breadstick from her friend. "Fine. But this too falls under the Fort Knox protection."

She looked over both shoulders to make sure no one was eavesdropping on them. In Blue Moon, it was a risk you took being in public. Your business was everyone's business here.

Enid Macklemore was working on a second bottle of wine with her friends Aretha and Xanna across the restaurant. Two tables away, Julio, the suave ponytailed cook from Pierce Brews, was staring deeply into the wide, violet eyes of Charisma Champion, school teacher and town astrologist who technically still should have been in school for the day.

Satisfied, Eden held up the breadstick and bit an inch off of the end and put it back down on her plate.

"You're screwing with us, aren't you?" Layla asked, eyeing the representation.

Eden shook her head. "I wish I was."

"And this was just head wound, pants off, naked? Not like ready to spelunk in your lady cave naked?" Sammy asked.

Eden closed her eyes. "You need to get laid. Like ASAP."

"Seriously," Layla agreed, still staring at the breadstick.

"So, are you going to?" Sammy asked.

"Going to what?" Eden picked up the breadstick and hastily took another bite of it before anyone guessed that they were playing *how big is Davis's schlong*.

"Are you going to have sex with Davis?"

The bread lodged in her throat, and Eden choked and coughed.

"Shit. Now I have to give her the Heimlich," Layla sighed, putting her napkin down and standing up.

Eden coughed, her eyes watering, and grabbed for her water. "Sit down! I'm fine," she rasped.

"Yeah, Layla. She's fine. She just choked on Davis's breadstick," Sammy snickered.

"I hate you both," Eden gasped.

"No, you don't," they said together.

"I do! And just to be very clear, I am not sleeping with Davis. Ever. Not in a million years would I let that man into my bed!"

"Well, I'm sure he'll be very disappointed," Franklin said, setting a plate of chicken parm in front of her.

12

She'd left the dishes from snack time next to the sink, intending to do them tomorrow. But Eden hadn't taken into account how that decision would haunt her while she chased the sleep her body begged for. She stared at the ceiling over her bed. Blinked. Then stared some more. Sleep continued to elude her.

It was because her brain was clogged with Aurora Decker's tea party to dos, with catering menus, and linen rentals for the Beautification Committee's reunion luncheon. This was the second request for midnight blue napkins. *Should she buy her own and add to her ivory, white, and grey collection?*

She wondered if Davis was comfortable next door.

His comment card, discovered by her two-man cleaning crew on his already neatly made-up bed had simply said: *Thank you, Eden.*

She wondered if he slept naked.

No! Eden rolled over and punched her pillow. She was *not* laying here not sleeping because she was wondering if Davis Gates slept naked... and if he was covered by a sheet or sprawled out like an Adonis in repose.

"Damn it," Eden muttered, kicking off her own blankets. Those dishes were going to get done and maybe while she was at it, she could scrub all thoughts of Davis—naked or clothed—from her mind.

She pulled on a cardigan over her sleep tank and shorts and padded barefoot into the hallway, past Davis's door. The inn was dark and quiet at this time of night and she sent up good vibes for a sound night's sleep for its inhabitants. Her guests' experience was paramount. White noise machines, luxurious linens, aromatherapy oils. Everything in each room was designed to soothe and comfort. Aunt Nell, her father's sister and owner of this fine old home, refused to turn over the keys to the inn until she was satisfied with each and every one of Eden's improvements.

Aunt Nell remained a silent partner in the property but had promptly fled to Arizona once the responsibility had been officially transferred to Eden. She still kept Aunt Nell up to date with financial statements, occupancy stats, and written proposals on all major decisions. But her aunt trusted Eden to not bankrupt them both and stayed out of it all.

Eden tiptoed through the lobby and cut down the back hallway that led to the kitchen. She flipped the light switches and gave a hefty sigh. Dirty dishes sat in heaps on both sides of her farmhouse sink. Both dishwashers were full of—clean—dishes that needed to be put away. She was off her game. And that she could blame entirely on Davis Gates.

With the resignation of someone who should have sucked it up, done all their work earlier, and now be dreaming of Channing Tatum, Eden picked up the mixing bowl crusted with dried batter.

She worked methodically if not enthusiastically, unloading one dishwasher and then the next before tackling the first stack of dirty dishes. A shadow fell over the counter next to her and she whirled around, tea towel at the ready.

Eden smothered a strangled scream. But the intruder held up his hands and she spotted the familiar bulge in those also familiar yoga pants.

"Davis! You scared the hell out of me!" His hair was mussed and he had pillow marks on one side of his face. The sleepy-eyed sexy look *so* worked for him.

"Sorry. I thought you heard me come in."

"And completely ignored you?"

"Well. Yeah." He shrugged, testing the limits on that ladies' V-neck tee.

Fair point. "What are you doing up at," she paused to glance at her watch. "1:30 in the morning?"

He looked a little embarrassed and not just because he was rocking her yoga pants and t-shirt as pajamas. "I missed dinner tonight, worked through it. I thought I could power through until morning." His stomach let out a long, low rumble. "I was wrong."

Eden turned away from the delectably sleepy sex god and started loading teacups and coffee mugs into the dishwasher. "There's always snacks available in the library."

"I wasn't aware."

She felt his gaze travel up from her ankles, her skin warming under his perusal.

She hadn't told him about the snacks. Hell, she hadn't even shown him the library. She hadn't exactly gone out of her way to make him feel unwelcome, but she certainly hadn't offered him the full guest experience. That was bad business karma. Just because the man had dented her heart a hundred years ago was no excuse to treat him poorly.

Aunt Nell would not approve the bad vibes. Even if Davis was "a real stinker."

"We're having pancakes for breakfast in the morning. I could make you some eggs to tide you over," she offered.

"Please. Don't go to any trouble," Davis insisted. "I can find the library and raid the snacks."

"You're a guest under my roof. The least I can do is make sure you don't starve to death. Your skeletal remains would scare off new visitors."

Eden pulled out a gleaming frying pan from the rollout drawer and placed it on the stove.

Davis eyed the eggs and cheese she stacked on the counter. "If you're sure it's no trouble."

If he were a regular guest, it wouldn't be any trouble. "I don't mind," she said lightly. *See? She could be nice!*

"Then the least I can do is the dishes." Davis stepped up to the sink, into her personal space and she was suddenly transported back to her hormonal junior year where his mere presence had her body lighting up. She backed up a pace and rapped her elbow on the stainless-steel island.

"Do I make you nervous?" he asked with a slow smile.

She snatched a cheery yellow bowl out from under the island and cracked an egg with a little extra force. "You infuriate me. You don't make me nervous."

"I infuriate you and you're making me eggs," Davis pointed out as she continued to crack eggs into the bowl.

"You're a guest." She whipped the egg mixture with violent efficiency. "And as such, you're entitled to certain amenities, services.

"Hmm." Davis's eyebrows winged up his forehead.

The flirtatious sound of his monosyllable set Eden's teeth on edge... and her blood warming. "Are you flirting with me?"

Davis systematically dried the mixing bowl with a dish towel, twisting it slowly around and around. "I'm weak with hunger," he explained, his eyes twinkling.

Shaking her head, Eden dropped a pat of butter into the pan.

"What's the craziest guest request you've ever accommodated?" Davis asked, changing the subject. He poked around under the sink cabinet and found the dishwasher detergent.

"Besides eggs at 1:30 in the morning?" Eden batted her lashes sarcastically at him.

"You're still funny. I always liked that about you."

Not in the mood to reminisce about their high school days, Eden answered. "Peacocks."

"Peacocks?"

"It was for this Jane Austen meets Woodstock marriage proposal. The intended loved peacocks, had a figurine collection of them. Her boyfriend wanted to have peacocks strolling the lawn here."

"Did you find some?" Davis asked.

Eden poured the egg mixture over the melted butter. "Of course," she sniffed that he had to ask. She always delivered. "I had to lock up Chewy and Vader because they kept chasing the birds. But that couple got their peacocks."

Davis's laugh filled the kitchen. "Did she say yes?"

The memory teased a smile out of her. "Most enthusiastically. She tackled him to the ground and the ring went flying. I had to wrestle it away from a particularly aggressive peacock."

"You do go the extra mile." Davis filled the dispenser with detergent and glanced in her direction.

Wordlessly, she closed the distance and stabbed the appropriate wash cycle buttons.

Davis grinned. "Team work.

"Mmm. So, what was so important that you had to work through dinner?" she asked, changing the subject and returning her attention to the eggs.

"My parents aren't big believers in technology and the

nine-year-old computer that housed our payroll program decided to die a painful death."

Eden winced, feeling his pain. "Back-ups?"

"Now there's a novel idea," Davis said dryly. "I should have known better when I asked my father if everything was cloud-based and he said 'isn't everything?'."

She bit her lip and reached for the gruyere. Maybe it felt a little nice to know that Davis too could suffer from the down-side of business ownership. That it wasn't all champagne and profits across the property line. "I take it, no, it is not cloud-based?"

"My father seems to believe that the internet lives in the sky and therefore is—"

"Cloud-based." Eden couldn't help but laugh. "My parents got rid of their Wi-Fi in the house because they said it was spying on them and killing their house plants." Her father's basement bumper crop of pot had actually dried up due to an irrigation issue, *not* the internet.

Davis laughed again and Eden felt a warmth in her belly. She ignored it and grated a light layer of gruyere over the fluffy eggs. Since she'd made them, she pulled two plates out of the cabinet, scooping eggs onto both. She turned and admired his work. The countertops gleamed and the dish-washer hummed quietly. He'd even scrubbed down the sink, Eden's personal definition of a clean kitchen.

"I suppose you've earned these." She handed him a plate. His fingers covered hers as he reached for it. Reflexively, she looked up into those soft brown eyes.

"Thank you, Eden."

Why did her name sound so good from his mouth? Why did the brush of his fingers warm her blood to molten?

"Thanks for everything," he said.

Her body's response to him pissed her off. Where was her

sense of self-preservation? If Davis were a cliff, her body would happily stroll to the edge and throw itself over.

"Stop. Thanking. Me." She'd been nice enough for one night. "I'm going to take these with me and get some sleep. Forks are over there." She gestured with her chin. "See you at breakfast."

She could feel him watching her as she left the room still clutching her plate of eggs. Why hadn't she ever felt this frisson of awareness with anyone else? She'd dated men, enjoyed taking them to bed. Yet, not one of them had set her body vibrating like a tuning fork the way that one, sleepy-eyed look from Davis did.

High school crush hangover, she decided. Her body just hadn't caught up with the reality her head and heart had embraced. Davis Gates was *not* the one.

13

After an accidentally intimate late night with Davis, Eden was enjoying her solitude the following afternoon. She had just dug into a round of bill paying and order placing when she heard the tinkling of the front door bell. On the monitor, she watched as Eva Merrill hurried inside, bundled up in a heavy down jacket and thick wool cap.

A moment later, her desk phone rang. Vader rolled over onto her back under Eden's desk and grumbled at the interruption to her nap.

"Eva's here to see you," Sunny chirped through the phone.

"Can you send her back?" Eden asked.

"Sure! Back where?"

"To my office. Where you called me," she enunciated. Sometimes Eden regretted not setting up shop literally anywhere but Blue Moon.

"Oh, right! Duh! Eva, you can go on back to Eden's office."

Sunny hung up before Eden could ask her for the cup of tea that she was dying for. Moments later, Evangelina Merrill —Cardona now—strolled into the room shedding winter layers.

"I hear someone has some big news," Eden said, staring pointedly at her friend's hand. Eva's eyes widened and her mouth opened into an O.

"How did you—Oh, right! The wedding!" Eva flopped down in the white upholstered chair in front of Eden's desk. "I'm so sorry I didn't invite you. It was a little... spontaneous."

"What did you think I was talking about?" Eden pressed, suspicious now. Eva had a history of keeping secrets, and in Blue Moon, that was right up there with stiffing delivery drivers and littering.

"Nothing," Eva said brightly.

Hmm. As a good reader of people and predictor of their needs, Eden was suspicious. She saved the spreadsheet she'd been editing. "Do you want some coffee?"

Eva rolled her eyes back. "I'd kill for some."

"Perfect. I was just going to make some tea. Let's go sit by the fire, and you can tell me all about the wedding," Eden suggested.

"Oh, tea sounds nice, too," Eva said frowning. "Less caffeine, right?"

"I can make you some tea instead," Eden offered cautiously. Her friend looked like she was ready to burst into tears.

"That would be really, really nice," Eva said, her voice shaky.

"Okaaaay. Tea it is." Eden led the way to the fireplace in the library. "How about you hang out in here, and I'll get it ready?"

Eva was already lost to the bookshelves. She was a romance novelist by trade, a lover of books, and Eden's shelves were stocked with gems from all genres. "Entertain yourself," Eden called over her shoulder.

She made a quick pit stop in her office and then put

together a tea tray in the kitchen. When she returned to the library with Chewy on her heels, sniffing after the cookies, Eva was curled in one of the leather chairs by the fire, one of her own books in her lap.

"I can't believe you have these," Eva said, stroking the burly fireman on the cover.

"Blue Moon's own," Eden said, setting the tray down on the hassock between the chairs. "How's the book coming?"

Eva beamed. "Great. Really great, thanks." Eva had used Sheriff Sexy as inspiration for a romance novel and had been shocked when life had followed art, leading her to her own happily ever after.

"How do you like your tea?"

"I don't know. I've never had any real tea before," Eva said, peering at the small plate of cookies on the tray.

"How about I fix you a cup the way I like it, and you can get started on the cookies?" Eden suggested.

Eva didn't need to be told twice. "Ohmygod," she said through a mouthful of raspberry bowtie. "These are amazing. I feel like I haven't eaten in days."

Eden slid a cup and saucer in front of her. "This is also for you," she said, handing over the card.

"What's this for?" Eva asked, wiping her hands on her jeans.

"Just a little congratulations."

Eden had a tabbed file folder full of greeting cards for every occasion. If one of her guests lost their elderly cat or got engaged or passed the bar exam, Eden had a card ready and waiting for them.

Eva opened the envelope and read quietly.

"My own happily ever after," she said, her eyes going damp. Eva made a choking noise and reached for her tea.

"Are you okay? You're not freaking out about the wedding

are you?" Eden asked. "Because you know you and Sheriff Sexy are meant to be."

Eva waved away the question. "No, not at all. Donovan and I are… great."

"Uh-huh."

"Seriously. I may have freaked out for the teensiest minute after the ceremony, but I'm happy. I swear."

"Right, because you look ecstatic," Eden pointed out.

Eva went from flushed and rosy to pale and sweaty in the span of a heartbeat. "Oh, God! I think I'm going to—" She bolted from her chair and dashed across the room to the brass umbrella stand by the French doors and vomited with enthusiasm.

Crap on a cracker. What was with people puking in the inn this week?

Eden approached cautiously. "Uhh, Eva? Are you okay?" she asked.

Eva straightened and wiped her mouth with the back of her hand. "I'm fine. Totally fine. Happens all the time."

"It does?" Eden asked, bewildered. She added *buy a new umbrella stand* to her mental to-do list.

"No! I'm pregnant and hiding it, okay? Geez, with the twenty questions, Eden! And now you made me tell my secret, and this is the worst!" Eva flopped face down on the striped cushion of the window seat.

Chewy decided to be helpful and climbed up on the cushion to spoon Eva with his eighty-pound body.

"Um…"

"Is everything okay?"

Eden whirled around to find Davis standing in the doorway looking fine as an Instagram model in dark trousers and a light blue shirt with the sleeves rolled up to his elbows.

He hadn't shaved today and had a sexy little stubble thing going.

He needed to leave her alone or her resolve to continue her intense dislike of him would start to crumble.

"Everything is fine. Great. Eva just..."

"I threw up in the umbrella stand," Eva wailed, working her way back to a seated position.

"I threw up in Eden's shower," Davis confessed.

Eva's lips reluctantly quirked. "Really?"

He nodded. "Like a geyser."

"It's been a real barf party around here this week," Eden sighed. She wished she had some rum for her tea. It would make everything just a little more manageable.

Eva tapped her forehead, looking at Davis. "Kitchen cabinet?" she asked.

"Fridge then cabinet," he said, brushing his fingers over the fresh bandage.

"If you two are done comparing war wounds—" Eden began, intent on getting Davis out of the room.

"Excuse me, Eden? Sheriff Cardona's here to see you," Sunny said poking her head into the room.

"Donovan!" Eva came to her feet as all of her six-foot-plus husband ambled into the room in his uniform.

"Hey, honey."

Eva danced over and placed a NC-17 kiss on her husband of three days.

"Newlyweds," Eden muttered.

"Don't take this the wrong way, Eva, but you taste a little like puke," Donovan said in a soft whisper.

Maybe tequila instead of rum, Eden decided.

"I threw up in the umbrella stand," Eva confessed.

Donovan didn't look remotely surprised.

"I hear congratulations are in order," Davis said, clapping Donovan on the back.

"Thanks," Donovan beamed, grinning down at his wife. For a split second, Eden wondered if Davis had ever looked that way at a woman and then decided instantly that she didn't care.

"Did you need something, Sheriff?" Eden asked, pinching the bridge of her nose between her fingers.

Donovan cleared his throat. His gaze flitted to Davis and back to Eden guiltily. "I'm afraid I'm here in an official capacity."

"Oh, for shit's sake!" Eden spat out. "That was fifteen years ago, and it wasn't my fault!"

"What's going on?" Eva asked.

"Is there somewhere private we can talk?" Donovan asked Eden. He pulled off his hat, revealing a mohawk earned during the height of the astrological apocalypse last week.

"Why don't we hold a town meeting, and you can interrogate me in front of everyone to see if I burned down Davis's house?" Eden suggested.

There was a noise in the hallway, and they all froze as a troop of six women giggled past on their way to the stairs.

Eva's gasp took the air out of the room. "Donovan! Are you accusing Eden of starting the fire?" she asked, drilling a finger into her husband's chest.

"Eva, I have to do my job."

Eden rounded on Davis. "So me opening my home to you earns me a visit from the sheriff? I can't believe you think I did this!" She couldn't believe she'd cooked this man eggs last night.

Davis stepped carefully into the fight that she was dying to have. "First of all, Eden, I never said I thought you had anything to do with it. In fact, that's exactly the opposite of what I told the fire chief."

"Donovan, how can you think Eden would have anything to do with this?" Eva hissed. Eden's heart softened at how offended her friend was on her behalf. Although Eva probably didn't know what had happened all those years ago.

"Then who decided I'm a suspect, Gates?" Eden demanded.

Davis let out a heavy sigh. "I'm guessing Donovan here got a call from my apoplectic father today. I told him about the fire. He didn't take it well."

"So he called the cops to tell them that *I* did it?" Eden said shrilly. The Moodys and Gateses had, for the most part, left law enforcement out of their feud. This would take things to a whole new level. She hated to think of the revenge her parents would want to extract now. If Donovan hauled her out of here in handcuffs, would they paint giant penises on the Gateses' fleet of electric cars again?

"That sounds like something he'd do," Davis said.

"A source called to express their very loud, demanding concern that we perform a thorough investigation," Donovan said over Eva's head. "Unrelated, is your father on any kind of stress management program or anti-anxiety medicines? Because he should consider it with his health history."

"Look," Eva cut in. "I get that you're in work mode, and you're not allowed to come out and say 'Of course, Eden's innocent, and I'm wasting everyone's time right now because Davis's dad is a—sorry, Davis—dick. But if you don't say those words right now, you're going to have to cook yourself dinner tonight." She crossed her arms over her chest.

If her friend hadn't recently vomited, Eden would have kissed her on the mouth.

"I *am* in work mode," Donovan insisted. "And, as such, I'm

not allowed to let my personal feelings cloud my judgment even if I would know *for certain* this is a waste of time and an unfortunate and embarrassing inconvenience for some of us."

Eva crinkled her nose and debated. "I'm not sure if you're forgiven yet."

Donovan closed his eyes and took a deep breath. "May I please just ask my questions so we can all put this behind us?"

"Fine, but I'm calling Beckett first," Eva announced. "Eden deserves legal representation."

Eden put her hands up. "Okay. Let's take a breath. Eva, thank you for wanting to protect me. But I don't need a lawyer. On the day in question, I was making and serving breakfast for my guests. There were about twelve people who can place me here during the morning. The *whole* morning. I have a list of their names and contact information."

Davis had remained quiet for far too long in Eden's opinion. "Is that good enough for your father?" she snapped at him. "Or would he prefer that the sheriff hauled me out of here in handcuffs?"

"I'm not going to answer that truthfully," Davis said with an embarrassed grin. "Let's just say my father is a hard man to persuade."

"Well maybe *someone* should try it sometime," Eden said, boring holes in him with her eyes.

Donovan cleared his throat. "If you have that list handy, I think we can call it a day."

"I'll get you a copy," Eden said primly. She strode from the room, head held high, and congratulated herself on not punching a hole in the plaster wall.

Back in her office with her stack of paperwork and ignored to-do list, she printed a copy of the guest information and folded it neatly, if a little violently, into an envelope.

She was headed in the direction of the library when she

heard Eva's voice coming from the sun porch on the back of the house.

"Yes, I *know* they're under the same roof, Bruce. But how are they supposed to fall in love if Eden's being questioned in *his* fire investigation?" Eva was hissing.

Eden ducked behind the doorway and held her breath... and her bile. *Fall in love? With Davis?* No wonder Bruce and Ellery had shown up on her doorstep with him. Those sneaky sons of Beautification Committee members had been waiting for an opening to force her and Davis together. And the destruction of his house had provided the perfect opportunity.

"I'm only saying that I don't think having Eden accused of a crime against Davis is very healthy for their relationship."

Oh, *hell* no. Eden crumpled the envelope in her hands. No one played puppet master with Eden's life. She tip-toed past the door and hurried into the library. Davis was gone, but Donovan was studying the shelves smiling boyishly at his wife's romance novels.

"Here are my witnesses," Eden said handing over the mangled envelope.

"Look, Eden, I'm sorry about all this. I'm just doing my job."

"Yeah, well, so am I. Any further questions, Sheriff?" Eden asked with a hint of frost. She'd forgive him. *Eventually.*

"No, ma'am. If you'll excuse me, I'm gonna find my wife and get out of your hair. Oh, and, if you don't mind, I'll take that umbrella stand and have it cleaned for you. Eva's... a little under the weather."

He hurried out of the library as if his pants were on fire with the vomit-filled umbrella stand under his arm. Eden gave herself a moment to just sit and stew, sinking into the chair in front of the fire and picking up her now cold tea. The woven tote on the floor next to Eva's chair caught her eye. As did the hot pink binder with the words *Beautification Committee Rules & Regulations* scrawled down the spine.

She cast a glance over her shoulder and, seeing no one, snatched the binder out of the bag. This could be the key to getting the nosy, matchmaking troublemakers off her case.

This could free her forever from Davis Gates.

She heard a noise in the hallway and unceremoniously stuffed the binder under her seat cushion. Eva reappeared, flushed and happy again. The joys of hormones and new marriages, Eden supposed.

"Sorry about... well, literally everything that happened in the last thirty minutes," Eva offered.

"Eh," Eden shrugged, trying not to feel guilty at her thievery. "Let's eat cookies and pretend everything is normal."

~

Dearest Beautification Committee Member,

Allow me to be the first to welcome you to the honorable, venerable, deeply respected keystone of our community. If you'll forgive me for waxing poetic, I like to think of us as the "heart" of Blue Moon Bend.

Our goal is a noble one: to make our community as happy, and therefore as secure and peaceful, as humanly possible. To accomplish such ends, we dedicate our energies to joining single citizens in love matches carefully orchestrated to the benefit of both parties and Blue Moon.

You have been chosen to join our ranks to uphold this magnificent, magnanimous cause. It is an honor you won't soon forget.

With Warm Regards,
Bruce Oakleigh
Beautification Committee President

14

Snack time was one of the highlights of Eden's days as an inn keeper. While some inns touted fancy tea time, Blue Moon stood for no such arrogance. Every day at 4 p.m. guests were treated to cookies and pastries and alcohol. It was a happy hour with baked goods. And it was quite popular.

Eden hurried onto the sun porch where a roaring fire warmed the room. Her tray was overflowing with pecan tassies, apple tarts, and cheesecake cookie cups. She smiled when she noticed that half of her guests were already here, laughing and mingling. The smile froze on her face when she noticed Davis in the corner pouring wine. *His* wine. With her dogs staring adoringly up at him. Chewy put his head on Davis's foot under the table. *Traitors.*

She'd been avoiding him since overhearing Eva on the phone with the Beautification Committee. Eden didn't see where it was any of his business that he was the other half of her intended match. This was a situation she could handle on her own.

"Now, this one is our Riesling," Davis said, handing Billie Sue a plastic cup with a healthy slosh of white wine in it.

"You'll be able to pick up on the tree fruit notes and maybe a hint of mango. It pairs best with savory dishes like a pork roast. Ah, Eden, perfect timing! I hope you don't mind if I offer your guests a private tasting?"

"How lovely," she said wrestling the sarcasm out of her tone. It wasn't her guests' fault that they were being served free wine by a penis-packing closet jerk.

Davis, blissfully unaware of her murderous thoughts, leaned across the table and snatched one of the cheesecake cookies from her tray. "Here, Billie Sue. Try it now."

Billie Sue nibbled at the cookie and took a dainty sip of the wine. Her green eyes rolled back in her head, painted eyebrows arching toward her hair line. "Oh. My. God. Sebastian! Come try this," she bellowed over her shoulder.

Eden tried to telegraph her rage through her eyeballs to Davis, but he was too busy entertaining her guests. They were all bellied up to his makeshift bar, asking questions and sampling.

"What a nice young man," Mrs. Hasselbeck, a sub-five-foot tall grandmother of seventeen, sighed as she shuffled by with her walker. "They sure don't make 'em like that anymore."

Eden bit back a sigh. Nothing in the world could make her argue with a guest. Not even when the guest was profoundly and painfully wrong. "No, I guess they don't," she agreed.

"My granddaughter's boyfriend has a neck piercing and calls her his 'old lady'." Mrs. Hasselbeck leaned in conspiratorially. "I hit him with my scooter at Easter. Pretended it got stuck in gear."

Eden couldn't hold back her laugh. "I'm sure he deserved it."

"He's a douchewagon, as the kids are saying these days. Not like that handsome Davis. Smart, charming, funny. And easy on the eyes." Mrs. Hasselbeck took her glasses off and cleaned them on the hem of her sweater where donkeys paraded across her chest. "He just needs a good woman to help him pick better clothing."

Davis was still rocking a horrific collection of thrift store finds until he was cleared to drive. Today his turtleneck could be described as a horrific mix of grey, green, and beige and was untucked over a pair of low-rise, orange corduroy trousers that sat snuggly on his hips. They made a whisper sound every time he took a step.

"Maybe he'll be lucky enough to find one someday," Eden said. Why did everyone have to love him so damn much? He *wasn't* the perfect gentleman that everyone thought him to be. And it annoyed her to no end that no one else could see it.

"Eden, I swear you are a hospitality genius." The sleekly dressed Nia was hitting the east coast for a road trip with her twin sister. The two had a goal of hitting all fifty states together and spent a portion of their year in the car, bickering and seeing the sights that the U.S. had to offer. "Setting up a tasting with our very own wine expert? Girl, you're a genius-level marketer!"

"Oh. Um. Thank you," Eden said, deciding now was not the time to announce that she'd never served Gates wine under her roof before. Or to draw attention to the fact that Davis had undermined her to push his own business.

"I love how this town is so damn neighborly," Nia's sister Tierra said, holding a dainty apple tart between glittering purple finger nails. She wore her hair in a short cap that framed her face and was dressed in a flowing caftan. "It's like you're all friends, and you want everyone to do well."

"Sounds like communism," Nia laughed.

"Actually, around here we call it *commune-ism*," Eden said, still glowering at Davis.

The sisters appreciated her humor.

"So, can we talk about Mr. Hottie Wine Man for a minute?" Tierra asked, shooting a glance at Davis as he grinned down at the 82-year-old Mrs. Hasselbeck.

"What about him?" Eden asked warily.

"If he's single and you're single, why haven't you two locked yourself in a bathroom with finger paints and a black light yet?" Nia demanded.

"Well, that's oddly specific," Eden evaded.

Nia pulled a folded piece of paper out of her back pocket. She cleared her throat, "Sexual Scenario Suggestions for November. Number One: Lock yourselves in a bathroom with finger paints and a black light. Number Two... Oh wait, that one's just a drawing." She turned her head. "I can't tell which end is up."

Tierra peered over her sister's shoulder.

"Where did you get that?" Eden asked, making a grab for the paper.

"It was an insert in *The Monthly Moon* that we got at the book store," Nia said, snatching the brochure back to get a better look at the illustration.

"Super weird guy behind the register at the book store, by the way," Tierra added.

"That's Fitz. He's... unique," Eden said in lieu of explaining that Fitz was a reformed pot dealer who now supplemented his used book income by stripping on the side. She, like the rest of the town, had seen the video the Pierces had shot when an unfortunate mix-up had Fitz flashing his pearly white butt cheeks at the Pierce women and was nearly arrested by Sheriff Cardona. Some things were better kept from tourists. Some things couldn't be unseen.

"Anyway, so why haven't you?" Nia asked.

"Why haven't I what?" Eden asked, setting the tray down

and arranging the cookies carefully on color coordinated plates.

"Why haven't you and Davis broken out the finger paints?" Tierra demanded. "He's so fine, I'd write a sonnet about him."

"He's hot enough that I can forgive him for his utter fashion failures," Nia said, eyeing up Davis's bleck turtleneck.

Eden bit back a laugh. "In his defense..." those words had never come out of her mouth in regard to Davis before. "Most of his wardrobe was ruined in an unfortunate incident recently. He's living it up in thrift store donations until he can go shopping. You should see him in yoga pants."

"Ooooh!" Nia and Tierra crooned, drawing the eyes of everyone.

Davis looked their way, and the twins wiggled their fingers at him.

"Ladies, would you like a sample?" Davis asked. He gestured at the open bottles of wine in front of him. But given the direction their conversation had gone, the twins erupted into flirty giggles.

"Davis, let me ask you something," Tierra insisted.

Oh, no.

"Ask me anything." He flashed them a charming grin that had Nia fanning herself.

That son of a bitch was even smoother than he had been in high school, Eden thought gritting her teeth.

"Why haven't you and our girl Eden here gotten together, yet? You're both beautiful, you live next door to each other, you're running successful businesses," Tierra ticked the items off on her fingers.

"Are you working for the Beautification Committee?" Eden asked. "Did a man named Bruce come up to you on the street and ask you to help in some matchmaking scheme?" *Damn it, she really needed to find time to read that binder she stole from Eva.*

She kept falling asleep halfway through Bruce's twelve-page introduction.

Nia and Tierra shared a "she's lost her damn mind" look.

"Let's start with a sparkling wine," Davis suggested, dancing around the line of questioning. Sparkling wine was for celebrating, and as far as Eden could tell, she had nothing to celebrate. Not with the man who had stomped on her teenage heart and helped destroy her reputation—possibly twice now—pouring *his* wine for *her* guests as if he owned the place.

"Fill us up," Tierra insisted holding up an empty cup.

"And tell us why you haven't asked this fine young lady out yet," Nia added.

"I asked him out," Eden said, regretting the words as soon as they were out of her mouth. The twins had no idea what kind of disaster story they were in for. But at least she'd wiped the smug smile off of Davis's face. The other guests crowded around ready for the gossip.

"Eden asked me to the HeHa dance when she was a junior and I was a senior," Davis began.

Tierra raised her hand. "HeHa?"

"Helping Hands," Eden answered. "It's a day of community service that ends with a big, formal dance."

"Did you pick her up in a limo?"

"Did you get her a corsage?"

"You didn't wear that, did you?"

The questions flew fast and loud around them.

"I actually stood her up," Davis said.

Eden felt a grim satisfaction at the looks of horror and disappointment on the faces of their rapt audience.

"That doesn't sound like you, sweetie," Mrs. Hasselbeck frowned.

"No, it was very much like him," Eden said, unable to hold back on the dig.

Davis didn't make a move to defend himself. "It was a mistake I've regretted ever since then," he said simply.

"Awh," swooned their audience.

"He showed up at the dance with another date," Eden added.

"No!" Nia gasped.

Davis nodded and poured a round of chardonnays. "I'm afraid so. I was young and dumb, and my parents didn't approve of me going with Eden."

"Star-crossed lovers! And now here you are under one roof for a second chance," Marty Bigelow, an insurance salesman from Idaho sighed dramatically.

Eden shook her head. What the hell was in the wine Gates was serving up? Liquid romance?

"That ship has sailed," Eden said with a cheery smile she didn't feel. "Now, who would like a pecan tassie?"

"But you two practically smolder when you're in the same room," Marty's sister-in-law Judith said, her dangling cat earrings jiggling with vehemence.

Davis met Eden's gaze, and Eden pretended not to notice said smolder.

"See? That's exactly what I'm talking about," Judith said pointing at them. "It's like he wants to rip your clothes off, and you want to break his face kissing it!"

"How much did you give these people to drink?" Eden demanded.

Her guests erupted into a loud discussion of all the reasons why Eden and Davis should give each other a second shot. Eden's polite proprietress smile was frozen on her face.

"Everyone. Everyone!" The room quieted down at Davis's

tone. "We both made mistakes, myself especially. And sometimes there are no second chances."

Someone in the small crowd booed.

"Besides," Eden added. "Our families have been feuding for decades. It would never work out."

Tierra grabbed the bottle of sparkling wine from the table and started filling cups. "This I've gotta hear."

"Well, it all started in 1960 when Davis's grandfather hit my grandma with his car," Eden began.

"That's not how it started."

She turned to look at Davis. "Excuse me?"

"No, it started when your great-aunt broke into my great-aunt's store and stole all her flour."

"That's not what happened," Eden argued. "Your great-aunt refused to sell my great-aunt any cake ingredients so *she* could win the baking contest."

"That actually does sound like something she'd do," Davis said, rubbing a hand over his dimpled chin. "Great-Aunt Vera was mean as a snake. She hit her husband with a rolling pin every time he asked what was for dinner."

"Great-Aunt Uversal wasn't much better," Eden admitted. "She chased me once with a riding lawn mower. She was 97 at the time. Got kicked out of two nursing homes for biting."

Davis's lips quirked at the corner.

"Look! They're bonding," Marty whispered as if Eden and Davis couldn't hear him.

"Wait, if your families were already feuding, what happened after you stood her up at the dance?" Nia asked Davis.

Davis held Eden's gaze.

"I accidentally set his lawn on fire and almost burned down his house."

~

BEAUTIFICATION COMMITTEE GUIDELINES

SECTION C: IDENTIFYING POTENTIAL MATCHES

Potential matchees are identified at committee discretion. Qualifications can include, but are not limited to: general physical attraction, compatible emotional neediness, and/or a satisfactory score in the proprietary Blue Moon Mate Compatibility Profile™.

15

After sharing the gist of The Incident with Eden's guests yesterday, Davis got the feeling he was persona definitely non-grata around the inn. Apparently, Eden was still sensitive about the whole fire thing. At breakfast this morning, she'd actually thrown a fresh blueberry muffin at his head when none of the other guests were looking. Vader helpfully caught the shrapnel of it in her mouth and trotted off under the dining room table to enjoy the spoils of war. He'd gone back to his room to change out of the black sweater vest with brass buttons into a more subdued checkered shirt with bull horns embroidered on the back.

"You busy?" Anastasia poked her head into Davis's office.

He'd been staring blankly at the newsletter template for the past half an hour and thinking about Eden.

"I've got a minute."

"Then I've got something for you to taste." She plopped down across from him and handed over a small glass beaker.

Davis picked it up and held it to the light. "Is this the blend?" he asked. Before the fire, he and Anastasia had spent a good week tasting and testing a new blend. Last year's Cayuga and Chardonnay grapes were getting a new life. It was a secret experiment he and Anastasia were working on behind closed doors. They wanted to nail down exactly the right mix before introducing the vintage to his father.

"Have a sip and you tell me." He and Anastasia had worked at rival wineries in California and had spent their first year at Blue Moon Winery going head-to-head over every decision. They'd finally settled into a groove once they both realized that the other wasn't out to ruin everything.

Davis wished he could come to a similar agreement with Eden.

He swirled the wine inside the beaker and watched the legs work their way down the glass. He sniffed deeply, catching notes of fruit and oak.

Anastasia sat patiently through the ritual. Wine was a multi-sensory experience. One had to be detail-oriented enough to hit all the right notes for each sense. Their batches were small compared to some other upstate wineries, but there wasn't a single vintage that Davis wasn't inordinately proud of.

He brought the beaker to his mouth and sipped lightly, letting the wine hit his tongue. It was crisp and dry, clean on his palate.

Anastasia smiled smugly and crossed her arms. "Winner?"

He swallowed, breathing out the aromatics. "Wow."

"Rack it?" she asked. Racking was the next part of the process once the proper blend was established. It was one of Davis's favorite parts of winemaking. Finalizing the flavor that would end up in glasses on dinner tables around the country.

"Rack it," he nodded.

Anastasia kicked her legs out and stretched. "How's the head?"

"For all intents and purposes, good as new," Davis said. "I got the okay to drive this morning."

"Good. That means you can stop dressing like a seventies porn star," she said eyeing his shirt.

"Not a fan of western flair?" he asked.

Anastasia wore the same thing every day. Jeans and a black sweater in the winter and jeans and a black tank top in the summer. She insisted her mental energy was better spent on the grapes rather than her wardrobe.

"Your father called me this morning," she said, changing the subject.

Davis picked up his pen and tapped out a beat on his notebook. "And what did he want?" He knew exactly what his father wanted.

"Oh, the usual. Wanted to know if the girl at the inn had been arrested. Wanted to know where you were staying. Wanted to know if he needed to call his cousin Ira."

Ira Gates was a bulldog lawyer who worked out of Boston and made a living suing the shit out of anyone who looked at his clients funny.

"Of course, I figured he could get this information from you if he'd just ask," Anastasia said.

Davis had been avoiding his father's calls since Ferguson had sicced the sheriff on Eden. He didn't want to give his father any more reason to fly home early.

"What did you tell him?" Davis asked.

"I told him your family pays me to tend the vines and make the wine, and if he wants me to take time away from that to play snitch, he's going to have to pay me extra and hire me an assistant." Anastasia took no crap and doled it out by the shovel full.

"Thanks for not telling him... anything."

"Maybe you all should work on your family communication so you don't have to put employees in the middle of it," she suggested pointedly.

A tremendous snore erupted from under Davis's desk.

"You got a girl under there so long she fell asleep?" Anastasia asked.

Davis leaned down to ruffle the mound of fur at his feet. "It's Chewy, Eden's dog. He followed me over today."

"Eden know you stole her dog?"

"I didn't steal him. He came willingly."

"Uh-huh." Anastasia rose. "Well, I'm getting out of here before you turn me into an accessory to dognapping. Enjoy the blend," she said, leaving the beaker on his desk. "I'm going to top up and head out."

"Thanks, Stasia."

Davis stared down at the dog slobbering on his shoe. "I guess maybe I should let her know that you're here," he said. He didn't need yet another reason for her to hate him. He thought they'd been making progress that night over eggs and business talk. But once again, his parents had bullied their way in, wrecking things.

He leaned down and snapped a picture of Chewy. Attaching it to a new email message, he wrote:

To: Eden

From: Davis

Subject: To Whom It May Concern,

Found. One narcoleptic dog with a snoring problem. Will return to rightful owner this afternoon.

He hit send. And waited for the reply. She had one of those watches that told her every time she got a text, received an email, or the temperature dropped a degree. He waited five full minutes before her reply came through.

To: Davis

From: Eden

Subject: Beware the back end

Tell Chewy to enjoy his last hours of freedom. He knows he's not supposed to cross the property line. In the meantime, watch out, he tends to let them rip in his sleep. He'll make your stink bomb seem like an air freshener.

To: Eden

From: Davis

Subject: Gas mask on

I'll bring him back for snack time. If no one lights a match in my office between now and then.

There. See? They could communicate without fighting. Without sniping at each other. He drummed his pen on the desk. He needed to move, needed to think.

The newsletter could wait, Davis decided. He wanted to get out and stretch his legs. "Come on, Chewy. Let's take a walk."

He led the way down the back hall of the building that housed the main tasting room and the event space and pushed open the door. There had been a time when he'd thought he and Eden could be the end to this ridiculous feud. That they could be friends, or dare he hope, something more. Buttoning an olive green wool jacket that smelled vaguely of mothballs, he signaled for Chewy. The dog trotted outside, a pile of yellow fluff and lolling tongue. "Let's walk the vines, Chew," Davis suggested.

Together they wandered down the slope to the neat rows of grapevines. They were coming up on Thanksgiving soon, which meant winter. The bulk of the harvest was already over. They had a small plot of late harvest grapes to deal with next month for ice wine, another experiment he'd yet to discuss with his father. Work had moved indoors for the winter. And while wine fermented and fined, Davis would focus on operations. Marketing and community outreach and the never-ending tasks that fell between operations and wine-making.

He'd been ready to come home to Blue Moon long before his parents gave him the go-ahead. This was home. And these sloping acres were where he belonged. California had been one long, fun adventure, but he'd never viewed it as more than a stopover. While he'd lived there, tended vines there, built a career there, his thoughts had always been of Blue Moon and, occasionally, the dark haired beauty he'd disappointed.

Chewy dashed ahead of him and trotted down the first row of vines. Davis took his time, breathing in the crisp air. There'd be frost tonight and snow soon enough. The winter was when he focused on planning. Last year had been a banner year for Blue Moon Wines, and he hoped to continue the trend.

He'd had several irons in the figurative fire before the actual fire. He was expanding his distribution to restaurants and scheduling weekend events in the summer that would bring people out for a night under the stars between the vines.

And now that he and Eden were on speaking terms—sort of—he hoped they could discuss a partnership of sorts that would benefit both businesses.

They weren't so different, he and she, Davis mused. They were both single-minded entrepreneurs who loved what they did. Who lived and breathed work. He admired that about her. And if she could forgive him for being eighteen, maybe someday they'd get their second chance at more than just a partnership.

She was still as beautiful as ever with that short dark hair and those wide blue eyes. Still had that edge to her. She still gave him that thrill in his blood when he caught her laughing.

He'd spent a very large portion of his years since high school regretting that he'd hurt her. Unfortunately, she'd spent those same years remembering that he'd hurt her.

He and Chewy walked the vines until his cheeks were pink and his hands were cold. "Come on, buddy. Let's go home," Davis suggested. Chewy's lopsided ears perked up and he pranced off in the direction of the inn.

Davis and Chewy found Eden frantically stripping bed linens from a suite on the third floor. "Wow, great room," Davis said, admiring the carved molding that circled the interior of the turret. The walls were a deep slate blue, the furniture heavy and masculine. There was an oversized chair angled to take in the view. The perfect spot for reading or daydreaming.

Judging from Eden's constant full-steam-ahead pace, he guessed that she rarely attempted the latter. He turned to admire her, in fast forward as she bent over the mattress. That view was even more spectacular.

"Thanks," she said dryly and dumped the pillow sham on top of the growing pile on the floor. Chewy jumped up on the bed and flopped down in his favorite napping position. "Chewy, I love you, but if you don't get your furry ass off this bed, I'm going to sell you to the gypsies," Eden threatened.

Davis snapped his fingers and Chewy cheerfully hopped off the bed. He wasn't sure why that pissed Eden off, but she was glaring at him like he'd just punched her grandmother in the mouth. He searched his memory, wondering if any of his relatives had done such a thing.

Seeking to ease the tension he grabbed the first pillow on his side of the bed and shucked off the fabric casing.

"You don't have to help," she snapped, hurrying into the bathroom and returning with an armload of damp towels.

"You don't have to do it all yourself," he pointed out, moving on to the next pillow. "Is there a linen emergency I wasn't made aware of?"

Eden dumped the towels on top of the sheets and returned to the bathroom. "No, just a husband who forgot his anniversary and desperately needed this room for the night. I have to get it turned over with fresh everything in the next two hours. Oh, and have a bouquet of baby pink roses waiting. And a gift."

She moved like she was the prima ballerina in a high-speed ballet. All grace and efficiency.

"A gift?" Davis asked, eyebrow cocked.

"Just anything I think a wife might like on her tenth anniversary to make it look like her husband hadn't completely forgotten," Eden said grimly.

"You're saving this guy's marriage," Davis pointed out.

Eden used her foot to shove the lump of laundry toward the doorway. She swiped an arm over her brow.

"Where are the fresh sheets?" Davis asked.

"Why are you being nice to me?"

"Do you really want to get into that conversation now, or do you want me to make the bed and dust or vacuum or whatever needs done while you go get flowers and a marriage-saving gift?"

She blinked at him. It was only a quick flash, but Davis saw it all the same. Relief.

"Are you screwing with me right now?" she asked.

"Despite my actions fifteen years ago, I'm not a horrible person out to screw you, Eden. At least not in that sense. There are other meanings behind the word that I'd be happy to discuss the potential of with you. Go. I've got this."

She hesitated. "Sunny's coming in in half an hour for snack time."

"Then she can handle the front desk. Just show me where the linens and those little bottles of shampoo are."

"Thank you." She said it like it pained her. And Davis felt a fifteen-year-old knot loosen somewhere in his chest.

"You're welcome. Now go."

She made it to the doorway before he stopped her.

"Eden?"

"Yeah?"

"Did he give you a budget on the gift?"

She shook her head. A slow smile spreading across her pretty face. "Nope."

"Make sure he never forgets another anniversary."

~

BEAUTIFICATION COMMITTEE GUIDELINES

SECTION 147, SUBPARAGRAPHS B-XXY: ASSISTED WOO-ING

In some trickier matches, Committee members may find it necessary to give the match a helping hand on the road to their happily ever after. While we are constantly striving to improve our capabilities, these are options that have served us well in the noble quest for true love:

The use of harmless fibbing in guiding matchees to each other.

Manipulating environments for amorous and romantic mood enhancement.

Crafting situations in which matchees will be required to spend large amounts of time together.

Creating false realities in which matchees are forced to reconcile their feelings.

Hypnosis (note: used only as a last resort and with varying degrees of success).

16

Eden put her hatchback in gear and accelerated down the driveway as quickly as she could without squealing her tires. Blue Moon was five minutes away, and everything in town was within five minutes of town limits. If she called ahead for the flowers, she could hit the jewelry store because Forgetful Husband was definitely going to make up for forgetting and swing by the grocery store for the essentials on the growing list on her phone.

She used her voice activation and dialed the flower shop.

"Every Bloomin' Thing. This is Liz. How can I help you?"

"Liz. I have a flower emergency," Eden told her.

"I just so happen to have some emergency flower arranging time available."

"Good because I need an over-the-top bouquet of baby pink roses that say 'I'm sorry for forgetting our tenth anniversary.'"

"Budget?" Liz asked, all business. As a flower shop owner, she had her fingers on the pulse of every stupid thing that spouses did to each other.

"Impossible to forgive," Eden said.

"That's what I like to hear. I'll have it ready for you in forty minutes."

"You're a gem. A miracle worker. People sing songs about you," Eden gushed.

"Yep. So how's it going with Davis?"

Eden drummed her fingers on the steering wheel and came to an abrupt stop at a stop sign. She gritted her teeth and eased through the intersection. "He's fine. Everything is fine."

"Such a shame what happened to him," Liz continued. "He's the nicest guy."

"Yeah, he's peachy," Eden said dryly.

"Well, I'm gonna get to arranging. See you in forty." Liz disconnected the call, and Eden cranked up her music. At least Van Morrison wouldn't insist on telling her how great the man who had dented her teenage heart was. Even if said heart-denter was currently turning over a suite for her. "No!" Eden smacked her steering wheel. She would not allow herself to entertain the idea that Davis Gates might not be the devil incarnate. He was a bad, bad man. And she couldn't be bought with a half-assed bed linen offering or late night conversations, or her dogs' obvious affection for him.

Resolve fortified, Eden headed toward Blue Moon.

The universe was working with her today. Eden squeezed into a parking space directly in front of Wilson Abramovich's jewelry store and hopped out. The damp chill of the November day seeped into her bones, and she envisioned a quiet night by the fire, maybe a hot bath. She'd earn it today. It was days like this that frustrated and energized her. She loved being around people, loved surprising them with things that made their day just a little better. And she would make sure that Forgetful Husband was not only forgiven but revered before he and his wife left tomorrow.

She pulled the glass door open, slinging her bag over her shoulder.

Wilson, the town's jeweler, was a tidy little man with a halo of gray hair fluffing out under his growing bald spot. He wore a watch on a chain and glasses that constantly slipped down his nose.

"Ah, Eden. How lovely to see you," he said, rising from the desk with a loop still attached to his glasses. "Oops. Now, I can see you," he said, swiping the contraption off his head.

"Wilson, I need something that will get a forgetful husband forgiven," she said, leaning over the display glass at all the sparkly perfection perched on plush pillows and waiting to adorn lucky men and women.

Wilson tapped his chin. "How forgetful was he?"

"Tenth wedding anniversary."

"Let's begin with gold and work our way up from there," he suggested, sweeping an arm toward a case at the front of the store.

Twenty minutes of discerning browsing later, they'd settled on the perfect gift—two, actually. Wilson handed over one of the tiny boxes to an assistant for wrapping and Eden scrawled her signature on the credit card receipt.

"I heard that Davis Gates is staying with you while Calvin's crew works on his house," Wilson said. In any other town, it would have been making small talk. But Wilson Abramovich was a member of Blue Moon's Beautification Committee. Matchmaking was in his blood... and his business. Ninety-nine percent of all engagements in Blue Moon were sealed with a sparkly something from his jewelry store. Wilson was fishing for information. *Damn it. She really needed to dig further into that binder.* She was on the chapter about laying the groundwork for a solid match. Suggestions included surveilling said couple and watching for flirtatious exchanges and identifying each half's definition of love.

"Yes," she said, pasting a smile on her mouth and slipping the unwrapped gift box into her purse. "He's staying in a guest room." She put emphasis on "guest room" lest Wilson delusionally believe Davis had moved right into her bed. Davis Gates in her bed. Her brain decided to run with that fantasy and Eden felt her cheeks flush scarlet.

Wilson accepted the wrapped box from his assistant and placed it carefully in a festive gift bag. "I must say, it's wonderful seeing you step up to offer Davis a place to stay."

"Because he's such a great guy?" Eden guessed. The entire town was convinced that Davis was a heart-of-gold sweetie pie with a quick grin and a desire to lend a helping hand. And maybe he was that... to everyone else. But to her, he was a sneaky, cowardly, dog-stealing son of a Gates. Who looked excellent in a suit, even better naked, and was occasionally quite thoughtful. Oh my God. She needed a vacation. Far far away from Davis and his nice ass.

Wilson chuckled under his mustache. "Well, that, of course. But also seeing you take the first step to bury the hatchet in this ridiculous feud is simply wonderful. Blue Moon has long suffered under the bad vibes created by your two families, and seeing it finally come to an end is something to celebrate. People won't forget how generous you've been," Wilson predicted.

Eden suddenly didn't feel like stomping her foot so much. In fact, there was a warm flush creeping over her cheeks.

"I'm just doing the neighborly thing," she mumbled.

Wilson handed over the gift bag. "It won't go unnoticed," he predicted, giving a not-so-subtle nod to the two Blue Moon Business of the Year awards on a shelf behind the cash register.

"Um. Thank you... for your help with this and... everything," Eden said, waving the bag.

"Good luck to your guest," Wilson called after her as she rushed out.

Eden checked her watch, ignoring the new texts from Layla and Sammy. She had enough time to swing by Farm and Field Fresh, the grocery store. Her personal cupboards were bare. She backed out of her space and drove down Main Street. Even on this gray day, the colorful people of Blue Moon were out in droves. Righteous Subs and Peace of Pizza were doing a brisk early lunch business, and there was a steady flow of customers in and out of Overly Caffeinated on the corner. She turned right on Lavender Street and then headed west on Karma Avenue. Farm and Field Fresh was a large brick building on the edge of town. It was organic and free trade, and it had three entire aisles of vegan and vegetarian foods.

Eden dodged the employee offering samples of beet juice smoothie just inside the door. But she did make a pit stop to taste a gluten-free, vegan oatmeal raisin cookie. It tasted a little like cardboard, but beggars couldn't be choosers. She pushed her cart into the produce section and grabbed her usuals for weekly lunches. She stocked up on organic, cage-free chicken breasts and her secret obsession: chili lime popcorn. She'd have a bag of it in front of the fire tonight and put her feet up, Eden decided.

She made it into the dog food aisle without being stopped for more than a quick hello or seventeen. In Blue Moon, even strangers weren't strangers. One trip around the grocery store and a visitor could meet half of the town if they weren't careful.

Eden's cart came to an abrupt stop. Mrs. Nordemann, dressed in the head-to-toe black of a widow committed to mourning the decades-old death of her husband, hovered near the aisle entrance. She rivaled Bruce Oakleigh and Minnie Murkle for Blue Moon's biggest gossip. There was a lot of competition for that title.

"Eden!" Her lined face broke into a calculating smile. "How lovely to see you in town. We've all been wondering when we'd see you. I thought perhaps that handsome Davis Gates was holding you prisoner in that beautiful inn of yours." Her wink was anything but subtle.

Eden's forced smile hurt her jaw. "No captivity," she said lightly and turned her attention to the bags of dry dog food. Vader and Chewy ate like small horses.

"Well, I think it's wonderful about you two," Mrs. Nordemann said conspiratorially. She plucked a six-pack of canned cat food off the shelf. Eden had been to Mrs. Nordemann's house every month for the last few years for Book Club and had never once seen a cat.

"What about us?" Eden asked, not liking one bit how for the first time "us" included Davis Gates.

"Abandoning your families' feud and embracing each other... as neighbors of course," Mrs. Nordemann added quickly with another wink.

"As neighbors," Eden echoed.

People were acting like they'd just signed a peace treaty. She hadn't realized how their little fifty-year fight had affected the rest of Blue Moon.

"And you were the one to take the first step. Why I wouldn't be surprised if that alone netted you the Business of the Year award."

Yes, the Business of the Year award was a small acrylic plaque with block lettering congratulating the recipient on vague "service to the community." Everyone knew that Eden wanted one more than a vacation to the Virgin Islands.

Earning that award would symbolize finally putting the past behind her. It meant that her hometown recognized that she was a responsible, upstanding adult who ran a successful business that brought tourism dollars to the community. It meant that everyone would finally have something good to say about her rather than reminiscing about why Blue Moon's landscaping service had to change their organic lawn fertilizer formula.

People still felt it necessary to remind her that the new, nonflammable formula wasn't as good as the old.

"Eden, hi!" Emma Vulkov, one of Franklin Merrill's red-headed daughters, waved to her from the mouth of the aisle. One of Franklin Merrill's red-headed *pregnant* daughters, Eden remembered. Lips zipped, she waved her greeting.

"Hello there, Emmaline." Mrs. Nordemann wiggled her fingers in greeting.

"Are we still on for Book Club, Mrs. Nordemann?" Emma asked.

"Of course, my dear. *The Pilot and the Puck-Up* by Pippa Grant. Have you started it yet?"

"Not yet, but I have it downloaded," Emma assured her grabbing a femur-sized bone off the shelf. Emma's teenage puppy Baxter had a bit of a chewing problem. Fortunately, he was also devastatingly handsome, so it was hard for his parents to stay mad at him.

"Well, I'll leave you ladies to your shopping," Mrs. Nordemann announced. "I've got to skedaddle!"

"Bye, Mrs. Nordemann," Eden called after her. She sighed with relief when the woman ducked around the corner. "How are... things?" she asked Emma, not sure if asking about the woman's pregnancy would immediately alert her to the secret Eden knew about her sister.

Emma brushed her short red hair back from her face.

"Things are good. Niko's painting the nursery and kicked me out because I was critiquing his trim work," she said cheerfully.

Emma had surprised Niko on Halloween with the news that the reformed ladies' man was going to be a daddy. The entire family was still celebrating, most likely the reason her sister Eva wanted to keep her own baby news under wraps for a little longer.

"How are you doing?" Emma asked.

Eden didn't hear the hint she would from most Mooners in the question. The subtle emphasis on "you" with a tilting of the head encouraging her to spill everything. Blue Moon residents were ruthless. Emma was still relatively new to town. She hadn't been there two full years yet, so there was still plenty of "normal" on her. They'd make sure it rubbed off eventually.

"I'm fine. Good. The inn is busy," Eden said.

"I heard you've got an unexpected guest," Emma said innocently.

Dang it. Emma was sneakier than she'd expected.

"Yeah, there was a fire at the winery, and Davis needed a place to stay for a few days. It's just temporary," she added quickly. "Sounds like it was a stink-bombing gone wrong."

"Only in Blue Moon, right?" Emma laughed and rolled her eyes.

"It's a shame that a prank can do so much damage," Eden said, thinking about the damage to her life having Davis under her roof was inflicting.

"How much you want to bet it was a senior citizen brigade hopped up on pot brownies and running amuck?" Emma joked.

"I doubt it. They really cracked down on what they call

'senior clumping' after the incident of 2003." Eden pointed out.

Emma blinked at her.

"Never mind," Eden murmured.

17

After picking up the flowers from Every Bloomin' Thing, Eden had just enough time to squeeze in a quick stop at her parents' house on the way back to the inn. The grocery store was out of dried lavender, Eden's not-so-secret ingredient in the butter she served with her biscuits. "Mom? Dad? Are you guys home?" Eden called pushing in the front door without knocking. There was no point. Half the time her parents were in their basement recording studio working on their guided meditation albums and didn't hear visitors troop inside.

"Back in the kitchen," her mother called.

Eden hesitated. "Are you fully clothed?" She'd walked in on her parents naked more times than she ever cared to catalogue. It was a major con to being born to hippies that didn't understand social constraints like clothing.

"Mostly," her father yelled.

"Ugh." Eden left the living room and turned sideways in the hallway to skirt past the overflowing bookcase her mother had found on the curb. There'd been no space for it, so her father had plopped it in the hallway to the kitchen temporarily. That was seventeen years ago.

The kitchen was bright and warm and in desperate need of updating. The yellow linoleum countertop peeled up on the corner of the peninsula. The wood paneling had been painted a street line yellow before Eden had been born, and no one had thought to change it since. There was a small collection of macramé plant holders hanging in front of the breakfast nook window. Her father was wearing underwear and an apron decorated with chickens.

"Jeez, Dad!"

"All the important bits are covered," he insisted. Ned Moody slid in at barely five-foot-eight. He had a scrawny build that, for some reason, her mother found irresistible. Lilly Ann was perched on the countertop swinging her bare feet while Ned fried eggs.

"Want a fried egg sandwich, sweetheart?" Lilly Ann offered.

"No thanks, Mom. I just needed to raid your lavender stash."

"You know where to find it," her mother sang, waving her braceleted hand in the direction of the pantry cabinet. "Oh! While you're here, there's something I wanted to talk to you about."

"What's that?" Eden asked, opening the cabinet door and wrinkling her nose at the chaos. Organization was not her parents' forte.

"Hmmmm," her mother hummed. Neither was remembering things.

"Was it about Atlantis?" Eden's older sister lived in New Jersey with her plumber husband and their six kids.

"Noooo. I don't think so."

Eden moved a sticky jar of paprika out of the way and stretched an arm into the back of the cabinet.

"About Thanksgiving?" Ned suggested.

"Oh!" Lilly Ann breathed. "I forgot about that, too. Sweetheart, your father and I aren't going to be here for Thanksgiving. Atlantis invited us in for the holiday, and then we're finally using that scratch-off money for a weekend getaway to Atlantic City."

Her parents were under the constant assumption that someday their ship would come in. They just had to "open themselves to the favors of fortune." Which meant buying copious amounts of scratch-off tickets and spending the second Sunday of every month at the casino and race track. They were still waiting for that ship, but having a damn good time doing it.

"That sounds like fun," Eden said, finding the collection of baggies behind a jar of Marshmallow Fluff.

Triumphantly she freed one of the bags. "Dad! This is not lavender." She tossed the bag to him and he stuffed it in his apron pocket.

"Huh. I wondered where that got to."

"Aha!" Lilly Ann's exclamation caught Eden's attention. "I remember what it was! And I am about to be absolutely furious with you!"

"Me?" Eden deadpanned.

"Yes you! My daughter who is harboring a horrible human being who doesn't deserve the lovely roof you've put over his head."

Hell. Eden had hoped—futilely—that her parents had missed the news.

"Mom, what was I supposed to do?" She finally wrestled a baggy of lavender out of the depths of the pantry.

"Well, first of all, you shouldn't have tried to burn the man's house down again," her father chastised.

"Dad! I had nothing to do with the fire!"

"That's what you said last time," her mother pointed out.

Ned scooped up an egg and dropped it on a piece of bread.

"Extra cheese on mine, darling," Lilly Ann said.

"Anything for you, buttercup."

"What were we talking about again? Oh, yes! I won't stand for my daughter opening her home to a Gates." Her mother said "Gates" as if it were a synonym for a murderer who had just punched a baby and told her mother to get back in the kitchen where she belonged.

"It's just temporary, Mom. And if it makes you feel any better, I hate having him there."

"That, that, that... *very bad* person," her mother, who was terrible with insults, began, "swapped out our organic weed control spray with a non-organic formula and then told everyone they were eating toxins when we brought spinach and black bean brownies to the bake sale!"

"That was actually Davis's father," Eden pointed out.

"What about the time we drove all the way to Cleary for Christmas shopping and were circling the shopping center parking lot for a space, and Davis refused to back out of his space for *an hour* until someone called mall security?" Eden's father asked, wielding the spatula like a weapon.

Eden rolled her eyes. "That was *you* in the parking space and Davis's grandma waiting for *you* to back out."

Her parents shared a frown. "Oh, yeah. I guess it was," Ned said.

Lilly Ann giggled. "That was funny. She was hanging out of her sunroof, honking with her foot and giving everyone the middle finger."

Ned snapped his fingers. "A ha! Davis Gates broke my little girl's heart when he stood her up for the HeHa Dance!"

"Awh, dad—"

"I'll never forget the look on Atlantis's face when she came home that night. Devastation." He shook his head in fatherly regret.

"That was *me!* Not Atlantis!" Eden groused.

"Are you sure?" Ned asked with a frown.

"I'm positive!"

"Then why are you letting him stay with you? He should just set up camp in a cardboard refrigerator box and panhandle for scraps," her mother said with a decisive nod.

Eden's watch buzzed. "Shoot! I have to go. I have guests coming in." She swooped in and pressed quick kisses to her parents' cheeks. "I'll call you later," she promised.

"Still mad at you," Lilly Ann called after her. "Love you!"

Eden made it back to the inn with minutes to spare. She wrestled the flowers and gift bag out of her backseat and high-tailed it in the backdoor. "Please don't be early. Please don't be early," she chanted through the kitchen.

"Are they here yet?" she hissed, poking her head out into the lobby.

"Who?" Sunny blinked.

Eden gritted her teeth. "The last-minute guests I told you about."

"Oh, them. Not yet." Sunny went back to bopping to a beat that only she could hear.

"Perfect!" Eden hustled across the lobby, gifts and flowers in tow. She dashed down the hall and came to a screeching halt in the doorway to the sunroom. Snack time was underway, and Davis Gates, her sworn enemy, her high school nemesis, was pouring wine and plating cookies like it was his job.

He was charming the small weekday crowd with Blue Moon stories.

His gaze flitted to the door and found her. While Mr. Tottingham stuck his snoot in a sample of merlot and called it "passable," Davis gave Eden a little smile and an "I've got this" wave off.

She didn't have time to argue. The front door bell tinkled, announcing new guests. Eden dashed upstairs, praying that Sunny would take her usual ten minutes of chatting and spacing out to check them in. She burst into the room and placed the flowers and gifts just so on the table in the front window. Impossible to miss.

Eden gave the suite a cursory glance. It smelled lightly of lemons, clean and fresh. The bed was neatly made, the pillows fluffed. The towels in the bathroom were folded wrong. Wrong but still acceptable.

What caught her attention was the towel on the vanity. Davis had fashioned it into a heart. It was thoughtful, sweet, and not at all what she expected from the man.

~

BEAUTIFICATION COMMITTEE GUIDELINES

SECTION IVXII: LEGAL AND MORAL RAMIFICATIONS OF MEDDLING IN CITIZENS' LIVES

While the Beautification Committee prefers to operate beyond the law, it is important that certain societal and legal guidelines are at least recognized if not followed to the letter. The quest for true love can't always be defined within the scope of what's "legal."

(Unrelated Editor's Note: Beautification Committee President Bruce Oakleigh would like to take this moment to remind committee members that no committee business should be discussed outside the committee, including any written comments about ignoring the law.)

18

The balloons were purple. The linens were pink. Trays of delicate frosted cupcakes and cookies decorated the buffet. The manicurists were set up in the corner of the sunporch armed with polishes and removers and ear plugs should the noise level become a problem. There was a glittering tiara at the head of the table waiting for the guest of honor. The music was poppy and kid friendly. And the dogs had been turned outside for a romp... far away from the nose-height baked goods.

Not a single detail had been overlooked.

Eden surveyed the sun porch with satisfaction. Miss Aurora Decker, daughter and stepdaughter to Gia and Beckett Pierce, was in for quite the birthday celebration.

She'd chosen a Sunday afternoon tea party for a dozen of her closest friends as her official celebration. The family party had taken place the day before.

Gia referred to it as Birthdaypalooza and announced that she had every intention of locking herself in her lady cave with an entire bottle of wine tonight to celebrate it all being over.

Eden might do the same. It had been a hectic week with her unintended guest and business as usual at the inn. Fortunately, Davis had left the inn this morning, and she didn't expect him back until later this evening. Not that she was keeping track of his schedule. She was still avoiding him.

Mainly because she was worried she might choke on the words "thank you." And also because of the whole "pack of rabid matchmakers breathing down their neck" thing. Eden had lived in Blue Moon all her life and was aware of the B.C.'s striking list of victories. Whether it was magic or hypnotic suggestion, she wasn't going to get close enough to Davis to find out why the B.C. was so successful.

Thankfully, the inn was a Davis-free afternoon. Just what she needed.

"Wow, Eden. You've outdone yourself." Mayor and town attorney Beckett Pierce, in his version of Sunday casual—dockers and a button down, hauled an armful of gift bags into the room.

"Thank you. Where's our woman of the hour?" Eden asked.

"She's with Gianna. I gracefully bowed out of driving half a dozen seven- and eight-year-olds over," he confessed.

"Chickened out, you mean," Eden teased.

"Gianna gets her bottle of wine and foot rub tonight. I got my quiet five-minute car ride."

From the grin on his face, Eden gathered that Beckett was looking forward to giving that foot rub tonight.

She directed him to the gift table and started pouring waters in thick goblets that she'd chosen with clumsy kid hands in mind.

Guests began to trickle in. Girls in frilly pink, reluctant-looking boys, and of course Aurora herself. She arrived wearing a feather boa and a tutu worn over star leggings. Her red curls exploded off of her head in a display of independence that said, "No, I didn't brush my hair for my own party."

"Bucket!" Aurora skipped over to Beckett and launched herself at him.

"Shortcake!" Beckett hefted his stepdaughter into the air despite having seen her minutes ago.

Gia bustled in mother-henning four other kids and juggling baby Lydia on her hip. Evan, Aurora's older brother, shuffled in with his hands in his pockets.

"Ready for the party?" Eden asked him brightly.

He sighed a worldly sigh for thirteen. "Family obligations."

"Well, if your family obligations allow, there's a library across the hall with absolutely zero eight-year-olds in it," Eden told him, nudging him toward the doorway so he could see.

"Awesome."

"This looks perfect, Eden," Gia sighed, handing the baby off to Beckett who gave them each a kiss on the head.

"If Aurora's happy, I'm happy."

More guests arrived—including a reluctant Joey Pierce and her soon-to-be-adopted son Caleb. Joey helped herself to two cookies off the adult treat table and promised she'd help with crowd control as long as she wasn't forced to play any dumb games.

Caleb ran over to a pretty little girl with black braids and hugged her.

"Jesus," Joey sighed. "He's his father's son." Joey was referring to her husband, Jax, an infamous flirt in his teenage years.

Eden busied herself making sure all the adults—there were few who actually stuck it out for kid birthday parties at this age—had refreshments. She stutter-stepped around kids and gifts on her way to the buffet when she spotted Davis dressed casually—why did he have to make jeans and a sweater look so effortlessly sexy?—standing in the doorway, his hand on a little boy's shoulder. Davis had a child's backpack slung over one shoulder. The boy was clutching a tablet and looking at the floor.

"Rubin!" Aurora called from the head of the table where she was blowing bubbles into her goblet of chocolate milk. She hopped off the chair and went to greet him. She bent at the waist to peer up into his face. "Remember? We look up, okay?"

Rubin bounced a little in his shoes and finally spared a glance upward.

"Good job," Aurora said softly.

"Mama, Miss Eden, this is my friend Rubin. He has autism, and he doesn't talk but has this cool tablet that talks in a robot voice for him. Say something cool, Rubin," she prodded.

Rubin turned his attention to the tablet in his hands.

"Want cake," the android voice announced.

"I can make that happen, Rubin," Eden told him. He shuffled from foot to foot.

"Rubin, you're supposta say 'please,'" Aurora reminded him.

Another button push. "Please."

"Come on. You can sit by me," Aurora said, guiding her little friend to the table.

"Davis, you are my personal hero," Gia sighed. "Eden, did you know that Davis is Rubin's family's inclusion mentor?"

A few years back, Blue Moon had started the Inclusion Committee. Where the Beautification Committee was an underhanded, ill-disguised matchmaking service, the Inclusion Committee served a real and lovely purpose. They worked to properly integrate new families into the Blue Moon community. The move was often a culture shock for new residents. And the town council wanted to make it a seamless transition by helping neighbors learn how best to make new families feel welcome.

"He actually volunteered to bring two kids that aren't his to a kid birthday party so their parents could get a break. It's swoon-worthy, isn't it?" She elbowed Eden in the side.

Eden refused to take the Beautification Committee-laid bait and remained silent. If the B.C. wanted her and Davis to fall madly in love, well, they could retire waiting.

"Your daughter is my hero," Davis countered. "Aurora's class takes turns visiting the special kids program. She's Rubin's inclusion buddy at school. She takes him to art class with her."

Eden made a mental note to add an extra layer of frosting to Aurora's cupcake. If this was the kind of generation Blue Moon was raising, the world was going to be okay.

Davis pulled a folded piece of paper from his back pocket.

"Here are some of the highlights on Rubin and his sister, Claudia. She's washing her hands." Eden skimmed the paper which included the specifics of Rubin's diagnosis, triggers, and likes and dislikes.

"When he gets overwhelmed, he starts 'stimming'—self-stimulatory behavior," Davis explained. "So we need to watch for hand flapping and pacing. Unfortunately, those are also symptoms of Rubin having a good time."

Eden nodded. "Got it. Any dietary restrictions?"

"Gluten- and casein-free... and I just realized I should have told you that before showing up with a kid to a birthday party." He smacked himself in the forehead.

"Gia has you covered," Eden promised. "She sent a three-page write up on all of the dietary restrictions complete with recipes, and I made sure all the treats are gluten- and casein-free."

Davis looked relieved. "Thank you. I appreciate that." He

looked down at his arm where Eden's hand rested. She snatched it away.

"Davis! I haven't finished telling you about the second season of *Guess Again*," a lanky girl in striped leggings and a hoodie announced earnestly from the doorway.

"I was hoping we weren't done yet, Claudia. Come here and meet Miss Eden first, and then we'll talk all the game shows you want."

"Just Guess Again," she reminded him. "Not all game shows." Reluctantly the girl sidled over.

"Miss Eden," Davis began the introductions. "This is Rubin's sister, Claudia. Claudia, this is Miss Eden."

"Nice to meet you," Claudia said flatly. "Now can we?"

Davis gave the girl a smile that made Eden's heart roll over in her chest. "Sure."

They wandered off in the direction of the snacks, Claudia peppering Davis with every known fact in the world about the game show.

"That one is a keeper," Gia sighed after him. "Claudia is on the spectrum as well. She's super smart but gets hung up on certain topics. Last year was that crazy video game that all the kids play. She can be a handful as well, just in a different way."

"She seems really sweet," Eden responded. "And Aurora is amazing with her brother."

"A single guy who steps up for a family like that?" Gia continued. "If my ovaries weren't already spoken for by that sexy hunk of man who just snuck a handful of candy into his pocket for Aurora later, they'd be in a hormonal uproar."

Eden didn't want to hear how amazing and wonderful and thoughtful Davis was. Certainly not from a Beautification Committee member. She preferred thinking of him as an undercover asshole and hated the fact that her up-close view of him this past week was showing her a different side to him.

A side that meant maybe she'd been very wrong for all these years.

"What's that about your ovaries?" Beckett asked, sliding his arms around his wife's waist from behind.

"Davis," Gia said, leaning back against him.

"Oh, right. Yeah, if I were into guys, I'd be into that," Beckett agreed.

Eden laughed despite herself.

"Okay, who wants their nails painted?" Aurora called out, adjusting her tiara.

"HONEY, maybe Lionel doesn't want his nails painted," Gia said as Aurora oversaw the navy blue polish go on the seven-year-old boy's fingernails.

"Mom, I went to Lionel's paintball and monster truck party last week," Aurora pointed out.

"It's only fair," Lionel sighed with resignation.

Eden hid her laugh behind her hand. Aurora was going to grow up to be the first president of the universe someday. She was sure of it. She took a moment to re-stack the colorful napkins that had fallen into disarray during the cupcake decorating.

"Listen, I hope you don't mind me crashing the party." Davis stood to her left, a pink cupcake with glittery sprinkles in his hand.

"I was just surprised to see you," she said lamely, adjusting the perfectly positioned veggie tray.

"It was a last-minute thing. Their parents just needed a break."

"And you were the one to give it to them," she said.

"Why do I get the feeling that this bothers you?" he asked.

"And how long are you going to keep avoiding me?"

She dropped the napkins in a heap. "Look, Davis. I'm trying my hardest to continue intensely disliking you, and you're not making it very easy."

His lips quirked. "I'm not sorry about that. Don't you think it's time we moved on from high school?"

Eden raised her gaze to his. "Where would we go from here?"

He stepped in closer, his arm brushing hers. "I'd like to get to know you without the pitchforks and I Hate Davis Gates t-shirts."

"I only wore that once."

"To my graduation."

"Don't tell me you've been dazzled by my ability to scrub a toilet and make crepes," Eden said lightly.

"Cards on the table? I've been dazzled by you since I was sixteen," he said running a finger around the icing of his cupcake and bringing it to his mouth. "That hasn't changed."

"Have you been drinking?" Eden whispered, leaning in to smell his breath. This was not how she'd seen her day going.

"No," Davis laughed. "I've been living under the same roof as you and it's bringing everything back. I liked you a lot at seventeen and eighteen when you were badass. Enough to think about you all those years I was in California. But now? Seeing the woman you've become up close, I'm floored."

"Davis..." Eden didn't know what to say to that. There was a time in her history that those words from this man would have had her throwing her arms around his neck. Even now, hearing them plucked a heart string or two.

"You can't deny the attraction." He stepped in closer and like clockwork, Eden's body revved at his proximity.

Flustered, she took a step back. "I'm working right now. I

don't have time to discuss this... this... whatever the hell this is." She kept her voice low.

"I know I've thrown you for a loop," Davis began.

"You haven't done anything to me," she said primly, despite the fact that her heart was climbing its way out of her throat. "I need to serve the tea." She took another step back to put some distance between them.

"Davis. We have a problem," Claudia said, appearing next to them. She pointed to her brother. Rubin was flapping his hands like a baby bird trying to take off.

"I'm on it," Davis promised. He crossed to the boy who was by now in full-on distress.

Rubin dropped the tablet to the floor and covered his ears, rocking side to side. He wailed, fat tears running down his little cheeks.

Eden felt her heart break for him.

"It's too loud," Claudia yelled.

"Okay, buddy. Let's get you out of here," Davis said, making a move to pick him up.

"Hang on. I got this! Guys, we have to be quiet for Rubin," Aurora announced, pushing her way into their little circle.

Rubin threw himself back onto the rug. Eden recalled the handout Davis had given her. *Loud noises and bright lights*, she thought. She flicked the switch turning the overhead lights off. Davis shot her a grateful look.

"What do we do?" a girl in a bright yellow dress with embroidered duckies on the skirt asked, leaning down.

Aurora shooed the kids back from Rubin. "Okay, people! Everybody be quiet and lay down!" She flopped down on the floor near Rubin and lay still. She gestured for the girl to do the same.

The other kids followed suit around the room. Eden

looked at Davis, shrugged, and joined them. The floor was hard and cool beneath her. But Davis was warm beside her.

"We should probably hum something," Aurora told them in a stage whisper. "Rubin likes music."

A quiet argument about exactly what to hum ensued. Claudia finally won by insisting that since it was a birthday party, they should be humming "Happy Birthday."

"We don't have to worry about any litigious repercussions," she whispered. "The copyright ended in 2016."

The party guests began to hum, painfully out of tune. They sounded like a defective kazoo band.

"You know," Eden lifted her head and whispered to Davis. "Believe it or not, this isn't the first party I've been to that's ended like this."

He grinned at her.

She looked away, not sure she could withstand the affection she saw in his face, and noticed Rubin wasn't crying anymore and Aurora was holding his hand.

Reaching over, Eden prodded Davis and pointed at the kids. She saw his lips lift at the side. And then his pinky finger was linking with hers on the rug. And she wasn't stopping him. She just held her breath and then hummed along.

~

BEAUTIFICATION COMMITTEE GUIDELINES

SECTION 432 B: CLOSING THE DEAL

Committee members can and will be called upon to help matchees "close the deal." The match is not officially successful until both matchees publicly agree that they are in a committed relationship. Matrimony is not a requirement for a match to be considered a success.

To help matchees to the finale (their happy lives together), the Beautification Committee's resources—manpower, budget, and creative energies—can be deployed in any manner seen fit by the Beautification Committee president. This includes but is not limited to: providing support for grand gestures, obstacle removal, and the swaying of public or private opinion on any necessary matters.

19

The inn settled into shadows and whispers behind closed doors for the winter night. Davis found it oddly comforting to have people around. He hadn't noticed how isolated he was tucked away behind the winery every night, his only companions the owls in the trees. Here at the Lunar Inn, there was a constant ebb and flow of people after dinners eaten and adventures had.

He was restless tonight. After Aurora's birthday party, he'd worked late in his office fine-tuning the media kit for the spring wine trail events and scheduling for winter pruning. He'd have a hand in that as well. For him to do his job well, Davis needed to know every grape, every vine, and every step to vintage.

His mother and father had divided and conquered. She in the vineyard and he behind the desk. But there was only one of him. And only one of Eden, too. He wondered if she ever felt it. The loneliness of being in charge.

There was a scratch at his door. From the chair at the foot of the bed, Davis stared at the closed door wondering if—or was he willing—it was a certain beautiful innkeeper on the other side. Unfortunately, it wasn't a lanky brunette who scowled at him every time he entered the room. It was a short, fluffy blond. Chewy sat down in Davis's open doorway and grumbled.

"What's the matter, Sir Chewsalot?"

Eden stocked healthy dog treats in every guest room should her visitors be so inclined to feed the fluffy beasts that roamed the property and Davis handed over the requisite snack.

Chewy gobbled it up and looked over his shoulder down the hallway. "Do you need to go out?" Davis asked.

As if in understanding, the dog's fat tail thumped on the hardwood.

"Are you allowed out at night?" He was having a conversation with a dog at 11:30 at night. He really needed to start dating again. Davis pocketed another dog treat just in case and let Chewy lead the way. Eden's door was closed, which wasn't unusual. But Chewy's insistence that Davis follow him was.

He glanced down at his gray sweats and moccasins and shrugged. Everyone around here had seen him in much worse the last few days.

Chewy led the way down the hall stopping every few steps to make sure Davis was still behind him. Someone had obviously given the dog a complex. It was probably his sister, Vader. Davis had seen her chase Chewy around Eden's huge dining table only to duck underneath with a satisfied doggy smile on her face while her brother continued his laps.

They entered the lobby at the center of the house, but instead of dancing at the front door as he'd seen the dog do every morning, Chewy trotted into the next wing, still casting apprehensive glances over his fluffy shoulder.

Davis followed him to the library. "You want me to read you a bedtime story?" he asked, stepping into the room.

"I can read all by myself, thanks."

The dry voice coming from the direction of the fireplace startled him. Chewy, with a dopey smile on his furry face, hopped up on the window seat next to his sister. Their tails thumped in unison.

"Sorry for the interruption. Your dog insisted I follow him," he said, slipping his hands into his pockets.

Eden glanced around the wingback of her chair and sighed. "He likes to collect people at night and herd them into one room."

One of the dogs let out a not-so-dainty snore. Eden shot them an affectionate look. Davis didn't feel unwelcome, exactly, so he tested the waters, wandering down a long wall of book shelves. He heard her turn a page. A thriller jacket caught his eye, and he pulled the book from the shelf.

"You can stay if you promise not to talk," she said without looking up from the binder she was studying.

Davis hid the curve of his lips. He crossed to the fireplace and dropped the book in the chair next to hers and held up a finger to her. She raised her eyebrows, and he left the room. He half-jogged the distance back to his room, collected what he needed, and was back at the library door only slightly out of breath.

"Thought you'd changed your mind," Eden drawled.

Davis placed the two wine glasses on the white washed pedestal table between their chairs. With a flourish, he unpocketed the corkscrew and made quick work of opening the bottle of merlot. She watched his every move, guarded. Wordlessly, he poured. Silently, she accepted the glass he offered.

He considered it an even bigger win when she sipped rather than tossing the wine in his face. Companionably, he sat, relaxing into the chair and picking up the book. "What are you reading?"

Rather than snarling at him, Eden held up the cover of the binder.

"Beautification Committee? Are you studying up for your membership test?" he teased.

"Har har," she said, tucking a strand of dark hair behind her ear. She was dressed comfortably in leggings and a long cardigan over a jewel-toned tank. Her bare feet were tucked up under her on the deep seat. A pair of soft gray slippers was neatly stowed beneath her chair. She painted the perfect picture of a quiet evening. Davis itched to paint her that way. "I liberated it from Eva's bag when she was here last week so I can figure out how to stop their idiotic plans."

Davis laughed. "Who's the unlucky target this time?"

"Let's see how funny you think it is when I tell you that you're one half of their current target."

"I beg your pardon?"

"You and me, Gates." She sipped again and gave the smallest nod of approval at the wine he'd poured. "They're taking advantage of your homelessness and trying to force us together."

"Huh," Davis said, cracking open his book.

"Huh? That's the best you've got? There's an entire committee scheming against you, and all you've got is 'huh'?"

Davis gave a one-shouldered shrug. "Well, you can't blame them. Not only have our families terrorized this whole town for fifty-plus years, you and I are both ridiculously good-looking."

Eden gave him a long blank stare before her laughter won out. It was a night of wins, Davis decided.

He shifted his attention to page one. "How did it go with Mr. Forgot His Anniversary this week?" he asked.

"Mmm, it's safe to say the Mrs. is appeased and he'll never forget another anniversary again. He can't afford it."

"I wondered when I didn't see them around the inn."

"They never made it out of their room," Eden said innocently.

"Must have been some gift."

Eden told him about the gift she and Wilson Abramovich had selected for the wife, a lovely crescent moon pendant with a tiny blue diamond. "And, if the bill for the jewelry isn't enough of a deterrent, I also had a very manly leather and metal bracelet engraved with their anniversary date for him."

Davis's lips quirked. "You're very good at what you do."

"Thank you." It was a simple acknowledgement of what she already knew to be true.

He sipped and gathered his wits to recite the speech he'd been waiting to give for fifteen years. He closed his book. "Eden, I never meant to hurt you, you know. I wanted to be at that dance with you," he said.

He saw the shutters come down in the tension that tightened her shoulders. She turned the page in her binder, feigning disinterest. "Then why weren't you?" she asked, picking at the binder's spine.

"My parents—"

"You know what. Forget I asked," she decided.

"I wish you could forgive me. I forgave you," he pointed out rashly. This was not part of his carefully planned speech.

She gazed at him, her face a mask, but he could see the emotions moving fast and sharp behind her blue eyes.

"*You* forgave *me*?"

"Frankly, I deserved worse," Davis admitted.

"Hmm." It was all she gave him. But it was better than a blistering speech about his teenage shortcomings. Of course he'd regretted letting his parents bully him into taking someone more "suitable." It was his MO, making other people happy—especially his parents.

"I was eighteen… painfully stupid," he began.

"Let's just go back to that whole not talking thing," she said flatly, her tone leaving no room for argument.

He let her have this round, not completely willing to piss off his hostess who had very generously opened her guest room to him.

They sat in silence, each pretending to read while lost in thought. Eden nudged the small plate of cookies toward him without looking up. He accepted the offering and bit into a cookie.

"Dear God, woman. What are these?" he asked, reaching for another one.

"Cappuccino cookies. Did you mean what you said at Aurora's party?" She blurted the words out and he knew she must have been mulling them over since he spoke them.

He nodded. "I'm very attracted to you, Eden. You're a beautiful, amazing woman. You've built this entire business from nothing. You were willing to overlook fifty years of feuding to give me a place to stay. Can you blame me for being dazzled?"

"Maybe the Beautification Committee is dabbling in pheromones or something. Doesn't it bother you that there are people out there pulling strings to make you do something you don't want to do?" Eden asked.

Davis gave it some thought. "You aren't something I don't want to do. And maybe the B.C. has our best interests at heart. I can see the benefit of someone calling the shots when you don't know what you want or what's best for you."

"You're a grown man, Gates. I think you can make decisions for yourself," she said dryly. "And there's no way in hell that I'm what's best for you."

One of the dogs gave a low rumble in their sleep.

Davis weighed Eden's words. He'd always been more interested in going with the flow than standing up and taking what he wanted. Really, what did he want that he didn't already have? A challenging job in the town he'd always loved. A family that—though annoying and disturbingly set in their ways—cared for him and wanted to see him happy. A loose circle of entertaining friends. He had all that plus purpose, community.

But what if there was more? And what if she was sitting next to him?

Eden sat up, her spine ramrod straight as she held up the binder. "Yes!" She jumped up, jamming her fist in the air. "Suck it Beautification Committee! I just solved our problem. There's no way they can match us now."

Reluctantly, Davis raised his hand for the high-five she offered.

"We'll be free of each other in no time," she said taking a celebratory swallow of her wine.

~

BEAUTIFICATION COMMITTEE GUIDELINES

SECTION Alpha Lima Echo B32: CONTESTING YOUR MATCH

It's best that matchees remain unaware of their right to contest their match.

20

Eden hid out in the classic literature section of the library's first floor, wanting the element of surprise to be in her favor. When Eva wandered by the stacks digging through her bag, dressed in jeans and a baggy sweater, Eden nabbed her.

"Looking for this?" She shoved the Beautification Committee binder in Eva's face.

"Damn it! How did you get that?" Eva demanded, snatching it out of Eden's hand. "I'm in so much trouble if they find out that a non-committee member got their hands on the rules and regulations."

"Relax, you didn't leave it lying around. I stole it out of your bag while you were busy puking in my umbrella stand."

"Sorry about that again," Eva blushed.

"Can we stay focused, please? I'm here to invoke my right to Section 718, Subparagraph G," Eden announced.

Eva stared at her blankly. "Your right to choose your own match?" she asked.

"No! Wait, that's a thing?" Eden reached for the binder

again. "Because I've got some strong feelings for Gerard Butler."

Eva fended off Eden's hands. "No! Bad! I can't believe you stole this from me! What does Section Whatever Paragraph Alphabet say?"

"Section 718, Subparagraph G states that I can dissent my match."

"Oh. That Section 718," Eva said, flipping pages. "I'm new to the committee, but I have a feeling this has never happened before."

"Because you jerks don't tell people they're allowed to fight the matches!"

"Well, no one's ever needed to fight a match before. I mean, come on, Eden. We've got a perfect record. That has to count for something."

"Davis and I do *not* belong together. We don't even like each other."

Eva looked over her shoulder to make sure no one was eavesdropping. "Look, whatever you do, just promise me you won't tell them that I'm the weak link who delivered committee secrets to a reluctant matchee."

"Fine," Eden said. "Go up. I'm going to wait until the meeting gets started before storming in and dissenting all over the place."

"Hey, guys!" Eva's sister Gia poked her head around the bookshelf. "What's going on?"

Eden and Eva shared a long look.

"It's probably better if you don't know," Eva decided.

EDEN FELT like an idiot pressing her ear against the conference room door listening for her cue. But it couldn't be helped. If she wanted her future to be free of well-meaning, ill-informed string pulling, she needed to present her case in exactly the right way.

And then she would be free of Davis Gates forever. No more bumping into him outside her quarters. No more eye contact over eggs at breakfast. No more watching him romp with the dogs in the yard. Eden's resolve wavered for a moment, before she gathered her wits about her. She just wanted to go back to the way things were before Davis moved in under her roof.

"Are there any public comments?" Eden heard Bruce Oakleigh's muffled voice through the door. That was her cue. She turned the knob and pushed. And in her haste, she tripped over her own feet, stumbling into the room. She didn't stop until she caught herself on the snack table, sending a dozen pink iced cupcakes tumbling to the floor.

"Awh." Gordon Berkowicz, a slim figure in unwashed tie-dye, lamented the sugary loss from across the room. The tables were set up in a U-shape with everyone facing a large whiteboard where Bruce wielded colored markers and a shocked expression.

Gordon's wife, Rainbow, an intimidating figure in pinstripes, gaped like a guppy at Eden. As bank president in the hippie-est town in the Northeast, it took a lot to surprise Rainbow.

Eva had her face buried behind her hands, but the rest of the committee stared in confusion.

"Eden, you can't be here," Bruce gasped. If the man had worn a string of pearls, he would have been clutching them.

Ellery's dark purple lips were pressed in a thin line, her eyes wide with surprise. "Is the building on fire? Do we need to evacuate?"

A murmur went up around the room and Gordon bolted from his seat. "Oh my God! I think this shirt is flammable!" He ripped off the long-sleeve tie-dye and tossed it on the floor. He nearly trampled Amethyst Oakleigh, Bruce's beehived wife—who actually was clutching her pearls.

"There's no fire," Eden shouted over the commotion.

Rainbow grabbed her husband by the belt and yanked him off of the windowsill.

"I have a public comment," Eden announced righting herself and accidentally smearing pink icing down the front of her black turtleneck. She fished her index cards out of her back pocket and cleared her throat. "I hereby officially voice my dissent for my match."

That got a bigger reaction than when they thought the building was on fire. Amethyst swooned into the arms of the unsuspecting Wilson Abramovich. Bruce bent at the waist to suck in shuddering gasps of air.

Gordon picked up a cupcake off of the floor and bit into it wrapper and all.

Bobby, the unflappable proprietress of Peace of Pizza, sat calmly like a goddess waiting to deliver judgment. While Ellery anxiously flipped through her binder, Eva was very busy studying her fingernails and not making eye contact with anyone. Her sister Gia sent her worried looks.

"According to Section 718, Subparagraph G, I have the right to petition the committee to cease and desist in their matching actions."

Binders slapped open and pages were turned with panicked enthusiasm.

"Holy crap," Ellery gasped. "That's a thing. She can do that."

A collective gasp went up around the room.

"How did you even know there was a Section 718?" Bruce demanded, grabbing at his graying hair until it stood out in tufts behind his ears.

"How did you know you were a match?" Rainbow asked.

Eden pointed toward the whiteboard.

EDEN + DAVIS = LOVE

She glanced at Eva who had her eyes squeezed shut tight. What had recently begun as an investigative assignment to infiltrate the Beautification Committee had turned into real loyalty somewhere along the way. Eden almost felt sorry for her friend. *Almost.*

"Per the Town Ordinance 17-06 of 1985, I observed suspicious activity at a committee member's home and let myself in," Eden lied. Blue Moon had an oddly specific ordinance granting townsfolk access to their neighbor's homes. "This binder was readily available, and while I made sure there was no imminent danger, I just happened to open the binder to Page 336."

"What danger did you think you witnessed?" Bruce demanded shrewdly.

"Um. Squirrels?" Eden hadn't quite worked out that part of the lie.

"Amethyst! I told you not to leave your binder lying around. This is why we have the fire safe in the basement!" Apparently, Bruce and Amethyst had a squirrel problem at home.

Amethyst hung her silvery beehive in shame.

"Let's not point fingers here," Eden said hastily. "I would like to present my case for being unmatched."

"Huddle!" Bruce called shrilly. The committee members abandoned their chairs and huddled up in front of the whiteboard. A heated conversation took place with the occasional head poking up out of their circle to look at Eden.

After a good three minutes of huddling, the committee members broke apart.

"We will now hear your dissent," Ellery said regally.

Eden consulted her index cards. "I would like to void this match based on the grounds that there are no mutual feelings of affection, that the match would exacerbate current emotional distress, and that the match was proposed as a way to benefit the community rather than based on the needs of the couple."

Bruce covered his face with his hands and let out a moan while the remaining committee members broke into loud commentary. Eden tapped her index cards against her jeans and waited.

"Huddle!" Ellery screeched over the commotion. Once again, the Beautification Committee members circled up.

They debated longer this time. Giving Eden not much else to do but stare around the room. She looked at the whiteboard again. Under the couple equation written at the top was a list of other names. Sammy Ames, Blue Moon's large animal vet and Eden's BFF, was at the top. Layla's was stuffed in the middle. Beneath the names—future victims, Eden supposed—was a number. $47,735. And beneath that was a bar graph shaded up to the $100 line. There was a list of suggestions next to the graph.

Fundraisers

1. *Beautification Committee Nudist Calendar*
2. *Bake Sale*
3. *Place Remaining Annual Budget on Horse in Race.*

Bruce peeked up out of the huddle "Ms. Moody, the Beautification Committee consents to hearing your reasons."

"Uh, I just told you my reasons," Eden reminded him, eyes flitting back to the whiteboard.

"Oh, of course. How silly of me." He ducked back into the pile, and the whispering started again.

Eden helped herself to a cup of punch while she waited and studied the figure on the board. It was the exact amount of damages to Davis's house. She'd heard him discussing it on the phone with Calvin Finestra at breakfast one morning.

Did that mean—

"Ms. Moody," Bruce said abruptly. "The Beautification Committee is prepared to vote on your petition."

Oh, crap. That wasn't in the binder.

They all regained their seats, and Eden swiped nervously at the frosting on her shirt.

"Please let me remind the committee that they are free to vote their conscience. Don't worry about the devastating blow this could deliver to the individual who campaigned for this obviously perfect match," Bruce announced dramatically.

If Bruce wasn't careful, she'd deliver a devastating blow... to his face.

"Try not to be swayed by the fact that the BC has a perfect record in matchmaking and never before have we abandoned a couple in mid-match," he continued.

The Beautification Committee members exchanged glances with each other.

"All those in favor of abandoning Eden and Davis when their tender love requires our support the most," Bruce began. His voice squeaked. "I can't look!" Bruce covered his eyes. "Amethyst, my pearl, please record the vote."

Eden counted hands. Eva, Gia, Bobby, and Gordon were her new best friends, voting to free her from Davis Gates. She wanted to make out with all of them... except for maybe Gordon, who was still shirtless.

"All those opposed to this frivolous claim and who wish to stay true to our mission statement of providing lasting love for those in need of it?" Bruce asked.

With his eyes still covered, Bruce joined Amethyst, Rainbow, and Wilson raising their hands.

Well, shit. Eden crossed her arms.

"Well?" Bruce demanded, peeking through his fingers.

"It's a tie vote," Amethyst said in her quiet, mousy voice.

"How is that possible? Who didn't vote?" Bruce demanded.

"That would be me," Ellery said, gnawing on her pencil.

"Ellery, we've been friends for a long time," Eden reminded her.

"Friendship has no place in the quest for true love," Bruce snapped. "I forbid you to be swayed by such platitudes!"

"Nice attitude, Bruce." Bobby rolled her eyes.

"What is your vote, Ellery?" Bruce demanded impatiently.

Ellery interlaced her fingers on the table in front of her. "I'd like to ask Eden a question before I cast my vote."

"Ask away," Bruce said grandly.

"Why don't you and Davis work?"

Eden blinked. "Uh. Well, first of all, our families don't get along for one. Two, we tried dating in high school, and it was a disaster. Three, we don't even know each other. We've barely spoken in fifteen years." She felt like an idiot, stumbling over an explanation that should have flowed as easily from her mouth as the Pledge of Allegiance. *Had she really softened this much toward the man?*

Ellery nodded, lips pursed. "I'm ready to vote."

"You are?" Eden asked with a sinking feeling as her stomach dropped into her feet.

"I am in favor of continuing our matchmaking for Eden and Davis," Ellery announced. The room erupted.

"What? Ellery! You're supposed to be my friend!" Eden pointed out.

"I'll be honest. I had my reservations over this match. I didn't think that you could ever get past what happened in high school. But as your friend, you didn't say that you found Davis gross or hateful or mean. You're just going to have to trust us. You two are a good match. It's time to forgive."

"Time to forgive?" Eden sputtered.

"Just sit back and let us handle everything," Gordon said, crossing his arms and kicking back in his chair. He tumbled over backwards and landed on his discarded shirt.

"Hear, hear," Bruce said banging a gavel on the table in front of him. "I motion to close the public comments section of this meeting. With a stern warning to our matchee that she should heed our advice."

It was a public declaration of war. And Eden was going to fight. She pointed around the room, ready to express her displeasure, when the number on the whiteboard caught her attention again. Something clicked into place, and she shut her mouth.

She knew exactly how she was going to win this war. And it would bring the Beautification Committee down to its manipulative, matchmaking knees.

21

Davis set aside his laptop to answer his room phone. "Gates," he said, still focused on the balance sheet he'd been studying.

"Davis, it's Eden. Can you meet me at Peace of Pizza?"

Davis shook his head and looked around the room. He was indeed awake. However, he wasn't quite sure how to make sure he hadn't stumbled into an alternate reality.

"Is everything okay?" he asked slowly.

"It's about to be."

"Well that's not at all vague or confusing," he quipped.

"Look, just come into town, okay? We need to talk."

With trepidation, Davis changed into his new chinos and a lightweight sweater in marled blue and pointed his SUV in the direction of Blue Moon.

Peace of Pizza was busy as it was most weeknights. Cars filled the parking spaces the whole way around the town square. He parked a block back and, shoulders hunched to the winter wind, pushed into the garlic scented, lava lamp-lit haven that was Peace of Pizza. He waved to Bobby, the dreadlocked owner who made a secret sauce that had pizza chains offering up big bucks for her recipe.

"Your girl's in the back," Bobby told him grimly, pointing a dough-covered hand toward a table. He didn't try to yell over the din and ask what she meant by "your girl." He spotted Eden sitting at a table for two, drumming her fingers on the checkered table cloth and scowling.

She saw him, and her face lit up. He felt his heart do a slow roll in his chest. *Wow. That was a beautiful smile.* And for the first time since high school, she was directing it at him.

"Hi—"

Before he could get the whole word out, Eden was on her feet and grabbing him by his coat. Her mouth met his in a sizzling shock of a kiss. Davis would have been less surprised had she decked him. Her lips were warm and oh-so-soft beneath his. The contact lit up every cell in his body. She felt like a warm fire in the dead of winter, bringing his body back to life, bringing his blood to a slow simmer and almost immediately jumping it to a boil. Eden made a sexy little moan and broke the kiss.

This was the moment he'd been waiting for for fifteen years.

Everyone was staring at them. There wasn't a single sound inside the pizza joint. Except for the pounding of Davis's heart against the confines of his ribs.

"Uh, what was that?" he whispered.

"Hi, handsome!" she said loudly. "I thought you'd like pizza for our date night."

Okay. He'd definitely slipped into an alternate universe. Was his name still Davis? He dug through his pockets for his phone.

"What are you doing?" she asked dropping her voice.

"I want to see if there's an app that can tell me I fell into an alternate reality."

"Sit, down," she hissed through clenched teeth. "I'll explain everything."

They sat, and Eden took his hand and beamed at him like he'd just finished telling her his favorite thousand things about her. He didn't know what was happening, but he liked holding her hand and he *really* hoped there was a second kiss coming.

"Can I get a pie for you all?" Bobby asked, approaching them as suspiciously as she would a live grenade.

"Bobby, could you make one of those specialty heart-shaped pizzas for us?" Eden asked with a girlish giggle.

Bobby looked back and forth between them with suspicion. "Sure," she said finally. "What do you want on it?"

"Green peppers," Eden said.

"Black olives," Davis added.

"The perfect combination." Eden batted her eyelashes. It was unsettling.

"Don't be messing around, girl," Bobby warned Eden before leaving the table. Eden immediately dropped the flirtation.

"How much damage did the fire do to your place?" she asked.

"What?"

"Money. How much money will it take to fix everything?"

"A lot," he hedged.

"$47,735?" Eden asked, leaning forward.

"How did you know that?" Davis had kept that number very quiet. Word traveled fast in this town, and he didn't need someone reporting to either of his parents that the tiny bit of smoke damage was actually a full-blown gut job.

Eden looked over both shoulders and crooked her finger at him. Helpless, he leaned in closer.

"I think the Beautification Committee burned down your house to get us together."

Something white hot and painful burned in his chest. Davis wasn't one to dabble in anger. It didn't serve much of a purpose to him. There was something to be said about going with the flow. But right now, he wanted to go set every one of the committee members' houses on fire. He suddenly got, first-hand, exactly how Eden must have felt all those years ago.

"What makes you say that?" he asked, red creeping in on the edges of his vision.

"Someone out of the blue decides to stink bomb your house, right? Who would do that? Teenagers in Blue Moon are too busy learning how to organize protests and brew organic temporary hair dyes. Someone wanted your house to be unlivable so you would have to come stay with me."

"So, they *burned it down*?" Davis gritted his teeth. It made an odd kind of sense. Mischief in Blue Moon was limited to streaking and unpermitted bake sales. Not property damage and arson.

Eden held up a slim hand. "Hear me out. I went to a committee meeting tonight to dissent the match. They had $47,735 written on the board at the front of the room with a list of fundraisers under it. Why would they feel like they owed you that money unless they were the reason there was a fire in the first place?"

Davis took a slow deep breath, wishing he could regain his peace, wishing she'd just kiss him again and make him forget everything else. But it was gone, lost to the bubbling lava in his gut. "They could have hurt someone. They could have burned down the entire winery, my family's legacy."

"Yes. They could have," Eden said, with a slow, dangerous smile. "And we're going to get them back."

"No offense, but your last attempt at revenge almost landed you in jail," Davis reminded her.

"There is nothing illegal about what I'm proposing. Even better, it's just diabolical enough to make those yahoos think long and hard about ever meddling in anyone else's life."

"I'm in. I don't care what it is. They could have ruined everything I've worked for," Davis said, his voice a low rasp of rage.

"I'm so glad to hear you say that, Gates. Because you and I are about to fall madly in love."

"WALK me through this again and tell me how much more satisfying this will be than turning them over to the police," Davis said, slipping another slice of pizza off the tray. It was a good plan, but for once in his life, Davis wasn't sure if it was mean enough.

"First of all, do you really want to try to have the sheriff's and mayor's wives arrested?"

"They burned down my kitchen!"

Eden laid a hand over his and he realized he was shouting. "What would having half the town arrested do to you, to your business, to your standing in the community?"

"They burned down my kitchen," he said again at a much lower volume.

"Honestly, it was probably just a stink bombing gone wrong."

"Still."

"Still," she agreed. "What does the Beautification

Committee prize above all else?" Eden asked sipping her iced tea.

"Their sterling reputation of perfect matches," Davis answered.

"Exactly. They want us to fall in love? Fine. We'll do it. And everyone in town will know it."

"But really we're just setting the stage," he prodded.

"That's right. You're going to dump me—again—in the most spectacular public breakup in Blue Moon history. By the time we're done, the entire town will know that the Beautification Committee is to blame."

"This might be the rage talking, but you're incredibly sexy when you're plotting evil schemes," Davis told her.

Eden laughed. Every time she laughed or smiled at him, the entire restaurant stopped and stared. They were witnessing fifty-plus years of animosity be replaced with what looked like a good old-fashioned, star-crossed love affair.

She leaned in over the table. "We're going to give them what they want most in this world. And then we're going to snatch it away from them."

He'd never been more attracted to a woman in his entire life than he was at this exact moment.

"How far should we go to sell it?" he asked huskily as he leaned forward over their shared heart-shaped pizza. "I mean, are we kissing in public?"

Eden met him halfway. "Whatever it takes."

This time it was his lips meeting hers, sealing the deal.

~

BEAUTIFICATION COMMITTEE GUIDELINES

SECTION T: Observation

All matches must be observed to ensure that the matchmaking process is proceeding in a healthy, optimal direction. Observation techniques deployed may include: undercover/in disguise surveillance, listening to and participating in town gossip, innocently overhearing match-based conversations, etc. Unfortunately, committee members are no longer permitted to employ any such listening devices or let themselves into the homes of matchees unless there are extenuating danger-related circumstances. Please see Town Ordinance 17-06 of 1985.

22

In celebration of their official weekiversary, Davis was taking Eden to dinner at Villa Harvest. She'd decided to take for a spin the long-sleeved red wrap dress she'd bought on a whim three years ago and never worn. The life of an innkeeper wasn't particularly glamorous, and the impulse buy was buried behind a collection of sensible, comfortable clothes that enabled her to cook, bake, and scrub vomit out of showers when necessary.

She put a little more effort than usual into her hair and makeup and was rewarded with Davis's abrupt stop in the lobby. Chewy, who needed a bit of grooming himself and couldn't see past the fur in his eyes, walked into the back of his legs and almost sent Davis flying into her.

"You look... wow," Davis offered, admiring her from head-to-toe. Eden felt the heat of his gaze and tried not to notice how nicely he filled out the navy suit he'd chosen. *Was that a vest? Oh, hell. She was a sucker for a man in a vest.*

"I see you finally got a chance to go shopping," she said. The suit made her nervous. His thrift store wardrobe had downplayed his blatant sexuality. It had masked his powerful shoulders and leanly muscled torso. Badly Dressed Davis had been less intimidating. Now, he was all charm and style. And she felt like she was an awkward seventeen again.

Sunny whistled at them from behind the desk. "Wowsers. You two look gorge! I'm taking a picture!" She whipped out her phone.

"Smile pretty, love of my life," Eden said, without moving her smiling lips.

"Smiling like the sweetest revenge depends on it," Davis confirmed.

"Make sure you put the filter with the little hearts on it," Eden called as they headed for the front door.

"Milady," Davis said, opening the passenger door of his SUV with a flourish.

"You're too kind and very, very handsome," Eden crooned. "I hope your seats recline so I can swoon comfortably."

Villa Harvest was doing a brisk business. Eden waved at a table of her guests who were enjoying a family-style serving of fettuccini and a heavenly basket of fresh garlic bread.

Phoebe, Franklin's wife, was standing in as hostess tonight looking stylish in all black. "Well, don't you two look delicious tonight?" she teased.

"We're celebrating our one-week anniversary," Eden announced, cuddling into Davis's side. It was weird how comfortable he was to touch. It was as if her body was making up for years of playing "Davis Gates is Lava."

Phoebe led them to a cozy booth near the fireplace.

Julia and Rob, from OJ's by Julia, occupied a table for two. "Hey, guys!" Eden greeted them as they passed.

Julia dropped her fork on her plate, scraping her purple bangs out of her eyes to get a better look. "Uh, hi, Eden and... Davis?"

Eden grinned and slid into the booth. This was the kind of

attention her teenage rebel self had wanted. Surprise, shock. Not just a blind acceptance of every weird thing she tried. Of course, that rebellious desire had come to an abrupt end in flames. And since then, she'd been trying to prove how nice and normal she was. This was the best of both worlds... even if it was completely fake.

Davis unbuttoned his jacket revealing more of the vest that had lust curling into a ball in her stomach and slipped into the booth next to her. "Uh, don't you want to sit on that side?" Eden asked.

"Why would I want to be that far away from my stunning girlfriend?" Davis asked threading his fingers through her hair playfully.

She opened her mouth, but no sound came out. His fingers in her hair, the proximity of his body to hers. His hard thigh was pressed against hers. She was getting dizzy.

"Are you okay?" he asked. "You look like you're going to faint."

Cheeks flaming Eden picked up her menu. "I was just playing the awe-struck lover," she insisted. *Or lust-struck hater.*

She made herself busy trying to focus on the calamari appetizer description.

"Hey, aren't the Berkowiczes in the B.C.?" Davis asked, sliding his arm around her shoulders.

Eden was suddenly breathless. "Yes. Why?" she squeaked.

"Two o'clock." Davis leaned in to nuzzle her neck, and Eden had to force her eyelids open to scan the room. She felt like he was pumping an aphrodisiac through his pores, and if she didn't get some space between them, she'd do something stupid... like Davis.

Rainbow and Gordon were cozied up at a table with Ellery, her husband Mason, and Kathy Wu.

"I guess we've got an audience to perform for," Eden said,

pretending to be enthralled with the gold flecks in Davis's warm, brown eyes. Like molten milk chocolate.

"Is this okay?" Davis asked, his voice husky, as his fingers stroked her shoulder.

She nodded in slow motion, her all-for-show smile wavering. She was supposed to hate this man. Not only had the resentment been bred into her, but she had her own personal experience of the Gates family douchebaggery. Why then did her traitorous body want to snuggle a little closer to his warmth? Why did her fingers itch to rake through his hair? And why the hell were her nipples trying to slice their way through her bra?

She knew the answer. She just didn't want to face it.

"I should probably know how you like to be touched." Davis's voice was low, almost threatening. Eden's underwear spontaneously caught fire. She pressed her thighs together in an attempt to suffocate the flames.

She swallowed hard and then choked on her own saliva. Desperately, she fumbled for her water glass.

"Are you all right?" Davis asked, patting her on the back.

Get it together, she told herself. She was not some sex-starved teenager with heart eyes. She was a damn grown woman with ambition and a brain and great shoes who ran a successful business. She was no longer an eyeliner-abusing high school junior desperate for love.

"Fine," she gasped out. "Absolutely fine."

She wiped the tears from the corners of her eyes and made herself settle stiffly against Davis's arm.

"I like having my hair played with," she told him and watched those brown eyes narrow. "And I love skin on skin contact." Eden leaned into him and boldly placed her hand on his thigh.

He flinched as if she'd just tried to punch him in the balls, and she grinned wickedly.

It was Davis's turn to reach for his water glass. He drank deeply, emptying it in three quick swallows.

Eden wiggled in her seat, confident that she'd just won some control back.

"Welcome to Villa Harvest." Their server was a shaggy-haired bean pole.

"Rupert, when did you start working here?" Eden asked. Rupert was the famously terrible waiter at John Pierce Brews —and Sunny's on again off again boyfriend. Emma Vulkov, brewery manager, had fired and rehired him twice now.

Rupert brushed his sheepdog bangs out of his eyes. "Oh, hey, Eden." His voice belonged to a 1990s California surfer. "I'm picking up a couple of shifts here every week. Emma needs some space from me sometimes."

"Ah," Eden said. Rupert stared at her expectantly for a long beat.

Davis cleared his throat. "Do you have any specials tonight?"

"Oh, sure." Rupert dug his notebook out of his back pocket. "You want to hear them again?"

"Or for the first time," Davis said amicably. He shot Eden a look that said they'd be lucky to get the food they ordered before the restaurant closed.

She squeezed his thigh under the table again, and Davis reflexively hit the bottom of the table with his knee.

Rupert didn't notice and carefully read off the night's specials. "So, I'll go ahead and put in your appetizer. And I'll give you a few minutes with the menus," he said as he tried to grab the menus from the table.

Davis wrestled one away from him. "We'll just hang on to this one. You know, so we can order dinner."

"Oh, sure." Rupert wandered away.

"What appetizer did we order?" Eden asked.

"We didn't."

"Where are you going?" she asked, as he slid toward the edge of the booth.

"I'm going to the bar to get us drinks. If we wait for Rupert, we'll be dehydrated skeletons."

"I'll take the biggest glass of wine you can carry," Eden told him.

"Anything your heart desires, beautiful." Davis said it loud enough that the Beautification Committee members lifted their heads above their menus like prairie dogs.

The flush that tinged Eden's cheeks was by no means scripted.

She studied the menu and traced a finger over the tablecloth to calm her nerves. Her phone buzzed in her purse and Eden jumped at the distraction.

Sammy: How did I miss the fact that you're dating Davis Gates????

Her text included a screenshot of a post from the Blue Moon Facebook group. It was Eden and Davis staring deeply into each other's eyes posted approximately two minutes earlier. The damn Blue Moon grapevine.

Eden: Long story. We're revenge dating.

Sammy: Is this like when you spite dated Ramesh Goldschmidt for half of junior year?

Eden winced. After the disastrous HeHa dance, she'd dated Ramesh until Davis left for college that summer. She'd ended up liking the guy. Just not as much as she would have liked Davis. It was not one of her finest moments. He'd dumped her gently for Windy Jones, who wouldn't have given him the time of day had he not spent six months in a relationship with Eden. They had married, moved to Buffalo, and ran a thriving orthodontist practice together. So she considered her karmic debt paid.

Eden: I'll explain later. It involves the B.C. BTW, you're next on their list.

Sammy: The HELL I am!

Eden smirked and stuffed her phone back in her clutch. It was always funnier when someone else was the target of the Beautification Committee's machinations.

23

Davis returned to the table with two glasses and a bottle of Blue Moon Cabernet Sauvignon. "I had to fight my way through the crowd," he said, dropping back onto the booth beside her. "It seems like Rupert has a lot of tables tonight."

Eden laughed loud and long. "Oh, Davis, you're *sooooo* funny."

He looked at her like she was losing her damn mind.

"Just play along," she hissed. "They're eating it up. We've already made the Facebook group."

"You really commit, don't you?" he asked.

Eden straightened her shoulders so defensively her neck cracked. "What's that supposed to mean?"

"Why in the hell would that piss you off?" Davis countered.

She shrugged it off and sipped. "Sorry. Reflex. I'm used to being pissed off at everything that comes out of your mouth. Please elaborate, and I promise not to bite your head off."

"Depending on what our appetizer is, that might still be a danger," Davis said, raising his glass to hers.

Eden squashed the eyeroll.

He laughed softly, and the sound of it rolled through her belly.

"I only meant that you put a lot of effort into everything you do. You're not just an innkeeper. You go out of your way to find out what a visitor's favorite chocolate is and then leave it on their pillow. You tailor your snacks to guest preferences. You hand draw maps of Blue Moon for guests and circle the places you think they'll really enjoy."

"That's just being a good businessperson," Eden argued. "You do the same thing with the winery. You're constantly listening and adjusting and learning so you can be better."

He drummed his fingers on the table cloth. "I like that you're as obsessed with work as I am."

She flushed, the compliment meaning more to her than any comment on her appearance. The Lunar Inn was her life. She'd breathed life into it and spent every waking moment trying to ensure every guest had the best possible experience. "I have a lot to prove," she admitted, thinking back to those five minutes that had defined her to an entire town.

"Believe it or not, I know how you feel. The only way my father was willing to relinquish control of the winery was by being forced into it with a heart attack. I want to prove to him that I am capable of not just matching his success, but taking our business to the next level."

"That might be something I find attractive in you, too," she admitted. "Your dedication to work. A lot of people just go to work and come home and forget about it until the next morning. You and me? We live it."

Davis clutched at his chest. "Did Eden Moody just admit to finding me attractive?"

She did roll her eyes now. "Don't let it go to your head, Gates."

He leaned in to her, her body uncomfortably aware of the proximity of his mouth. And she thought he might kiss her. And it might mean something besides revenge and painting a pretty picture for their audience. Her lips parted, eyes locking in on his mouth. She could feel the heat from his body as it caressed her face.

"Well, don't you two look gorgeous together?" Summer and Carter Pierce stopped next to their table.

Eden jumped back against the booth in flustered surprise.

Speaking of gorgeous, the Pierces were a stunning blend of Summer's urban chic and Carter's rough-around-the-edges, earthy sex appeal. Carter's arm was slung possessively around his wife's slim shoulders.

"Date night?" Eden asked.

"Jax lost a bet and had to take the twins for the night," Carter said with a quick grin under his thick beard.

Carter and Summer were parents to two-year-old twins, who were as cute as they were mischievous.

Summer slid into the booth across from them tugging Carter with her. "Listen. I just wanted to say how happy I am for you guys. I know there's been a lot of bad blood between your families over the years, and it's really beautiful to see you two so happy."

"And sorry for crashing your dinner," Carter added wryly.

Summer wrinkled her pert nose at him and cuddled into his side. "As an old married lady, it just makes me so happy to see you two together. I think the whole town has been waiting for this for a long time. So, what are you guys doing for Thanksgiving?"

Eden blinked. She knew Summer well enough. The woman had been a Mooner for three years and had apparently embraced the nosy neighbor residency requirement. She was stylish and smart and head over heels in love with Carter.

Eden found it hard to believe that Summer Pierce, let alone the entire town of Blue Moon, could be so invested in this fake relationship.

Rupert appeared before Eden or Davis could respond and dropped off three bowls of minestrone soup.

Eden and Davis shared an eyeroll. "Look, dear. Our appetizer," Eden laughed.

"He was our waiter, too," Carter told them. "You might want to deliver your dinner order directly to the kitchen."

Eden had just dipped her spoon into the soup when Summer spoke up again. "So, as I was saying, Thanksgiving?"

"Oh, well. My parents are out of town," Eden began.

"My family is still on the west coast," Davis added.

"We were probably just going to do something quiet..." Eden trailed off, looking to Davis for help. Did newly dating couples spend the holidays together? What was the protocol?

"We're hosting a progressive dinner at the farm. Drinks at Jax and Joey's, dinner at our place, and desserts at Phoebe and Franklin's," Summer told them, flipping her blonde hair over her shoulder.

"That sounds like fun," Eden said, thinking back to her family's last Thanksgiving. Her dad had burned the tofurkey, and the pumpkin pie hadn't set. After dinner, Atlantis's kids had hosted a screaming contest in the living room.

"You're more than welcome to join us," Carter put in stretching his long legs into the aisle.

"You should come," Summer said, more insistently.

"Oh, I, uh." Eden looked at Davis. A fake relationship was one thing. Faking their way through an entire holiday with members of the Beautification Committee in attendance was something else.

"We were just planning something quiet," Davis began.

"I'll have Joey text you and tell you what to bring,"

Summer said triumphantly despite the fact that no one had uttered the words "yes, we'd love to come."

"Oh, but…" Eden's protests fell on deaf ears. She elbowed Davis in the ribs.

"We couldn't impose like that," he coughed.

"It's the opposite of an imposition," Summer insisted. "The crowd is so big, it's literally the more the merrier. And I'd just hate to think of you two alone on Thanksgiving." She looked up at her husband. "Shall we get back to our quiet, child-free house?"

The look Carter gave his wife was positively sinful.

"It was great seeing you," Carter said as he scooted out of the booth and took Summer's hand.

"Can't wait for Thanksgiving," Summer said without tearing her eyes from Carter. They jogged out of the restaurant like two horny teenagers with the keys to the car.

"Uh, what the hell just happened?" Eden asked.

"I think we just got invited to the Pierce family Thanksgiving," Davis said, stirring his minestrone.

"I was going to stay home and eat pizza in my pajamas while binge watching *Gilmore Girls*," Eden complained. She had guests booked for the holiday, but they were all repeat visitors in town to see family and would require very little attention from her. Thanksgiving with her parents traveling would have been a much appreciated, quiet day off.

"I was going to work on some ad mockups for the wine trail and scan some expense receipts," Davis grumbled.

His nerdiness eeked the attraction factor up another notch.

Eden sighed. "I don't know if our fake love can hold up to the scrutiny of the family that accounted for most of Wilson Abramovich's engagement ring sales for the last three years."

24

"Well, crap. How are we supposed to rub our fake relationship in Blue Moon's face if there aren't any Mooners here?" Eden pouted.

Their big movie date was a bust. Besides the elderly ticket taker and the baby-faced snack stand staffer, the entire theater was empty. There was no one present to witness and report on their canoodling.

"I guess everyone must be at the high school basketball game," Davis speculated.

Eden frowned down at her fresh popcorn. "Maybe we should just call it a night? Try to be a public spectacle when we have an actual audience?"

They'd gone out on the town three out of the last four nights, working hard to sell their romantic relationship. His social life had never been this active. A quiet night in would involve them going to their separate rooms. Davis looked her up and down in the dim theater lighting, pausing to admire the way the ice blue V-neck sweater hugged her subtle curves.

He finally had Eden Moody all to himself. He wasn't going to waste this opportunity.

"If we leave now, Snack Stand Toby will report it," he said, leading the way down the aisle. "Everyone will start speculating that we got into a fight—because what new couple doesn't want an entire theater to themselves? And then the Beautification Committee will worry that this isn't the slam dunk match they think it is."

He picked a row, paused, and gestured for her to enter first. Eden hesitated. And Davis wondered if she was nervous about being so close to him in such an intimate setting. It was an idea he didn't mind.

"You go first," she insisted. "I like to sit on the aisle."

Everything was a power play with Eden, but Davis considered her agreeing to watch a movie alone in the dark with him a bigger victory.

Ever since she'd kissed him that first time at Peace of Pizza he'd been able to think of little else. She'd caught him by surprise as had the kiss itself. That supposed fake lip lock had unlocked a very real hunger in him. And blown every teenage fantasy he'd ever had out of the water.

Davis waited until Eden settled in next to him before sliding his arm around her shoulders. She tensed against him. "There's no one here," she pointed out.

Yep. And he was going to take advantage of that fact. Davis was pretty damn sure one of his more colorful Eden-centered fantasies in high school had involved an empty movie theater.

"Someone could walk in late. This way we make sure they get the happy couple picture," he told her.

"Hmm." She remained unconvinced, but Davis was feeling particularly persuasive today.

With what he took as reluctance, Eden offered him her popcorn bag.

He took a handful and lazily stroked his free hand over the softness of her sweater sleeve.

"Have a good day?" Davis asked.

"Uh. Yeah," she said, giving him the side-eye.

"What? You don't want to make small talk?" he teased. "Just pretend I'm one of your guests."

Eden cleared her throat. "I'm not actually used to talking to someone every day. This whole 'dating' thing is kind of weird. I mean, we talked yesterday when we went for custard and checked out the high school art show. And the day before that was our dinner date. More talking."

"You can't be *that* rusty at dating," Davis pressed.

She crinkled her nose. "It's been a while since I've dated anyone seriously... or fakely. What about you? Were you Mr. Monogamous Relationships before you moved back?"

It was his turn to clear his throat. "I dated. Had a handful of long-termish relationships, but nothing that ever felt serious."

"What about since you moved back?" Eden wasn't pretending to look at the blank screen anymore. She was staring right at him.

"You mean before you swept me off my feet?"

"Har. Har."

He grinned at her. "Dating in Blue Moon is... difficult," Davis decided.

"It totally is," she agreed. Davis felt like he'd won big on a scratch-off. They *agreed* on something. "I've actually never dated anyone from town since high school. Everyone's always—"

"Watching," he filled in.

"Yeah. It's hard to focus on being funny and smart and charming and girl-next-door-y when an entire town is watching your every move, waiting for you to get your feelings hurt and damage some personal property again."

He shifted in his seat. "I hope you don't feel that people are still judging you on that."

"My mug shot ran in *The Monthly Moon*. Your parents still call me Vandalism Moody every time they see me. And rumor has it that same mug shot hangs in your tasting room so your employees know not to serve me."

Davis shook his head. "I took it down my first day back. And my parents are professional grudge-holders. You can't take it personally. Someday, I'll tell you the story of the Cleary department store clerk who dared to refuse my mother's expired coupon."

Eden smiled wryly and he knew there was more to her feelings than what she'd grudgingly shared.

He leaned in just a little closer. "You know what I just realized?"

She ran her tongue over her lower lip. "What?" she asked softly.

"You're literally the girl next-door. I'm living every guy's fantasy right now."

Brave and ballsy Eden Moody was suddenly staring into her popcorn as if it were the most fascinating food in the universe. She took in a breath and blew it out. And then she was drawing herself in, behind those tall walls she'd built because of him.

"So, do you think the Beautification Committee is trying to frame me or was that just a really unlucky byproduct? Because if I'm being investigated for arson, wouldn't it be harder for you to fall madly in love with me?" she asked, changing the subject.

The mention of the fire had his eye twitching in response. Sometimes he forgot why they were doing what they were doing. Sometimes he got caught up in the smiles and the intimate touches without thinking about their primary objective.

The absolute irresponsibility of using arson in matchmaking… well, it was imperative that they dismantle the organized insanity.

"I don't think any sane person can begin to understand the motivations of the Beautification Committee. But I'm not letting you go down for arson. I promise you that, Eden."

She gave him a small smile. "Thanks."

"What are friends for?" He offered her his green tea icy and was gratified when she took a sip from the straw.

The lights dimmed around them.

Sharing snacks and conversation. Cuddled up together in the dark. Yeah, he'd just taken Eden on their first *real* date.

25

"I need you to come to the brewery tonight and drink all the alcohol they put in front of me," Eva announced on speakerphone.

Eden was elbow deep in flaky pastry dough. "Is this a joke?"

"No! You owe me. You stole my B.C. binder. And I still haven't told anyone about the B-A-B-Y."

"Most of Blue Moon knows how to spell," Eden said dryly.

"I'm watching Lydia. With siblings like Aurora and Evan, who knows what this kid can spell." Lydia was a baby that babbled and drooled and batted her impossibly long lashes at Beckett and Gia Pierce, keeping her parents firmly wrapped around her chubby little fingers.

"I was planning to get a head start on my kitchen inventory," Eden began, searching for an excuse. She and Davis had been busy traipsing all over town so Blue Moon could witness their fake love in all its faux glory. He had a meeting tonight, and she'd been looking forward to a night in with no pretenses.

"Eden!" Eva screeched. "I am begging you as my friend to

help me cover my secret B-A-B-Y and come hang out with us. I'm sure you can pry your lips off of Davis's face for two whole hours. Especially since I know he's meeting with the Pierces tonight about wines and beer."

"Two hours?" Eden clarified.

"Yes! *And* I'll buy you dinner."

Eden sighed, sending up a cloud of flour. "Ugh. Fine. But I sort of hate you for all of this."

"You can't hate me. I'm part of the reason you're finally swooning over Davis Gates. I basically did you a huge, inappropriately invasive favor."

Eden hmm-ed her response. "What are we wearing?"

JOHN PIERCE BREWS was a welcome respite from the biting November wind. The old stone barn had been renovated by the Pierce brothers and turned into a comfortable gathering space with craft beers and farm-to-table food. Eden shrugged out of her coat at the host stand and waved to Cheryl, the tattooed bartender. Cheryl winked and pointed to a long table in the corner.

The bar area was loud and crowded, a sign of small business success that Eden could appreciate. It wasn't long ago that this very barn sat abandoned and empty. Now it was part of the fabric of Blue Moon socialization.

And at the very center was the Pierce family. The Pierce-Merrill-Cardona women were an intimidating sight. Blonde and chic Summer sat at the head of the table nursing a glass of wine and toying with the earrings that dangled from her lobes. Joey with her model-worthy resting bitch face sat on Summer's right. She was still dressed for riding in jodhpurs and boots, but she'd yanked her long dark hair out of its perennial ponytail. Emma, Eva, and Gia were red-headed versions of the same fine-boned, ivory-skinned heritage. Emma was the edgy, fashionable one with a short, trendy haircut. Gia looked as though she'd been born in Blue Moon with her long curls and sexy tunic. Eva looked... well, mostly relieved when she spotted Eden approaching. She was dressed in a chunky oversized sweater the same color as her pale cheeks.

"Eden!" They greeted her enthusiastically, and for a moment Eden was actually glad she came. It had been too long since she'd gotten an evening out with girlfriends. Sammy and Layla's schedules were a hindrance to any actual social life.

"Hi, everyone," she said, taking the empty seat next to Eva. Eva nudged her beer toward Eden. "What did I miss?" she asked.

"You missed Emma whining that we made her hang out here," Gia teased.

"It's my night off, and you guys made me come to work," Emma groaned and picked up her water. "All I want to do is get up and yell at everyone."

"That's why we made her sit with her back to the room," Summer explained.

"I can feel them congregating at the service bar while food gets cold," Emma insisted.

"Too bad you can't drink to take your mind off of it," Joey said cheerfully as she sucked down the last of her Long Island iced tea.

Emma tossed a wadded-up beverage napkin at her friend and stuck out her tongue.

Eden picked up her pilfered beer and drank.

"Now that we're all here, I move that we discuss exhaustion levels," Eva said.

"Exhaustion level conversation is how we start our nights out," Summer filled Eden in. "We talk about how tired we are from all the crap we have to do—"

"And all the crap we *think* we have to do," Gia added, pointing a finger.

"We bitch and moan about it for five or ten minutes and then drink and talk about sex," Joey interjected. "That's my favorite part."

"I'll start," Emma volunteered. "You guys were not kidding about this pregnancy exhaustion. I went to bed at seven last night and didn't wake up until nine this morning." Emma was famously a night owl. She and her husband Niko had started their relationship with late-night workouts at the twenty-four-hour gym.

"Just wait until that baby gets here," Gia said. "Lydia is getting her molars or growing a second head. All week, she's been waking up at two and again at five. Then I have to be on my A-game to make sure Aurora wears pants to school and Evan..."

"Yeah, try to come up with one complaint about Evan," Eva teased her sister. Evan was known as Mini Mayor around town. He and his stepfather, Beckett, were cut from the same cloth.

Joey snorted. "It's the smart ones you have to watch. They know how to act like a good kid."

"Oh, like you're *soooo* worried about Reva," Summer said, elbowing her.

Joey and her husband Jax were in the process of adopting seventeen-year-old Reva and her six-year-old brother, Caleb.

"I'm smart enough to remember what seventeen felt like."

"Seventeen with Jackson Pierce is different than seventeen with Arnie Einhorn," Emma snorted.

"I'll drink to that," Joey grinned.

"Back to exhaustion, I have twins," Summer reminded them. "And they're two. And I'm afraid I'll never be able to turn my back on them."

The women around the table laughed.

"Eva, we know you're probably exhausted being a newlywed and all," Gia said fluttering her lashes at her younger sister.

Eva turned a pretty shade of pink and beamed.

"Awh," they cooed.

"I *am* a little tired," Eva admitted.

"That sheriff would wear any woman out," Summer said with a long, slow wink.

Eva studied the gleaming bands on her left hand. "I still can't believe we did it. Got married, I mean. I can totally believe we have all the sex."

Eden laughed. Lila, the pierced-nosed, pixie-cut server popped up next to her. "Sorry it took me so long, Eden. Busy night! Can I get you a drink?"

Eden ordered a glass of Chardonnay, and they placed their dinner orders.

"How about you, Eden?" Joey asked. "What exhausts you?"

Eden picked up Eva's beer. "Life," she told the table. She had a business that required twelve-hour days usually seven days a week, parents who were too irresponsible to be left alone for long, and a revenge plan that depended entirely on the man who had broken her delicate, squishy, teenage heart.

"I'll drink to that," Joey said, lifting her glass.

"On to the happiness portion of our conversation," Emma declared.

Eva leaned in to Eden. "So we talked about what makes us exhausted, and now to balance the conversation so we're not a bunch of whiny assholes with first world problems, we talk about what makes us happy."

Kids and new shoes and more help at work were all enthusiastically discussed. Joey's horse breeding program was taking off. Summer's online magazine had reached another major advertising milestone. And Gia's yoga studio was busy enough that she'd brought on a second part-time instructor. Emma, her business success already evident in the hustle and bustle at the bar behind them, talked about the room she and Niko were turning into a nursery and Niko's photo shoot in Miami at the end of the month. Eva's backlist of books was selling well, and she and Donovan were thinking about taking a honeymoon now that the fuss and chaos of the month-long astrological shitstorm was behind them.

"I think we can guess what's making you happy, Eden," Summer said, wiggling her eyebrows.

"You mean, *who* is making her happy," Gia teased.

Oh, right. Her hot, fake boyfriend.

Eden plastered an expression on her face that she hoped would pass for bashful. She wasn't really prepared to lie to half of Blue Moon to their faces tonight. "I'm very happy," she promised them vaguely.

"It's been a long time coming," Joey pointed out.

"Okay. I'm asking it. I've been in the dark long enough," Emma announced. "What exactly happened with you two? What was The Incident everyone keeps talking about?"

Lila returned with Eden's wine, and she took a healthy gulp to buy some time. It didn't help. They were all still staring at her expectantly.

"Why didn't you just ask Joey?" Eden asked. "She was only a few years behind me in school. She knows."

Joey crossed her arms over her chest. "I'm not a gossip," she said haughtily.

Eden leaned back in her chair and wished the floor would swallow her up.

"You don't have to tell us," Gia said, patting her hand from across the table.

"Yes. She does," Eva and Emma announced together.

"Ugh. Fine. I asked Davis to the HeHa dance. He said yes and then showed up with Taneisha instead."

"Taneisha?" Gia gasped. "Was she this beautiful as a teenager?"

"Yep," Eden said flatly.

"Why would he have done that to you?" Summer asked.

See? Davis wasn't the Mr. Wonderful everyone thought him to be, Eden thought. Only now she couldn't gleefully announce that since she was supposed to be falling in love with him. The thrill of victory she expected didn't wash over her.

"I don't know the specifics. I didn't really give him a chance to explain. There wasn't anything he could have said that would have made it not hurt."

"Agreed," Joey announced.

"Of course, you agree," Summer sighed. "You held a grudge for eight years."

"A grudge that deserved to be held," Joey shot back.

"You guys, the first time Joey saw Jax when he moved back to Blue Moon, she slapped the crap out of him in the kitchen," Summer tattled. "It was so hot!"

Eden laughed along with the rest of them. Joey and Jax had been high school sweethearts when they were in an accident just before graduation. Jax had left Blue Moon—and Joey—that night. It had taken a lot of time, a lot of Pierce charm, and a rescue dog to thaw her feelings toward him.

"Okay, so that's the why," Emma prodded. "What was The Incident? What did you do to get back at Davis?"

Eden covered her face with her hands. "This is so stupid. It's so embarrassing," she complained.

"We're all friends here," Eva said, patting her on the shoulder.

"I was mad," Eden began.

"Rightfully so," Joey cut in.

"So, after the dance, I took my cousin Moon Beam with me to his house."

The women around the table leaned forward in anticipation.

"I was just going to toilet paper his precious El Camino. I swear, it was totally innocent."

"I wish I had popcorn right now," Gia whispered.

"Anyway, Moon Beam was smoking like a rebellious teenage chimney at the time. She flicked her butt into the grass, which hadn't had a good rain in forever. And it turns out the organic lawn fertilizer was highly flammable."

A collective gasp went up around the table.

"So, there I was in my pretty dress with my rolls of toilet paper, and the entire front lawn is ablaze. Moon Beam, who was one infraction away from being sent to live on a commune with our Aunt Martha, took off."

"That explains a lot," Joey said. "I knew you weren't the arsonist type."

"I had to run up the driveway and ring the bell to tell them their yard was on fire. The flames were racing toward the house. I was hysterical and Mr. and Mrs. Gates were screaming at me. The Monthly Moon photographer arrived right before the fire company and spent the next half hour shooting my mugshot. Hazel Cardona arrested me in front of Davis and Taneisha... his next-door neighbor."

The table was in absolute silence.

"It looked like he'd dumped me and I tried to set his house on fire. It was humiliating."

"Oh, Eden," Summer said with sympathy.

Eden stared down at the table. She could still smell the acrid scent of ash and smoke... and shame.

"You know how Blue Moon is. There were about fifty people on the scene, watching Sheriff Cardona read me my rights. I was still in my dress for the dance."

She took another gulp of wine.

"I told the sheriff it was my fault and left Moon Beam out of it. My parents got the charges plead down to trespassing and vandalism. Moon Beam worked at the Fry and Fly for an entire year to pay me back for the fines. But for fifteen years, I've been the girl that tried to burn down Davis Gates's house."

She'd never told anyone but her parents the real story. And they didn't believe her. They thought she was just acting on behalf of the feud. Everyone, including Davis, still believed that she'd been responsible for the fire.

"So, you really didn't set the fire?" Joey asked in disbelief.

Eden shook her head. "Nope. My own parents didn't believe me. I figured why bother to try to convince anyone else?"

"That's awful," Gia said with sympathy. "You must have felt so alone."

She had. And if Eden were being honest, sometimes she still did.

"Listen, I believe every word. Your cousin Moon Beam saw a target on Jax's pants and tried to get in them when he moved back to Blue Moon," Joey told Eden.

"Davis's parents freaked out, which caused my parents to freak out on them. I had to go through an entire semester of Impulse Control class and a year of community service," Eden confessed. "And ever since, I've been the unstable bad girl of Blue Moon."

"That's so sad and funny and crazy," Summer said.

"On the bright side, you two put it all behind you and now

you're together!" Gia said. "I'll admit, I was skeptical at first, but from the pictures, you two look so happy. I'm really glad we matched you."

"Pictures?" Eden frowned.

"Wait? You're not allowed to talk about Beautification Committee business," Joey pointed out.

"Oh, it's okay," Eva told them. "Eden knows she was matched. She even showed up to a meeting to contest it."

"We can contest our matches?" Joey screeched, slapping her hand down on the table.

Gia clamped a hand over her own mouth.

"Shit. What's it going to take to make sure that never gets repeated," Eva hissed.

"Five-hundred bucks," Joey shot back.

"That's extortion!"

"Okay, fine then. Dedicate your next book to me." Joey steepled her fingers, her long legs stretching out under the table. Joey devoured Eva's novels like chocolate-covered pretzels.

"Arg. Fine. Deal."

"I can't believe all this time we were allowed to contest our matches," Summer muttered.

26

The cabernet was a rich red in the tasting glasses Davis distributed. "This particular blend is heavy on the currant and vanilla."

Beckett Pierce held up the glass to the light and swirled the wine, his apocalypse-earned black eye from Sheriff Cardona had faded to a dull yellow. Jax knocked it back like a shot. Carter shoved his youngest brother.

"Don't you know anything about wine tasting, Hollywood?"

Jax ignored his brother's ribbing and opened the tap to fill a sample glass with a dark ale. "This is our Joey's Porter," he said, passing it over the bar. "Smooth. Strong. A kick in the ass, just like its inspiration."

The Pierce brothers may have started the brewery to honor their late father, but the beers themselves were inspired by the women in their lives. Davis wondered what kind of wine would bear Eden's name. Something red, sinfully smooth, with a full body—

"You gonna drink it or moon over it?" Jax joked.

They'd all known each other since forever, as was the case

with anyone born and raised in Blue Moon. He'd been closest in age to Carter, but the Pierce brothers came as a package deal and Davis had spent a good deal of his high school career being entertained by all three.

Davis sniffed and then sipped, tasting the beer much the way he would sample wine. The notes of coffee and chocolate caught his palate. They were in the midst of a very friendly negotiation on serving John Pierce Brews at the winery and Blue Moon Wines at the brewery. Apparently, his new truce with Eden had lifted an unspoken business embargo for anyone who didn't want to be perceived as choosing sides.

"Look, I vote that we all just say yes now instead of pissing around," Jax said, tossing back a sparkling wine. "Ooh! Bubbles."

"What's your hurry, Jax?" Beckett, the attorney and Blue Moon mayor, hedged. Beckett liked to think through decisions, weighing all the angles.

"We've got, what? Two hours allotted for this meeting, right?"

Carter shrugged and waited.

"We wrap this up now with handshakes, and we can sit back, order up a bunch of wings, and watch the game without wives or kids."

Carter and Beckett shared a look of longing.

"Deal?" Beckett said, standing and offering Davis his hand.

"Good with me." They shook, sealing the deal and sticking a fork in the business portion of the evening.

"We'll work out the specifics later," Carter promised.

Jax got on the phone behind the bar. "What kind of wings do you want, Gates?" he asked.

They placed an order with the kitchen for an astronomical amount of bar food.

"I'm texting Vulkov and Cardona," Beckett suggested. "The

wives are all out together working on some fundraiser or something, and the kids are spread out with an army of babysitters. It's Man Night."

Davis started to stopper his bottles. "Hang on. We'll double fist to celebrate," Carter insisted, pulling down wine glasses from above the bar. They were in the private bar area on the second floor of the brewery. Used mainly for special occasions or Pierce family meals, it was a generous space with its own bar and restrooms and a dozen tables spread out. There was a steel cabled railing overlooking the main bar area below.

Davis poured himself a merlot and accepted the lager Jax poured for him. He planted himself on a bar stool and wondered when he'd last watched a game with friends. The winery had kept him busy, had basically consumed his life. And the fire had been a major setback. And then there was Eden picking up all of his spare time and confusing him with a fake relationship that felt way too real.

It was nice to be normal for a little while.

The sheriff and Nikolai Vulkov arrived together minutes later. Niko shrugged out of his leather jacket and made a mad dash for alcohol.

"Emma can't drink," he said by way of an explanation as he reverently picked up a beer.

"Meaning?" Davis asked, watching him swallow two-thirds of the glass's contents.

"Meaning I can't drink either," Niko said, pausing for a breath and then polishing off the rest of the beer. "Ahhh, I've missed you," he crooned.

Carter smirked. "Why don't you just tell Emma the truth? That you're cheating on her with a frosty blonde."

"It's called being supportive," Niko said dryly. "I'd think a father of twins would know what that was."

Jax held up a piece of popcorn chicken, and Beckett nodded and rose. Jax gave the chicken a toss, and Beckett caught it in his mouth, shooting his arms up victoriously.

"A father of twins knows what support looks like," Carter shot back, amused.

"What? A vasectomy?" Niko teased.

"If that will make Summer's life better, I'm not afraid of getting snipped."

"My buddy back in L.A. went with a bunch of his friends. They all got them done together. Like a really painful spa day," Jax told them, chucking another piece of chicken at Beckett.

"Are you guys done with two?" Niko asked Carter.

Carter shrugged. "I think so, but every time one of you jackasses has a baby, Summer sniffs them and starts talking about how much she misses the baby stage."

Beckett rolled his eyes. "I'm currently in the baby stage, and I'm very much looking forward to Lydia going off to college. She's getting molars or growing a tail and isn't sleeping."

"Not making me look forward to next year, guys," Niko confessed. "I'm already terrified that I'll screw this kid up somehow."

"Oh, you will," Carter told him cheerfully.

"Should have just adopted a couple of older ones," Jax said smugly. "Ours came potty-trained and with all their teeth."

Jax, the youngest of the Pierces, had just over ten years on the daughter he and Joey were adopting.

"What about you two?" Beckett asked Donovan and Davis. "Now that you're settled down, has the f word come up?"

"Family," Jax explained.

"Ah. Well, Eden and I just started dating," Davis hedged. "We've got time to figure that out."

"How about you, Cardona?" Jax asked. "You working on a pack of baby sheriffs?"

Donovan sucked his beer down the wrong pipe and choked. But it was the stupid grin on his face that alerted everyone to the real issue.

"Are you kidding?" Niko asked. "You guys are having a baby?"

"Shut the fuck up," Donovan said, looking over both shoulders as if worried that his tiny wife would appear and murder him for spilling their secret.

"Holy shit! I can't believe Emma didn't tell me," Niko said, reaching for a glass of wine.

"Emma doesn't know. *No one* knows. We found out after the wedding. Like ten minutes after the wedding," Donovan confessed.

"That's what you were doing in there?" Carter asked. "We all thought you were having sex."

"That, too," Donovan grinned. "But seriously. None of you can say a word to anyone, especially your wives. And when Eva does decide to tell you, you have to pretend to be surprised."

Each of the men traced their fingers over their hearts in an X, Blue Moon code for "I promise." It was legally binding.

"It's crazy to think that three years ago, you were all single," Davis pointed out. So much had changed in their lives, and he had to admit he'd never seen them happier. He felt... a pang. Just that little hint that maybe there was something great out there that he was missing out on.

Jax reached out with his arms and rolled his eyes back in his head. "Join us. Join us."

"We literally just started dating," Davis pointed out. He left out the part where they were only pretending to date. He also didn't feel inclined to reveal that the more time he spent with

Eden, the less fake it all felt. She was challenging. Exciting. Interesting. All of that on top of the fact that he'd always found her irresistible.

"You've got a lot going on, man," Beckett said, slapping him on the shoulder.

Davis reached for another hot wing from the tray.

"Any luck with the insurance company?" Donovan asked him.

Davis shook his head. "Until investigators can prove it wasn't me setting the fire to perpetrate insurance fraud, they aren't paying up."

"Man, that sucks. And you have no idea who did it?" Beckett asked.

Davis stared into the eyes of the man whose wife had played a role in burning down his kitchen and lied to his face. "No idea."

DONOVAN PROMISED to check in with the fire chief and the inspector the next day. But Davis wasn't holding on to any hopes there. He'd talked to his financial advisor earlier in the day, and she had confirmed that he could borrow against his retirement savings. It would hurt. A lot. But at least his house wouldn't rot and fall down waiting for the cash to fix it.

And as angry as he was with his irresponsible town, charging the Beautification Committee with arson wouldn't make life better for anyone.

No, he'd stick with the plan. Borrow against his savings and be back in his own house in a few weeks. They could blow up the Beautification Committee together. And then Eden would have her guest room to herself again.

They'd be back to where they started: virtual strangers sharing a property line.

That part didn't sit well with Davis.

"Hey, that doesn't look like a fundraiser meeting," Carter said. He was peering over the railing into the bar below.

Beckett and Davis joined him and spied a table full of beautiful women.

"Yes!" Jax pumped his fist in the air. "Joey's drinking Long Islands. They always make her frisky."

Davis watched as Eden leaned in and shared a laugh with Eva. Her dark, loose curls fell over her forehead, obscuring one wide, blue eye before she brushed it back. She had always been not just attractive but fascinating. He'd spent the last fifteen years watching her from a distance, and now that he had the opportunity to be up close and personal with her, God he was enjoying himself.

"Gentlemen," Carter said, slinging his arms around Donovan and Niko's shoulders. "We have excellent taste in women."

"I'll drink to that," Beckett said, his gaze warm on his wife.

"What are the odds that they'll be pissed at us for cutting loose tonight?" Jax asked warily.

Beckett cuffed him on the back of the head. "We just busted them lying about organizing a fundraiser, genius. We're covered."

"That's because your wife's logic outweighs her desire to win a fight." Jax didn't sound like he was complaining. It was rumored that he and Joey argued just so they could make up.

"Let's go test the waters, gentlemen," Donovan said, heading for the stairs. "And remember, if one of you says the word 'baby' down there, I'm going to tase you."

27

"Well, well, well. Look what's coming our way," Summer announced to the table, staring in female satisfaction as the crowd in the bar parted for a half-dozen gorgeous men.

"Mmm," Emma sighed. "We sure are lucky, aren't we?"

It should be illegal to have that many good-looking men in one confined space, Eden decided. And leading the way was *her* man. Her *temporary* man, she corrected silently. Davis was getting his fair share of rapt attention from the estrogen-carrying bar customers.

He was dressed for business in slate gray slacks and a light blue button-down. He'd forgone the tie and rolled up his sleeves. His hair was thick and attractively mussed. And his brown eyes were firmly on Eden. God, there was something in that gaze. Something possessive, primal. And why did she think that maybe it wasn't just for show?

"Ladies, my friends and I couldn't help but notice how beautiful you are," Niko said suavely. He trailed a finger down Emma's neck, and she grinned up at him. "Can we buy you a round of drinks?"

"How's your meeting, *Jax*?" Joey demanded with a glare.

Jax strolled around the table and gathered his wife's hair in his fist, tugging her head back to kiss her. "Objective achieved early. How's your *fundraiser*, Jojo?"

"Fundraiser?" Summer snorted. "Ow!"

Joey gave her a swift kick under the table.

"Maybe we should just call a draw on this one, Joey," Gia suggested, hopping up to press a quick kiss to Beckett's cheek.

Davis made eye contact with Eden, telegraphing a question. *How should we play this?*

Eden gave a small shrug and a nod. Play along.

He leaned down, closing the distance carefully, and Eden felt like she'd spontaneously combust from the anticipation. She felt it every time a kiss was called for. Hell, she'd even instigated one or two lip locks when they weren't absolutely necessary just to have his mouth on hers again.

Finally, his lips met hers, firmly, sweetly. It was a chaste kiss, but he shoved his fingers into her hair, holding her lightly at the top of her neck, and Eden's pulse started to hammer.

He pulled back slowly, keeping his hand where it was, and she opened her eyes.

"Hi," he said softly.

"Hi," she blushed.

"Awh, you two are so damn cute," Gia sighed across the table. She rested her head on Beckett's shoulder. "Isn't new love cute?"

"Adorable," Beckett agreed dryly. "The Beautification Committee is a genius."

Eden tensed, and Davis tightened his fingers on her neck.

"I'm sensing sarcasm," Gia said, hands on hips. "They matched us. And look at Eden and Davis! Eden's trusting our expertise enough to throw herself into this relationship to give them a real chance at happiness."

What was that feeling settling in the pit of her stomach? *Guilt?* That was ridiculous. Those people basically firebombed a residence in the name of matchmaking. They had to be stopped. She felt Davis give her neck another squeeze as if he were reading her mind.

"According to my watch," Summer interrupted. "We have forty-five minutes before we need to relieve babysitters. Are we going to spend it arguing, or has ladies' night become date night?"

~

THERE WEREN'T ENOUGH CHAIRS. So, Eden sat on Davis's lap. She tried to perch at first, her back military straight. But her thighs soon began to cry foul holding her entire weight. Davis solved the problem for her, by slinging his arm around her waist and pulling her back against his chest.

He rubbed lazy circles with his thumb on the back of her neck while they talked. The conversation buzzed around them, but Eden had trouble concentrating on anything but Davis's fingers.

He'd asked her how she liked to be touched. *Was he using that information against her? Was he just playing the game? Or was this something more?* She couldn't figure out his game. All she wanted to do was curl up like a cat in his lap.

"You look beautiful," he whispered in her ear. His lips brushed the delicate skin of her ear lobe, and Eden shivered.

She looked down at the gauzy white blouse she'd donned over slim, black biker pants. "Thank you," she said, her cheeks turning scarlet. Her voice sounded robotic. Davis Gates was seducing her, and she was falling for it.

He stroked his hand down her back and she felt the

warmth of his palm scorching her skin under the thin layer of clothing.

"I've been thinking about our arrangement," Davis said softly.

Eden stiffened. Nothing he said next could be good. Either he'd decided he didn't want revenge and she'd have another reason to go back to despising him, or he wanted more... and that was... something she wasn't prepared to think about. "You have?" she said evenly.

"Look around us. Would it be so wrong if we had what they have?"

She couldn't help herself. Eden looked around the table at the happy couples. The love, the intimacy, the *connection* was palpable. It was beautiful, this sharing, this building a life together. And for one shining second she could see them, walking the vines, sharing a bottle of wine on the porch, watching dogs and kids play in the yard...

"Eden Moody! You get off that horrible man's lap right this minute!"

"Mom?"

Lilly Ann in her date night caftan peered over Ned's shoulder in horror. They were wedged between two high-top tables, the occupants of which were rearranging themselves for better views of the impending fight. Eden's ashen-faced father looked as though he'd just walked in on his own parents in the middle of a swingers' party. Her mother didn't condone physical violence, but with the murderous expression on her face right now, Eden wondered if she was willing to make an exception.

"How could you?" Lilly Ann howled flinging both arms out wide, tangling pint glasses in her bell sleeves. "How could she, Ned?"

Eden's father shook his head slowly, morosely. "Where did we go wrong, Lilly Ann?"

Eden could have given them a list of all their wrong turns, but she didn't feel that now was the appropriate time.

She jumped out of Davis's lap, conscious of the stares directed their way. Just another weeknight in Blue Moon with a family feud spilling out into a public restaurant.

"You are a bad, bad man," Lilly Ann announced, wielding her finger like a wand at Davis. "And I hope you are rendered impotent and your children are redheads."

"Hey!" The trio of redheads piped up from the table.

"No offense," Lilly Ann said. "You three are simply stunning."

"How can I be impotent *and* have children?" Davis whispered. Eden elbowed him in his very solid abs.

"Mom, Dad, I can explain," Eden began.

They stared at her expectantly, hurt and disappointment radiating off of them.

"Well?" Ned prodded.

"How about we step outside?" Davis suggested. He rose, dropped some bills on the table, and grabbed their coats.

"I'm not stepping anywhere with you!" Lilly Ann shrieked. "You'll probably shove me in front of a moving car!"

"Enough! Mother. Outside, now!" Eden grabbed her mother's arm and started dragging. She didn't stop until they made it outside the brewery.

Ned stomped along behind them with Davis on his heels. "I got this," Eden told him.

But Davis shook his head. "Not leaving."

Lilly Ann blew a raspberry in Davis's direction.

"Oh, real mature, Mom." Eden's breath puffed out into the night air on a silvery cloud.

"After everything his family put us through, you're just

willing to forgive and forget? His second cousin Wooster stole my hamster!" If Ned's voice got any higher, the dog population of Blue Moon and its surrounding areas would be arriving at any moment.

As it was, Eden could hear Joey's dog, Waffles, howling from the horse barn just down the road.

"I'm not even going to point out the irony of you two growing up in the hippie-est damn town on the entire east coast and complaining about forgiveness," she said, putting her hands on her hips. "For the record, Davis and I are *not* dating!"

"Oh, so you're just having sex then?" The rage had gone out of Lilly Ann. Apparently having sex with one's enemies was fine.

"Oh my God, Mom! We're not even doing that," Eden hissed out. "We are nothing. There is nothing between us but a plan to get revenge on the Beautification Committee for trying to match us *and* for burning down Davis's house in the process."

That shut them up, Eden thought triumphantly.

Davis was looking at her. His face was in shadows, but she could feel something radiating off of him. Disappointment? She couldn't tell.

"The Beautification Committee tried to match the two of you?" Lilly Ann pointed at them both.

"Yes," Davis answered.

Eden's mother threw her head back and cackled. "That's the most ridiculous thing I've ever heard."

"Okay, Hilarious Hilda. It's not *that* funny," Eden said.

"You two would be a horrible couple," Lilly Ann pressed. "I mean come on. You dress like you're in a motorcycle gang, and he's all Mr. Suits over there. You're a beautiful, sweet, kind soul, and Davis—no offense—is the demon spawn of those Gates monsters."

"None taken," Davis said amicably. He draped Eden's coat over her shoulders.

"They thought it would put an end to your stupid feud that has apparently tortured your friends and neighbors for fifty years," Eden explained.

Ned waved a hand dismissively. "That's ridiculous. Everyone loves our feud."

"Dad," Eden rubbed her temples in exasperation. "No, they don't. The whole town wishes we'd all just bury the hatchet."

"Oh, I know exactly where I'd bury the hatchet," Lilly Ann said looking at Davis darkly. "Right between your mother's—"

"Mom!"

"What? I was just going to say butt cheeks."

"Help me out here, Davis, please?" Eden begged.

He stepped forward into the spotlight cast by one of the brewery's exterior lights. "Eden and I would appreciate it if you could pretend that you don't know that our relationship is just a means to revenge." He looked at her as he said it.

Oh, yeah. He was definitely... annoyed? Angry? She couldn't read him. But she'd deal with him later.

"In fact, if you want to be upset about it to everyone else, that would be great. You'll be helping us... me," Eden added. It wouldn't hurt to have the Moodys showing no sign of backing down on their end of the feud to further prove the Beautification Committee wrong.

"You expect us to not only recognize but also participate in a temporary truce in the battle we've been fighting our entire lives?" Ned demanded.

"Oooh! We could fake disown you!" Lilly Ann said fingers

fluttering as she got into the spirit. "I've always wanted to disown a child!"

Her mother had interesting life goals.

"I don't know about this, Buttercup," Ned said to his wife. But Lilly Ann was committed.

"Now, you'll need to make sure you're selling it," she instructed Eden. "Don't let your natural dislike of each other cloud your acting ability."

Eden decided now was not the time to point out that her parents had spotted them together inside and blew their collective gaskets after buying the ruse.

"Okay, Mom," Eden said, pushing them in the direction of the parking lot.

"I think we should make sure," Lilly Ann insisted.

If Eden's blood pressure got any higher, her head was going to explode.

"Kiss her," Lilly Ann ordered Davis.

"Excuse me?" Davis paled, his eyes beseeching Eden in the dark.

"Mom, it's been a long night. Why don't you and Dad just head home—"

"If I'm going to get into character as a mother whose daughter has deeply disappointed her, I need to feel it, Eden."

Lilly Ann had once been the understudy for Annie in the Blue Moon High School's 1980 performance of *Annie Get Your Gun*. The experience had convinced her that she was born to be an actress.

"Eden, be a good girl and kiss your fake boyfriend."

She needed to move out of Blue Moon. Or get her parents to move, Eden decided on the spot. Maybe she could ship them off to Aunt Nell in Arizona?

"I'm not sure if I'm comfortable with this," Ned wheezed.

"Dad, do you have your inhaler?"

He patted the pockets of his ancient barn coat and corduroy blazer underneath.

"Davis, as your future fake mother-in-law, I demand that you kiss my daughter!"

Eden started to argue again. But Davis caved. His hands closed around her upper arms, and he reeled her body into his. Helpless, she slid her arms under his coat and around his waist, drawn to the heat there.

He brought his mouth to Eden's abruptly and held them there.

"I don't like this. I don't like this one bit," Ned said from behind them. Eden could hear the puff of his inhaler.

"Put some feeling into it, Gates!" her mother shouted. "Make me hate you!"

Eden felt Davis's lips curve under hers and without any warning, he dipped her backward. She clung to him, afraid of falling. But he held her close, keeping her suspended above the walkway.

She melted into the kiss, opening for him and sighing into his mouth. Eden didn't hear her mother anymore. Didn't even remember the woman's name. Once again, she was flooded with pure, unfiltered desire. Her body didn't understand that this was just a game. It just wanted more.

Davis broke the kiss first and righted her. It was only then that Eden became aware of her mother's wailing.

"Mom! *You* told him to kiss me!"

Lilly Ann paused in mid-histrionics. "I'm acting!" Her eyeroll was audible. "Have I taught you nothing? Come on, Ned. Let's go home and make love and eat brownies."

"Bye, guys," Eden said, raising her hand in a wave.

"I'm not speaking to you, Eden. Not until you come to your senses," her mother shouted with an exaggerated wink. "Love you!"

28

It was after midnight. But rather than sleeping, Davis was laying on the bed staring up at the ceiling thinking about the woman one wall away. The woman who was apparently not questioning the "fake" part of their relationship like he was. Was she really that good of an actress? That committed to revenge?

He heard the soft knock at his door and debated not answering it. Then hated himself for hoping it was her. He climbed out of bed, not even bothering to pull on a shirt.

"About tonight," Eden said by way of a greeting. She stood framed in his doorway in a cardigan over a scoop neck tank and short, cotton boxers. To him, the combination was more of an aphrodisiac than a thousand dollars of sheer lace lingerie.

"What about it?" He dared her to say something about the kiss.

"I'm sorry about the things my parents said." Her gaze skimmed down his bare chest, and was it his imagination or did they linger on the low waistband of his cotton pants?

"They don't know any better. It's been indoctrinated into them to hate you and your family."

"That's not why you're here, Eden," he told her quietly.

Her eyes narrowed at him. "Really? You want to take the first time I ever apologize to you and tell me I'm lying?"

He reached out before he thought better of it and skimmed his finger over her cheek, along her jaw, and down her neck. A pink flush followed his touch, and Eden drew in a sharp breath.

"You can't sleep for the same reason I can't sleep."

She was moving closer to him, and he doubted Eden was even aware of it.

"Why can't I sleep?" she asked softly.

"Because you can't stop thinking about that kiss."

Her breath was shaky. "I don't know what you're talking—damn it." She grabbed him, nails raking the bare skin of his shoulders. Her lips found his.

He spun her and kicked the door shut behind him. He had fifteen years of pent-up need trying to claw its way out of him. The kiss was hungry, rabid. Her hands swooped over his chest, his torso. Fingernails dragging, electrocuting his skin.

This was real. This wasn't some act designed to confuse or distract. This was truth.

He shoved the cardigan from Eden's narrow shoulders and thanked his lucky stars that there was only one thin layer to go.

Breaking from the kiss, Davis moved his lips over the sensitive skin of her neck. Eden slid her hands into the waistband of his pants and gripped his ass cheeks.

"You can't tell me you don't feel this," he whispered. He rocked his hips into her, his erection a fraction of an inch away from escaping the top of his pants.

"Of course, I feel it, Davis." She squeezed his ass again, nails digging crescents into his flesh.

"Then stop fighting it." He wasn't sure if he was begging her or ordering her. It didn't really matter because she'd just slid a hand down the front of his pants to cup his balls, and his mind had gone inconveniently and completely blank.

Heart racing, he dropped his forehead to hers.

Still palming his balls, she commandeered his mouth and took control of his entire being. At that moment, there was nothing more that Davis wanted than Eden naked and breathless beneath him... or on top of him depending on her inclination.

He slid his shaky hands under the hem of her tank top and dragged it up and over her head. "God, you're gorgeous." He spent a breath admiring her flat stomach, her long, lovely torso, and those small, perfect breasts. Rosy tipped and pebbled, they begged for his attention. He shoved her back into the room until the backs of her knees met the mattress. Following her down on top of the quilt, he reveled in the feel of her soft breasts flattening against the hard of his chest.

Her intake of breath at the contact had him smiling victoriously into her hair. She used her hands and the heel of one foot to free him of his pants.

"God," she murmured when his erection fell heavily against her stomach. Eden gripped his shaft.

"Eden, I'm not interested in doing this if you hate me," he told her, his voice raspy and thick.

She flashed him a cocky arch of her eyebrow and squeezed him. "Liar."

His teeth in her shoulder changed her tune. "Ow! Okay! Okay! Maybe I don't hate you."

"Maybe?" He rescued his cock from her hand and lined it up between her legs, probing at the crotch of her shorts. God, he could feel how hot she was for him through the cotton. He hadn't thought this through, wasn't sure what the consequences would be once there was no turning back. But for once, he didn't particularly care. He finally had Eden right where he'd always wanted her.

"Damn it. Of course you're packing," Eden sighed. "Is there anything about you that isn't perfect?"

"Yeah, I made a big mistake my senior year of high school."

"Sweet talking will get you an orgasm."

He leaned down and, with her watching him, took one tight tip of her breast into his mouth. She arched off the mattress. "Damn it. You know what you're doing." She said it like an accusation.

"Lose the shorts, Eden," he told her before closing his lips over her nipple again and stroking it with his tongue.

"Not sure if my body can follow commands right now," she panted.

He helped her, and together they stripped her shorts off one leg. They were still hooked around an ankle, but it was good enough. There were no barriers between them now.

She reached between their bodies and recaptured his shaft in her talented fingers. She stroked him in long, tight pulls. His vision was going gray around the edges, and Davis wished there were more lights on in the room. He wanted to see her, wanted to burn every moment of her spread beneath him into his memory.

He rolled to his side and brought one hand down to cup her sex.

"Gah!" she breathed.

"Is this okay?" he asked, dipping his fingers through her divide. Eden's legs tensed, trembled, and then fell open.

"Okay," she repeated.

"How about this?"

Davis worked the pads of his fingers over the tiny bundle of nerves. She opened her mouth in a silent scream.

"Davis I'm—" Eden couldn't get the words out because he was plunging his fingers into her, his thumb dragging over her, stroking her.

She came in an instant, an orgasm so quick and fierce that her leg trembled against him. His cock ached to feel her hungry pulls from the inside.

"More?" he asked her.

She nodded, her eyes squeezed shut. "God, yes. Please."

He settled between her legs, his hungry tip brushing that sweet flesh. *Home.*

Shit. "I don't have any protection," he told her, kicking himself for failing his teenage boy pledge to always be prepared for sex.

Eden let out a noise somewhere between a sigh and a growl. But she wasn't shoving him off of her and storming out. "Vanity. Bathroom," she panted.

"You do not stock condoms in your guest rooms."

"Of course I do. Tampons and floss, too."

He didn't know why he was surprised. Eden was a professional at anticipating her guests' needs. And he was literally dying to see if that talent continued in the bedroom. With a wave of regret that bordered on pain, Davis levered up and off of her.

"Hurry!" she called after him.

He hit the bathroom at a dead run and disgorged the contents of the small walnut vanity. He found the condoms under a sewing kit and next to a stain remover pen and extra rolls of toilet paper.

Davis was a little too enthusiastic to get back to the bed.

He caught his knee on the open vanity door and pitched forward almost running headlong into the door.

"You okay?" Eden called.

He was too busy destroying the condom wrapper to answer her.

"Davis?"

She was halfway off the bed by the time he made it back to her. If she'd changed her mind, he was going to die from the worst case of blue balls doctors had ever seen.

"Are you okay?" he asked, a little breathlessly. His knee throbbed, but it was nothing compared to the similar sensation in his cock.

She was staring at him dazed and wide-eyed. He realized he was fisting the root of his shaft. There was no romance, no suave charm in his stance. He looked aggressive, desperate, *demented*. But Eden didn't seem to mind.

She reached for him and snatched the condom from his hand. "Gimmie." And with that, she was gripping his dick in the vice of one hand while she rolled the condom on with the other.

Yep. He was a dead man.

Davis dropped his head back and let out his breath in one long, slow exhale. The feel of her fingers, the vision of her eager and naked on her knees, both were seared into his brain. And if he didn't start thinking about balance sheets and profits and losses, he was going to embarrass himself and disappoint the woman he'd wanted his entire adult life.

With the condom in place, Eden dropped her hands to her sides, and they eyed each other up. Naked, inches from touching. Every nerve in Davis's body felt alive and ready to report pleasure back to his brain.

"I want you to be sure," he said, the words coming out thick and heavy.

She nodded, still staring at his naked body.

"Say it, Eden."

"I'm sure." There was a weight to her quiet words. And Davis got it. They both knew this would change everything, but neither of them could predict just how. And as carefully as he usually considered consequences, nothing short of a "no" from Eden's swollen lips would stop him. Not even an impending return to the feud they'd both fought since birth.

When he didn't move fast enough for her, Eden took the lead, looping her arms around his neck and pulling him in to her. She was still on her knees at the edge of the bed, but now they were skin to skin. It was enough to send his system into overdrive.

"I don't want to rush this," he murmured, trailing kisses over the sharp edge of her jaw, nipping at her skin.

She raked a hand through his hair, pausing to give it a sharp tug. "Gates, this has been fifteen years in the making. I don't think anyone could accuse us of rushing."

"You know what I mean," he told her, nuzzling at her neck. "If I want this night to erase the last decade and a half, it has to be perfect."

She nudged his chin up. "Forget perfect, Davis. I want real."

He saw the lust slide through those blue eyes when his erection pulsed against her torso.

"I want you tonight. Forget our history. Forget our families. Just be right here with me and forget everything else."

He didn't need any further encouragement. He was pushing her backward and sprawling over her. The crown of his cock nestled between her thighs, exactly where it belonged.

She arched under him, breasts flattening against his chest, hips rocking against him.

He didn't need anything else.

With one brutal thrust, he finally possessed Eden Moody, the girl of his dreams.

"Holy. Shit," she breathed.

How could something he'd imagined since puberty be even better than every fantasy he'd ever concocted? How could being buried inside Eden be better than any other sexual experience to date? It took him a long minute before he gauged himself ready to move. And the slow drag of her walls over his erection felt like heaven. If he was going to die tonight, it was going to be happy... with a fulfilled woman beneath him.

"I can feel your heartbeat," he gritted out next to her ear, all his concentration on the sensation of the slow slide back inside her.

"I think I'm having a heart attack."

He grinned, mouth moving over her shoulder. Her nails dug into his back, harder with every stroke. It had never been like this, would never be like this again. Not with someone else. His body had just claimed Eden as its mate.

Feud and family be damned. Revenge forgotten. Sense and logic deserted.

And for the first time in his life, Davis felt like the selfish thing was the right thing. Eden wasn't getting away this time.

She brought her bent knees up higher, and he used the change in angle to thrust lazily against her tender bundle of nerves.

Biting her lip, she squeezed her eyes closed, relishing in his slow, methodical seduction.

"You feel like magic," she whispered dreamily.

The non-sex-having, feudal Eden would never have confessed that. He wondered what other truths he could coax out of her using orgasms as truth serum.

He brushed his lips over hers. "I love how you feel."

They were moving together, and he could feel that long, slow build in the stutter of her muscles, in the way she held him tighter.

"It's too much. You make me feel too much."

"That's right, beautiful," he coached her.

The sight of her sprawled beneath him, soft and pliable and so greedy for pleasure, had him quickening the pace. It was too much and not enough at the same time. The towering wave that they were teetering on would give way, and neither of them would be the same afterward.

Eden's eyelids fluttered open as if hearing his thoughts. He shifted a hand to cup one of her breasts and gently worked his thumb over her nipple.

"Oh shit," he breathed out the oath on a long groan.

"Davis, I'm not ready," she said, squirming beneath him. Fighting the inevitable. But she arched against him, her body demanding what her heart was afraid of.

He felt the heaviness in his balls, felt the tingle at the base of his spine. The headboard rocked into the drywall with each sure thrust. There was no quiet, no carefully orchestrated seduction. Only a bottomless desire and a race to the top. "I've got you, gorgeous. I'm going with you."

And staring into each other's eyes, they gave themselves over to the wash of pleasure. The trembling squeezes of her walls set him off. He flexed his hips into her as the orgasm carved him out. He bucked into her over and over again until her hungry squeezes and his pulses subsided.

29

Her limbs were heavy and warm. The bed beneath her was too comfortable to leave, but someone had to make breakfast for hungry guests. Bleary-eyed, she reached for her phone on the nightstand to see how many minutes of sleep she could squeeze in before her alarm shrilled.

Only there was no phone, no nightstand.

And holy hell, there was someone else on the mattress next to her. Intertwined with her.

Eden went rigid as a board and sifted through her sleep-addled brain. Davis Gates. Naked. Tossing her a handful of orgasms like he was on a lust-themed parade float.

She was indeed in the small guest room she'd dumped Davis in, cuddled up under the covers. She peeked under the quilt at the long arm that was nestled between her breasts.

"I can feel you overthinking everything," Davis's sleepy voice filled her ear.

Embarrassed and confused, Eden tried to sit up. But he only pulled her closer. "Good morning, gorgeous."

Eden fought at his grasp. He let her go, and she bounded

out of bed, scrambling for whatever clothes she'd worn the night before. "I can't believe we did this," she whispered. "Oh my God. If anyone sees me leaving your room..." She'd had glorious, beautiful sex with the man and slept in his bed! Sharing a bed was saved for very serious sexual relationships. She didn't just fall into bed and *stay* there with any man. But with Davis, she'd curled up, sated as could be, and gotten a solid six hours of sleep without so much as waking up to roll over in the middle of the night.

She had a crick in her neck, and her crotch was deliciously sore from overuse.

"Why can't people know?" Davis asked with amusement. He propped himself up on his elbow and watched her hop into her shorts. They were on backwards, but at least it was a small barrier between the two of them.

"What do you mean, 'why can't people know?'"

"We're supposed to be dating. Wouldn't that also involve sex?" There was that smug smile again.

Eden stopped mid-hop. "Oh my God. You're right. I'm so used to not liking you. This is all just part of our cover. I mean, of course, professional appearances still need to be maintained. We can't just saunter around the lobby naked, but this is totally allowed." She sounded like a babbling idiot.

His smile dimmed by degrees. Davis sat up and swung his legs over the side of the bed. He stretched his arms overhead, and Eden gave herself a few seconds to admire the view. He was all lean muscle in the back and shoulders. He looked great in a suit but even better out of one. Because that's how the world worked. Every layer that she peeled back from the man only revealed something better, smarter, sweeter, sexier.

Davis rose and padded barefoot into the bathroom.

"What are you doing?" she called after him, feeling like a

lovesick girlfriend. Why didn't she just pass him a note in Household Management class?

"I'm starting the shower for us," he called out. "You don't have to start breakfast for another forty minutes."

"Us?"

"Unless you want to serve up eggs smelling like sex. Your call."

Thirteen minutes and a tidy pair of orgasms later, a much less panicky Eden stretched like a cat in the pool of sunshine at Davis's window.

"Wow," she said for the third time. "You really know how to wake a girl up."

He strolled out of the bathroom, wearing nothing but one of her white, fluffy towels. His hair was still damp at the ends.

"What are you doing tonight?" Davis asked, hooking his fingers in her shorts and pulling her closer.

Eden beamed up at him. "I don't know. Do I have plans?"

He picked up her hand and kissed each knuckle, melting Eden from the inside out. "You have a date. With me. For ice cream."

"That sounds really good," she said, the good feelings settling in her stomach like comfort food.

"Say seven?" he asked.

"Okay," she said dreamily. "Sounds great. I'm going to go… dry my hair… make breakfast." She was in a sexual stupor. She needed to leave this man's room before she said or did one more stupid thing. "Bye, Davis."

"Bye, gorgeous."

She opened the door on her face and rubbed the cheek that took the blow. "Ha. Oops. Okay. I'm just gonna…"

She stepped out into the hallway and made a mad dash for her room before she could humiliate herself any further.

Safely ensconced in her living quarters, Eden cupped her

hands to her flushed cheeks. "What the hell have I done?" she whispered.

She felt amazing. Like she'd just let go of years of pent-up frustration and anger and disappointment and banished them with a sexual rite of passage. She didn't want to overthink this, didn't want to wonder why one night with Davis had erased years of bad feelings.

Eden spotted her phone on her nightstand where she'd left it last night and grabbed it. No guest emergencies, thank goodness. But there was a group text conversation from Sammy and Layla.

Sammy: Rumor has it you and your parents threw down at the brewery. Do you need help disposing of the bodies?

Layla: Rumor also has it you and Davis left the brewery together and that the BC has doubled down on you two. SPILL THE BEANS!

Eden carried her phone into her bathroom and plugged in the hair dryer. She debated blowing them off and focusing on her day until she could make sense of all the crazy feelings that were careening around in her system.

Eden: Sorry. Spent the night watching Wheel of Fortune *reruns. Catch up soon?*

"*Wheel of Fortune* reruns" was their code for having a sexy story to tell.

Sammy: Holy shit. Holy freakin' shit! I can pencil you in at 10:30 this morning barring any emergencies. Lay? What's your deputy schedule look like?

Layla: Same. 10:30 at the inn. There'd better be coffee, some of those little sugary things, and an orgasm count.

Eden: You guys are ridiculous.

Layla: WILL THERE BE LITTLE SUGARY THINGS?

Eden served up poached eggs over avocado toast with sides of sausage—turkey and vegan—to her early risers. And she did it with a smile permanently etched on her face. After drying her hair, she'd fussed a little with her makeup and chose a pretty cranberry wrap blouse and navy skinny pants.

If she felt good, she might as well look the part, she decided.

Davis skipped breakfast to head out for an early meeting with the vintner. But not before sending her a sweet text.

Davis: I have a feeling I'll be thinking of you and smiling all day long. Thanks for an amazing night, gorgeous.

If Eden were the swooning type, she would have let her knees buckle so she could collapse on the fainting couch in the east suite. But she was far too practical for that. Instead, she took inventory of the towels and toiletries and double checked that the linens were fresh. The room was, as usual perfection. It's subtle gold walls showcased local artists' oil paintings in natural themes. The windows were a perfect frame for the rising sun. The entire space smelled lightly of lemons and sage, the work of her cleaning crew. Eden placed the bottle of wine the guests had ordered next to the two glasses on the sideboard.

She heard the bark of a dog downstairs and checked her watch.

Layla: We're here. Make your ass magically appear or we'll start knocking on doors.

They would too. Nothing stood between her friends and sex news. She gave the room another quick once-over and skipped down the stairs to meet them.

She caught Sammy with her hand in the candy jar at the front desk and Layla snooping around the guestbook.

Vader was nudging Layla's free hand for absent pats.

"Isn't it a beautiful morning, ladies?" Eden sighed grandly.

"Oh, boy. There's a lot of orgasms written on her face," Sammy said, unwrapping a peppermint.

"I hate you a little bit right now," Layla groaned, leaning down to bury her face in the dog's yellow fluff.

"Come on. I'll feed you and fill you in," Eden promised. She led the way into the now empty dining room. Breakfast service ended at nine. Late sleepers were directed into town or to the stash of donuts, pastries, and fruit Eden refilled daily in the library.

Layla's eyes lit up when she saw the tray of lemon blueberry scones. "Dibs on the entire tray." She picked up one of the dainty side plates and began loading it to capacity.

At home here, Sammy helped herself to the coffee carafe while Eden made herself a cup of tea.

They sat, basking in the sunlight that poured through the wall of windows, and sipped in silence for all of four seconds.

"Okay. Let's get this show on the road. Why do you look like you just spent all night practicing the *Kama Sutra*?" Layla asked, through a mouthful of crumbs.

"You do look like a Zen orgasm master," Sammy added thoughtfully.

"Davis and I had sex—three times—and it was amazing, and I can't stop smiling, and my body has that really great "used" feeling today. Like every time I sit down, I think about him and us and last night..."

She trailed off, taking in the open-mouthed gapes of her friends.

"What?"

Sammy collected herself first. "Uh. We've just never heard you babble over a sexual experience before."

"I'm not babbling," Eden argued.

Layla snorted. "Totally babbling."

"We're not making fun of you," Sammy insisted.

"Maybe a little." Layla held up her index finger and thumb. "A tiny bit."

"No more scones for you," Eden said, flipping her friend off.

"Come on. We'll behave," Sammy promised. "Tell us what happened."

"Did you go all rebel without a clue after your parents threatened to dismember you?" Layla demanded.

"Disown me," Eden corrected. She hadn't had any time to check the Blue Moon Facebook group, the gossip mecca for residents. There was probably misinformation out the wazoo in that little corner of the internet.

Layla stared at her for a moment and shook her head. "I can't believe I'm doing this." She pulled her wallet out of her back pocket and tossed a twenty in Sammy's direction.

"Yes!" Sammy snatched up the bill and kissed it.

"What's this about?" Eden asked, picking up a cookie.

Sammy tucked the money into her shirt pocket. "Ten years ago, I bet Layla that you and Davis would end up together."

Eden gasped. "You did what? You're supposed to be my friend."

"I *am* your friend, and you *are* dating Davis." Sammy's logic was infallible.

"I'm *not* dating him," Eden snapped. "I'm fake dating him to get back at the Beautification Committee."

Layla held up a finger. "Hang on. You're fake dating but real banging Davis for revenge?"

When she put it like that, it sounded stupid and immature.

"Is this like when you spite dated Ramesh in high school?" Sammy asked.

"No! It's not like that," Eden argued. "I'm an adult now—"

"An adult who is fake dating her next-door neighbor."

"I want my money back," Layla said, holding her hand out to Sammy.

"They burned down his house!" Eden realized her mistake a moment too late. Layla's eyes sharpened. She was all cop now.

"They did what now?"

"It's just a theory. We don't have any evidence," Eden said quickly. Getting half the town arrested for arson wouldn't do anyone any favors.

"How about you let the police assess that?" Layla suggested with professional politeness reserved for really obnoxious citizens right before they got cuffed.

"Oh, sure. Because you really want your boss to investigate his own wife?" Eden let the words hang there between them.

"Shit," Layla swore.

It was well-known that Eva—wife of Sheriff Cardona—and her sister Gia—wife of Blue Moon's mayor Beckett—were members of the Beautification Committee as was Beckett's paralegal and right-hand woman, Ellery. Hell, there was a bank president and town councilman in play as well.

"What the hell am I supposed to do with this information?" Layla demanded.

"Nothing! It's purely speculation that they plotted to make Davis's house unlivable so he'd have to come stay with me."

"They burned down his kitchen and made the whole town smell like burrito farts for two days."

"I heard Davis can't get the insurance money to start the repairs," Sammy put in. Vader trotted up to her and stuck her head in the vet's lap.

"Why does she like you so much when you give her shots and check her rectal temperature?" Eden wondered.

"I save the good treats for her," Sammy said, squishing Vader's big face between her hands. "Isn't that right, sweetie pie?" She fished out a dog treat from her pants pocket.

"Where's Chewy?" Layla asked, glancing around for Vader's lazier counterpart.

"Probably with Davis."

Sammy and Layla exchanged eyebrow wiggles.

"What?" Eden shrugged. "He goes with him to the winery sometimes."

"But you're only fake dating?" Layla clarified.

"Yes!

"Still confused. If you're fake dating, why did you have real sex?" Sammy asked, sipping her coffee.

Before Eden could formulate a response, Layla stepped in. "Have you seen Davis? What single woman could be under the same roof and not want to jump his bones and rip those sexy-ass suits off of him?"

"It was just a... fluke," Eden insisted. "We ran into my parents at the brewery last night, and things got heated and... then they stayed heated when we got back here."

"I'm keeping the money," Sammy announced.

"It was just sex," Layla argued.

"One time! A fluke!" Eden put in. They didn't need to know about round two this morning.

"I'm inclined to let it ride and see what the outcome is,"

Sammy decided, ignoring Eden. She handed over another treat to Vader.

"Shake on it?" Vader put her paw in Layla's offered hand.

"Awh. What a good shake, but I meant the mean vet lady," Layla told the dog.

"It's not happening again. There's no real relationship there. We can barely tolerate each other," Eden argued.

"Barely tolerate is better than hate," Sammy mused.

"A fluke. Never again," she told her friends. She was also reminding herself. The whole point was to teach the Beautification Committee a lesson. Not to complicate things or lose her head over a man she was too scared to trust again.

Eden's watch signaled giving her a much-needed excuse to duck out of the conversation. "Hang on, I've got someone at the front desk," she said.

She stepped out of the dining room, leaving her friends arguing over if she had sex with Davis again would that constitute the relationship they'd bet on.

"Mornin', Eden," Liz Berkowicz, the face of Every Bloomin' Thing, poked her head over a massive bouquet of pretty fall flowers. Oranges and purples and reds as deep as blood. "Got a delivery for you."

"Wow," Eden said, taking the flowers out of Liz's hands and putting them on the front desk counter. "Stunning as usual. Who's the lucky recipient?"

Liz gave her a funny "duh" look. "One Eden Moody according to the card."

"Me?"

"Looks like you made quite the impression last night."

Eden grabbed the card.

For a night fifteen years in the making.

Davis

Eden's heart did that funny flip-flop thing again in her chest. But she shook it off. This wasn't real. This was part of the plan. She reminded herself. It was a smart move on his part. Everyone would be talking about the bouquet, the note. This fit *the plan*.

"Thanks, Liz," Eden said. She didn't have to work hard to paste a lovesick smile on her face.

"Sounds like you've got quite the admirer," Liz pressed, fishing for details.

"The feeling is... mutual," she choked out.

"Well, have fun admiring each other," Liz said, giving her a slow wink. She walked out whistling, leaving Eden staring at the flowers.

"Well, well, well. Someone was a good girl," Layla said strolling out of the dining room with Sammy on her heels.

"Holy hell," Sammy said. "Where can I get a fake boyfriend who'll give me real orgasms and flowers?"

30

He hoped the flowers weren't too much. He'd gotten carried away, riding the high of last night. Any doubts and concerns he'd had over whether Eden had feelings for him had been erased. No one could fake that kind of connection. Not even Eden Moody.

Davis whistled his way into the belly of the winery. Stainless steel tanks lined the walls, filled with the winery's future. Primary fermentation was over, and now the new wine was settling, transforming into something else. New beginnings. And weren't there a lot of those going around?

Chewy danced at his heels. The dog had made himself a mascot of sorts at the winery. Visitors loved him. And he loved their affection... and the dog bed Davis had installed in his office. Vader joined them some mornings. But spent most days at the inn.

Davis felt like Chewy's seal of approval carried weight with Eden. And he was willing to take all the help he could get to win her over. Not just temporarily. Last night had clinched it. He was going to make Eden Moody his. Parents and pasts be damned.

He'd dated women, had sex with several of them, and even lusted after a few of them. But nothing had prepared him for Eden naked and willing and demanding. He recalled enough of his high school poetry classes to realize the course of his life had changed last night. And while it would be a rocky transition, he was willing to do what it took to make her his. Even if it meant disappointing his family.

He just had to make sure no one told his father yet. Not until he found the right way to break the news.

"Gates!" He found Eden striding toward him. Her gray wool coat was open to reveal a ruby red sweater that hugged her lean torso and slim fitting pants. Her short hair framed her face in dark curls. Her lips were painted red and currently curved in a frown.

She was magnificent.

And she gave him the unshakable feeling that he was watching his future storm toward him.

The fluffy Vader trotting over to him for a quick pat before teasing her brother into a romp through the tanks.

She stopped abruptly in front of him just inches away from touching him. "About the flowers."

"You got them."

"They're stunning," she said, her tone softening a degree. "But I don't want you to think that we're going to repeat last night. This is a fake relationship."

She paused to peer over her shoulder to make sure there weren't any eavesdroppers present.

"And I don't want to confuse either of us with... physical feelings."

She crossed her arms in front of her chest and waited.

It wasn't entirely unexpected. He'd gotten to her, and she was running scared, trying to put him back in a neat little box.

"Is that so," he said, his voice calm, amused.

"Look, I just don't want you developing real feelings for me when all of this is just a ruse—"

"What was last night? You didn't have to go that far to convince the B.C."

She sputtered and paced around him. "Last night was... a fluke. It won't happen again."

Her foundation was rocked. He could see it in those blue eyes. A hint of panic. She was grasping desperately at straws rather than face the fact that they had something real. Something elemental. Something that needed to be explored.

"A fluke, you say." He rubbed a hand over the jaw he'd neglected to shave this morning.

She nodded briskly. "Fluke. Never again."

"We're still going for ice cream tonight," he said, giving her no wiggle room to get out of their date.

"Well... I guess that's okay," she hesitated.

"We still have to convince everyone else that we're in a relationship, don't we?" he reminded her.

"That is the plan," she said lamely.

"Good. There's a town meeting tonight. I thought we could go to that together, too. You know, make an appearance. Lay it on thick."

"I guess that's a good idea." Her eyes narrowed, as if she were trying to figure him out like a puzzle.

"Great. Have time for a tour?" he offered, checking his watch.

"Oh, I..." she looked around her as if for the first time. "I can spare a few minutes."

"Welcome to Blue Moon Winery's tank room," he said, spreading his arms showman style. "These stainless steel tanks are where the magic happens."

"I feel like I'm on an episode of *MTV Cribs*," Eden said with an eye roll.

Davis ignored her. "This is where the pressed, fermented juice is stored. We call it new wine. The sediment sinks to the bottom, we pump the wine into a new tank, and repeat the process. This is what makes the wine clean and smooth."

"How long does that take?" Eden asked studying the tanks.

"About two months."

Davis flexed his teaching muscles and explained the process as he led her into the next room where hundreds of oak barrels were stored and then into the bottling area. The dogs tagged along.

"I'm amazed at how much of the process is automated," Eden said as Davis smoothly escorted her past the sun-filled tasting room where a handful of guests were bellied up to the bar being charmed by staff.

"We try to honor tradition while embracing innovation," Davis told her, leading her up the stairs to his office.

"That sounds like a line of bullshit."

He laughed. "That's my father for you." He pushed open the door, waved her inside.

The dogs shoved their way past her. Chewy settled down immediately in his plaid dog bed under the window. Vader sat on top of him. "Guess I'd better get another bed," Davis observed.

Eden looked at her dogs in a pile and swallowed hard. "You don't have to do that." She was guarded again. He caught the direction of her gaze, and it wasn't at him. It was at the three Blue Moon Business of the Year awards displayed on the shelf behind him.

"A good boyfriend would be accommodating," he reminded her, drawing her attention back to him. "Now, tell me what you think of these," he said opening a document on his computer.

She made a move to lean over his shoulder, but he tugged her into his lap instead.

"Davis. We don't have to be like this alone." He heard the warring notes of panic and passion in her voice and didn't feel the least bit bad for purposely pushing her buttons.

"Consider it practice for when we're out in public." He rubbed a hand down her back, letting his fingers brush the strip of skin that appeared between the waistband of her pants and the hem of her soft sweater.

"You wouldn't be taking advantage of the situation, would you, Gates?" Eden asked.

"Heaven forbid. I'm just dedicated to selling it." He danced his fingers up her spine, under the sweater, and felt the prickle of goosebumps on her silky skin. "Now, tell me your thoughts on these label designs."

He opened the file from the design firm and turned over control of the mouse to her, never ceasing his gentle caresses.

She clicked through the designs one at a time, pausing to compare two side-by-side. Her ramrod straight back started to relax against him, and he relished the surrender.

"This one," she said, finally pointing at the screen. "It's slick and whimsical. Kind of like your winery, bringing class to our little hippie, backwoods town."

She'd chosen the one he'd been drawn to, the one his father had nixed for being too "fun."

He lifted her hair from her neck and placed a soft kiss at her nape. Davis delighted at the full body shiver that skated up her spine.

"I don't think you need that much practice," Eden said dryly, once again tense in his lap.

"Mmm. But I like touching you," he confessed.

She took a shaky breath and shifted in his lap to face him. "Davis," she said, warningly.

"Don't you trust yourself, Eden?" He pressed his fingertips to her neck, rubbing in slow, lazy circles.

"Look. Last night was… great. Really great. But I don't want to complicate things."

"Who's complicating anything?" Davis asked, skating his teeth over her neck.

"Holy—Gah! Davis!" She was sprawled across his lap, one hand simultaneously holding on tight and pushing away. One breast was pressed into his chest, and his knee had parted hers from below. Exactly where he wanted her.

She watched in what looked like fascination as he ran his free hand over her knee and up her thigh. Back and forth, each time rising higher, growing bolder. He gripped her waist with his other hand, just under the curve of the breast he'd worshipped last night.

It had been mere hours, yet it felt like a lifetime again.

"Do you like it when I touch you, Eden?" he asked.

She stared at the track of his hand as if it were mesmerizing.

He was hard as marble, his cock fighting against the confines of his slacks as if they were a prison. But he didn't attempt to go any further.

"Fluke. Fluke. Fluke." Davis heard Eden chanting under her breath.

"Do you regret last night?" he asked her.

She shook her head hard. "No! I mean, no," she said with more calm. "It's not that. I just think it's not a good idea for a repeat performance. It'll… complicate things."

His fingers skated higher up her thigh within an inch of where he wanted to be. "I see," he said, teasing her with his mouth at her ear. "And you want uncomplicated."

She nodded without speaking.

"Then we'll keep things uncomplicated," he agreed

amiably. He stalled the motion of his hand. He felt her tense against him, coiling tight.

She opened her eyes, lashes fluttering.

"Damn it, Gates," she breathed.

He would win. It was his last coherent thought before Eden kissed him. Her mouth was hot and demanding under his. She cupped his face in her hands, and he slid her higher in his lap so she could feel how hard and ready she'd made him.

"Still a fluke," she murmured against his lips. He would have agreed, would have placated, but she used the opening to sweep her tongue inside his mouth and kiss him until he forgot his own name. He slid his hands under her ass and rose, dropping her on his desk. She yelped and pulled the keyboard out from under her.

"Kiss me like that again," he demanded.

For once obliging, Eden gripped his tie and dragged him down to her. He felt her fingers in his hair, the heat from her center against his erection when he rocked his hips into her. He shoved his hands under her sweater, all finesse abandoning his fine motor skills in favor of speed and need.

"Yes," she hissed when his hands coasted over the satin cups of her bra. Her nipples budded against the fabric.

He didn't have a condom here. Why would he? But he was willing to get creative if it meant he could have Eden right here like this.

"Hey, boss, I've got—holy shit." Anastasia busted into the office and immediately spun back around to leave. "Sorry! Ohmygod. Sorry. Shit."

Vader sprang to attention and got tangled up in Anastasia's legs as they both tried to bolt for the door.

Eden jumped off the desk as if she'd been electrocuted. "I should go," she announced in a near shout.

"No! I'll go," Anastasia insisted, stepping over Vader only to run into Chewy who'd decided to rouse himself and join the fun.

"No, you two have work to do," Eden said, wedging herself in the doorway with Anastasia and the dogs.

Davis sat back and watched with anguish and amusement. If a very intimate moment had to be interrupted, at least he could enjoy how much it rattled Eden.

"Um." Eden stepped over Vader, getting one leg into the hallway. "I'll see you tonight?" she asked, her blue eyes zeroing in on his face.

Davis nodded. "Tonight."

"Okay. Good. I'll, uh, take the dogs. And give you some space. Oh, and thanks again for the flowers."

Still blushing, she hauled the dogs out by their collars.

Anastasia still wasn't making eye contact with him. She stared up at his diploma framed neatly on the wall. "You tell your parents anything yet?" she asked.

"Nope." He'd cross that burning bridge only when he had to and not one minute sooner.

31

She changed for the third time and felt like a complete idiot. Especially knowing that Davis was one wall away and probably just wearing what he'd worn to work today. She'd made it exceptionally clear that there were no real feelings between them, she decided, tugging at the hem of her ivory sweater. And then she'd kissed the ever-living hell out of him.

Mixed messages. Just like her outfit. On the exterior, it was a nice boatneck sweater with skinny jeans. Underneath, she'd sprung for purple lace with interestingly placed cutouts. Not that she was expecting another fluke.

"Nope. Not happening again."

Her subconscious wondered why she'd bothered shaving her legs if that were the case. She shut it up with a sip of the wine she'd poured. Davis's wine that she'd snagged from the helpful hostess in the tasting room on her walk of shame from his office.

It had been a long, busy day, made only longer by her excitement over tonight. It was a town meeting and ice cream. Nothing special. Except for seeing Davis again.

"I'm just excited about teaching the B.C. a lesson," she insisted to her reflection.

Her reflection wasn't buying it any more than her head was. Eden stuck her tongue out at herself and went digging through her jewelry box for earrings. Simple hoops. Nothing too sexy. She went with her favorite pair of over-the-knee boots. *Not* because they were sexy as hell but because they'd keep her legs warm in the winter chill.

She reviewed her efforts one last time, making sure to ignore the excitement she saw dancing in her eyes.

"Not a real date. Not a real date. No more flukes."

She chanted it to herself as she shoved her arms into her pretty gray cape coat. "You're in charge," she reminded herself as she closed the door behind her.

"You certainly are," Davis agreed behind her. She jumped rapping her elbow on the door and yelping. "Ouch! I was just, um… hi."

"Hi, yourself," he said, giving her an admiring look. He looked too good for ice cream. A black wool coat hung open over designer jeans and a black sweater and white Oxford. He looked preppy and delicious.

"When did you stop dressing like a hippie?" Eden blurted out as his hand settled at her waist and he leaned in for a soft kiss on her cheek. The change in him when he'd come home from the West Coast had been profound, at least on the surface.

"Right around the time when I realized no one would want to buy wine from or go out on a date with a guy in a handknit poncho," Davis quipped. He slid her hand into his and led the way to the lobby.

"Goodnight, Sunny," Eden called.

The pretty blonde was rolling silverware into napkins at

the front desk and singing along to a pop song playing on her phone.

"Night, you two! Have fun," she winked flirtatiously.

"Seriously," Eden said when they were buckled into her car, Davis behind the wheel.

"I'm being serious. I left Blue Moon at eighteen and landed in a different world. Sure, there were hippies out there. I spent some memorable weekends in Berkeley. But for the most part I was skulking around wineries and learning the business. People aren't as forgiving of shaggy hair and rumpled clothes in that arena. And once I put on my first suit, it just felt good. I felt like I could be taken seriously," he admitted.

"Did you lose any other pieces of Blue Moon out there?" Eden asked, curious about the years he'd been missing from her life.

She'd sped through a degree in hospitality management all the while begging Aunt Nell to turn over the keys to the old monstrosity of a mansion she left vacant for six months every year when she traveled.

"A few. But I missed this place."

"You didn't visit," Eden pointed out, realizing too late that meant she'd noticed his absence.

He kept his eyes on the dark road ahead. "My parents felt it was best if I stayed in California and soaked up as much of the business as I could. I got winery jobs every summer and landed an internship and then a job with a vineyard in Napa."

"Your parents," Eden said, keying into his mention. "We're polar opposites there. I spent my entire high school and college career trying to tear myself away from my parents. It seems like you've spent your life being the good son."

Davis steered the car toward town, his hand reaching down to take hers. She didn't pull away even though part of her was shouting "fake relationship" loud enough to make her ears ring.

"My dad's heart attack has a lot to do with compliance. He had two actually," Davis said.

Eden shot him a glance. "I didn't know that."

"The first was when I was young. Four or so? I just remember him being very sick and my mother insisting that we not do anything that would upset him. He's always been tightly wound. It just became my job to keep him from exploding."

Eden bit her lip and considered. She'd had the freedom to be a rebel, even at times an asshole. Maybe Davis had grown up so "good" because he'd had to. "Give him what he wants to keep him happy?" she asked.

"Sounds like bad parenting advice for a tantrum-throwing toddler," Davis joked.

"If you spend all your time making your dad happy, when do you get what you want?"

"Who says I don't already have it?" he asked. He slid the car into a space on the opposite end of the town square from the movie theater. McCafferty's Farm Supply loomed in front of them. Despite the weather, Blue Moon's downtown was bustling. People wrapped in hand-knit rainbow scarves and brightly colored winter coats browsed store windows and warmed themselves inside the town's many shops.

"I am sorry about your father." She squeezed his fingers a little tighter. "I know I'm a Moody and I'm supposed to celebrate Gates' traumas. But I'm still sorry. And for what it's worth. I kind of liked the ponchos. Hippie Davis was pretty cute."

He gave her one of those underwear singing smiles. "Maybe if you're lucky I'll dig one out later?"

They laughed together and Eden marveled at the easy intimacy.

"Coffee, meeting, then ice cream?" Davis suggested.

She approved his priorities. "Perfect." He reclaimed her hand on the sidewalk, and together they weaved in and out of couples and families braving the chill.

They looped around One Love Park, heading in the direction of Overly Caffeinated when Eden came to a sudden stop.

"Get your hot apple cider!" Ellery called to the foot traffic in the park from a makeshift stand under a banner that said Support Your Local Beautification Committee. She wore a glossy black vinyl coat, black jeans, and a mile-long black and gray scarf. Her husband, Mason, was dressed like a regular person in a heavy winter coat and a ski cap. He took his mittens off every time he needed to count out change.

"What the hell is this?" Davis whispered to Eden.

"I think we're looking at the Beautification Committee's fundraiser for your fire damage."

"So, if I bought a cup of apple cider, I'd be funding my own fundraiser?"

He looked disappointed, and Eden laughed. "Are you really that big of an apple cider fan?"

"Well, yeah. But I'm not giving those pyromaniacs a dime."

"Hot apple cider for a good cause!" Ellery screeched, scaring Mason into dropping a roll of quarters.

Eden pulled him toward the stand. "The least a girlfriend can do is buy her boyfriend a cup of apple cider on a cold night."

"I'm not having you pay for my fire damage," Davis argued.

"Don't be a baby," Eden said lightly before stepping to the front of the line. "Ellery, Mason, what brings you two out on a night like this?" Davis let out a sound that was eerily similar to a growl, and she elbowed him.

"Oh, hi, guys," Ellery said, eyes wide and guilty. "We're just doing some… fundraising."

"Tell us more about this good cause," Davis demanded. Eden stepped on his foot, and he winced.

"What good cause?" Ellery asked, batting her spider-like lashes.

"The one on your sign," Eden said, pointing at the poster behind Mason.

For a Good Cause

"Oh, *that* good cause," Ellery laughed nervously. "We're uh, um. Raising funds for… you… and neighbors like you," she added quickly. "To make our community… better."

"Interesting," Eden said. "Isn't that interesting, Davis?" she asked.

He still looked mad enough to say something stupid that could ruin their entire plan. Eden ducked under his arm and cuddled into his side. "How much for a cup?" Eden asked.

"Oh, um." Ellery blinked. "Five dollars?"

32

"I can't believe you gave those arson-causing bastards five bucks," Davis complained.

Eden was still laughing as he held the door to the movie theater for her. "It was worth it just to see the look on your face." She swiped at the corners of her eyes, clearly enjoying herself. "I can throw the cider away if you want me to," she offered.

He clutched the paper cup protectively. "No use letting it go to waste."

Town meetings were one of the things he'd missed the most when he'd moved away. The smell of the movie theater popcorn, the press of bodies dressed in bib overalls and decades-old tie-dye. It had all seemed normal to him growing up, debating socially acceptable behavioral standards that would never be up for public discussions anywhere else in the country.

Moving to California for school and then work had given Davis some much needed distance. And with that distance came an even deeper appreciation for his hometown. Romantic, fading frescos decorated the ceiling held up by painted pillars. There was a podium, flanked by folding chairs on the skinny strip of stage in front of the heavy velvet curtain.

After a quick stop at the concession stand, he guided Eden to the right-hand side of the stage. "The acoustics are better over here," he told her.

She shot him a funny look that turned to pure lust after he handed her a snack pack of chocolate coconut granola, her favorite in high school. They settled into the third and fourth seats from the aisle, just out of the draft of the overhead vent. He knew this theater, knew this town inside out. He'd been more than ready to come home before his father's heart attack gave him the reason.

"You look like you're about to watch your favorite movie," Eden commented, popping a handful of colorful candy into her mouth.

Conversation buzzed around them as neighbors caught up with each other despite the fact that most of them had seen each other earlier that day. It was a small town, impossibly close-knit. Which was both a blessing and a curse.

"This is my kind of entertainment," he told her. "Beckett's going to get up there and announce something ridiculous, and then seventy-two of his constituents are going to have questions and even more ridiculous solutions. It's better than any movie."

Eden chuckled at his enthusiasm. Davis used her good mood to sneak a coconut cluster from her hand.

He pretended not to notice the looks shot in their direction. Smug from Beautification Committee members, curious from feud historians.

"Mind if I sit?" Eden's friend Layla in full deputy regalia tapped the seat next to Davis. He caught a glimpse of the look Eden shot Layla. It was a warning.

"Help yourself," Davis said, offering his bag of popcorn.

Not one to pass up a snack, Layla dug a healthy fistful from the bag. She stretched her legs out under the seat in front of her, the picture of relaxation.

"I take it you're not here in a professional capacity?" Eden asked.

"I'm on duty, but since every single citizen is in this building, I figured it would make sense to be here. Plus, I wanted to see Cardona and the mayor in their stupid powdered wigs."

Bruce Oakleigh had finally successfully lobbied for town officials to wear the powdered wigs of their ancestors for official town meetings, a town ordinance two years in the making. It horrified the straight-laced Beckett Pierce, which entertained the entire rest of the town who had voted unanimously for the motion.

"What are you two crazy kids doing after this?" Layla asked.

Eden leaned forward in front of Davis. "What is this? An interrogation?"

Layla let out a low whistle. "Someone's feeling persnickety tonight. Don't worry, Davis. Just feed her something chocolate and tell her she's pretty, and she probably won't rip your face off later. I mean, they don't call her Moody for nothing."

"It's my last name, assface," Eden sniped.

Layla gave a careless shrug. "Don't mind her, Davis. I mean, I don't need to remind you that she's basically a loose cannon."

Eden bared her teeth at her friend. "I know what you're doing, and if you want twenty bucks that much I will give it to you."

"It's the principle of the thing," Layla sniffed.

Davis had a feeling he was missing an important key to the conversation.

"If you two get in a fight, who's going to break it up?" he wondered out loud.

Eden sat back in her seat in a huff. "I need to make new friends," she grumbled.

Layla grinned triumphantly as if she'd won a tough victory.

The lights flickered, signaling that the festivities were about to start. People started filling in the auditorium seats.

Davis took Eden's hand and squeezed it. The purpose was two-fold. One, he wanted to hold her hand. Two, it was one less appendage she could throw punches with. He didn't want to get thrown out of the meeting before the fun started.

The lights flickered again and then dimmed. The speakers crackled on, and the opening strains of "Eye of the Tiger" blasted through the theater.

Beckett Pierce, in powdered wig and a suit, slumped his way to the podium at center stage. The town council members plus Sheriff Cardona took the stage behind him, filing to the single row of seats next to the podium. Millie Murkle, Blue Moon's police station manager and dispatcher, jogged up to the front of the theater and snapped about a dozen pictures of Donovan sitting miserably between Bruce Oakleigh and Elvira Eustace.

He felt the weight of Eden's gaze on him and schooled his features into an impassive mask. She leaned in. "Don't pretend you're not enjoying this," she whispered.

"I don't want you to be embarrassed by your boyfriend fanboying over a town meeting," he returned.

Eden snickered behind her hand and Layla leaned forward and gave them a hard look. "I'm not losing my twenty to Sammy," she hissed.

"Next time you sleep over, I'm shaving your eyebrows off," Eden threatened.

"Don't threaten an officer of the law," Layla whispered back.

"Ladies, if we could save the threats for later?" Davis suggested, drawing a line in the air between them with his arm.

On stage, Beckett was making a slashing motion over his throat. The music cut off abruptly.

"Ladies and gentlemen, thank you for braving the cold tonight and coming out so close to Thanksgiving," he began. "As you know, our HeHa Festival is almost here, and we wanted to take this opportunity to make sure we're as organized as possible."

Davis grinned. Last year's HeHa had been an organizational disaster. Information about drop-offs had gone out with a typo in the address and forty-seven bags of winter clothing were deposited onto Juan Garcia's front yard. His pet ferrets had escaped—again—and burrowed into the bags of down vests and heavy sweaters. It took two hours for the dozen volunteers to find the ferrets.

"It's come to my attention that our co-chairs for the HeHa Festival have both stepped down, citing irreconcilable differences, which really only applies in divorces," Beckett said into the mic. A low rumble of speculation rolled through the crowd.

"Who were the chairs?" Eden asked.

"Charisma Champion and Fitz," Layla whispered.

Charisma, with her long black hair and purple glitter tunic, stood up. "I'd like the record to show that I was willing to work with Bill Fitzsimmons, but he made it *impossible.*"

Beckett leaned into the mic. "There is no actual record."

A rat-tailed, skinny hippie in a Save the Bay t-shirt that didn't quite cover his pasty belly rose on the other side of the theater. "And *I'd* like the record to show that my schedule is a complex organism."

"There's still no record," Beckett put in.

"You own a bookstore that's open twenty hours a week," Charisma shot back.

"I'm *also* an exotic dancer," Fitz announced.

A crowd-wide shudder made its way through the building as everyone remembered the Facebook video of a nearly naked Fitz being hauled out of the barn at Pierce Acres during Phoebe Merrill's bachelorette party.

"You spent two days last week restocking your underground bunker!" Charisma was working herself up to a full-fledged fit.

"Well, someone has to be prepared!"

Beckett rubbed his forehead and closed his eyes as if in a bid for patience.

"It's your fault that we have three weeks until the festival and absolutely nothing in place!" Charisma shouted.

"Let's try to get back on track here," Beckett said, shouting into the mic to be heard over the din. "We're looking for two volunteers to chair the event which, just as a reminder, includes a day of community service and a town-wide dance."

Rainbow Berkowicz got to her feet. "I volunteer Eden Moody and Davis Gates to co-chair."

Davis lost his smile.

"Oh, hell no," Eden said next to him. Layla snorted out a laugh.

"Seconded," Ernest Washington said from under his denim cap.

"That's *not* how asking for volunteers works," Eden muttered.

Davis mentally rolled through his to-do list which

included zero room for organizing a huge community event. Although, it *would* also give him even more time with Eden...

Beckett cheered considerably as the burden of public service in Blue Moon was passed to someone else. “Great. If anyone has any questions about HeHa, please see Eden and Davis after the meeting.”

“What the hell just happened?” Eden whispered.

“We were just thrown under the Blue Moon Volkswagen bus,” Davis answered.

Beckett picked up his gavel and banged it ceremonially. “On to the next order of business. It’s been brought to the council’s attention that the rumor that businesses do not have to pay their taxes is circulating again. Once again, it is very, very important that you file and pay your taxes every year. For more on this subject, please welcome Mason Smith.”

33

"I can't believe that just happened," Eden breathed out a silver cloud. The chaos of the town meeting was behind them in the theater where half of the town was still throwing tax questions at the sweet and sweaty CPA. The quiet of an empty One Love Park was in front of them.

"I can believe it," Davis said, leading her across the road into the park. "We live with a bunch of manipulative sociopaths."

"It's not like you have time to deal with this. I mean, you've got the insurance company, the fire damage, plus all of your usual work." Eden ticked off the items on her fingers. "And why are you smiling at me like that?"

Davis scraped the grin off his face. "It's kind of nice seeing you mad on my behalf for a change."

"Don't look at me like that," she said, poking a finger into his chest.

"Like what?" he asked innocently.

"Like you want to kiss me."

He took a step closer to her, and Eden felt her heart climb into her throat. Anticipation twined nicely with the knowledge that she should *not* want Davis Gates's mouth anywhere near her. Eden slapped a hand to his chest.

"Fluke," she reminded him.

"Sometimes lightning strikes twice," he countered.

"You're just trying to get in my pants," Eden said, annoyed that her voice was so breathless.

"They're very nice pants."

"Davis," she gave a half-laugh. "We have a big problem. The entire town is counting on us organizing the best Helping Hands Festival ev—" The realization hit her like an ice cream truck on a sticky summer day. "Oh, my God! That's it!"

"What's it?" Davis asked, bringing her hand to his mouth so he could brush kisses over her knuckles.

"We're going to get into a huge fight at HeHa and break up!" It was so poetically perfect. "Think about it. This all started for us when you stood me up for the dance. The B.C. is counting on us spending this time together and falling deeply in love. But *we*," she poked him in the shoulder, "are going to make sure history repeats itself."

Davis was looking slightly less lusty and a little more nauseated. "Run this by me again?"

"We're going to stage the most spectacular breakup in the history of Blue Moon during HeHa. They'll be talking about it for years to come! This is perfect!" In celebration, she launched herself at Davis and kissed him square on the mouth.

"Is it weird that I get turned on by how turned on you are by revenge?" he mumbled under her lips' advances.

"Not weird. Revenge is hot. Keep kissing," she ordered.

"Wait." He gripped her by the shoulders and held her back a step. "Does this mean we're still dating?"

"Fake dating," she reminded him.

"Good enough," Davis said, drawing her back in. His mouth quickly devoured hers. Eden felt her knees go weak.

"I think we're going to fluke again," she whispered into his mouth.

"Thank God."

"My parents left for their Thanksgiving trip," Eden said, sliding her hands under Davis's jacket. "Their house is a block from here."

~

ONLY NED and Lilly Ann would forget to lock their front door before leaving for a week-long trip. Eden pushed open the front door and picked up the stack of catalogues under the mail slot. "Welcome to Casa de Moody," she said, flipping the switch for the overhead disco ball her parents used to light the small living room.

It was a cramped space made even smaller by the two full-sized couches and throne-like wingback chair in pink velvet her mother insisted they needed "for company." The last time her parents entertained had been Eden's fourteenth birthday.

There were bookshelves crammed full of books, trinkets, and family photos behind every oversized piece of furniture. One shelf partially blocked the large bay window. The carpet was orange shag. The table lamps were draped with pink gauze for mood lighting.

"Wow," Davis said, stuffing his hands in his pockets. "I'm surprised I didn't burst into flames walking in the door."

"They must have deactivated the Gates deterrent system," Eden teased. She took his hand and slid his coat off of his shoulders. "Now, where were we?"

"I believe I had my tongue down your throat like a teenager," Davis recalled.

"You're a funny guy, Gates."

"Just think of all those years you missed out on my humor. Guess we'll have to make up for it now."

There was nothing fake about the way his eyes raked her body when she shrugged out of her coat. And, damn it, there was nothing fake about the way her body thrummed with anticipation.

She backed her way to the stairs, Davis following her. "Want to see my room?" she asked, arching an eyebrow.

"I've been waiting fifteen years for that invitation," he told her.

She bit her lower lip, refusing to be charmed by him. She turned and jogged up the stairs to the landing. "Coming?"

"God, I hope so."

Giddy at the sound of his footsteps, Eden hurried ahead and pushed open the door to what had been her bedroom for eighteen long, happy, painful years. The walls were still papered with the dozens of posters—Evanescence and Nirvana and Foo Fighters—she'd hung. She rolled the switch for her lava lamp and was delighted when it began to glow orange.

"Always the rebel," Davis observed from the doorway.

The twin bed stood between them. Her black rose comforter had been traded in for a cheery checkered throw that matched nothing for guests that her parents never hosted.

Davis stood on the other side of the small bed, tension in every muscle, waiting for her.

Eden bit her lip and took the plunge. She unhooked the clasp on her pants and shimmied out of them.

Without tearing his eyes away from her, Davis toed off his loafers and ditched his pants. His thighs were lean and muscled, and she caught a glimpse of the growing bulge in his black briefs. It made the throb in her core intensify. He straightened, waiting again.

Eden closed her fingers on the hem of her sweater and slowly dragged it over her head. When she heard his sharp intake of breath, she was thankful she'd gone with the purple lace set and the condom in her purse.

Just another fluke, she assured herself. She wasn't setting herself up for pain. Not this time. They both knew the score. Temporary. Pretend. If they had a little fun in the process, what was the harm?

Davis shucked his sweater. She saw her own nerves mirrored when his fingers fumbled with the buttons on his shirt.

His shirt landed in the pile of clothing on the floor, and Eden looked her fill at his broad chest, his lean torso, tapering to those sexy AF briefs. Nothing was left to the imagination as his erection swelled.

She, Eden Moody, made him feel like this. There was a power in knowing that. And a responsibility. But she'd revel in the first and ignore the second. Just for tonight. Just one more time.

"I used to wish you'd show up here in the middle of the night and throw rocks at my window," she whispered. *Where had that come from? Why would she tell him that?* Confessions like that weren't meant to be shared.

Davis held out his hand across the bed. With the slightest of hesitations, Eden took it. "What would have happened if I did?"

She tugged, pulling him onto his knees on the bed with her. "I'd hoped something like this."

Eden took her time kissing the man who'd been the boy she'd dreamed of. The boy who'd dented her heart. The boy she'd never quite forgotten.

She coasted her hands up his arms, across his chest, and down his stomach, enjoying the feel of him quiver the closer she got to the waistband of his briefs. He stroked her back, her hips, her sides, skimming his palms over the outer curves of her breasts.

"You're beautiful, Eden."

Fantasy Davis had told her dreamy seventeen-year-old self that.

"You're not so bad yourself," she whispered back, slipping her hands into the back of his briefs to squeeze his ass cheeks.

"I love it when you touch me," he told her, sliding his hands into her hair to angle her face for a kiss.

It was too intimate, too gentle for a fluke. Eden couldn't pretend this was something it wasn't.

She couldn't handle the words. They would dent her heart again. But she could move the two of them from sweet to desperate, where soft words wouldn't reach through the haze.

Eden shoved her hands into the sides of his underwear, sliding them down those thighs until his erection sprang free and proud. It jutted toward her, craving her touch. Reverently she grasped it in an eager fist.

"Go slow," Davis whispered, dropping his forehead to hers.

Not this time.

She gave the shaft one long pump, reveling in the feel of his muscles bunching, tensing with need. There was no room for words here. He let her stroke him and busied himself by unhooking her bra and tossing it on the growing pile of clothing.

"I have a condom in my purse," she said before she could lose herself in the sensation of those warm palms cupping her soft flesh. Her nipples budded to points against the rough of his hands.

"I dream about you every night," he said, ghosting his lips over her cheek, down her jaw.

"Shut up," she warned him, stroking faster, harder.

"I see you like this. Naked, breathtaking."

He worked her underwear down her legs, held her steady while she slid out of them.

"Shut up, Davis," she said, harsher now.

"You're my dream come true."

There was only one way to get him to shut the hell up.

Eden dropped to all fours and slid her mouth over the crown of his cock. He made a noise somewhere between a groan and a growl, and she felt it reverberate between her thighs.

She slicked her mouth over him, taking him into her throat.

"Fuck. Eden." He wasn't in control and poking holes in her resistance now. *He* was defenseless against *her*.

She drove him wild with her tongue, her mouth, until he couldn't take it. Davis fisted his hand in her hair and pulled her up his body.

His erection, wet and steely, throbbed against her stomach.

He took her down to the mattress, but Eden wasn't going to let him set the pace there either. She rolled, coming out on top of him. She straddled his hips and once again gripped that proud hard-on. She could feel the pulse of blood beneath her hand.

He wet his lips when she reached for her purse on the nightstand. Her hands trembled when she fished out the condom, and Davis helped her unwrap it. Together, they rolled it down his thick shaft.

She didn't give him any time to think, to anticipate. Eden rose on her knees, positioned him at her entrance, and sank down on him. She was so full, she had no room for breath in her lungs. The air left her on a strangled cry. But it was enough for Davis's thin sheen of control to shatter.

He gripped her hips with strong fingers and thrusted with his hips, forcing the last inch into her.

She cried out in a pleasure so sharp it bordered on pain. Her muscles tightened involuntarily around him.

"So tight," he gritted out.

But then she was moving. Slowly at first, rocking her hips and relaxing around him. Eden dropped her hands to his shoulders, and Davis raised himself up to take one of her breasts in his mouth. Sweat sheened her skin as she rode him. Here, on the very bed she'd daydreamed about her high school crush. In the room that she'd wandered, making up a dozen sweet fantasies. And now he was under her, their bodies connected, their goal unified.

He met her with enthusiastic thrusts that made the headboard slap against the wall. Words, strangled by passion, worked their way free of her throat. "Yes. More. Now."

He abandoned one breast and took the other into his magical mouth, and when his lips closed over her tender peak, her body responded with a gut-wrenching orgasm that built and crested in a swift explosion of pleasure that took her by surprise.

She screamed his name as her body convulsed in climax.

"I've never seen anything more beautiful in my life," he gritted out as she collapsed against his chest, sweat-slicked and almost sated. But Eden didn't want that intimacy, that vulnerability. She was too raw.

She slid off of him, her body instantly demanding she return to his heat. He was rock hard for her. "Your turn, Gates," she breathed. She turned around on all fours facing away from him. She needed the distance, needed to be able to look away from the softness she saw in his eyes.

Eden felt him rise to his knees, and her body sang an angels' chorus when he aligned the head of his cock with her still pulsing entrance.

He eased into her inch by inch. She dropped her face to the blanket beneath her, stifling her cry. How could he feel so perfect inside her? How could this feel so damn right? His fingers flexed into her hips, and he began to move.

She felt every ridge, every vein, every inch of his thickness as it coasted in and out of her. He wasn't talking now. No, casting a glance over her shoulder, Davis was a tableau of lust. His jaw clenched tight, nostrils flared, eyes glassy.

Davis using her body for his pleasure was the most intimate thing Eden had ever experienced.

She went pliable under him, letting him draw her hips back to bottom out on every thrust. A movement against the wall caught her eye. Eden's old vanity mirror captured the two of them in their passion, framing them dead center. Their gazes met in the mirror, a new terrible kind of intimacy that there was no escaping. She wanted to look away, wanted to pretend that what was happening right now meant nothing. But she couldn't.

His gaze held her prisoner, just as his body made her a captive. She saw the cords of his neck stand out as he let out a soft grunt and another. She couldn't tear her gaze away from the building pleasure she saw in his face.

He grabbed her, more roughly than he probably meant and pulled her up so her back was to his chest. Still watching their reflection, Davis cupped one breast and dipped his free hand between her legs to stroke between her folds. He hooked his chin over her shoulder, and Eden gave herself over to him.

She felt him swell impossibly thicker inside her, knew he was close. That knowledge danced her own pleasure closer to the precipice. His fingers worked her, insistently taking her higher.

"Davis," she whispered.

His breath came out in a growl. His thrusts came faster, shallower. His arm banded her to him, thumb brushing her swollen nipple. No escape.

"Come, Eden. Come with me."

As if their bodies had been waiting for that command, Eden felt her release build dangerously fast. His fingers were magic between her legs as his cock worked its own kind of miracles within her. She never had a chance. She was with him. And when he buried himself inside her on one more brutal thrust, she closed around him, gripping him like a vice. Their orgasms erupted together. She felt the pulse of his pumps as her own walls closed around him again and again. Until they were both empty and spent. It was sweat in her eyes, she told herself.

Certainly not tears.

34

"I used to walk down the alley to see if your light was on." Davis found his voice rusty, his throat raw. They were wrapped around each other in her tiny bed. Adding to the intimacy, he was still semi-hard inside her. He couldn't bring himself to pull out and sever their connection.

"Until the fire," she said dryly. He couldn't see her face, but he could hear the sadness in her voice.

He shook his head. "Even after."

She was silent for a long moment, and he wondered if she'd dozed off.

"I didn't set the fire, Davis," Eden said finally.

He guided his fingers over her stomach, up over a breast. "I know."

"You do?"

"Moon Beam confessed to me about a week after it happened. She told me about the toilet paper, the cigarette. That you took the rap so she wouldn't get sent off to the commune."

"Some good it did. Her mom sent her away a year and a

half later for getting caught in the backseat of a Volkswagen with no pants and Beckett Pierce.

Davis laughed softly against her shoulder. "But she got that extra year because of you."

Eden moved against him restlessly. "I've spent all this time thinking you thought I was a crazy arsonist. I *agonized* over that, Davis. You could have put me out of my misery. Why didn't you tell me you knew?"

"How was I supposed to? You wouldn't talk to me."

"Because you devastated me. Did you tell your parents it wasn't my fault?"

"I tried. They weren't in a very open-minded mood."

"My parents didn't believe me either. They were so proud of my commitment to the feud I didn't even get grounded."

"But you did have to go through a semester of Impulse Control."

"That was horrible. Mr. Reynolds spent the first three weeks offering up alternatives to setting a fire so I could consult a list next time I had my feelings hurt."

"Mmm," he sighed. "What were some of your alternatives?"

"Knit a scarf, using the needle and yarn as weapons of peace."

"Of course."

"Oh, and there were the thirty-minute guided meditations on abundance, not scarcity."

"I see." He brushed his lips over her hair, inhaling the scent of her shampoo.

"Apparently you were just one fish in the sea, Mr. Reynolds told me. I didn't have to have my heart set on you when there were so many others. Grouper, halibut, sharks, salmon—"

"Salmon are freshwater fish."

"Yeah, well, Mr. Reynolds' analogies were lacking in many areas."

"Well, while you were listing fish, I was agonizing over the fact that I let my parents force me into taking Taneisha to the dance." He interlaced his fingers with hers.

"How did they do that?" she asked, wondering if there was an excuse in the world that would make her understand.

He sighed heavily. "They'd heard that we were planning to go to the dance together. My dad was so angry that I'd even consider betraying the family like that. I'd never seen him that mad. My mom was worried he was going to give himself an aneurysm... or another heart attack. They told me you asked me out as a joke. That you were going to embarrass me at the dance."

Eden gasped and sat up. "I would never—"

"I know. *Now.* But back then, my parents had never lied to me. I tried to call you, but your dad wouldn't let me speak to you. He told me you were going to the dance with Jordan Catalano."

She covered her face with her hands. "Jordan Catalano was a character from My So Called Life. I told my parents that so they wouldn't be suspicious."

"My parents insisted everyone knew and you were just going to humiliate me. I pacified him by promising to take Taneisha to the dance and I thought I could straighten everything out with you when I got there. And then I saw your face. Then you were so angry, there was no way to undo it. And then you were dating Ramesh like you'd never really cared about me."

Eden felt guilt bloom hot in her belly. She'd shut him down every time he tried to talk to her. She'd embraced the grudge and carried it proudly like war colors.

"I spite dated Ramesh. I'm not proud of it," she said before he could interrupt. Her confession hung between them in the soft orange glow. "I was seventeen. I just wanted to protect myself, and I stupidly thought the best way to do that would be to date someone who wasn't you. Don't get me wrong. I ended up liking Ramesh a lot. He was smart and nice and funny. But he wasn't you."

"I'm here now."

"And Ramesh is happily married to the woman he dumped me for."

"And all is right with the world."

"What about Taneisha?"

"She lived next door. Her date had just dumped her for a gig in Cleary with his folk band."

"Hang on. Someone dumped Taneisha the Most Beautiful Woman in the World?" Eden demanded.

Davis chuckled softly. "No one survives high school without a few scars."

Eden heaved a sigh. "Now what?"

Davis stilled his hands on her. "Now, what do you want?"

"Don't you think after all this you should figure out what *you* want?"

"I'm starting to get an idea," he admitted.

35

"What if we use the high school as the meeting point for the community work day teams?" Eden suggested, circling the high school on the map Davis had sketched up.

Davis pushed the basket of cheese fries out of the way. They were bellied up to the bar at Shorty's sports bar drinking beers and eating greasy food to avoid the chaos at the inn. The entire building had been overtaken by twenty senior citizens celebrating their sixtieth high school reunion.

They partied harder than a high school class on spring break. Eden had found one woman face-down in the upstairs hallway and assumed the worst. Her surprised shriek when the woman came to and started singing "Great Balls of Fire," roused the entire second floor of the inn.

It was Davis who had suggested they head out for the evening instead of cozying up to the fire in the library.

"You mean instead of clogging up town square with a bunch of cars and people who don't need to be there?" Davis joked. "You're an organizational genius."

"Ah, but *you're* the one who suggested posting all of the drop off locations and hours in the Facebook group," she reminded him.

"Well, well. If it isn't Blue Moon's most popular couple." Shorty dropped two fresh beers in front of them. At six-foot, five-inches, Ed, as his mother called him, was the runt of the Avila litter and the proprietor of the only bar in town. "It's nice to see you two getting along."

"Teamwork makes the dream work," Eden quipped, offering up a no-look high-five to Davis.

"Everyone's talking about you two today," Shorty told them, swiping a towel over a spill and pocketing a five-dollar tip.

"We haven't done anything newsworthy today," Davis told him.

"Not according to this." Shorty slapped a copy of *The Monthly Moon* down on the bar in front of them. The front page was a grainy picture of Eden and Davis at the town meeting staring dumbly at the stage.

From Feudal Followers to Star-Crossed Lovers: Will Falling for Moody Burn Gates Again?

"My parents are going to have a conniption," Eden groaned.

"I heard they dismembered you," Shorty said.

"Disowned," Davis corrected.

Eden turned the page and swore ripely. She jumped off her barstool.

"What? What's wrong?" Davis demanded.

"That little weasel Anthony Berkowicz."

"What about ol' weasel-faced Berkowicz?"

"I'm going to kick his ass!"

Davis slapped cash on the bar, grabbed the newspaper, and jogged out in Eden's angry wake.

"CAN I ask you why we're purchasing whiskey and a ladies' razor?" Davis ventured.

Eden slapped the newspaper he was holding. "Page two." She added a can of shaving cream to their basket.

Davis flipped open the paper and read. "Oh."

"Yeah. *Oh.*" She rounded on him, wielding a second pack of razors. "Do you know how hard I've worked to move past all that? To get people to see me as Eden Moody the innkeeper, not Eden Moody the front lawn arsonist? I was *this close* to the Blue Moon Business of the Year. And I *know* it's just a stupid award," she snapped before he could say anything. "But I wanted that stupid award. I wanted people to finally forget all about high school and see me for who I really am."

"And Anthony Berkowicz writes a feature article on our high school relationship," Davis said, understanding.

"Page three is just my mugshot," she said, hysteria high in her voice. "And this! This right here!"

She shoved the paper into Davis's face.

"I can't read it that close." His voice was muffled by the newspaper.

"He suggests that setting fires are part of my 'woo-ing' repertoire." She ranted and raved, pacing the supermarket aisle.

"At the risk of being reminded that no one in the history of freaking out has ever calmed down by being told to calm down, let's take a breath and think. I'm here. I'm on your side."

Davis was right. She wasn't doing herself any favors having a meltdown. She needed to think and plot.

"If you'll excuse me," she said with an abundance of calm that she didn't feel. "I think I'm going to go freshen up."

Head held high, she marched past him to the restroom between the gluten-free treat aisle and the selection of goat milk soaps.

The ladies restroom was a lovely lavender and silver theme with a mural of the goddess Athena on the wall above the baby changing station. The mirrors over the sinks had inspirational quotes written on them. After a quick foot check under the stall doors, Eden lined herself up with the You Look Beautiful mirror and dialed Sammy.

"I am losing my damn mind!"

Sammy yawned mightily. "Huh?"

"I'm sorry. Did I wake you?"

"I was up early for horse sonograms," Sammy yawned again. "What's up?"

"No. Forget I called. Go back to sleep."

"I'm awake and eating directly out of a carton of Rocky Road. What's up?"

"I'm hiding out in the women's restroom at Farm and Field having a life crisis."

"Mm-hmm," Sammy answered. "Any particular impetus for said life crisis?"

"I take it you didn't see *The Monthly Moon* yet," Eden said dryly.

"Hang on. Let me bring it up online." Eden heard her friend's fingers on her keyboard.

"Oh. Well, shit… oh my God. Is that a picture of you two naked?"

"What?" Eden hissed.

"Nothing. Forget I said anything. It's kind of grainy. You're in the front seat of a car. Wait, I thought you said it was just a fluke."

"It was," Eden insisted. "And so were the next seven times."

"Seven? I really need to start dating," Sammy sighed.

"Can we focus on my pain and suffering first? I promise we'll get to your dismal dating life in a second."

"Sorry. Focusing. So you've fluked eight times, and the town paper has just labeled you an unstable fire bug. Okay, go."

"Sammy, I feel like everything is out of control. I've worked so hard to build this reputation, to not have people look at me as some irresponsible, arsonist teenager. And one time in bed with Davis, and I'm back to where I started."

"Eight times," Sammy corrected her.

Eden could hear Sammy's ice cream spoon hit the sink. All of her years of work, of pushing to be seen as more than just a teenage screw-up, and now she was staring down at her teenage mugshot. The sad little Goth girl with eyeliner running down her face in the tracks of her tears. When she looked in the mirror she saw a woman now, lusting after Davis Gates—a man she could never have—and running off the rails.

"No one in town takes *The Monthly Moon* seriously. We've all been the target of 'local vet dates Bigfoot' headlines. And everyone knows what a smart, kind, amazing business woman and asset to the community you are. So, I'm guessing what you're really freaking out over is the fact that you can't stop inviting Davis into your pants."

Eden toed the purple tile mural on the floor. "Maybe."

"You've spent your entire adult life hating the guy, and now everything's different."

"Also, maybe."

"Have you considered that perhaps the universe is trying to tell you something about your quests for revenge?" Sammy asked.

"Quests?"

"Didn't you just spend fifteen years holding a grudge against Davis? And are you or are you not currently involved in a plot to foil the Beautification Committee?"

"Yeah, but they deserve it."

"Uh-huh. Don't get me wrong. You probably couldn't find a Mooner who wouldn't agree with you. However, what did this town drum into our heads every day since kindergarten?"

"Believe in karma and do no harma." Eden recited. "What are you getting at, Sammy?"

"What if you've spent a decade and a half fighting what you really want?"

"You think I want Davis?"

"Um. Duh. You're Eden Moody. You don't accidentally sleep with anyone."

"Maybe it's just really good sex. I mean like superhuman amazing sex."

"Stop rubbing it in, jerk."

"I'm having a life crisis. I can't be held responsible for the word vomit coming out of my mouth."

"Look, babe. If you like Davis, date Davis. Forget the B.C., forget your parents. And, most of all, forget high school. Stop being held hostage by the past."

"What if holding grudges is my thing?" Eden asked the question that turned her stomach to acid.

"What if you have control over what your thing is? What if your thing is Davis's thing? And by thing, I mean penis."

"You're awfully wise when you're woken up at 9 p.m. on a Tuesday night."

"They all come to the single, Rocky Road-eating vet for knowledge bombs," Sammy sang.

"I need to think," Eden decided. She needed some time, some space, and a lot of brain power.

"Then get out of the bathroom before someone drops a deuce, and go think."

36

"How would you two like to buy some rice flour cranberry almond orange zinger muffins? Only eight dollars apiece!" Amethyst Oakleigh announced cheerfully from the table in the Farm and Fresh vestibule. She was bundled up in a mint green parka with a rainbow beret and scarf distorting most of her face. Wilson Abramovich sat next to her in a puffy vest and an ivory turtleneck sweater.

The doors opened, and a rush of cold night air barreled inside followed by a tropical wave of heat from the overhead heaters. They'd missed this little fundraiser when they entered the side door and Davis wished they'd gone out the same way they came in.

Eden stopped and stared at them. "What are you raising money for?" she asked pleasantly, the death threats in her blue eyes going unheeded. Davis knew that benign tone. It was something to be feared, and those poor B.C. bastards had no idea what hell was about to rain down on them.

"You know what? We just had rice flour muffins for dinner," he said, wrapping an arm around Eden's waist. "We're going to leave. Right now."

Davis steered her toward the exit before she could show the Beautification Committee exactly what they could do with their rice flour muffins.

She took a deep breath of the crisp winter night. "Thanks for that. Apparently, I have a problem with my temper and holding grudges... and never moving forward from the past."

She sounded so forlorn he reached down into the bag and fished out the pack of Sour Patch Kids he remembered her loving in junior high. He handed them over, and she clutched them to her chest like a beloved stuffed animal.

"I have to know. What were the razors for?" He'd left those on the shelf, but he had purchased the whiskey while she was in the bathroom.

"I was going to shave that weasel's eyebrows off if he didn't print a retraction. I could easily give him a real reason to think I'm unhinged," she seethed.

"Uh-huh." Davis tucked her into the passenger seat of his SUV and crossed around to the driver's side. "How about the whiskey?" he asked, settling in behind the wheel.

"Just thirsty," she pouted.

He started the engine and looked at her. "We're a team, right?"

She shrugged, ripping open the candy and shoveling a handful into her mouth. "Yeah, I guess."

"Then let's handle this as a team."

"You want to shave one eyebrow while I get the other?" she asked him hopefully.

"I have an even better idea."

"Better than shaving Anthony 'Weasel Face' Berkowicz's eyebrows?" she challenged.

"Don't open the whiskey, yet. We have a couple of stops to make."

~

"Why are we parked in front of my aunt's house?" Eden asked, peering out the window at the tidy electric blue ranch house. Garden gnomes were organized in a semicircle around the front porch.

Davis pointed toward the house where a window opened and a pair of denim clad legs appeared. The legs slid out of the window followed by a torso and a lot of straight blonde hair.

"Moon Beam?"

The blonde slunk around the gnomes, skirted a large rhododendron, and then opened the back door to Davis's SUV.

"You guys didn't have sex back here recently, did you?" Moon Beam asked, gingerly sliding over the seat.

They had two nights ago, but Davis didn't see any reason to share that knowledge with Moon Beam.

"Why are we picking up my cousin?" Eden demanded.

"We're going to pay Weasel Face a visit," Davis announced. "And what are we leaving in the car?"

"Cigarettes and anything else flammable," Moon Beam recited, popping a tube of lipstick out of her skin-tight jeans and leaning between the seats to apply it in the rearview mirror.

"Why were you climbing out of your mom's window?" Eden asked her cousin.

Moon Beam rolled her eyes dramatically. "Mom's on this 'you need to act like an adult' kick. Gag. Anyway, she got me this part-time job at the Snip Shack. Reception, hair sweeping. And I have to be there early tomorrow, so I'm supposed to be in bed like a loser."

"What has he dragged you into?" Eden asked.

"Something that I should have dragged myself into years ago. Mind if I smoke?" she asked.

"Kind of," Davis told her.

"Yeah," Eden said.

"Ugh. Fine. I'll wait."

Eden peered out her window. "Where are we going?"

Davis pulled onto Main Street and whipped his SUV into a parking space in front of the police station. "Here."

"I'm not talking to the police," Eden announced, crossing her arms over her chest.

"Not there." Davis rolled his eyes. "There." He pointed up to where lights were blazing on the second floor. The offices of *The Monthly Moon*.

"Why didn't you let me buy the razors?" Eden asked, gleefully hopping out of the car.

"Because we don't need to shave his eyebrows. Ladies, if you'll follow me." Davis led them inside and up the brightly lit stairwell that smelled vaguely of stale coffee and old carpet. On the second floor, he paused outside the glass door labeled *The Monthly Moon Where Blue Moon News Breaks First Once a Month*. The tagline took up the entire door. "The plan is you let me do the talking until it's Moon Beam's turn to talk," he said to Eden. "Got it? No screaming or punching or shaving. And no setting anything on fire."

Eden and Moon Beam nodded solemnly, and he was instantly suspicious.

Davis tried the door and found it locked. He buzzed the button next to the door.

"Monthly Moon. Everything you ever wanted to know about your neighbors," a voice crackled over the speaker.

"It's Davis Gates. Let us in, Anthony," Davis said.

"I'm sorry. Do you have an appointment? Mr. Berkowicz is very busy. He *is* our editor-in-chief, you know. News is constantly breaking. You can't expect to just walk in all willy-nilly and get some face time with him."

Moon Beam pressed her face up against the intercom. "Hey, how do you walk willy-nilly?"

Davis gave her a helpful shove away from the speaker. "Anthony, I know this is you. Open the damn door. We have a scoop for you."

"Well, why didn't you say so?"

A buzzer sounded, and Davis opened the door before Anthony had second thoughts. The newspaper office had fudge brown carpet and industrial gray walls that were papered with what looked like the front page of every issue of *The Monthly Moon*. Overflowing filing cabinets took up one whole wall with a bank of windows overlooking Main Street on another.

Anthony Berkowicz, esteemed editor-in-chief and son to town fixtures Rainbow and Gordon Berkowicz, was wearing pajama pants and eating ramen noodles with his slippered feet propped up on his desk. Empty bottles of Diet Sprite and YooHoo crowded the surface.

He wore gamer headphones slung around his skinny neck. Davis heard a crinkle and saw Eden stress eat the rest of her pack of candy.

"Do you live here?" Moon Beam asked, eyeing the six cartons of Chinese takeout in and around the trashcan.

"I'm a newspaper man. I live with the news. So, what's the scoop?" Anthony demanded. "I start working on next month's issue in three days so we need to move fast."

"Good because you're going to need the entire issue for the retraction I'm demanding," Eden said through clenched teeth.

"Sexy news sells, sweetie pie."

Someone was about to die. Davis decided it might as well be him and stepped between Anthony and Eden. "What did you just call my girlfriend?" he said, pretending to snarl.

Anthony's feet hit the floor. "Uh, sorry. I didn't mean to be disrespectful, sir… I mean, ma'am."

"Look," Davis began. "We're here about the exposé you printed about us."

"Oh, yeah," Anthony grinned. "That was some of my finest work."

"It was also five pages of lies," Eden snapped.

Anthony shrugged his bony shoulders. "Listen, journalism is all about attracting advertisers. I can't land Farm and Field or the bank with boring news."

"Your mother is the bank president," Eden pointed out.

Anthony's gasp nearly knocked him out of his chair. "I'm *shocked* that you'd insinuate my family would practice nepotism!"

Moon Beam, who had cigarettes to smoke, stepped in. "Look. Eden didn't set the Gates' yard on fire, dumbass. And she sure as hell didn't burn down his kitchen."

Anthony held up his hands. "Look, it's not my job to investigate—"

"Oh, for fuck's sake." Davis grabbed a notebook off the top of a counter buckling under the weight of yellowed newspaper. He slapped it down in front of Anthony and fished a pen out from under a half-dozen candy bar wrappers. "Shut your mouth and open your ears. Moon Beam? Talk."

"This isn't how my process works," Anthony whined. "First I need to formulate questions. Then I need to record the interview. Then I need to—"

Davis growled in Anthony's face.

"Or, I could just try this way," Anthony said, picking up the pen.

37

Feeling restless, Eden knocked on Davis's door after they'd returned to the inn from setting the record straight with *The Monthly Moon*. But his room was empty.

She tip-toed into the lobby and checked the security monitors. His car was still in the inn's small lot. But Chewy was conspicuously missing from Eden's couch, and she had a feeling the two were together. She drummed her fingers on the desk.

She was restless after the rollercoaster of the evening and had hoped some naked fun would help her shake the feeling. She was going to have to stop calling them flukes, she supposed.

The entire town would finally know the truth of what happened all those years ago. And Davis Gates was the one who'd stood up for her.

She didn't want to analyze the warm feeling in her stomach. She wanted to go about her life without the drama and chaos of the past few weeks. But did that mean she wanted to go back to her pre-Davis life?

Wandering back into her quarters, Eden trailed a finger over the back of her sofa. She loved her rooms. Her own private oasis. The cozy living room with its white-washed trim and gold walls was decorated with off-white furniture and framed family photos. Tall windows offered a view of the acre of green lawn behind the inn. If business continued this very nice upswing, she'd be able to up the landscapers and yard crew to once a week and save herself a few hours of lawn mowing two or three times a month.

She paced into her bedroom. Here were more ivories and beiges. Serene and simple. Thick bedding, luxurious window coverings, and a cozy seating area tucked into a nook of windows that looked toward the winery, a view she'd shunned until recently. There was a tiny utility room that doubled as kitchenette and laundry room for when she didn't feel like using the inn's facilities.

Her tour complete, Eden returned to the living room. She'd loved this house. Had spent hours here whenever her aunt was in residence. And when she'd been forced to take an elective in college her sophomore year and landed in Hospitality 101, it had all come together. Bring the old home back to life and share the town she so loved with an endless stream of visitors.

She'd built this business from the hardwood floors up. Usually the thought satisfied her. But tonight she was still restless. Still distracted. She debated, looking at the stack of paperbacks on her side table. She could sit and read until she was tired. Her pleasure reading had taken a backseat in recent weeks. Hell, maybe even months. The inn had never had a busier off-season. It was time to think about hiring more part-time help.

And now, her free time was spent juggling HeHa organizational challenges. And with Davis... well, that was a whole new level of distraction.

Dammit. She'd thought of him again. That settled it. She'd just send him a casual text.

Eden: Have you been dognapped?

Relief loosened her when she saw the dots on her screen.

Davis: Just checking the vines. Pruning starts next week. Chewy's with me.

She bit her lip. Debated.

Eden: Want some company? Of the human lady kind?

Davis: Meet me in the vines out front. Dress warm.

The vineyard was in all its frosty majesty under the nearly full moon. Eden picked her way down rows of silver vines, the frozen ground refusing to yield beneath her feet. She could hear him, that quiet, steady tone and knew he was talking to Chewy. She'd invited Vader. But the dog was smarter than the rest of them, choosing the comfort and warmth of bed.

"Try not to piss on every single vine, Chew."

Eden smiled and shifted the bag in her hand when Davis's form came into view. "Marco."

He turned and she could see his quick grin in the moonlight. "Polo."

Eden ignored the turmoil in her head and went instead with the lightness in her heart. She stepped into his open arms and placed a soft kiss on his mouth. "Should I ask what sent you on a midnight walkabout through the vines?" she asked.

Davis slung an arm around her shoulders. They'd both made affectionate moves without an audience. Eden decided not to worry about what that did or didn't mean.

"Just clearing my head," he told her. "We'll be pruning soon. Earlier than last year. The cold came faster."

They walked slowly down the row as he talked. It was peaceful being surrounded by the promise of another harvest, Eden thought.

"What does pruning do? How long does it take?" she asked, enjoying the cadence of his voice. It settled her thoughts. Stirred her blood.

He explained the process, the purpose, with Chewy trotting faithfully at their heels.

"What's in the bag?" Davis asked.

"Ah! I almost forgot." She plucked the bottle from the bag and held it aloft.

"Your whiskey," Davis said, holding the bottle to the moonlight.

She shook her head. "*Our* whiskey. I figured after tonight I owed you at least half."

"We're partners." He said it as if he meant it. As if their little revenge plot relationship were real. "What are we celebrating?" he asked.

She looked around them in the dark, at the dormant vines, the frost tipped ground, and sighed. "New leaves?"

"I like that," he said, his voice low and dangerous.

The shiver that worked its way up her spine had nothing to do with the cold.

"Can I show you something?" he asked.

~

Davis's house was small, charming, and smelled of stale smoke. He shut the front door behind them, and her gaze went immediately to the stretch of plywood that blocked off the fire damage from the rest of his home.

"Davis, this is awful. I'm so sorry," she breathed.

"Hmm? Oh, that." He glanced in the direction of the mess formerly known as his kitchen and scratched the back of his head. He nudged the thermostat out of the fifties.

"It makes me angry all over again," she told him. "Maybe this was a mistake? Maybe we should have gone to the police?"

He shook his head, took her hand. "No, you were right. What good would come from having half the town arrested for what was probably an accident?"

"An accident caused by a team of dumbasses."

"No argument there," Davis said wryly, tugging her toward the stairs.

"You're not taking me to bed, are you?" she asked, stalling on the first step.

He looked at her over his shoulder. "Scared you can't resist me?"

She scoffed. "Excuse me! Who resisted you for one and a half decades? That's gold medaling in resistance."

Davis opened a door off of the second-floor landing, his cocky expression daring her to enter. Eden breezed past him into the tiny bedroom. It had the musty smell of an empty house mixed with the scents of smoke and soot. She stopped when she saw the easel.

"Well, well. Unexplored depths," she murmured. "You always were good in art class. May I?"

At his nod, she handed him the bottle and flipped through the canvases stacked against the wall and was pleasantly surprised by landscapes, still life, and even the occasional abstract. Bold colors, beautiful light. “These are great, Davis. Really great.”

He took a swig and crossed his arms, watching her. “It’s a hobby.”

“I didn’t think you had time for hobbies.” She paused on a painting of rolling grass of emerald green, her inn in the distance. Fanciful and vibrant. “I want this one by the way. If you say I can’t buy it, I’ll smuggle it out under my shirt.”

“It’s yours.”

Her heart leapt. She’d hang it in her quarters, in the bedroom. Davis studied his feet. “My father would prefer if I didn’t have time for hobbies.”

“Doesn’t he care about a well-rounded life?” Eden asked, holding out her hand for the bottle.

His laugh was short. “Definitely not. If there’s any room for anything besides business in your life, you’re not working hard enough.”

“Said the man who worked himself into two heart attacks.” She studied the bottle and took a drink.

He pointed at her and winked. “Bingo.”

“How’s he going to handle what we’re doing?” she asked. Eden wasn’t sure which part of “what they were doing” she was referring to. Banding together for revenge. Having sex. Being... friendly.

Davis gave a shrug that had the teenage rebel inside her swooning. She passed the bottle back to him.

“Cross that bridge when we come to it, I guess.”

“Even if they don’t come home until we’re broken up,” Eden said, pulling the painting of the inn out of the stack and then flipping through the rest, “you’ll have a lot of explaining to do.”

“Sometimes I’m tired of explaining... and asking for permission,” he sighed. He leaned against the door frame, an exhaustion that had nothing to do with being tired slumping his shoulders.

"He doesn't trust you to make decisions?" Eden asked.

"Ferguson Gates doesn't trust anyone but himself to do the right thing. And if it's something different from the way he's been operating for the past thirty-plus years, it's automatically wrong."

"So, you work around him."

His fingers worried the label on the whiskey. "And maybe it makes me feel like ever so slightly less of a man."

Davis's words, his raw honesty hung in the room between them. She rose and crossed to him. Her fingers circling his on the bottle.

"Maybe it's time to stop asking for permission."

"Maybe it is."

"For what it's worth, Davis. Ferguson should be thrilled to have you at the helm. No one cares more about the winery and this town than you do." *It was the truth and he deserved to hear it.*

He studied her, his brown eyes looking into hers, searching. "I want to draw you," he decided.

"Ohmygod, yes!" Eden said, surprising him. She laughed at his shock. "Um, hello. Have you seen *Titanic*? 'Draw me like one of your French girls'? It's like the sexiest scene of the entire movie."

Eden pulled the bottle from his grasp and flopped dramatically on the tiny loveseat he'd crammed against the wall by the room's closet. "Make sure you get my good side."

"You are a piece of work," Davis said, pulling a sketch pad off the shelf and arranging his charcoal pencils.

"No, no, Davis. I'm a piece of *art*."

38

Loose-wristed, Davis let the charcoal move over the paper in quick, sure lines. "This is just a quickie," he told her.

Eden turned her head to look at him, a feline smile on her face. "I like quickies."

He was always half-hard around her. It was impossible not to be. Everything about Eden Moody was alluring. The lines and curves of her frame, the wicked way she used her mouth, the never-ending energy she put into life. Not to mention the fact that she was as obsessed with work as he was. He loved that she was driven, ambitious. That she lived and breathed a passion to build and grow something.

"Mind if I run something business-related by you?" he asked, watching the way her face changed as she studied the whiskey she'd rested on the flat of her stomach.

"Mmm, you *know* it gets me hot when you talk business," Eden teased.

He grinned. "Thinking about offering weekly art classes at the winery. Open it up to the community—and tourists. Serve wine, learn to paint or draw."

She lolled her head to the side, eyebrows arched. "That's brilliant."

"I could teach some of the beginner classes," he continued, capturing the curve of her lips on paper. "Bring in other artists here and there."

"And everyone would drink your wine, learn more about your winery. You'd be deepening the relationship."

"Exactly," he said, shading lightly under the graceful line of her neck and jaw. "I want Blue Moon to feel connected to the winery and vice versa. Right now we're sort of separate. We don't do anything beyond the usual tastings. There's nothing that draws locals, our people, in."

He liked the way she was smiling at him. Fondly, with an underlying desire that he doubted she even realized was there. "What are your other ideas?" she asked.

"Private tours of the vines, the process. Bringing in a group during harvest to show them how it works. Grape stomping vs. pressing. How we choose the grapes, how we blend them, how we name them."

"Again. Smart. You're building that connection between your customer and your product. Making them feel invested. They'll come back for the vintage that they helped create."

"And maybe they'll stay at your inn," Davis mused.

Her gaze sharpened and he drew the heavy lids, the inky lashes, liking the anything-but-aloof expression.

"Are you suggesting a partnership?" she asked, sitting up and swigging from the bottle.

"You're not running and screaming in the opposite direction," he observed.

"What about the breakup?"

Eden slumped back against the couch cushion. "There's nothing that says we have to go back to hating each other after we break up."

He felt a single tendril of something—was that hope?—curling into his gut and taking root.

"Are you saying we could stay… friendly?"

She was looking everywhere but directly at him. Eden gave a surly, one-shouldered shrug. "I don't know. Just thinking out loud."

Davis held out his hand for the bottle.

She made a move to hand it over and then dangled it just out of reach. "Can I see?"

"I'm not done."

Eden rose and closed the scant distance between them to peer over the top of the sketchbook. He wanted her to like it. Wanted her to see the way *he* saw her. All feline grace and sultry energy.

"Mmm." She studied the stylized sketch with an impassive face.

"Mmm good or mmm terrible?" he asked.

She took the sketchbook from his hand, placed it and the whiskey on the floor, and straddled him on the chair.

"I was right," she said, lips brushing his.

"About what?" He was already out of breath, and she'd barely touched him. Such was the power of a turned-on Eden Moody.

"Just as hot as it was in the movie."

"You'll have to take your clothes off next time," he suggested, hands sliding up her sides.

"Oh, I can take them off this time."

He laughed softly. "You're a hell of a girl, Eden."

"You're not so bad yourself, Davis."

When she kissed him, he felt a slow, lingering hunger burn its way into his gut. "I thought we weren't going to do this again," he reminded her, lips moving over hers possessively.

"I can't seem to stop myself," she whispered against his mouth. "Not sure I want to."

He liked the sound of that and rewarded her by gripping her hips and dragging her across his already aching cock.

The noise she made was purely carnal, and Davis counted his lucky stars that some idiot thought to stink bomb his house, putting him in this exact position.

She tasted like whiskey and sin. Better than any wine he'd sampled. She grinded against him, both of them desperate for the friction that would take them to the top. Davis slipped his hands under the hem of her sweater finding her skin, soft and warm to the touch.

"God, I love it when you touch me," she said, biting his lower lip.

Davis's vision started to gray. This is what was missing in his life. This raw need and Eden willing to fill it again and again.

He coasted his palms up and over her breasts reveling in the sharp rasp of her breath. He memorized the texture of satin skin and lacy bra. Her busy fingers were plucking at the buttons of his shirt with a charge of desperation. Matching her, he shoved her sweater up and over her head, swiping the straps of her bra down her shoulders.

"You are so fucking sexy, Eden," he breathed.

"Gah" was the only response she could manage, and Davis loved it. He buried his face in her breasts as she boosted herself up to release him from his pants. Together, they wrestled their clothes into submission, freeing enough flesh for contact. Once freed, they no longer had all the time in the world. It suddenly became a matter of life and death to be inside her.

Reading his mind, Eden hovered over him, notching the head of his cock against her sex.

"Condom, condom, condom," he chanted, sweat breaking out on his forehead.

"Shit. All I brought was whiskey."

"I don't have any in the house." Davis imagined his teenage self shooting him two middle fingers before curling into the fetal position and weeping.

Eden stared into his eyes. "I'm on birth control," she said, teasing her lower lip between her teeth. "Diligently taken at the same time every day." Since she found out Eva got knocked up.

"What are you saying?"

"You don't have any festering diseases, do you?"

He was so busy staring at her cherry red lips that he could only shake his head.

"Neither do I."

"So, we..." His fingers flexed on the sexy ass curves of her hips, demanding that he yank her down onto his shaft.

"If you're okay with it."

His control was slipping through his fingers like grains of sand.

"I'm okay if you're okay."

She lowered herself down, taking the first inch of him. *Heaven. Perfection. Ecstasy.* He meant to let her set the pace. Meant to let her have control. But that small taste of what awaited him was too much.

Gripping her hips, he pulled her down, thrusting up.

Her head fell back, mouth open on a soundless cry.

There was no relief. Now the need was fiercer, cutting at him like jagged glass.

Go slow, he cautioned himself. But his body wasn't interested in listening. Davis shifted his grip to hold Eden by the hips and ass. He lifted her and drove home again. This time she rocked against him, and they both were lost.

Nothing could compare to the wet glove of Eden clutching his cock as she panted his name in his ear. In this moment, he wanted to personally write thank you letters to every member of the Beautification Committee. Because without them, he wouldn't be slamming into Eden's body like his life depended on it.

Her breasts heaved and bounced with each powerful thrust. He couldn't take the temptation, letting his tongue snake out of his mouth to lick her.

"Ohmygod," Eden chanted. Her fingers bit into his shoulder with a shock of pain.

The finish line, what they were both recklessly racing toward, shimmered on the horizon.

Davis shifted in the chair, changing the angle, and Eden choked out her appreciation. "Why do you feel so damn good?" she hissed. "Why?"

He hoped she was being rhetorical because there was no way he could answer her. There was something here. People who didn't like each other didn't get to heights like this. Their connection was deeper. He didn't just want her. That much was clear.

"Davis?"

He could feel her quickening around him, knew she was close. The slick slide of her around his shaft was systematically driving him insane.

The groan that tore its way free from his throat sounded inhuman, primal. His balls tightened, and he tensed feeling the tingle at the base of his spine. He was taking her with him, forcing her to the edge so they could fall together.

She was chanting incomprehensible things, her eyes squeezed shut. He latched on to one perfect pink nipple and drove into her. Harder. Faster. That sweet nipple pebbled in his mouth against the roughness of his tongue. She rode out his thrusts until he felt her clench around him. There was no surviving that. He poured himself into her as she came.

"God, yes! Davis!"

He released her nipple with a *pop* and took her mouth as they rode out their releases in sync wrapped around each other. *Partners.*

Mom: Just saw The Monthly Moon's article on your cousin setting the fire at the Gates house. Why didn't you tell us it wasn't you?

Eden: I did! You didn't believe me!

Mom: Well, whose fault is that?

Eden: Yours!

Mom: I guess I never gave Moon Beam enough credit for family loyalty. I owe her an apology. You're retroactively grounded.

Eden: head desk GIF

39

Thanksgiving followed suit with the rest of November in Blue Moon—fifteen degrees colder than it should have been with a mess of snow flurries that flirted with freezing rain.

The shit-tastic weather was tempered by the town's reaction to the special edition of *The Monthly Moon*. Eden lost count of the number of neighbors who came up to her on the street and lied sweetly to her face, claiming that they never believed she'd set the fire to begin with. But Eden was feeling magnanimous—or maybe that was orgasmic—and graciously accepted their sort-of apologies.

Moon Beam was enjoying her newfound notoriety as an accidental teenage fire-starter. "It gives me a bad girl edge without the fear of being packed off to the commune," she'd insisted.

With the weather and the extra workload of planning HeHa festivities, Eden had considered backing out of the Pierce family invitation. Her fireplace and sweats would have made up for missing out on turkey and homemade gravy, but the Pierces were a tenacious lot.

On Thanksgiving morning, an inch of snow fell, and Summer and Phoebe had both texted Eden to make sure she and Davis were still coming. To drive the point home, Joey had called her on speakerphone shouting above what sounded like a wrestling match between Jax, their foster son Caleb, and Waffles the family dog and issued the ultimatum that they "better get their asses over to the farm."

"We could have spent the day naked in bed," Davis lamented beside her. They'd been spending most of their recent nights that way. And Eden was growing rather fond of their new hobby. Sex.

He stomped his feet on Jax and Joey's front porch, dislodging the snow from his shoes. The house was a cozy-looking log cabin with a wide porch and gabled roof. It was a quick walk from the back door to Joey's beloved stables where Pierce Acres had launched a wildly successful breeding program thanks to Jax's apology stallion.

"Hold on to that thought," Eden told him. "If we play this right, we can be back at the inn and naked by four." She tightened her grip on the two bottles of wine Davis had thoughtfully brought for their first stop.

"Count me in."

"No eating too much or drinking too much," Eden cautioned. Sex on a full stomach was no one's idea of fun.

Davis's hand found its way to the nape of her neck, and he gave her an affectionate squeeze when she rang the doorbell. "Three hours. We've got this," he whispered.

The door flung open, and two dogs raced past them into the front yard. Waffles, the scruffy mixed herding dog, was happily nipping at the heels of a small black and white pony —scratch that—Summer's rescue Great Dane Valentina, who dashed ahead of Waffles in a game of tag.

"Sorry about that." Reva was Jax and Joey's foster daughter. A high school senior, she had a serious face and quiet nature. The girl had been raising Caleb on her own after their mother skipped town before Sheriff Cardona and Jax and Joey intervened.

She was wearing yellow and orange leggings decorated with turkeys and an oversized hoodie.

"Someone didn't get the dress code message," Reva said, eyes skimming Eden's jeans and forest green blouse.

"Joey was serious about that?"

"How the hell else are you supposed to eat eight hundred pounds of food if you don't have an elastic waistband?" Joey demanded, appearing behind Reva and glaring at their apparel. "Rookie mistake."

Their hostess was decked out in gray sweat pants and one of Jax's old t-shirts.

Eden shot an apologetic look at Davis. She'd assumed Joey's "don't get dressed" message was a joke.

Eden held up the wine. "We can just go home if the dress code is—"

"Get your asses in here." Joey wrestled the wine out of her grip and motioned for them to come inside.

The house was full of holiday smells and the laughter of every member of the Pierce family, dogs included. There was music playing in the background that no one could hear over the din of family and fun. Reva went back to the couch where she and Evan were watching *National Lampoon's Christmas Vacation*. Aurora and Caleb were sneaking appetizers off of the dining table and taking them upstairs to Caleb's room. Joey had outdone herself with the spread. Eden's pants felt tighter just looking at the plates of bruschetta and stuffed mushroom caps. Most of the action centered around the kitchen island where Jax played bartender for the adults in the family. Phoebe was sitting on a stool critiquing his martini shaking.

"Thank God you're here," Eva said, appearing at Eden's side. "Taste this!"

She pressed a glass into Eden's hands.

"What is it?" she asked, sniffing the purple liquid.

"Cranberry apple cider sangria," Joey answered, leaning in to bite Jax's earlobe.

Eden turned her back on the festivities. "Why haven't you told anyone yet?" Eden hissed.

"We're spilling the baby beans at the main meal when Donovan's parents will be here," Eva whispered. "Just a few more drinks and you won't have to cover for me anymore!"

Eden chugged the drink and handed Eva the empty cup.

"The lovebirds are here," Beckett announced. He juggled Lydia over to his hip and dropped a kiss on Eden's cheek. He shook Davis's hand.

The greetings flew fast and furious with everyone talking all at once. Joey opened one of the bottles of wine and proceeded to pour half of it into Phoebe's super-sized wine glass.

Eden found Davis being pulled from her grasp as the Pierce men decided to congregate in Jax's office to talk "man" things.

Summer herded her two-year-old daughter Meadow onto the rug with the bribe of coloring books and crayons. Meadow's brother Jonathan was laying on Mr. Snuffles, Franklin and Phoebe's sinus-challenged pug, while Grandpa Franklin read him a story.

"Have you guys read the new book club selection?" Summer asked over her shoulder.

Phoebe slapped the counter with enthusiasm. "Yes! Amazing. I challenge any of you not to like it."

"Freaking hilarious," Eva agreed.

"You had your babies vaginally, didn't you?" Phoebe asked Gia innocently.

"Um. Why?" If Gia thought it strange that her mother-in-law was questioning her vagina, she didn't show it. The Pierces were uncomfortably close like that, and Eden felt a little twinge of sadness that she didn't get her own overly involved family antics today.

Her parents had called that morning from Atlantis's house over a noise factor much the same as the one in the Pierce house now. It made Eden feel just a bit homesick and happy that she hadn't stayed home alone.

"Because Pippa Grant will make you pee yourself laughing," Phoebe announced. "I woke your father up laughing in bed over the hockey players autographing people's foreheads."

"So, Eden, speaking of romantic comedy," Gia prodded, smugly popping a pickle into her mouth. "How are things going with you and Davis?"

The Beautification Committee was everywhere.

"We're great," Eden insisted, smiling brightly and helping herself to a glass of wine. "He's wonderful. I just feel awful for him being displaced from his home for the holidays." She couldn't help herself, reminding the guilty of their crimes. She shook her head sadly. "It's so disheartening to know that someone was malicious enough to want to hurt him like that. I mean, he's homeless for the holidays. Can you imagine?"

Eva and Gia looked like Eden had just run over their favorite baby bunny with a lawnmower.

"It is really unfortunate," Phoebe agreed, sloshing the wine around in her glass. "It almost makes me question just how safe this town really is."

"Me, too," Eden agreed seriously, enjoying the way the sisters squirmed. "He's homeless, and because of this mean-spirited prankster, the insurance company won't pay out." She sighed. "Davis may not show it, but he's really hurting. We're really hoping the police find out who did it."

Eva's lower lip trembled. *Home run.*

Sure, maybe it was mean to poke them on a holiday built around gratitude and sharing. But because of the Beautification Committee, Davis didn't have a home in which to celebrate Thanksgiving. Eden went in for the kill. "I just feel bad for the police."

"Why's that?" Eva asked, glancing nervously in the direction of Jax's office.

"Well, think about it. This is a small town. Your husband, Layla, Colby, they know everyone," Eden pointed out. "Imagine having to charge someone you know or care about with arson."

She shook her head, enjoying the stricken looks. "And can you imagine the trouble he could get in if it turns out to be someone he knows? He'd be accused of covering it up, collusion. His career could be sunk, too. It's just a really ugly situation," Eden tut-tutted.

Satisfied that she'd reminded the Beautification Committee to add "thankful for not being in jail" to their holiday to do list, she topped off Phoebe's wine glass and her own and went to browse the appetizer selection. She was debating whether she should be judicious with her choices or embrace the gluttony of the holiday when a pair of hands slid around her waist.

She leaned back into Davis's familiar body.

"How's it going so far?" he asked quietly, plucking a canape from her plate.

"Not bad. They tried to pump me for info on how happy and in love we are, and I laid the mother of all guilt trips. By the way, you're secretly devastated by the fire," she whispered in his ear.

"Got it. I'm secretly devastated, and you're head over heels for me largely based on my performance in bed."

"Gossips," Eden teased.

40

He'd underestimated the volume of food of a progressive Thanksgiving meal and overestimated the settling effect of the walk from Jax and Joey's to Carter and Summer's. They'd moved *en masse* from the log cabin near the barns to the pretty white farmhouse where turkey, tofurkey, and every holiday side dish known to man awaited them.

Given the number of guests, Carter set up the tables on the first floor of the little red barn next to the house. The wood floors were swept spotless and a potbelly wood stove in the corner warmed the room to cozy.

Eden wedged her green bean casserole onto the overladen table that was covered in a cheerful turkey-themed tablecloth. The legs buckled as if they couldn't withstand one more addition to the feast. "I'm already full," she confessed to Davis.

"You? I had two beers and six of those pigs in a blanket," Davis complained. "I thought the walk over would make some room. It just gave me more time to realize how full I am." Eden patted him on the back, and he had to resist the urge to burp.

Summer appeared in the doorway with two casserole

dishes piled on top of each other and Meatball the beagle sniffing after her hoping for spills.

"Good God. We're going to die here, aren't we?" Eden whispered to him.

He put his arm around her, though the effort hurt his full stomach. "We're in this together. And by my count, there are at least one-hundred dogs here that we can slip food to."

"You're so sexy when you're smart," Eden told him.

"Remember the plan. Naked Thanksgiving Sex," he reminded her.

She pressed a hand to her stomach and nodded. "Okay, we can salvage this. No more booze. Tiny portions."

Vegetarian Carter lugged in a gravy boat labeled "vegan." "This is the last of it," he announced, balancing it on top of the broccoli casserole and broccoli salad.

Summer bit her lip and swept Jonathan up in her arms. "I think Mommy got a little bit carried away."

"Cake?" Jonathan asked.

"Not 'til later," Aurora told her cousin with regret.

"Well, we are feeding an army," Carter reminded her.

It was true. Davis surveyed the room. Couples and kids and dogs—and was that a goat peering in the window?—gathered together. His own family holidays were... quieter. More sedate. Bryson was the cook or, more accurately, the amateur chef in the family and would create artistic, gourmet "cuisine experiences" with Davis's or Tilly's help. They would enjoy a few bottles of wine, a tiny helping of some sculptural dessert, and call it a day.

The Pierces made messy and complicated look... fun.

"Here come the Cardonas," Phoebe said, pointing at the drive as Donovan's parents pulled up in their shiny pick-up truck.

Davis noticed the look that passed between Donovan and Eva. Excitement, nerves, and pure joy.

"Hey, y'all," Hazel Cardona greeted them as she and Michael made their way inside.

"We figured you Pierces would go completely overboard, so we brought antacids and gas pills as our contribution." Her husband Michael held a plastic drug store bag aloft.

A cheer went up, and Davis made mental note to get his hands on that bag.

"Now that we're all here," Eva began. "Um, Donovan?"

There was a cheerful pop of a champagne bottle. "Since we had so much to celebrate this year," Donovan said, pouring a round of champagne into plastic cups, "we thought we should have a toast."

"What a lovely idea," Phoebe sighed. Her gigantic wine glass had made the trek from Jax's to Carter's and had been refilled.

The cups were distributed, and all gazes landed back on Donovan. He tucked his wife under his arm and promptly lost the power of speech.

Noticing her husband's predicament, Eva cleared her throat. "So. Um. We're pregnant."

There was dead silence around the table. Phoebe was the first to recover and ran squealing for Eva. Eden, Davis noticed, looked decidedly unsurprised.

"Well, this is the first I'm hearing about this," Jax said loudly.

Carter punched his brother in the shoulder.

"Why don't you look surprised that we're going to be an aunt and uncle?" Gia demanded, poking Beckett in the arm with one hand while she wiped away happy tears with the other.

"Who? Me?" Beckett asked.

Donovan made a slashing motion over his throat, and then his father and mother were pulling him into a back-slapping hug.

Franklin was taking his turn hugging his youngest daughter. "We're going to need a bigger bunkroom," he announced. "All of these wonderful grandbabies!"

"Congratulations, Eva," Carter said warmly.

"Why aren't you congratulating Donovan, too?" Summer asked, her eyes narrowed shrewdly at her bearded husband.

Emma gave a very un-Emma-like squeal. "We're going to have babies together," she said, wrapping her sister in a tight hug. "Baby buddies. Isn't that a wonderful surprise, Niko?"

"The best kind of surprise," he agreed.

Summer pointed an accusing finger at her friend. "Nikolai Vulkov! You're not surprised either."

"Mayday. Mayday," Jax whispered to Davis.

"Jackson Scott," Joey's voice rang out.

Jax picked up Caleb and held the boy in front of him as a shield.

"You sneaky sons of b—ears," Joey corrected herself at the last second. "You knew!"

Eva gasped and stared up at Donovan. "You *told* them?"

Donovan was back to speechless.

"It wasn't his fault. We were talking about vasectomies and kids, and he didn't tell us, but he got this..." Davis trailed off, feeling the weight of a roomful of female glares. Eden cautiously stepped in front of him.

"He got the stupid, goofy 'I'm going to be a daddy' look," Jax said, jumping in to swim with the sharks.

"Leave it alone, man," Beckett sang under his breath. "Don't try to save him."

"I can't believe you told everyone," Eva said, hands on her hips.

"We practically beat it out of him," Davis insisted.

Donovan shot him a look of gratitude.

"Honey, I—" he started but stopped when Eva dabbed her eyes with a festive cartoon turkey napkin.

"No, it's okay. I just had hoped we could have this big surprise."

"Shit," Donovan swore. "Baby, please don't cry."

"I'm not crying," she wailed.

"It's the hormones," Emma told everyone, tears streaming down her own cheeks.

"I only told Eden," Eva sobbed.

"You told Eden?" Donovan asked, all eyes flying to Eden.

Davis moved to stand next to her in case the mob got out of control.

"Huh? Oh, me?" she asked guiltily.

"That was just because I threw up in her hat stand! I had to explain!"

"Umbrella stand," Eden corrected.

"Regardless of who knew and who didn't," Phoebe said, standing with only the slightest wine-induced wobble. "I think we can all agree that we've been blessed and that a new baby is nothing but wonderful news."

Now, Donovan was tearing up and swallowing hard.

"We have a whole new generation who will grow up here running wild," Carter said, clearing his throat at the emotion that had lodged there. "What more could there be to life?"

"Your father would be so proud of all you boys," Franklin said, raising his glass. "You too, Donovan."

Beckett nodded silently, pulling Gia into his chest.

"What the hell is wrong with everyone?" Joey demanded wiping her eye on the back of her sleeve. "Can we at least eat before the hysterics start?"

Donovan swiped away Eva's tears.

Phoebe raised her glass and slipped her free arm into Franklin's. "I'd like to propose a toast. To family."

"To family," they echoed.

Davis felt a little tickle at the back of his throat and noticed that Eden's eyes were a little misty. He hip-checked her gently, and she gave him a watery smile.

Maybe there was something to be said for a big, sloppy family holiday? Maybe there was something more than balance sheets and grapes and marketing initiatives.

Maybe plantings and harvests were only the beginning.

41

The walk from the farmhouse to Phoebe and Franklin's home was slower and punctuated by the moans of the overfed. Even the dogs and kids were moving at a snail's pace. Meatball gave a lazy bark as Waffles trotted in slow motion in front of him.

Meadow stopped where she was on the path and held her arms up to her Uncle Jax. "No more walking," she insisted. Not to be outdone, Jonathan threw himself on Donovan's mercy.

Jax settled the toddler on his shoulders with only a small groan.

It was getting dark. They were long past their 4 p.m. estimate. But they couldn't very well skip out on dessert. It would be rude. And very, very smart.

"If one more thing goes in my mouth, I'm going to throw up all of my internal organs," Eden announced to Davis.

He squeezed her hand, and she realized how right it felt to have his fingers twined with hers, just as their shared suffering twined together.

Davis gave a sad shake of his head. "I've never eaten so much in my entire life. That's more than I usually eat in a week. I think I'm just going to lay down in this field and wait for birds to eat me. My carcass will feed them for the entire winter," he predicted.

Eden laughed and then clutched her stomach. "Please, don't make me do that again. I almost threw up."

"I think it's the tofurkey that's sitting like a bowling ball in my stomach," he told her.

"You didn't have to eat it," she pointed out.

"I didn't want to be rude."

"How many gas pills is too many?" Eden wondered. "Because I'm so bloated I could be a parade float."

They helped each other up the wide front steps of Franklin and Phoebe's pretty little craftsman cottage. Tucked away on a swatch of green grass at the back of the farm, it was a little slice of country heaven.

The lights were already on inside, welcoming them.

"Sweet baby cheeses! How many pies is that?" Eden hissed to Davis.

"Eight. Eight entire pies... and then that looks like a cobbler."

Eden clamped a hand over her mouth. "Can we even do this?"

Davis glared at the desserts like he would a cloud of aphids. "You listen to me, Eden Moody. We can and we will do this. And then we will go back to the inn and get naked."

She admired his blind, stupid faith in their sex drive.

Franklin busied himself lighting a fire in the great room's fireplace. Aurora, who had eaten as much as two adults, was sniffing around the pies. "Can I have apple and pumpkin and cheesecake?" she asked Gia.

"Christ, Shortcake. Are your legs hollow?" Beckett asked ruffling her red curls.

"Gram, do you have whipped cream?" Aurora asked Phoebe and grinned up at Beckett.

The crowd groaned at the question.

"In the fridge, sweetheart." Phoebe had given up on the wine. "I'm going to make the biggest pot of coffee in the universe," she announced. "Anyone want?"

"Can you just inject it directly into my veins?" Summer asked.

Davis steered Eden to the couch by the fireplace. "Maybe if we just sit down for a few minutes, we won't feel like vomiting anymore."

With effort, Eden propped her denim clad legs up on the coffee table. "My biggest regret in life right now is that I wore jeans. I think they're cutting off my circulation."

Summer flopped down in the overstuffed chair next to the couch with a groan. "Rookie mistake not wearing pjs. The rest of us just get to go home and fall into bed."

Summer was wearing a cute matching set of lavender thermal pajamas.

"Mama! I sit with you?" Meadow demanded.

"Okay, baby, but you're going to have to climb up here yourself, or Mommy's going to puke on your cute little head."

"Okay, Mama!" Meadow scrambled up onto the cushion next to her mother and promptly flopped into Summer's lap.

"Why, God? Why?" Summer wheezed.

"Do you do this every holiday?" Eden asked.

"Sure do!" Jax poked his head between Eden and Davis over the back of the couch. He was digging into a piece of pumpkin pie slathered with a tower of whipped cream.

"How can you eat, man?" Davis asked him.

"It's his super power," Joey said, slinking up behind them and laying across the back of the couch. "He can eat anything all day long."

"Jackson always was an emotional eater," Phoebe called from the kitchen. "Now, who's ready for pie?"

Groans and maybe some dramatic gagging sounded throughout the entire first floor of the house.

~

"WOULD you think less of me if I took my pants off right now?" Eden asked Davis.

Davis was behind the wheel after losing the coin toss. To be fair, he hadn't lost. He'd just been too full to bend over and look at the coin.

"I unbuttoned mine two hours ago," Davis told her as he steered them toward the inn. "Took my shoes off too. Can overeating make your feet swell?"

"What about naked Thanksgiving sex?" Eden asked, shimmying out of her jeans. "Ahhhhh."

"Still happening," Davis insisted grimly. "I'm a man of my word. I deliver what I promise."

Right now, the only thing less appealing than getting naked and bouncing around was the leftover pie that had been foisted on them. Phoebe gave them two to take home. Eden planned to serve them to her guests tomorrow morning for breakfast with fresh juices from OJs by Julia.

Davis eased the car down the lane. Jax and Joey's foursome were illuminated in the headlights as they walked home.

"Besides the obscene amount of food, that was actually kind of nice," Eden ventured.

"They make family life look… fun," Davis agreed.

"Yeah. They do," Eden agreed with a heavy sigh.

"What's that? Is that a dog?" he asked, pointing at a pair of yellow eyes reflecting the car's headlights.

Eden peered through the windshield. "Is that a goat?"

One minute the shadowy figure was hunkered down behind the tree, and the next it was jogging into the midst of Jax's family.

"No! Bad goat!" Jax's high-pitched screech rattled the car windows.

Davis braked hard, and Eden's seatbelt locked against her.

They watched as the goat danced into the headlights leering at Jax. Reva and Caleb doubled over with laughter.

"Ha! You Satanic son of a bitch!" Jax shouted yanking something from his coat pockets. "That's right, Clementine! I came prepared. Cornbread!"

Jax wound up like a major league pitcher and tossed what did appear to be cornbread into the field.

Clementine stared him down as if plotting his goat-trampling death.

"Oh, this isn't good," Eden breathed, smothering a laugh behind her hand.

"Get out of here, Clementine," Joey said, howling with laughter. She stepped between her husband and the offending farm animal.

The goat weighed its options. Cornbread? Or Jackson Pierce's pants?

"She still wants to eat you, Jax," Caleb giggled into his mittens.

"Should we get out and help?" Davis asked.

"I can't outrun a goat right now."

"Shoo," Joey said, holding one hand over her full-to-bursting stomach and waving the other at the goat. "Go on. Leave him alone this one time."

Clementine feinted to the right and dodged left, getting within biting distance before Joey blocked her.

"You told me you were going to untrain her!" Jax reminded his wife.

"I've been busy having a family and breeding horses, jackass. Do you want me to step aside?" Joey offered amicably.

"No!" Jax grabbed his wife by the shoulders and hid behind her back. "Just make her go away."

"If I laugh any harder, I'm going to vomit forty pounds of food," Davis told Eden.

Clementine made her move. She dodged toward Joey again, and when Jax shrieked, the goat turned and jogged after the cornbread he'd thrown.

"Was that goat smiling?" Davis asked.

THE INN WAS STILL STANDING when they returned. Eden's phone had been blissfully silent during the day. She only had a handful of guests tonight, and they were all in town visiting family, so their needs were few.

The dogs met them at the kitchen door, and Eden held the door so they could romp outside. "Watch out for runaway goats," she warned them.

Davis helped her stash the pies in the commercial refrigerator, and together they trudged down the hallway to their rooms. They paused outside of Davis's door, staring at it. "Do you want to maybe change and come over to my room?" Eden offered. She'd never invited him into her space before. They spent almost all of their naked time in his bed or his backseat or her parents' house.

"Yeah. That'd be good," he said.

She unlocked her door and shuffled inside, dumping her purse, coat, and pants as she went. Normally, she was a tidy person to the point of obsession. But tonight was not the night for cleanliness and organization. Tonight was for food comas.

She wrestled her way into a pair of stretchy leggings and a

black tunic with an open back. If a guest needed her, she would at least look somewhat presentable. Flopping down on the couch, Eden let out a heavy sigh. Despite the unbearable bloating and stomach pain, today had been... good.

It was interesting watching a family with so many moving parts celebrate together. She'd seen festive family celebrations before, plenty under her own roof. She wondered if she would ever be part of the celebration rather than the organizer or a guest? Would it ever be her family celebrating, arguing, eating until they burst?

She was happy here in the business she'd built. She'd spent so much time building it, she hadn't really given much thought as to what else she might be missing out on. But watching Donovan fawning over sweet Eva, seeing the heated look Summer and Carter shared over the heads of their kids, it made her wonder. Would she have that? Could she have it? And why was it, when she tried to envision it all, that it was Davis's face she saw?

There was a soft knock at her door. "Come in," she called rather than getting up off the couch.

Davis, in athletic pants and a Taco Tuesday t-shirt, came in followed by the dogs.

"Awh, thank you for letting them in," Eden said.

"I figured I'd save you the trip."

"Bless you."

She felt his weight at the end of the couch and opened her eyes she hadn't realized were closed. Turkey made her eyelids so heavy.

Davis picked up her feet and put them in his lap. "We can just rest here for a few minutes. Get our energy up to get naked."

"Sounds good," she said.

"You have a really nice place here."

"Thanks, Davis."

"I had a good time today," he told her.

"Me too."

"Makes me wonder if maybe there's something to the whole marriage, family thing."

"Hmm," Eden hummed.

"You ever feel that way?"

"They make it look easy," Eden told him. "Can you imagine our families sitting down for a holiday meal?"

His silence had her opening her eyes again, and she realized what she'd said. "Not that we're in a real relationship or anything like that. Or that our families would ever be forced to spend time with us as a couple," she corrected hastily.

"Of course not."

She let the silence fall again. "Davis?"

"Hmm?"

"Happy Thanksgiving."

They were both asleep in under a minute.

42

It may have been the turkey talking or some side effect of too many gas pills, but Davis couldn't stop thinking about Eden's comments. Imagining their families sitting down to break bread was, of course, ridiculous, impossible even. But she'd said it, and he couldn't stop mulling it over, looking for a solution. Even now, when he was supposed to be helping Eden educate the volunteers on their HeHa roles.

They were crammed into a conference room on the second floor of the library facing a dozen of Blue Moon's finest citizens and a few more who wandered in off the street looking for a snack and some conversation.

"So Rasheeda, you're going to be in charge of the kids with the donation cans, right?" Eden asked, a statuesque woman in her fifties.

Rasheeda nodded. "I've personally handpicked ten of the cutest kids in town. She pressed a button on her cellphone screen and a slide show appeared on the wall. "We've been practicing the puppy eyes and the quivering lips," she said, scrolling through photos of adorable, devastated looking kids.

"You're a genius, Rasheeda," Eden announced. "Now, let's talk winter coat drive. What have we collected so far, Ms. Friendly?"

Ms. Friendly was the meanest teacher at Blue Moon High. She sniffed in derision, her mousy brown hair was wrapped around her scalp like a python settling in for the night. "I still don't see why we aren't *only* accepting donations during the HeHa festival," she griped. "Going through the donations cuts into my lunch, snack, and meditation breaks at school."

Before Eden could formulate the passive-aggressive, polite response Davis could see her working on, he smoothly stepped in. "I know it's an imposition now," he said with sympathy. "But just imagine how relieved you'll feel that you aren't responsible for carting fifty garbage bags of winter garments from the park back to the high school so they can be picked up." He flashed her a devastating grin and Ms. Friendly fluffed her *very married* hair in appreciation.

Eden narrowed her eyes at Davis, but he only winked.

Moving on, she scanned the agenda he'd printed. "I think that's everything. We've got the chicken corn soup covered, the canned good pick-up scheduled, and all volunteers have been added to the email list and Facebook group." She checked off each item with the zest of a list lover. And he found it incredibly sexy.

"Are there any questions?"

They fielded another ten minutes of questions that would be asked only in Blue Moon.

Can I bring my pet ferrets to the funnel cake stand?

Will there be a designated nudist area?

Will The Man be recording us with drones?

Nope. NO! And maybe. Just kidding.

The volunteers filed out of the room talking about charity and ferrets. "Nice job, partner," Davis said, raising a hand.

Eden slapped his palm. "We work well together, don't we?"

"Kind of makes you wish we'd have done all this sooner, doesn't it?"

"What, you mean burned your house down?"

"Har har." He nudged her toward the door. "I have a feeling this is going to be the best HeHa in the history of Blue Moon." It was time they had a talk. About what happened after revenge. About where they stood... together.

"So, listen," he began as she locked the door behind them.

But a ruckus interrupted them. Two conference room doors on opposite sides of the hallway were open.

"I need safety pins or else the whole world is going to see Bruce's butt cheeks," Ellery called over her shoulder as she barreled out of one room into the next.

"We're trying to make money, not get sued," Rainbow muttered under her breath as she followed Ellery. Instead of her usual boxy suit, Rainbow was wearing a long flowing skirt in purple and... pasties on her otherwise bare and ample bosom.

"Holy shit," Davis murmured. He'd intended only to turn around but rapped smartly into the wall instead.

"Oh, like you haven't seen your share of these," Rainbow said, rolling her eyes.

"What's uh... what's going on?" Eden asked, clearing her throat, looking everywhere but Rainbow's boobs.

"Oh! Eden! Davis! How lovely to see you," Bruce said, poking his head out of the second room. Bruce was wearing an olive wreath on his head and a very short Greek tunic that bared his chest and gapped over his ass. There was a large white screen set up behind him and a camera on a tripod. Nikolai Vulkov, Emma's husband and famed photographer, was sitting on a folding chair with his head in his hands.

"Oh, hey… Bruce. What's hanging? I mean jiggling. Shaking! What's shaking?" Eden asked in a strangled voice.

"Bruce, Amethyst's body paint is dry," Gordon announced wielding an airbrush. "Do you want to come see before her shots?"

"Please excuse me." Bruce sidestepped with dignity across the hall, accidentally flashing his ass to two librarians who were minding their own business shelving books.

"Uh, Niko," Davis called into the now empty room.

"I'm not looking up unless you promise me you're fully clothed," Niko said miserably.

"Fully clothed," Davis promised.

Warily, Niko raised his gaze.

"What the hell is going on?" Eden asked.

"I love my wife very, very much. That's what's going on," Niko said.

"Emma roped you into this?" Davis clarified, eyeing the props. Plates of grapes, gold chargers, an acoustic guitar.

He nodded. "It was some kind of emergency, according to Gia and Eva. They need to raise money. When they said a calendar, I didn't think it would be a barely concealed nudity calendar. I live here four days a week. How can I look these people in the eye ever again? Pasties on the bank president! I've been staring at Bruce's ass cheeks for the last thirty minutes!"

"They're trying to raise money with a nudey calendar?" Eden shot Davis a triumphant look.

"Something about budget concerns. Do you have liquor on you? I'll literally drink anything if it gets me through this," Niko begged.

"Sorry, man," Davis said, slapping Niko on the shoulder.

"I'll text Emma," Eden promised. "I'm sure she can send someone from the brewery."

"Please hurry. I have to shoot my sisters-in-law dressed as mermaids next. I've shot naked super models painted in oil on an airfield in Paris. I don't think I can do this."

"We'll send help," Davis promised lamely as Eden towed him toward the door.

"Let's get out of here before we see Gordon's junk—Oh God. Never mind."

They raced down the hall in the direction of the atrium and away from Gordon Berkowicz's skinny form.

"The Beautification Committee claims another innocent victim," Eden giggled over her shoulder when they hit the stairs.

Davis dashed down the stairs behind Eden wondering if they'd just gotten an even better revenge than they could have planned.

43

They laughed to the point of hysteria the whole way home.

Davis wiped his eyes as Eden maneuvered the inn's twisting drive. "I'm going to say it. Seeing Bruce like that was worth a burned-down kitchen. I feel avenged."

Eden laughed. "I honestly didn't think they'd take things this far. I almost wish we would have gotten a peek at Amethyst's body paint."

"We'll see it in the calendar."

The inn loomed before them, and Chewy and Vader romped toward the car. Eden parked, and together they skirted the side of the building and entered through the kitchen, the dogs on their heels.

"Did you two have a good time?" Davis asked, ruffling first Chewy's fur and then Vader's. Vader wasn't playing as hard to get anymore where Davis was concerned. She leaned into his leg and stared adoringly up at him. Eden had to concede the point that her dogs adored her former mortal enemy.

"I've got a bottle of champagne stashed in your fridge. If you feel like celebrating," Davis said, eyes on Eden.

"I just might have two slices of apple pie hidden in the pantry," she said, raising an eyebrow at him.

"You've never been sexier."

"You just want me for my baked goods," she teased.

"That's a reason. But not the only one." Davis's words hung between them like she could reach out and touch them.

Eden cleared her throat. "Let's celebrate our victory with spoils."

They snuck through the lobby with glasses and plates. Behind the desk, Sunny had her earbuds in and was singing so enthusiastically that she missed them slink past her.

Still giggling, Eden let them into her room and closed the door. "So, how does it feel to make the Beautification Committee dance like a puppet?" Eden asked.

Davis popped the cork on the champagne, and Eden remembered the bright joy she'd felt the last time they'd shared a glass. The happiness on Eva and Donovan's faces as they made their announcement. The shared love around the table. *Family. Future.*

And here they were toasting revenge. It didn't quite have the same golden glow.

"If they didn't still owe me a kitchen, I'd be willing to call it quits right here and now," Davis announced, pouring her a frothy glass.

"What *are* you going to do if the insurance company doesn't come through?" Eden asked.

He shrugged. "Well, obviously the naked calendar will go viral, and the Beautification Committee will be able to pay me back in no time."

Eden laughed. "That's very optimistic of you."

"How could it not be a huge money-maker with Bruce Oakleigh's ass?"

"I'll never un-see those cheeks," Eden predicted. "But if

the nudey calendar is a flop—pun intended—what will you do?"

"I've got retirement savings as a last resort," he told her, draining his glass.

She winced. "I hope the insurance money will come through."

"Me, too." He refilled both their glasses. "Would you miss me?"

"You're my next-door neighbor," she hedged.

He twined his fingers with hers. "I'm asking if you would miss seeing me every day."

She sipped, the bubbles tart on her tongue. "I've grown somewhat accustomed to seeing your face," she said airily. "As well as the rest of your body."

"What would you say if I told you I didn't want this to end?"

Every muscle in her body went rigid. Her seventeen-year-old self had fantasized about this moment, or its teenage equivalent, about seven million times. Her adult self had spent years building walls around her heart so it would never happen.

"I'd say that you were blinded by Rainbow's ta-tas," she said lightly.

He swiveled on the couch to face her. "Eden. I'm serious." Handsome. Earnest. Hopeful.

She took a hasty gulp of champagne and wondered why it burned her throat.

"Why can't we make this work?" he asked.

How could this be happening? They'd united with the express purpose of exacting revenge on the Beautification Committee, not proving those Cupid-complex imbeciles right.

She shook her head. "Look, Davis. It's nothing personal,

but we *can't* work. We've got fifty years of bad blood between us."

"Don't you think it's time we put a stop to a half-century of idiocy?" Davis demanded. "How many people have told us how relieved they are that we've 'changed our town's karma' by not fighting like our parents and grandparents?"

"That's *not* a reason to be in a relationship, Davis."

"Agreed. But to you, it's a reason *not* to be in one."

Eden sputtered. She wasn't prepared to argue this. They'd both known the score. There was no future for them.

"That's not the only reason. It's just the obvious one."

"Fine. What are the less obvious reasons?" he demanded.

Eden was silent for a long minute.

He grabbed her hand, squeezed it. "You feel it. I know you do. We work, Eden."

She let out a long sigh. "I'm not looking for someone right now." The words sounded lame.

"You don't have to be looking to find something," Davis insisted. "I love being with you. You're smart. You run a crazy successful business that you're obsessed with. You're so beautiful sometimes it hurts my eyes to look at you. You make me laugh. It's gotten to the point where I can't wait to talk to you about my day, about your day. We may have started this as a fake relationship, but what we've got now is real. And I know you feel it, too."

Eden squirmed in her seat. "I *do* have feelings for you," she said, choosing her words carefully. "I can see us being... friends. But how would us staying together teach the Beautification Committee anything? They'd see it as a victory and just line up the next victims, start their next fire."

Davis's jaw clenched and released. "That's your priority?"

"It's *our* priority! That's what started this whole thing. I don't want to quit until we've achieved what we set out to do.

Teaching them not to meddle in people's lives. We're saving an entire town from well-intentioned arson."

"I get that. Just like I get that you're looking at this as a way to kind of rewrite your own history."

"That's *not* what I'm doing," she argued. *It was exactly what she was doing.* But he owed her. Because of him, she'd spent her entire adulthood thus far trying to prove herself to an entire town who was content to think of her as a vindictive teenage arsonist.

It was her turn to have people like her, appreciate her, believe in her. And if that was selfish of her, then so what?

"Eden, who really wins in that scenario? I still won't have my house rebuilt. You'll be a victim in the eyes of the whole town. And the Beautification Committee will implode after one blemish on their record. But, if we give us a real shot, don't we both win? We have something here." He lifted her hand to his mouth, kissed her knuckles.

"You haven't thought this through," Eden began. "Things are complicated. Do you want to reward the Beautification Committee for pulling strings and setting fires? Do you want to bitterly disappoint your parents? Because I'm guessing that my parents are a walk in the park compared to yours. And what if I say yes? What if I'm all in, and then your parents come home and you change your mind?"

"I was eighteen, Eden. I was stupid and immature. I know better now."

She sat up straighter. "Do you? You tiptoe around your father every day. Planting secret grapes, lying to him to protect his fragile health, banking good ideas for the one day that he might be open to hearing them. You're no better at standing up to your parents now than you were at eighteen."

Davis looked down at their joined hands and slowly withdrew his. The abandonment hurt her heart. But he had to hear her.

"Can they recover from the disappointment, the betrayal? Could we? Because I know what will happen. If you choose me now, our families will find a way to make us regret it. And eventually, we'll resent each other for it. Am I worth hurting your family over?" She took a deep breath, let it out slowly. "Because I don't know if you're worth hurting mine."

His jaw clenched. He needed to understand. This wasn't the plan. They weren't in the cards.

"If that's what you want," he said flatly.

"It's what *we* want," she said, hating the fact that she missed his touch already.

"So, we're breaking up," he said, leveling a long look at her.

"It's not like we have to go back to being mortal enemies after HeHa. I mean, we've already done that," she joked.

"Right. Ha."

"And there's no reason why we can't continue enjoying... the status quo until next week," she ventured.

"Actually, I don't think that's a good idea. One of us is obviously more attached to the status quo than the other. And if you don't see a future for us, I don't see a present." He stood abruptly.

She scrambled to her feet after him. "What about HeHa? What about the... plan?" She felt like an asshole even asking.

"Don't worry. By this time next week, you'll have everything you wanted," he said grimly. "Good night, Eden."

Davis Gates was too good to even slam the door, Eden thought, as it quietly clicked shut behind him. She'd rejected him, insulted him, and then reminded him she still needed to use him as a tool for revenge. And he was too damn gracious to even slam her door.

Where was this tightness in her chest coming from? They

were a *team*. They had a *goal*. They couldn't just give up now. Not when she was this close to having every wrong in her life righted. It wasn't fair of him to ask her to give it all up.

Shit.

She sank back down on the couch and picked up one of the happily bubbling glasses of champagne that taunted her. She'd gone from celebrating a victory to drowning her sorrow.

44

It was the second skillet of eggs she'd charbroiled. But Eden couldn't really rouse herself to care as she scraped the burnt mess into the trashcan. Even Chewy turned his never-discerning nose up at the pan.

She dumped the pan into the sink and shoved her hands into her hair, mindful of the headache that had been her only companion recently. It had been three days. Three miserable days since she'd told Davis they had no future. And then he'd gone and got all righteous on her, claiming that they had no present.

"Just what exactly was wrong with enjoying our time together?" she asked Vader. The dog looked at her brother and back to Eden. "I mean seriously. What kind of a future did he expect? We *agreed*. We had a *deal*."

Chewy backed himself into the pantry and feigned sudden hearing loss.

"Oh, sure. Go ahead and avoid me, too." Eden's flailing hand bumped the pitcher of utensils sending serving spoons and spatulas flying.

Davis was avoiding her. Every morning he left—or more

accurately, snuck out—while she was cooking breakfast, and he didn't return until late at night. He responded to her HeHa texts and emails tersely, ignoring the invitations to snack time and quiet nights in the library by the fire. She hadn't worked up the nerve to ask him to be seen with her in public to remind the Beautification Committee what a "great" job they'd done with the pairing that was about to explode.

He was sending her a message. They now had a business-only relationship, something that up until recently Eden would have been happy with.

"I don't know why everyone's acting like this is my fault," she continued to the empty room. "What was wrong with getting a little enjoyment out of our situation?" She wielded a set of tongs in the air, trying to find the mad that had gotten her through Day One. But mad had given way to something murkier, more desolate.

She missed him.

Her bed, a perfectly comfortable sanctuary pre-Davis, was now an infinite wasteland of sleeplessness and memories of orgasms past.

"How does that even work? We've only been together a few weeks, and that was in a fake relationship!" Davis had no right to deprive her of sleep. Everything was essentially the same as it had been prior to the stink bomb. She'd been happy then, hadn't she? And, if it had all been fine then, why wasn't it fine now?

"Because I miss him," she confessed to no one.

That suit-wearing, grape-smushing, sexy picture-drawing man had gotten into her head. And quite possibly her heart. The inn was tainted with memories, both sexy and sweet. It was unforgiveable. Turning her home, her business, into an altar at which to mourn the death of a relationship that was never supposed to be real.

"It was all supposed to be fake!" she railed.

"We're too late. She's screaming at her kitchen cabinets." Layla ambled in wearing running tights and a hooded sweatshirt liberated from a long-forgotten college boyfriend.

Sammy yawned her way through the swinging door in sweatpants and a cozy tunic sweater. "Told ya we should have come yesterday."

"What are you guys doing here at six o'clock in the morning?" Eden asked wearily. She didn't have a meal for her own guests, let alone food to feed her constantly hungry friends.

"Saving your guests from blackened eggs." Layla wrinkled her nose at the ruined breakfast remains.

"Supporting our friend in her time of need," Sammy countered, tossing two bags of store-bought biscuits on the counter.

"What. Are. Those," Eden demanded. Not-from-scratch biscuits were never welcome at her inn.

Layla pushed her down on a stool. "Sit. I'm on coffee." She bustled over to the coffee center, starting a thermos for the guests and a pot for the kitchen.

"I'll make the gravy." Sammy dunked Eden's skillet into the sink and scrubbed at the mess.

"Gravy? What the hell is going on?"

The dogs—sensing nice, normal, friendly people—tap danced out of the pantry to join the fun.

"We're making sausage gravy and biscuits for your guests before you turn anyone else off with your fruit and stale bagels like yesterday," Sammy explained. "It was the talk of the town."

Eden laid her head in her hands and moaned.

Layla put a mug of coffee in front of Eden. "Spill it."

Eden looked down at the mug.

"Not the coffee. You and Davis."

Eden sighed mightily. "Our pretend relationship is now

one-hundred percent pretend. And even that will come to an end at HeHa when we rub the Beautification Committee's noses in their failure."

"Isn't that what you wanted?" Sammy asked innocently, drying the skillet with a dish towel.

"Yes. At least I thought so, but we had this fight."

"Did it involve makeup sex?" Layla asked.

"No, and apparently that's the problem."

"Davis didn't like being used for some no strings attached fun?" Sammy surmised.

"I wasn't using him," Eden argued, though the allegation sat in her belly like a tray of ice cubes. "We had a deal. This was just temporary. Pretend. We were going to get our revenge and go our separate ways."

"You're still getting your revenge," Layla pointed out, watching Sammy dump two pounds of sausage into the buttered skillet.

"Yeah, but Davis is barely speaking to me," she said miserably.

"I thought that's what you wanted," Sammy reminded her. "Didn't you just want to go back to the way things were before the fire?"

"I know what you two are doing," Eden said darkly. Vader put her big head in Eden's lap, her tail swishing. Eden stroked a hand over her dog's smiling face.

"And?" Sammy prodded.

"And you're right, and I'm wrong, but that doesn't change anything," Eden insisted.

"Let's go back to the part about us being right," Layla suggested.

"So maybe I got a little attached to Davis," Eden sighed. "It was bound to happen, what with all the awesome sex and that time that he sketched me."

Sammy spun away from the stovetop. "He sketched you? Like *Titanic* sketched you?"

Eden nodded.

"God. That's so hot," Layla groaned.

"Yeah, well now things are pretty iceberg-y between us."

"So, he wanted more, and you didn't," Sammy prodded.

They'd been over the big picture on the phone two days ago, squeezing in a video call between animal appointments, small town disturbances, and guest needs.

"It's not that I don't want more," Eden hedged. "It's just I don't see how more is possible. My parents hate him. More importantly his parents hate me. He's not a rebel, guys. He's a go-along to get-along kind of guy. And while that works in a lot of situations, it doesn't make for a good romantic relationship. He already dumped me once for them."

"Eden, he was eighteen. No guy is lady-smart at that age," Layla pointed out.

Eden's thoughts turned back to their conversations. The concessions Davis made to his father, the sneaking around, the bypassing, the biding his time. Why would that Davis suddenly decide to draw the line and take a stand now?

She put her head down on the counter. "I have so many feelings." And none of them were good. Her watch vibrated on her wrist.

Mom: Are you done dating that doofus yet? I want to make sure I'm there to witness the big breakup!

Eden groaned.

"So, what's the actual problem here?" Layla asked, popping the biscuits into the microwave.

"The problem is I don't know what I want," Eden told her. Which was a lie. She knew what she wanted, but it wasn't possible. Davis Gates would never defy his parents to be her happily ever after.

"Well, you've tried mortal enemies, and you've tried hot and steamy bed buddies," Sammy said. "Why don't you try being friends?"

"Friends?" Eden repeated. The word felt funny in her mouth. Were the feelings she had wrapped up around Davis friendly? Or were they much, much more?

45

"Next, we're going to take a little of the green and a little of the blue and mix them together on your palette." Davis demonstrated, holding his palette up so his students could see.

Aretha, a skinny woman in her fifties who had narrowly avoided assault charges stemming from a fight she started at the bookstore during last month's astrological apocalypse, raised her empty wine glass.

The tasting room attendant, Coriander, a helpful pink-haired college dropout, hurried over with a new bottle of Pinot Grigio. The dry run for Blue Moon Winery's paint night wasn't very dry. The class had already put away four bottles, and they were only twenty minutes into the class.

"Good," Davis said, even though half of his students had mixed the wrong colors. Following instructions wasn't Blue Moon's strong suit. Residents didn't like anything that challenged their creative freedom. Which was why twenty-two women and Fitz were abstractly slathering acrylics on canvas. Davis had considered a step-by-step landscape or even the standard bowl of fruit. But there was something satisfying about turning everyone loose on their own blank canvases with minimal direction. "Now, try out that fan brush in the shade you just created."

He put his palette down, picked up his wine, and strolled down the first line of tabletop easels. They'd reconfigured the long tasting tables into stations fit for amateur painters.

Kicking off yet another venture hadn't been on his to do list. Not with the fire, the winery, the HeHa Festival, and then, of course, Eden's sudden claim that the feelings he knew she was feeling weren't real...

Something had happened, a head injury or perhaps a visit from the ghost of feuds past, and the woman was suddenly hellbent on being his friend.

She'd been leaving little breakfast sandwiches wrapped in paper bags outside his room every morning. Texting him funny pictures of the dogs. Leaving candies on his pillow like she did for the rest of her guests. And she'd insisted on planning the winery's first paint class.

She was the one who had found the bulk discount art supplies online and the one who posted about it in the town's Facebook group. And now that same crazy woman was currently glaring at her canvas in the next row between her friends Sammy Ames and Eva Cardona.

It was her consolation prize for him, Davis assumed. She'd turned him down flat, claiming no interest in a relationship beyond their current arrangement that was due to end in three days. So here, have a paint night.

Unfortunately for her, Davis wasn't interested in a consolation friendship or her pity art class. He'd been busy avoiding her rather than seeking her out. He'd missed every Snack Time and breakfast this week, and when she'd come knocking on his door two nights ago, he'd pretended he was in the middle of a conference call. So she'd organized this whole thing as a sort of apology. An olive branch. A friendship bracelet.

And he wasn't biting.

The look she was shooting him now, the one he was studiously ignoring, singed him. She was as miserable as he was. Davis was sure of it. And they were still supposed to put on the "happy couple" face for the Beautification Committee until HeHa. That happy couple face might be the death of him.

A glance over Freida Blevins's shoulder showed Davis the violent swath of turquoise she was working across her canvas. "Nice job, Freida," he offered.

"I'm a natural," she insisted, shimmying her shoulders, silver cactus earrings dancing from her lobes.

Mrs. Nordemann worked her paint brush with a rigid wrist and the tip of her tongue peeking out of the corner of her unpainted lips. Near as Davis could tell, she was painting the Grim Reaper in a sea of morbid purples. But the reaper was smiling, and so was Mrs. Nordemann.

He continued his rounds, offering advice and compliments until he got to Eden's row. He didn't even care about revenge at this point. The whole thing felt like one big loss. They'd all have been better off if the Beautification Committee had left them alone.

What was upsetting him now was the fact that Eden honestly believed that he wouldn't take a stand for what he wanted. That he wouldn't stand up to his parents. Which was ridiculous. He was a grown man and—

The thought stopped him mid-stride. Reality—and Elvira Eustace's fuchsia and tangerine masterpiece—punched him in the face, searing his eyes with the technicolor truth.

When *had* he stood his ground?

When had he fought for... *anything*?

Eden hadn't been insulting his manhood. She'd been citing an observation, and if Davis couldn't be counted on to stand up to his father when it came to grapes and wine labels, how could he be counted on to stand up for her?

He stopped behind her, drawn to the familiar scent of her shampoo. It twisted the knife in his gut. The way her shoulders tightened, he knew she could sense him behind her. Davis saw the prickle of goose bumps on her neck above the collar of her silky, sheer blouse.

"How does it look?" she asked shyly, never taking her eyes off of her canvas.

Davis couldn't resist. He leaned in, his chest brushing her back. She tensed against him, then relaxed, remembering their pretext. Her canvas was a tangle of darkness. Navies, purples, and grays warred over the white in bold brushstrokes. One didn't have to guess what was on her mind. Turmoil. Doubt.

And it gave Davis great satisfaction. Eden Moody might not be ready to admit her feelings for him, but she couldn't keep them out of her painting.

"Very nice." He let his lips brush the curve of her ear. She dropped her paintbrush with a clatter on the table, drawing eyes.

His blood emptied out of his head in a mad rush to his rapidly hardening erection. This was the other reason he'd been avoiding her. He couldn't control his impulses around her. It would be too easy to fall back into her bed while she talked friendship and he felt more. Much more.

And Eden felt it, too. She just had to believe in him. And it was up to him to give her a reason to believe.

He left her staring after him and strolled further down the aisle, a smirk on his lips. He felt fifty pounds lighter.

For the first time in his life, Davis knew what he wanted.

And he wasn't going to let anyone stand in his way. Now, he just needed a plan.

"Excuse me, Davis?" Kathy Wu waved him down. "We were all just wondering when you're scheduling the nude painting class."

Davis had the misfortune of a swallow of wine going down the wrong pipe. "I beg your pardon?" he coughed.

Fitz raised his hand, his tight waffle weave shirt unbuttoned to his sternum. "If you're not interested in posing, I can make myself available for a small fee."

46

"Those are my terms." Davis said. He was sitting cross-legged on the red velvet floor cushion in Gia Pierce's darkened yoga studio. Not exactly neutral ground, but if he wanted to make this deal, concessions had to be made. Plus, Eden would flay the skin from his bones if she knew what he was doing.

His plan was... well, complicated. And it involved asking the enemy for help.

Ellery stared at him for almost a full thirty seconds in silence, her lips painted what looked like a navy blue tonight giving her pale skin a bluish tint. "I'd like to consult with my colleague," she said finally.

Davis raised his palms. "By all means."

Ellery ducked her pigtailed head toward Eva's red curls. Eva had worn head-to-toe black in honor of their covert meeting. Top secret, back yoga room negotiations with the enemy called for stealthy wardrobe.

They'd recovered quickly after Davis had dropped the bomb on them. He knew what they'd done. What they were responsible for. What they owed him. And then he told them exactly what *he* owed them.

To their credit, neither woman dissolved into tearful groveling. They were smart enough to admit nothing.

They whispered to each other for an interminably long time. Long enough for him to braid several of the tassels on his meditation cushion.

"Okay," Ellery said stoically. "We accept your terms."

"With the addition of a few of our own," Eva added.

Davis narrowed his eyes. "Tell me."

"We want the credit, of course," Ellery began.

Davis twirled a braided tassel, considering. "If you've earned it, you'll have it."

Ellery rolled her eyes. "None of this would have happened if we hadn't matched you two," she reminded him. "You'd still be all by your lonesome at the winery while your next-door neighbor avoided you for the rest of your life. She would have eventually met and married someone else, and you would have had no idea how good you two would be together."

"Yeah, and I'd still have my kitchen," Davis pointed out.

"I'm sure whoever is responsible for that unfortunate accident feels terrible," she said through gritted teeth.

"Hypothetically speaking, whoever is specifically responsible may have run off the rails without the knowledge or permission of his—or her—fellow committee members... I mean friends," Eva added. "I'd hate for you to think that all of his or her friends would have ever in a million years even entertained—"

"Such an asinine idea," Ellery finished for her. "One that I'm sure whoever is broadly responsible is working tirelessly to correct.

Davis sighed and stopped fiddling with the tassels. "I apologize. I didn't come here to rub anyone's noses in their flammable mistakes. Whether you're responsible or not."

Ellery nodded. "Understood. And I'm sure *no one* meant to cause such extensive damage given the fact that all any smart matchmaking person needed to do was get you and Eden near each other and nature would take its course."

"That was the whole plan?" Davis asked.

Ellery and Eva nodded. "Not every plan is super complex. You guys have a whole history of sparks—forgive the pun. We knew if we could get you around each other temporarily those feelings would explode."

"You're truly diabolical people," Davis sighed.

Ellery beamed as if he'd given her a compliment. "We have a lot of experience in matters of the heart. Now, let's get back to business."

Eva nodded. "Okay. So, you have to promise not to make any copies or distribute this information that we give you to anyone under penalty of serious punishment," Eva added.

He was more than curious what kind of serious punishment the Beautification Committee could dole out. But after the stink bombing, he wasn't willing to find out.

"Uh. Agreed."

"You also have to promise that you won't ever hint at who might be responsible for that thing that I'm not mentioning in order not to incriminate any of my acquaintances," Ellery said, her eyes wide.

"Getting half the town arrested for arson does not serve me," Davis told them.

Ellery jerked her chin toward Eva's bag. "Give him the book."

Eva handed over a neatly bound notebook and interlaced her fingers in her lap. "Now that that's over. Let's talk strategy."

"If you'll turn to page five in our Eden Moody dossier, you'll find a list of her motivating factors," Ellery began.

"Wow." Davis was impressed and concerned. "Do you have one of these on me?"

"It's probably better if we just focus on Eden for now," Eva suggested.

"Is all of this going to cause a problem with you and your husband?" Davis asked her.

She flushed and placed a hand over her stomach. "This isn't a literal get out of jail free card, but I think with your idea and this little bundle of joy, we'll all be good."

"And the Beautification Committee will never commit another arson again," Davis prompted.

"We'll certainly try our hardest," Ellery promised brightly. "Now, let's look at Eden's rebellious tendencies. I feel like this could be the key."

Eden Moody, you are cordially invited to an emergency meeting of the Beautification Committee at 7 p.m. tonight. Emergency attendance is mandatory.

47

"What are you doing here?" Eden asked, spotting Davis on the library steps. *And why did he have to be so good-looking?* He was still dressed in what she'd come to think of as his winery "uniform"—slacks with a crisp button down, and today he'd added a vest. Lord, that vest.

Wordlessly, he held up a notecard like the one she'd received that morning.

"Do you have any idea what this is about?" she asked. With the exception of the handful of HeHa organizational meetings they'd hosted and a very strained paint night, Davis had avoided her like she was a sticky toddler in need of a nap since "the talk."

He shrugged. "Not really."

She wasn't sure if it was the winter air or Davis's obvious disinterest that chilled her more under her vegan leather jacket.

She jogged up the steps behind him. "So how was work today?" she asked. Was it weird that she missed talking to him about work and business and life? No. Normal people who weren't sleeping together could talk about regular things, couldn't they?

"It was fine," he said, holding the door for her.

He couldn't even slam it in her face like a jerk. Like she would have been tempted to do if their roles were reversed. *Damn polite bastard.*

"How was your day?" he asked, falling into step next to her.

"It was... entertaining. The Magnolia twins—have you met them, yet?"

He shook his head and waved at the librarian behind the desk.

"Well, they're celebrating their fiftieth birthdays and a divorce, and they got into an argument in the hallway with Mr. and Mrs. Hadad over—get this—80s hair bands."

"Mmm," he said, gesturing for her to go ahead of him on the stairs to the second floor.

"Yeah, the Magnolias are huge fans of Cinderella, and the Hadads felt that Def Leppard was a better representation of the best of the 80s." She was blabbering, nerves overtaking her mouth and making it work like a ventriloquist's dummy. And she couldn't stop the words from vomiting forth. "I'm thinking there's some leftover astrological apocalypse vibes going on. It could explain a lot of things."

"You mean, like us?" His tone was neutral, almost friendly. But the connection they'd shared was painfully absent. It was like chatting with a next-door neighbor. *Not* a man who had brought her to orgasm on the tasting room floor at midnight.

Rather than letting her answer, Davis rapped his knuckles on the conference room door and opened it at the brisk, "Come in."

They filed into the room. The full committee was in attendance and looking somber. Bruce, in a snowflake embroidered sweater vest, gestured toward two folding chairs at the front of the room. The whiteboard had been wiped nearly clean. No more Eden + Davis = Love. The only thing that was left was the fundraising bar graph filled in to $250.

Gingerly, Eden sat and crossed her arms over her chest. Nerves skated through her veins. Eva and Gia were avoiding eye contact with her, but Ellery offered her a sad smile and a little wave.

Gordon and Rainbow were, thankfully, dressed. Wilson and Bobby had their heads together over a committee binder. Amethyst looked as though she were stress-eating a cupcake.

"Eden and Davis," Bruce began. "It is with a heavy heart that I inform you that your match has been canceled."

"Canceled?" Eden repeated. Davis had no reaction next to her.

"Yes. I'm afraid it's come to our attention that this is no longer a fit match, and we cannot in good conscience proceed. To do so would be..."

"Disastrous," Ellery filled in.

Bruce nodded, his shoulders slumped. He pulled a handkerchief from his pants pocket and blew his nose noisily.

What did this mean? Had she won? What about the public breakup? The plan? Eden's mind was a whirl of confusion.

She raised a tentative hand. "May I ask what prompted this decision?" *What did it even matter?* The Beautification Committee no longer had a perfect record. And she was free of Davis Gates.

"I'm not at liberty to discuss committee business," Bruce hedged.

Bobby rolled her eyes. "Oh, for Pete's sake! Eden, do you love Davis?"

Did orgasms and friendship equal love? What? No! She was

losing her damn mind. Just being next to him was confusing her.

"I do not," she said carefully. "But I don't hate him anymore. In fact, I think we've gotten to be quite friendly." Naked, thrusting, coming. That kind of friendly. That wasn't love. And neither were their quiet evenings in front of the fire talking about plans and taxes and guests and customers. It wasn't the way her heart flipped over in her chest when he smiled at her across a room or the way he took her hand in his.

No, love was something else. Wasn't it?

"There you have it," Bruce said, rubbing his eyes as if to ward off a migraine.

"You can't have a love match without love," Gordon waxed poetically.

"You both are free to go," Ellery announced.

"Wait. What happens now?" Eden asked, her mind spinning. Were there forms to sign? Apology gifts? She glanced at Davis who was looking at his watch.

"Nothing happens now," Bruce moaned.

"We'll make a public announcement in the next issue of *The Monthly Moon*," Wilson explained.

"Then we'll begin reviewing our matching process to see where we went wrong and if we'll be able to continue our services in the future," Gia said, her voice laced with regret.

Bruce stifled a sob. "Decades of hard work. Over."

"On the bright side, you go back to exactly the way things were before," Ellery said with a half-hearted smile.

Eden flinched.

"Thank you for your efforts," Davis said formally, rising from his chair. His gaze returned to Eden, and she blushed furiously. "See you at HeHa this weekend," he said.

"Wait!" Eden began. But she had nothing. "So, that's it? We're free to go?"

Davis nodded politely to the committee members and left the room. Eva and Gia looked at her, two sets of puppy dog eyes trained on her.

Eden rose, slinging her bag over her shoulder. She hadn't even needed to take off her jacket before being handed the victory she'd worked for.

"Um, I'm sorry it didn't work out," Eden said lamely and walked out of the silent room. She closed the door quietly behind her and leaned against it, wondering why she didn't feel victorious.

48

HeHa was here. All of Blue Moon turned out in One Love Park bundled up against the harsh December wind. It had snowed overnight, but four inches of the white stuff wasn't going to stop the town's population from an entire day of do-gooding.

They'd divided and conquered. Eden was in charge of the park festivities while Davis was off coordinating the volunteer teams at the high school. There were senior citizen walkways to shovel, leaky windows to seal, and watery hot chocolate to choke down.

Helping Hands Day was hands down—ha—Eden's favorite day of the year. Usually. The entire town mobilized to do their part, no matter how large or small, to make life a little better for someone else. Blue Moon was blanketed in good vibes... except for Eden.

She was mired in a sticky quicksand of regret, self-loathing, and general confusion. And it was all Davis's fault. She shook her head to clear the thought. It was a deeply ingrained habit to blame him for everything. This time, the bad mojo was all on her. Exactly what did she have to complain about? Davis had gone and given her everything she wanted, a Davis-free, Beautification Committee-free life.

Eden was back to pre-stink bombing. Except now she had the knowledge of what it felt like to come on Davis's hard cock while he whispered dirty little nothings in her ear. And she'd never experience that again. She told him what she'd wanted, and he'd delivered.

Only now she wasn't so sure that what she *thought* she wanted was what she *actually* wanted. This last week without him? Well, it had none of the shine of her pre-sex-with-Davis life. She had to face facts. Having sex with Davis, having *feelings* for Davis, had ruined her life.

"Can I sign up for the last two weeks in February?" Mildred, everyone's favorite liquor store clerk, dragged Eden's attention back to the present. The freezing cold, lonely present where her only concern was supposed to be signing up volunteers to cook food for townsfolk in need.

Mildred snorted when she looked at the month of August. "Mrs. Nordemann's going to have her hands full. The Merrill girls are both due right around then!"

Eden gave a half-laugh and thought of her friends starting families... in their healthy committed relationships. Well, if she ignored the fact that Eva was an accessory to arson and hadn't told her husband, yet. But they were building something *while* running successful businesses. *Was she missing out by focusing only on work? Did she want more?*

She pressed a hand to her fluttering belly through the layers of thermal and down.

"I expect you and Davis will be joining in on the baby train," Mildred said cheerily. "Oh! There's Mervin Lauter. Yoo hoo!" Mildred scampered off to torture someone else with offhanded comments about their life choices.

Word hadn't spread yet, and Eden didn't blame the Beautification Committee for being slow to admit their first spectacular loss. She hadn't felt like sharing the news herself. It was a far cry from the gloating she'd planned on doing had it all gone to plan.

The Beautification Committee's loss didn't feel like her win. Eden tried to tell herself it was because she was cheated out of the big public breakup with Davis taking one for the team and finally being the bad guy. She'd been counting on the vindication. But that didn't explain the emptiness she felt every time she lay down in her bed... alone.

The fact was, they were all losers in this situation.

The B.C. failed at a match. Davis was still out of a kitchen. And Eden was... so damn lonely without Davis Gates.

Eden rubbed her gloved hands over her face. She'd used what happened in high school as a defining moment. And she's shaped her entire adult life around trying to prove to everyone that she wasn't that vengeful teenager. But look at what she'd done. Hadn't she just proven to herself that she was still that same wounded person?

She needed to talk it out. Needed to make sure she hadn't already made a huge mistake. Because right now, she was fairly certain she had.

"Damn it," she whispered to herself and then flashed an apologetic smile to Maizie, the waitress at Peace of Pizza, and her boyfriend, Benito, as they flipped through the calendar.

"Everything okay?" Maizie asked her.

"Good. Great. Really good," Eden insisted. She whipped out her phone, intending to text Sammy or Layla. But the wallpaper on her screen halted her fingers. It was Davis on the floor in front of the fire in the library. He was reading while her dogs snuggled up against him.

"Oh my God. I love him." It hit her like a bat connecting

with a piñata. This feeling. This gross, unsettled, yearning in her belly was *love*.

Maizie and Benito looked at her sideways. When in the hell had she fallen in love with Davis? A hundred memories flooded through her. Davis winking at her from his locker. Washing her dishes. Threatening Anthony Berkowicz. Bringing her to orgasm the way only a man who loved a woman could.

She was an idiot. A huge, stubborn, ridiculous idiot who wanted to be right more than she wanted to be happy.

Layla appeared, looking serious in her uniform. "Excuse me, folks. I need to borrow Eden for some police business."

"She didn't set the Gateses' yard on fire, deputy. Didn't you see *The Monthly Moon*?" Maizie insisted.

"Technically, she still could have set Davis's kitchen on fire," Benito pointed out. "That one hasn't been solved yet."

Maizie threw an elbow into her boyfriend's ribs.

"Noted," Layla said, dragging Eden out from behind the table, through the do-gooding crowd, and behind the homemade preserve collection tent.

"Are you okay? You look like you're going to pass out," Eden observed.

"I jogged here from the police station."

"I can see the police station from here," Eden pointed out, looking at the brick façade not two-hundred yards away.

"Shut up. I had like three funnel cakes, and I'm still full from Thanksgiving," Layla wheezed. "Listen, I have news on an investigation that I shouldn't be telling you about."

Eden grabbed her friend's hand in a death grip. "You're not going to set me up like that and then not tell me, are you?"

"I *can't* tell you," Layla insisted, shooting a furtive look over both shoulders.

"Do not make me stuff a fourth funnel cake in your pretty face," Eden threatened. "Is this even remotely important?"

"This directly affects you. Since it involves your ex-boyfriend and him moving out of your inn and back into his house," Layla hissed.

"What?" Eden gasped. If Davis moved out of the inn, her shot at winning him back went with him. He was so mad at her, he'd probably erect a security fence between their properties. "This is terrible!"

"A few weeks ago, you couldn't wait to kick his ass out," Layla complained.

"That was before I realized I loved him!"

"Crap! There goes my twenty bucks. I never should have bet on anything with an astrological apocalypse going on."

"I will give you twenty bucks if you tell me why Davis is moving out!"

"Okay, okay. Chill out with your talons," Layla said, carefully removing Eden's gloved hand from her arm. She looked over both shoulders, her blue eyes wide and sugared up. "Listen. You didn't hear this from me, but the insurance company paid up. Or they will."

"How? When did this happen?" Everything was going to go back to exactly the way it had been pre-stink bomb. And that wasn't good enough anymore.

"Would you mind putting your hands in your pockets? If you're not trying to saw through my parka with your nails, you're gesturing like a wild woman."

"Layla!"

"Okay! Apparently even arsonists are feeling the HeHa Spirit. The sheriff got this note. It was a confession."

"The Beautification Committee confessed?" Eden hissed.

"Sort of. It wasn't signed, but Cardona has to be suspicious, right? He's not an idiot. So, with a confession—and probably a hunch that he might have to put his new bride and baby mama in jail—the sheriff decided the case was closed. He contacted the insurance company personally to let them know that Davis didn't have anything to do with it. Criminal mischief yadda yadda. Anyway, they're paying up."

Eden scrubbed her hands over her face. At least one of them was a winner. Davis would get to fix his house, and then everything would go back to normal...

"You look like you're sucking on a lemon," Layla observed.

"I do not."

"Huh. Coulda fooled me. Anyway, I'll see you at the dance tonight."

Eden wasn't going to the dance. Heart-broken women didn't dance. They stayed home, hugging the pillow that still smelled like their fake ex, and beat themselves up for being idiots.

49

"Show of hands. Who's mapping the sidewalk wear?" Davis was at the high school organizing the second wave of volunteer crews while Eden maintained order in the park.

A ragtag group of winter-wear clad individuals raised mittened hands.

"Great. All we need to know is where the walkways need repairing on the north side of the park between Patchouli and Lavender streets. Take note of the closest address and document with pictures of the issue if possible."

A half-dozen colorful hatted heads nodded. They'd had so many volunteers this year that Davis and Eden had—separately—put their heads together with Beckett Pierce to come up with a few new tasks. Including sending people out to document sidewalk cracks.

They were desperate.

Davis consulted his tablet. "Okay, that just leaves the work crew for the high school sheep shelter." Blue Moon High saved money on landscaping by using grazing sheep on the school's lawns. The sheep lived like kings and queens in a small barn behind the football field.

Another seven or eight hands raised. "Head on up to the barn, and Huckleberry Cullen will set you up with cleaning supplies," Davis instructed them.

His group disbanded cheerfully, heading off to fulfill their civic duty.

He glanced at his watch, pleased that he still had some time before he needed to make his triumphant return to the park. Eden was going to be very surprised with what he had cooked up. And probably mad. But Davis had learned a thing or two in these past few weeks. And that was all her fault.

"Davis."

He felt the familiar tensing of his shoulders at the voice he knew as well as his own.

"Dad? What are you doing here?" Davis welcomed his father with a one-armed hug and a clap on the back.

Ferguson looked... good. Healthy, fit, tan. He was dressed casually—for Ferguson—in a cashmere coat over pressed jeans and a thick wool sweater. His silver hair and thick, archless eyebrows had recently enjoyed their monthly trim.

"I flew home early with Bryson and your mother. And it looks like not a moment too soon." He slapped *The Monthly Moon* into Davis's chest. "You owe us an explanation."

"I think that is the least of our problems," Davis said wryly.

"You may think so, but if you willingly got mixed up with a woman who tried to burn down your house, not once but twice, I can't help but question your judgment! By the way, we stopped by the winery first to leave our luggage. But your house *was burnt to the ground*!" he finished on a shout.

"I'm sorry for lying to you, Dad. I didn't want you to worry, and I thought I'd have it fixed by now. And you know as well as I do that Eden wasn't responsible for either fire, Dad."

"I know no such thing," Ferguson snapped, his cold words coming out in an icy cloud. "I know that she's trouble, and she's distracting you from your work. I left the winery in your hands, Davis. The family is counting on you."

The icy weight of responsibility and family expectations settled in Davis's gut with an uncomfortable familiarity. His father always made him feel like a noisy kid getting in trouble for having too much fun. Ferguson may have spent the last thirty-five or so years in Blue Moon, but no amount of peace, love, and nosiness could mellow the man.

"I'm aware of what's at stake, Dad."

His father shook his head sadly. "I knew you weren't ready to take the reins. I shouldn't have let myself be pressured into it."

"Don't confuse *your* inability to relinquish control with *my* business acumen," Davis said coolly.

"Acumen?" Ferguson's flat eyebrows winged up his forehead. "Is that what you call slipping unapproved grapes into the vineyard? Or this ridiculous painting class idea? Who comes to a vineyard to paint? We sell wine! You need to listen to me, Davis."

"And you *need* to let go." Davis's voice rang out across the now empty parking lot.

His father's jaw dropped. And Davis realized this was the first time he'd ever stood his ground with the man.

"I'm your son *and* your operations manager. But that doesn't mean that I'm a child or some irresponsible employee who wants to ruin everything you've built. I want to grow what you started. I want to put my mark on it, just like you did. And I want to live my life the way I see fit."

Ferguson sputtered.

"Dad," Davis said solemnly. "You built something great

here, and I want my chance at it. I'm tired of having both arms tied behind my back because you don't trust me."

Ferguson threw his hands up in the air. "How could I trust you when you continue to make bad decisions? That Moody girl—"

"Already told me I don't have a chance with her. But she's what I've been waiting my whole life for, Dad. There's a lot more to life than just work. Community, family, love. Maybe you need some reminding. Eden reminded me. She's smart, funny, brilliant at business. You'd be lucky to have her as part of the family."

"Part of the family?" Ferguson's face changed from a ruddy tan to beet red.

"Calm down," Davis warned him.

"Don't tell me to calm down! I'm sick of being told to calm down!"

"Your heart—"

"Is fine! I'm in the best damn shape of my life. Bryson has me eating vegetarian. Your mother hired me a personal trainer. And I meditate now!" he growled, obviously not thrilled with any of it.

"It's working so well for you," Davis said dryly.

"I'm tired of being treated like I'm an invalid."

"I'm tired of being treated like a child," Davis shot back. "I can't be *you* anymore than *you* could be *your* father. But if you can't trust me with the business you started, if you don't believe that I have the vineyard's and the family's best interests at heart, then maybe it's time that I follow in your footsteps and walk away."

It was a pot shot. But one his father needed to hear.

"I didn't *walk* away. I was forced out."

"Why? Because your father didn't think you had the family's best interests at heart?" Davis shot back.

"That's not fair, Davis."

Davis sighed, closed his eyes for a moment and felt the December sun on his face. "You know what's not fair? Me blaming you for keeping me from what I wanted. That's all on me. I'm responsible for my choices just like you're responsible for yours. Now, it's your turn to make a choice, Dad."

Davis took a breath and ignored the set of his father's jaw.

"I respect you, and I love you. And I will always be your son. But you need to decide if you want me running this business. Because I'm going to want to make changes, and some of those changes might someday involve Eden Moody. If I can wear her down and she can get out of her own damn stubborn way. So, you have to choose, let me run the winery or hire someone else who will do your bidding."

"What has this girl done to you?" Ferguson demanded.

Davis shook his head sadly. "You're missing out on so much, Dad."

"I don't need to be lectured by you, too. I've got Bryson doing enough of that."

Davis checked his watch, winced. "Maybe you should listen to one of us. Now, if you'll excuse me, I have someplace I need to be."

Walking away felt good. As did the fact that his father was still standing, not doubled over clutching his chest. One way or another, this was their new beginning.

~

Dear Sheriff Cardona,

We are writing to confess our role in the unfortunate and completely accidental fire at the home of Davis Gates. We are an innocent group of teenagers, only meaning to cause mischief with a silly stink bomb, and had no intentions of committing arson.

Please accept this confession in the good faith it was intended. We hope this absolves Mr. Gates of any wrongdoing. He was not in on our stink bombing plan.

We would also like to point out that if Blue Moon homeowners were required to install commercial sprinkler systems in their homes as the very intelligent and community-oriented Mr. Oakleigh recommended last year, the fire would have been immediately extinguished. Perhaps we should revisit this noble motion at the next town meeting?

Warmest Regards

A Pack of Regretful, Wayward Teenagers Who Have Learned Our Lesson

50

She was a gigantic idiot. She'd orchestrated her own unhappiness and refused a relationship with a man that she had L-word feelings for. Just to be right.

Eden paced the five steps in front of the volunteer meal booth over and over again. She looked at her watch. "Oh, God. I think I'm going to be sick."

"Did you eat as many funnel cakes as Layla?" Sammy, dressed in a bright red parka with a navy scarf wound around half her face, asked cheerfully.

"No. Much stupider. I pushed Davis away because I was convinced that I wanted revenge, not love. I made him break up with me because I didn't want to be with him, only to realize I'm in love with him and ruined everything."

"Well for shit's sake! It's about time you figured it out." Sammy slapped her on the shoulder.

"You knew?"

"Uh. Duh. Come on, E. One look at your heart eyes when you were together and then one look at your sad puppy face when you screwed it all up. Of *course* you're in love with him."

"I am the biggest, dumbest, jerkiest ass on the planet!"

"You're just stubborn. You've wanted to get back at him for so long, you couldn't see anything else but that. Not even the fact that he went out of his way to tell all of Blue Moon that they were wrong about you. Basically, you're making this all about five or ten minutes that happened fifteen years ago. And deep down, I think you know revenge won't make you happy."

"Why is everything you're saying right?" Eden wailed. She shoved her gloved hands into her hair, accidentally raking her hat from her head. "I set this whole thing up to blow up the Beautification Committee and prove to the whole town that Davis isn't this wonderful amazing guy. Only he *is,* and he wanted to give us a real try, and the stupid Beautification Committee *was* right about us... until I ruined it. They gave up on me. They gave up on me, Sammy. That's how much of a mess I am."

"Awh, babe." Sammy came in for a hug. "You're not a mess. You're human."

"I thought I was going to fix everything. Prove that *I* wasn't the bad guy. That Davis was. And then I could win the Business of the Year award, and my life as a contributing adult to Blue Moon could really start."

"You are a contributing adult. And people know that. I think you're the only one in town who still holds high school against you."

"Davis's parents hate me," Eden said, hating how whiny and weak she sounded. "He'd never be able to stand up to them over this. And I couldn't ask him to do it. I couldn't ask him to choose me over them. Not when I'm... such a mess of an adult. I'm no better now than when I was a teenager."

Sammy took her by the shoulders and gave her a good shake. "Eden Moody, you are going to get that stupid, shitty idea out of your head. Stop judging yourself on one mistake."

"I held a grudge for fifteen years!"

"One long mistake" Sammy corrected. "You are a smart, beautiful, kind-hearted, successful woman, and Davis Gates would be lucky to have you."

"But I don't know if he'd choose me," Eden said.

"You have to give him the chance. A real chance, not one of these fake bullshit chances with a pretend relationship and a revenge plot."

"How? How do I do it?"

Sammy shrugged. "I don't know." Then suddenly her eyes lit up. "Why not ask the Beautification Committee? They're sneaky smart."

"The Beautification Committee? That's ridicu—brilliant!"

Eden yanked her phone out of her pocket with so much enthusiasm it fell in the snow between them.

"Slow your roll, crazy town," Sammy said, plucking the phone off the ground.

"This is a disaster. This should have been an amazing day that everyone felt good about, and I had to ruin it," Eden muttered as she dialed. "Hello? Ellery? This is Eden. I made a huge mistake, and I need you to help me fix it. I love Davis."

"Oh, hey Eden," Ellery said, sounding not nearly as urgently excited as she should have in Eden's opinion.

"Help me fix this," Eden pleaded.

"Gosh, Eden. I don't know if there's anything I can do. Maybe you were right, and you two just aren't a good match? You should probably trust your gut."

"Ellery! We're a great match! We're perfect for each other. Or at least we will be as soon as I let go of the past and face the fact that I was totally wrong about him. I was wrong about everything. Help me!"

"Oh, Eden. I have to go. Mason needs something. We'll talk tonight at the dance," Ellery said cheerfully.

Eden stared at her phone. "I'm not going to the dance," she said to no one.

Sammy gave her an awkward pat on the shoulder. "Sorry, slugger."

"Well, well. If it isn't the latest generation of Moody riff-raff." Tilly Nuswing-Gates needed to work on her insults. She wore head-to-toe ivory, most likely special organic ringspun cotton. Her naturally graying hair was swept back from her pinched face in a classy twist. She looked exactly the way a wealthy, gracefully aging hippie with environmental leanings should look.

It was muffled by her scarf, but Eden thought she heard Sammy hiss.

"Mrs. Gates, I didn't know you were back in town. Davis hadn't mentioned that you would be back in time for HeHa."

"I'm sure there are a lot of things my son doesn't tell you," she said coolly. "Also, we didn't tell him we were coming."

In Blue Moon, even the villains weren't good at being bad.

"That could be a factor," Eden said carefully.

"My ex-husband is, as we speak, talking sense into our son. Which is what I'm doing with you. You and Davis do not belong together. The day your grandfather ran over my great-uncle's foot at the tractor pull put this all in motion. Our families are destined to be enemies."

"I'm sorry you feel that way," Eden said lamely. She wasn't prepared for a throw down with Tilly Nuswing-Gates. Not when she was already beating herself up.

"Well, I'm not sorry you're sorry," Tilly said primly.

"Wait, is that really what started it? I heard your mother locked my great-aunt in a pantry during a Christmas party."

Tilly scoffed. "That was in retaliation for your grandparents walking your screaming toddler aunt past their open windows every night at two a.m.

Eden vaguely remembered a story to that effect. "Don't you think this has gone on long enough?" Eden pressed.

"I am not going to bury the hatchet just so you can take advantage of my poor, sweet, kind-hearted, innocent son."

"Davis is an adult. And so am I. And if we choose to be together, there's nothing you can do about it." There was nothing *to* do about it. She'd already made the choice: a life without Davis.

"Over my dead body and possibly your father's since he can't survive without me!" Eden's mother was hauling ass down the sidewalk, her cheeks flushed pink with cold... or rage. "You and that, that, that... *heathen* are not to spend one more second of time together."

"We've spent a lot of time together. Naked. In your house." Eden said, stabbing her mother's buttons and hitting a few of her own in the process.

Lily Ann's gasp of betrayal nearly leveled her. Ned held her up, fanning her face. "I can't go back in that house," she shrieked dramatically.

"Don't worry, sweetheart. We'll just move. We'll move away from the bad mojo."

"Why don't you just have your daughter burn it down?" Tilly suggested smugly.

"Don't you tell my parents what to do," Eden said, waving a gloved finger at the woman.

"You and Davis do *not* belong together!"

"I couldn't agree more," Lily Ann shouted.

"See? Look at you two getting along," Sammy said cheerfully. "The feud is practically over. Yay."

Lily Ann and Tilly glared at each other for so long Eden wondered if they'd frozen in place.

"What's going on here?" Ferguson Gates jogged up with his handsome husband Bryson on his heels. "Tilly, don't waste your time talking to these people. They're incapable of a rational discussion."

"Ferguson!" Bryson laid a leather gloved hand on his husband's sleeve. "That's inappropriate."

"Your mother's incapable of a rational discussion," Eden's father puffed out indignantly.

"See?" Ferguson shot back.

"Frankly, sweetheart. It's true. Your mom can't discuss anything rationally," Bryson offered.

"I'm still insulted," Ferguson insisted.

"I don't care what that joke of a newspaper said, I know your daughter is responsible for our front yard and Davis's fire!" Tilly shouted at Eden's parents.

Anthony Berkowicz, who had been busy capturing the drama on his phone, gasped. "How could you say that, Mrs. Gates? It's in a newspaper. It *has* to be true."

"There is no reason to attack a well-respected institution such as *The Monthly Moon*," Rainbow Berkowicz said coldly. Eden thanked her lucky stars that, given the weather, the woman's breasts were buried under a heavy wool coat and several layers of peace sign scarf.

"Is there a problem here?" Sheriff Cardona, bundled up against the cold, pushed his way through the crowd.

Eden had had enough. "Everyone just stop it! *None* of this matters anyway. Davis and I are already broken up, so you can all just shut up and go on with your nasty little feud."

"Oh? Well, good. Why didn't you say so?" her mother demanded.

"Then our work here is done," Tilly announced, looking down her nose at Eden.

"I'm afraid it's true," Bruce Oakleigh said, pushing his way to the front of the crowd. "Eden and Davis are a failed match. We made a terrible mistake trying to pair them."

The crowd gasped.

"Bruce, it wasn't a terrible mistake. I made a terrible mistake," Eden insisted. "I love him!"

"If you really loved him, why would you have fought the match?" Bruce asked in theatrical disbelief.

"Because maybe I wanted to make my own decisions. And I was wrong." She covered her face with her hands. "When the Beautification Committee set the fire, I thought I could use Davis to get revenge—"

"The Beautification Committee set the fire?" Sheriff Cardona wasn't so easy-going right now. "Eva!"

His wife, bundled in a navy wool coat, flinched. "Yes, my love?"

Donovan hung his head and took several slow deep breaths.

"To be fair, you know Eva couldn't have been involved since the fire happened during your wedding," Ellery pointed out, joining them with a smug smile on her navy blue lips. "In fact, I happen to have iron-clad alibis for every single committee member for the time of the fire."

Eva ran a hand over her flat stomach. "I swear I didn't have anything to do with it. But I know for a fact that it was an accident."

"I am going to lock every last one of you in a cell," Donovan growled, pointing his finger at the committee members.

"Technically you don't have cells," Eva reminded him. "Just cubicles."

"I will drive your asses to Cleary just to use their cells."

"What's that sound?" Sammy asked from the inner circle of the crowd.

"Sounds like the marching band," Ellery said.

"Ellery!" Eden grabbed her arm. "I need your help. I screwed up with Davis. I want to be with him."

"Never happening," Tilly shouted. "My son will never be anything but a neighbor to you!"

"They're headed this way!" someone in the crowd announced.

The crowd parted as the entire Blue Moon High Marching Band stomped its way through the park led by none other than Davis Gates.

51

Davis blew smartly on a whistle and the band came to a halt. "Eden Moody," he yelled. "I have something to ask you."

Eden had to give him credit for drama. Blue Moon would be talking about this moment for the next fifteen years.

"Davis, what's going on? Our parents are ready to throw down," she whispered, pretending like fifty percent of the town's population wasn't eavesdropping on them right now.

He blew the whistle again, drowning her out. "Drumline!"

Six kids with braces and acne burst into an enthusiastic drumroll.

"Color guard," Davis shouted over the music.

A dozen teens dumped their flags and rifles on the ground, tripping over each other to unroll a banner.

HeHa?

She cocked her head. This was indeed HeHa Day. She wasn't really clear on what the question was.

"Eden Moody?" Davis yelled. "Would you do me the great honor of going to the HeHa Dance with me?"

Eden's heart climbed into her throat.

Their mothers' screeching was drowned out by the ongoing drumroll.

"We're gettin' tired here, Miss Moody," one of the drummers yelled. "Maybe you could say yes already?"

But Eden was already in motion. She pushed through Ned and Ferguson who were standing toe-to-toe engaged in a staring contest. She danced around Tilly and Lilly Ann as they hurled ridiculous insults at each other.

And when she got to him, Eden threw herself into Davis's waiting arms. "I thought I told you we shouldn't date."

He grinned at her. "I do recall you making some kind of ridiculous speech along those lines."

"And you're still here. Asking me out."

"That I am."

"I'm such an idiot," she told him over the chaos.

"But you're my beautiful idiot," he said with a grin.

"What about them?" she asked jerking a thumb behind her where things had gotten physical. Their fathers were flicking each other in the chest, and their mothers were locked in some sumo style embrace. Sheriff Cardona was radioing for backup.

"They can be someone else's problem for a while," Davis said with a wink.

Eden grabbed the whistle that hung from his neck and blew it shrilly.

"Yes, Davis Gates, I will go to the HeHa Dance with you!"

The part of the crowd that wasn't related to them erupted into cheers. The marching band played a celebratory riff.

And Eden and Davis were too busy kissing to notice the Beautification Committee encircling their fighting parents.

~

"Are you sure I look okay?" Eden asked, smoothing the skirt of her lace sleeved minidress in dark green. She hadn't been planning to go to the dance, so wardrobe pickings were slim.

"You look amazing," Sammy said. Her low-maintenance friend was dressed in a simple black dress, tights, and Uggs that were currently propped on Eden's coffee table.

"You need another layer of mascara," Layla reported. Layla was low-maintenance on the job, but after-hours, she was a freaking knockout. She'd styled her enviable blonde locks in loose waves and topped them with a Santa hat. Her fire engine red dress hit her at mid-thigh, and her gold stilettos made her look like a super model had wandered away from a holiday-themed shoot.

Eden hustled back into her bathroom and swiped on another coat of mascara, took a deep breath, and called her face done.

"Are you sure he'll show up?" Eden asked, poking her head out of the bathroom doorway. "I mean his parents are here, and Davis isn't exactly good at disappointing them."

Under that layer of giddy excitement was the icy edge of old, not-so-dormant fear.

"Judging from their faces at the front desk, I'd say him dating you is less of a disappointment and more of an epic betrayal," Layla said cheerfully.

Given the fact that the Gates' home was still occupied by its renter, and Davis's house was unlivable, Ferguson and Tilly were very reluctant guests of the Lunar Inn for the next week. Bryson, however, was having the time of his life. "You're not making me feel better," she told her friend.

Sammy put down her phone. "Babe, look. This is your shot. Your chance to start something amazing regardless of past, regardless of ridiculous families. This is your new beginning, and you look fucking amazing."

Eden pitched forward onto the couch and strangled her friend in a tight hug.

"It's okay to be excited and nervous," Layla pointed out, cracking her gum. "This is big, and it's real."

"And you owe me twenty bucks," Sammy added.

Layla didn't even grumble when she dug into her gold sparkly clutch.

"You're not going to make her wait to see if he shows up at the dance?" Eden asked.

Layla leveled her with a look. "He'll be there."

And just like that, the yacht-worthy knot that had tied itself in her stomach loosened. Eden took a steadying breath. "Then let's get our asses there so I can make sure Fitz doesn't accidentally spike the kids' punch again." The HeHa dance had offered separate adult and kid refreshment tables after the unfortunate gelatin shot incident of 1997. Since then, the adult punch bowl was traditionally spiked with some form of alcohol that got reluctant adult limbs dancing and mismatched partners making out in dark corners.

It was all part of the tradition.

THE HIGH SCHOOL gymnasium was looking festive in a crazy, someone-got-carried-away kind of way.

When the HeHa fiasco had been dumped in their lap, Eden and Davis had also inherited the mess that was the dance committee. They'd scrapped Charisma Champion's plans for a black and white mime-themed event—and ignored Fitz's suggestion for an event that would pay tribute to farm life during the Great Depression—and went with traditional holiday.

It was magical. Christmas, Hanukah, Diwali, and Kwanzaa had thrown up over every square inch of the gym.

Eden had to hand it to the decorating committee. Navy blue and silver panels of material hung from the ceiling. Twinkle lights cast a soft, holiday glow around everything that stood still long enough to get swagged. Bing Crosby crooned from the sound system, and the dance floor was festooned with stick-on snowflakes.

The entire population of Blue Moon was under this roof, tired and happy from a day of giving. They were decked out in a wide range of festive finery. There were ugly Christmas and Hanukah sweaters, some on purpose and some not. There were pretty gowns on senior high girls and baggy suits on their nervous dates.

There were potted trees scattered about representing every holiday of the season. There was even a tree of meditation mantras, and guests were encouraged to take a mantra. Eden snuck one from where it hung on a branch.

Today is your new beginning. Don't screw it up.

"No pressure or anything," Eden said wryly.

"Wow."

She turned and her heart soared. Davis was here, in a navy blue suit, a vest, and a sexy tie, looking at her like she was a goddess.

"You're here," she breathed.

"You think I'm dumb enough to stand you up twice in one lifetime?" He reached for her, took her hand. "I've been waiting fifteen years to ask you this."

"Ask me what?" she asked, nerves and anticipation dancing through her veins.

"May I have this dance?"

Eden congratulated herself on not swooning there on the spot. Sure, maybe she stumbled over her own feet on the way to the dance floor, but Davis was there to steady her.

He swept her into his arms beside Mrs. Nordemann and Ernest Washington. Ernest was wearing his cleanest coveralls over a green elf sweater. The Volkswagen salesman looked positively festive next to Mrs. Nordemann's long black cocktail dress.

"You look stunning," Davis said to Eden.

"Oh, aren't you sweet?" Mrs. Nordemann responded, fluffing her gray hair. "I tried a new eyeliner."

Eden cleared her throat. "And it looks wonderful on you. Purple is definitely your color."

Davis spun her away melding into swaying couples and silver and gold lights from the DJ booth. "I meant *you* are stunning," he said again.

"You don't have to sweet talk me, Gates," she teased.

"I'm not sweet talking you. I'm wooing you. It's what boyfriends do."

"Are we really doing this?" Eden asked.

"Hell yes, we're doing this."

"What about our parents?"

"What about them?"

"They're not going to be happy," she reminded him. Eden needed to make sure Davis had thought this through.

"Eden," Davis said, tilting her chin up. "Our parents' problems are their problems. You and I can and will create our own."

She took a deep breath and the plunge. "Are you doing this just to make me happy?" It was the last question that she had before she'd give herself over to the glee, the hope. If he wasn't in this for himself, they were going to have problems bigger than a family feud.

His hands tightened on her hips, and she reveled in the feel of his touch. "Eden, I'm doing this for purely selfish reasons. I want to be with you."

"That's why you didn't listen to me when I said we needed to break up?" she pressed.

"For once in my life, I am crystal clear on what *I* want. What's right for me. And believe it or not, that something is you."

She snuggled closer to him and felt him harden against her. "I owe you an apology for the last fifteen years."

"Eden, we've spent enough time in the past. You can spend the next fifteen making it up to me."

"Davis, I was so wrong about you, about not giving us a chance. I've been so wrong about so many things and I'm terrified that it's all too late. That you won't be able to forgive me."

"Sweetheart, you were forgiven before you did anything worth apologizing for. I just had to figure out how to make you realize you were head over heels for me. We've both made mistakes. Hell, there are multi-generational mistakes at play. But I'd rather talk about our future."

"Oh? And what does that look like to you?"

"I'm foreseeing special overnight wine tour packages. Discounts on wine purchased at the inn. Private winery tours or paint classes for inn guests."

"You're turning me on," she teased. "You know I love it when you talk work."

"I see us living together, arguing about wine labels and guest room linens. Unless of course, my father does fire me—I gave him the option today. Then you can hire me as your assistant innkeeper. I'll scrub toilets for you and mow the lawn."

"You didn't tell him to fire you!" Eden gasped. "The winery means everything to you!"

He nodded, stroking those warm palms over her back. "I most certainly did. If my father wants an operations manager who kisses his ass, he can hire outside the family. I'm done with the status quo. It's me and my ideas, or the family legacy gets turned over to a stranger. You, on the other hand, mean everything to me. I'll walk away from the winery, but not you, Eden. Never again."

"I love you." Eden blurted it out before she could chicken out. He'd shown up with a marching band after she'd rejected him. The least she could do was tell him how she felt.

Davis froze, mid-sway on the dance floor. "I beg your pardon?"

"Don't feel like you have to say it back," she said quickly. "I just wanted you to know that I don't know how or when it happened, but I'm in love with you, and before you showed up with the marching band, I was trying to figure out how to back out of the whole break-up thing. I'd rather be happy than right. Although in this case, I wasn't even right. And I'd rather be happy and wrong with you." And now she was babbling.

"Done?" Davis asked with a warm smile.

She nodded, not trusting herself to open her mouth again.

"Good. Because I love you, Eden Moody. And someday we're going to get married and have babies and dogs and force our families into regular social situations. But for now, it's just you and me, and I'm really happy about that."

A crop of goosebumps erupted on every square inch of Eden's body. Tears prickled the back of her eyes as Bon Jovi wailed over the speakers. And somewhere deep inside her, a seventeen-year-old girl finally got her win.

52

Leaning heavily on his high school gym class dance lessons, Davis whirled Elvira Eustace around the floor. Their feet tapped out a fun beat while hologram snowflakes fell from the ceiling of the gym, highlighting Elvira's salt and pepper curls.

"Ladies and gentleman," a voice shouted over the music. "If I could have your attention for one moment." Bruce Oakleigh blew into the microphone on the blue and silver swagged stage. He was wearing a blue sweater vest with a chubby snowman on it. The music cut off abruptly.

"Thank you. Gather 'round. Gather 'round." He waved the crowd toward the stage. "As you know, we like to present the Blue Moon Business of the Year Award during our annual HeHa celebration."

Davis felt Eden tense next to him.

"Every year, the city council strives to recognize a business that exemplifies Blue Moon's mission of inclusivity, community service, and all-around excellent karma. Or, depending on our town budget, it is awarded to the business that makes the largest donation."

"You have got to be kidding me," Eden hissed.

"I'm just kidding, folks," Bruce chuckled, holding up his hands.

Davis squeezed Eden's hand and held his breath.

"As always, the committee had its work cut out for it in determining the business that best exemplifies our mission. But this year, we had a clear winner. This year's recipient not only made it a point to be involved in the community, to give back in creative ways, and to show a vast growth that goes beyond mere economics and success but was also willing to embrace their neighbors in a very literal sense."

"Pick me. Pick me. Pick me," Eden muttered under her breath.

"This year's recipient was brave enough to put their happiness in the hands of his or her community, which is a level of vulnerability and openness that we should all strive for."

"Moveitalong," Ellery coughed into her hand at Eden's elbow.

"This year's recipient, if I may wax poetic for several minutes—"

"Bruce, we've only got about ten seconds before people start sitting down and falling asleep," Beckett pointed out, taking the stage and doing his mayoral best to move things along.

Bruce looked disappointed. "I suppose it's too much to request a fanfare or a drumroll when we announce Eden Moody's name?"

Shrill whistles cut through the crowd. Sammy and Layla reacted with raucous hoots and squeals.

"What did he say?" Eden asked, squeezing Davis's bicep. "Was that *my* name?"

"Get up there, gorgeous," he said, giving her a gentle shove toward the stage.

The DJ played a riff as she walked across the stage, and Davis looked on with satisfaction. Yes, few things were more rewarding than seeing the one you loved get something they so desperately wanted. She was radiant. And she was his. He'd fought for her and earned her.

Bruce shook Eden's hand and leaned into the microphone. "Unfortunately, due to budget constraints, we couldn't afford a trophy this year, but you will have the satisfaction of knowing that had there been a trophy, you would have received it."

Eden made eye contact with Davis, and they both shared a private grin. *Of course* there was no trophy this year. He'd give her one of his... or better yet, he'd have one made for her, Davis decided.

"Eden Moody," Bruce said grandly. "You are a shining example of everything we hope our citizens will embrace in Blue Moon. You're a hard worker who isn't above volunteering her time and opening her doors to the less fortunate."

Davis wasn't sure how he felt about being labeled "less fortunate."

"You have worked tirelessly to build a business, and we're all proud of the adult and entrepreneur and wonderful human being you've become."

It looked to Davis that Eden's eyes were extra bright under the stage spotlight.

She graciously accepted the invisible trophy, posing mid-hearty handshake with Bruce for Anthony Berkowicz and *The Monthly Moon's* camera.

Still gripping Eden's hand, Bruce leaned into the microphone again. "The Beautification Committee would like to take this time to invite Davis Gates to join us on stage," he announced.

If Bruce was intending to have Eden and Davis share the

Business of the Year award, he was about to be incredibly disappointed.

"Come on up here, Davis," Bruce said again.

Eyes on Eden's face, Davis climbed the risers onto the makeshift stage.

Bruce dropped Eden's hand, abandoning the invisible trophy, and gestured to someone in the crowd.

"While we're doling out the good news here," Bruce said. "We'll keep the ball rolling with another happy announcement."

He positioned Davis next to Eden before turning back to the crowd.

"Davis, this is truly fortuitous timing. All of Blue Moon is aware of the tragedy you suffered due to that unfortunate and *completely accidental* fire. Which is why it's my great pleasure to announce that you're the winner of our special Helping Hands Raffle!"

Amethyst Oakleigh took the stage wielding a large glass jar. The crowd, hopped up on good deeds and sketchy adult punch, cheered as if a multimillion dollar lottery winner had just been introduced.

Davis had never heard of the Helping Hands Raffle before, and judging by Eden's expression, neither had she.

"You may not recall entering this completely above-board raffle, but I can assure you did!" Bruce laughed like a nervous Santa Claus. "Here are your winnings! Two hundred and thirty-six dollars!" He handed it over to Davis in a large pickle jar crammed with wadded-up dollar bills.

That explained where the $8 muffin money went.

Bruce shoved the microphone into his face.

"Um. I don't know what to say," Davis told the crowd. They looked at him expectantly as if the pressure of their attention would turn him into an eloquent public speaker. Eden slipped an arm through his. "Thank you for this win?" he said into the microphone. The crowd applauded enthusiastically.

"Wonderful. Wonderful," Bruce crowed. "Eden, do you have a few words you'd like to share about your Business of the Year Award?"

Eden stepped up to the microphone elbowing both Davis and Bruce out of the way. "As a matter of fact, I do. I have a lot to say about this town."

Davis held his breath. He knew exactly what old Eden would say and it would involve a middle finger or two.

"The first thing that needs to be said is thank you."

Davis let his breath out in a soft sigh.

Eden glanced over her shoulder at him and gave him a slow wink. "It's an honor to be part of a town that is so invested in the health and happiness of its residents. And while we may not always agree on methods, good intentions are at the root of every act... no matter how hair-brained or ridiculous or destructive they may seem." She gave Bruce a long look that had his neck turning pink.

She admired her pretend, invisible trophy. "It's no secret that I set out to beat out the winery for this award. And now that I have it in my hands—so to speak—I understand that we're all in this together. This invisible award is for each and every one of us who make the lives of our friends and neighbors better. Every one of you deserves a piece of this trophy because together, we are more than just people and businesses and private agendas. We're a community."

Fitz lit a lighter and held it aloft. Other flames flickered to life around the gym. Those without lighters turned on their cell phone flashlights.

"Community! Woo!" hooted Rupert Shermanski from the back of the crowd.

"Um, thank you. Oh, and I'm sorry for doubting the B.C.

and messing up your plans. That's all I—thanks," Eden said, backing away from the microphone.

Bruce chuckled. "Oh, this was our plan all along. We knew all we had to do was get you two under the same roof."

"But I broke up with him," Eden reminded Bruce.

He waved away her words. "All part of the plan, my dear. You wouldn't have realized how wrong you were until you got exactly what you thought you wanted."

Her jaw dropped and Bruce gave her a wink.

"Diabolical," Davis whispered.

Bruce resumed his unofficial master of ceremonies role, leaving Eden blinking in shock. "If you'll notice, there's a collection jar at the back of the room. The Beautification Committee performs its essential community services at no charge..."

"Come on," Eden whispered, tugging Davis off stage.

The change in his pickle jar rattled as he hurried down the steps after her. Rather than rejoining the crowd, Eden jerked her head toward the hallway.

They pushed through the door, leaving the winter wonderland behind them for the energy-efficient LED-lit hallway.

"What are we doing?" Davis asked as Eden linked her fingers with his and pulled him further into the belly of the school.

Fifteen years later, and these halls still smelled like desperation and homemade deodorant.

"Living out our high school fantasies."

"I don't know what your fantasies were, but I'm fairly sure we could be arrested for mine," Davis pointed out.

She towed him down the hallway, change jingling.

The first classroom they passed was lit up and Eden came to a screeching halt outside the door. "Are those—?"

"Our parents," Davis observed. His mother and father and Bryson were seated in the front row of the classroom. Lily Ann and Ned were sprawled out in the back row. The front of the room was occupied by most of the Beautification Committee. Ellery was lecturing about something on a whiteboard under the title Feuds Are Bad. She didn't seem happy with the answers she was getting from her pupils.

"Are they re-educating our parents?" Eden asked.

Just then Lily Ann spotted them in the hallway. She fluttered up to the door, abandoning her desk. "Get us out of here, Eden!" she shouted through the glass window. She tried the doorknob, and it rattled but didn't turn.

"Are they locked in there?" Eden asked, trying the knob on her side.

Ellery pushed her way to the door, hip-checking Lily Ann out of the way. "Everything is fine! All under control. Go away!" she yelled over Lily Ann and now Tilly's screeches. Ellery yanked the window shade down.

"I don't even care if that's considered abduction. They've already committed arson. Might as well work their way through the felony As," Davis admitted.

They continued their stroll down the hallway they'd last walked together as teenagers. The lockers, then a dingy school bus yellow, were now partially hidden under a colorful mural of flowers, doves, rainbows, and peace signs.

She tried every door they passed. One opened in her hand, and she stuck her head into the room. "Whoops! Sorry Phoebe. Franklin. Didn't know this room was occupied," Eden said shutting the door with a decisive click. "Looks like our favorite town grandparents are enjoying some private time," Eden said sheepishly.

Davis smothered a laugh with a cough.

"A ha!" Eden said, triumphantly turning the door knob on the Household Management and Partnership classroom.

"Have a couples roll-playing script you want to work on?" Davis asked, stepping into the room. It was much the same as it had been fifteen years ago with lab tables.

She turned to face him, ran her hands down his shirt, and let her fingers linger on his belt buckle. "I was thinking maybe we could practice the fine art of make-up sex."

Davis felt his blood empty from his head. He dumped his pickle jar on a nearby lab table and grabbed her hands. "Eden, I..." He had no words. Hadn't he fantasized about a moment like this for most of his senior high career?

53

She locked the door and pulled the shade, enjoying the tangible nerves that Davis was firing off behind her. "I have twenty minutes before my volunteer shift in the inclusivity room," she told him.

Eden turned on the salt lamps at the front of the room before returning to him.

"Don't you want to spend that time basking in the congratulations of your friends?" he asked, his voice raspy as she turned and loosened his tie and worked the buttons of his shirt.

"I want to spend that time closing our circle. It all began here," she said, conversationally as she reached under the skirt of her dress and shimmied out of her underwear. "And I'd like our new beginning to *get off* to the right start."

His erection was already straining impressively at the confines of his black trousers.

"I feel like I should point out that this is reckless and irresponsible," he said, swallowing when she tugged his shirt free of his waist band.

"That's what I'm going for."

"Just so long as we're on the same page," Davis breathed a second before his mouth crushed down on hers.

In one swift move, he backed her against the wall, her shoulders erasing yesterday's class assignment from the whiteboard. His hands were everywhere, turning her skin to fire, her core to lava.

"Oh, fuck," was his strangled response when he found her thigh-high stockings under her dress. "You're my fantasy come to life, you know that?"

She shook her head, letting the words wash over her. She'd set out to rewrite her past and had narrowly avoided reliving it instead. But nothing—not even her own stubbornness—would take this future away from her.

"Twenty minutes?" Davis whispered, moving his lips over the throat she bared for him.

"Closer to eighteen now," she laughed huskily.

"I can work with that," he promised.

When he kissed her, she sighed out his name. There would be no more denying what she felt for Davis Gates.

With a swift move, he lifted her up locking her legs around his hips. Her skirt rode higher than what could be considered publicly decent. He held her there, one-handed, against the wall while he worked his fly down and then stalled.

"You're sure this is okay?" he asked. He was already panting with the need.

Eden loved him like this. Disheveled, dangerous, delicious.

With one thrust, he was filling her.

"Oh God. Oh God," she chanted.

He laughed softly against her neck.

She squeezed him with her legs until he forgot about laughing and started to move inside her. Pinned between his hard body and the wall, Eden could do nothing but take the pleasure Davis delivered.

His thrusts were quick, frantic.

The sound of flesh moving over flesh echoed in the silence of the room. Sweeter than words, the sound of their bodies and breath twining together was a kind of music.

He slammed into her, sure and hard, again and again. His hips hammering her against the wall as she clung to his shoulders.

"Eden," he growled out her name.

"I love you," she sighed the words on one long breath as she felt the tightening, the quaking, of her muscles as her body prepared to let go. "I love you, Davis."

He groaned low. "I've waited so long for those words."

"I know the feeling," she gasped on a particularly masterful thrust.

"Hang on to me, gorgeous," he ordered.

She obliged as her body surrendered to the wave of pleasure he brought down on her. He captured the scream with his own mouth. Kissing her as he pounded into her, her orgasm instantly forcing his. Her world went technicolor, bright and bold and oh-so-beautiful. She felt him, loved him, craved him. They shuddered together, whimpering against open lips desperate for breath. For life.

"You are incredibly efficient with your time," Eden said, huffing out a breath. She reached up to shove her hair out of her face.

"Wait 'til you see what I can do with only five minutes," he teased, slowly lowering her back to the floor.

"I'm not sure I could survive it. I think I'm going to like for real dating you."

With a cocky grin, Davis handed over her underwear. "I'm a catch. Everyone's been telling you for years."

"Yeah, yeah."

The knock at the door had Eden losing her balance and falling back into the wall.

"Miss Moody?"

"Claudia?

"Yeah. Listen, are you coming into the inclusivity room soon? I want to tell you about the prize packages on *Guess Again*. I brought pictures in case you're not an auditory learner."

Eden looked at Davis and patted a hand over her heart.

"That sounds great, Claudia. I'll be there in three minutes," she promised, scrambling to straighten her dress. "How's my hair?" she whispered to Davis.

"It's a disaster. I love you, Eden."

The swift joy that those words brought was humbling and exhilarating.

"Want to join me in the inclusivity room?" she asked. "Rubin's there, too."

"Wouldn't miss it."

They started down the hall. "Hey, I know this is moving fast. But what would you say to hosting both our families at the inn for Christmas?" Davis said.

They stared at each other for ten seconds before they collapsed in laughter.

EPILOGUE

"We're insane."

"We need to have our brains scanned," Eden agreed.

"Why did we think we could do this?" Davis asked peering through the small round window of the swinging kitchen door. "Did you take all the knives off the table?"

"These people could kill each other with dinner rolls. What are they doing now?" Eden whispered.

"They're sitting there in total silence staring at their plates. Except for Atlantis's kids. They just crawled under the table with the dogs. I think Bryson's already under there with them."

Eden blew out a breath and swiped her damp palms over her ruby red sweater. "At least someone's having fun."

It was Christmas Day.

And while the rest of Blue Moon was bellied up to tables laughing with family and singing carols, the Moodys and the Gateses were suffering through their very first dual family function.

The table was set with silver chargers and antique lace.

Davis had personally selected the skinny Douglas fir that stood proudly in the corner of the Lunar Inn's dining room. The food included something guaranteed to please every single family member. A fire crackled cheerfully in the hearth, and classic Christmas carols played on low in the background. The alcohol had been limited to an appropriate amount of wine.

And their guests were behaving as if they were facing life in prison.

It was going better than Eden had expected.

She plucked the open bottle of wine out of Davis's grip and drank.

"We can get through this. The first time is the worst, right? They have to get used to not hating each other," she said, wiping her mouth with the back of her hand.

"Agreed. We can't let this fester until we have kids and they get arrested at a tee ball game for fighting."

Eden handed the bottle back to him and Davis drank deeply. She ran a soothing hand down his back, the charcoal gray cashmere soft to the touch. "We've got this," she promised.

"Listen, gorgeous. I know we talked about telling them. But I think we're pressing our luck. It might push us over the edge into actual bloodshed."

Eden handed the bottle back and nodded. "Agreed. I think telling our parents that we're building a house together on the property line and turning your house into an annex for the inn would be asking for trouble."

"It would be asking for nuclear war."

She rested her head on his shoulder. "Honestly, I'm surprised they haven't gone for each other's throats yet."

"Whatever retraining the Beautification Committee put

them through seems to be working," Davis observed. "Did you see my mom when she started to call yours a buttface?"

"Yeah, what was that rigid muscle spasm thing?"

"You don't think the B.C. used electroshock, do you?" Davis mused.

"Whatever they used, it's a Christmas miracle," she said dryly.

"Do you still love me even though our parents are assholes?" Davis asked, putting the wine down on the counter and pulling her into his arms.

She dropped her head to his chest. "Davis, I'd love you even if our parents were serial killers. Are you sure it's not too much?"

"You're everything that I want in this life. And nothing, not even a group of middle-aged adults acting like cranky-ass toddlers, is going to change that."

She sighed. "Okay. Just checking in."

He pressed a soft kiss to her forehead. "What you and I have is bigger than anything they can dish out," Davis promised. "Besides, if I could convince my father to retire into consultancy, I think we can keep them from murdering each other during the holidays."

"I love the hell out of you, Davis Gates."

He hadn't let her down. Not when she'd been too scared and blind to admit that she loved him. Not when his father had held his position at the winery hostage for a week. Not when his mother threatened to have an aneurysm when he'd invited them to Christmas at the inn.

Davis was sticking.

Meanwhile, Eden's parents had vacillated between a grumpy acceptance and overdramatic despair. Both were manageable.

"I love the hell out of you, Eden Moody," Davis said, fondly brushing a curl off her forehead.

Eden brightened. "You know, the worse time they have here, the earlier they'll leave."

He caught her drift immediately. "And the sooner we can commence Naked Christmas Sex." His hands slid down to cup her butt, pulling her flush against him.

"How are you already hard with World War III brewing in there?" she teased.

"We have a lot of time to make up for," Davis insisted. "Fifteen long years. Wasted."

There was a high-pitched shriek from the dining room.

Davis tensed. "Shit. Did someone just get stabbed?"

Eden snuggled closer, cuddling his erection with her hips. "Nope. That's Atlantis's kids starting their screaming contest."

"You know, I sure could use a preview of coming attractions before we go back in there," Davis suggested, backing her up against the kitchen island.

She met his mouth hungrily, feasting on what he offered her. The newness was still there, but so was the abiding belief that *this* was what she'd been waiting for. This man, who saw her and loved her just the way she was. This commitment. This beautiful relationship.

She didn't know if it was the Beautification Committee's manipulations or just some kind of timely magic. But she'd unlocked herself from the shackles of her past, from a half-century of bad blood. And the next fifty years were looking pretty damn great. Even if both their families were certifiably insane.

Eden slid her hands under Davis's sweater, letting her fingers play across his abs.

"You are worth every second of every inconvenience, every fight, every fire—"

She pinched him, and they both laughed.

"God, I want you naked," she murmured against his mouth, desire flaming into a four-alarm fire.

The door swung open, and Bryson hurried into the kitchen. "You two might want to get out here with the dessert... and more booze," he suggested.

"On our way," Eden promised.

"You're doing well. In another decade or two, they might start using each other's first names," Bryson said cheerily.

Davis waited until Bryson disappeared through the door. "How hard do you think it would be to convince them all to move out of town?"

"I think it's worth a shot," Eden said with a grin.

She plated up the last slice of cheesecake. "Ready?"

He squared his shoulders. "Ready. The sooner we get them out of here, the sooner we can have Naked Christmas Sex."

"I like those priorities."

EXTRA EPILOGUE

BLUE MOON 1966

The fine spring day brought Blue Moon residents out of their stuffy homes and into the sunshine. Winter bones creaked, and vitamin D deficient bodies slowly awakened with the season. Storefronts threw open their doors to welcome foot traffic. Husbands brought their sedans to gleaming shines in driveways with the aid of garden hoses. Wives mixed up the year's first batches of lemonade and iced tea.

Neighbors gossiped over backyard fences while they hung out the laundry to dry.

"Isn't it a fine day, Cordelia?" Laura Beth asked.

Cordelia brushed her bouffant back from her face and dropped the folded table cloth on the picnic table. "Never a finer day," she agreed. "How's little Tilly feeling today?" Laura Beth's baby had been to the doctor twice that week.

Laura Beth waved a hand dismissively. "It was just what we thought. We've got ourselves an ornery baby girl. Nothing wrong with her but her attitude, the doctor says."

Cordelia giggled. "Just remember, if you can't take another

minute of her crying, rubbing just a dab of paregoric or brandy on her gums will get you a few hours of peace."

"And what do I give myself?" Laura Beth laughed. She slipped a pack of cigarettes out of her apron pocket and handed one over the fence.

They blew twin streams of smoke up toward the beautiful, blue sky.

"How's your little Ned doing? He was just the cutest little thing in his Easter outfit," Laura Beth crooned.

"He's just the sweetest little blessing." On cue, Cordelia's backdoor banged open and a little boy in matching baby blue shorts and shirt with a crisp white peter pan collar emerged.

"Mama! The lady with the makeup is here!" Little Ned piped up.

"I forgot all about the Avon lady," Cordelia said, stubbing the cigarette out in the ashtray on the picnic table.

"Send her next door when you're done," Laura Beth insisted. "I'm almost out of my persimmon lipstick."

"I'll do that. And you and Bert are still coming over for cocktails Saturday night, aren't you?" Cordelia said, starting for her backdoor.

"Wouldn't miss it. I'll bring my fondue pot!"

"Perfect!"

The women waved and returned to their respective springtime afternoons.

One house down, a pick-up baseball game was brewing behind the white picket fence of Jenny Zhao's big backyard. It was a rag tag group of children who had been cooped up for too long. The bases were Jenny's mother's underwear, yanked from the clothes line. The bat was a stick plundered from the unruly garden of Bruce Oakleigh's mother. The ball, a monogrammed golf ball discovered in the alley behind the Nuswing home.

Johnny Pierce, who was already quite tall for his age, took a practice swing with the stick while Jenny warmed up her throwing arm.

"Bend your knees more," Bruce called helpfully to Johnny.

Johnny pulled his ballcap lower on his brow. Jenny took the mound—two pairs of her father's coveralls folded neatly on top of a patio cushion.

"Now, I'll go second. You go third. And Jillian, you're up after that," Bruce announced to the rest of his team. Organizing was his specialty as his mother had repeatedly told him. He kept his room spotless, always took out the garbage, and had spent a week making nametags for his classmates before the first day of school.

There was a satisfying crack as the golf ball and stick connected, and the kids watched as the ball sailed up, up, up.

"Home run!"

"Foul ball!"

A good-natured argument broke out as the ball continued its flight over the Nuswings' manicured backyard before finally dropping behind the Moodys' fence.

"Awh, man!"

"Game over!"

Bruce waved his hands. "Wait! I'll get it," he insisted. This was the first game he'd been invited to, and he wasn't letting it end on the first pitch.

He jogged out the back gate of Jenny's yard down the alley past the Nuswings' garage to the Moodys' fence. He tried the gate and found it locked. With a running leap—he had an audience after all—Bruce scaled the fence, his shoes slipping on the wood, his fingers gripping the pickets like he was one-hundred feet off the ground, not two. With a graceless heave, he rolled over the top of the fence and landed face down on Mrs. Moody's garden.

Hauling himself up, Bruce scoured the backyard for the missing golf ball.

"Hurry up, Bruce!" Jenny called from two yards away.

"Didja find it yet?" Jillian yelled.

"Be a hero, Bruce," he murmured to himself. "You can do it."

He tiptoed closer to the house, not keen on Mr. Moody bursting forth and starting an awkward conversation about "when I was a boy..."

Finally, he spotted it under the picnic table. The white ball with red initials. BN. Burt Nuswing. He crawled under the bench and grabbed it triumphantly.

"I got it!" he announced, holding it aloft so his friends could see.

"Throw it back," Johnny called, waving the stick in the air.

Bruce wasn't exactly the best thrower, and Jenny Zhao's backyard looked like it was a million miles away.

"C'mon, Bruce!" someone else yelled.

Bruce glanced around the yard. Maybe if he got up on the picnic table, he could throw the ball farther? With a shrug of his seven-year-old shoulders, he climbed up on top of the Moodys' spotless white picnic table and took a deep breath.

"Hurry up! We wanna play!"

He took a deep breath and got a running start. Things didn't go quite according to plan.

His wind-up was great. But he released the ball just a smidge too early. Early enough that the golf ball hit the brick of the Nuswings' house and ricocheted right through the Moodys' window.

And Bruce didn't exactly come to a stop at the end of the picnic table. He had too much momentum. And that momentum carried him right off the end of the table and into the low fence that divided Nuswing yard from Moody. The fence crumpled against his flying body like that folding chair under his Great-Uncle Artie last Thanksgiving.

"Uh-oh!" the resounding cry rose up from Jenny's backyard. Bruce was tangled in some kind of flowery vine, but other than having the wind knocked out of him, all his pieces and parts seemed to be working.

"Run, Bruce!" Jillian howled.

Bruce brushed himself off, ripping the vines off his legs as he ran after his friends down the alley.

"WELL, that was quite the hub-bub over on Martha Washington Avenue today," Bruce's father announced when he unfurled the newspaper at the dinner table.

"Mabel told me she heard Elton Moody accuse Bert Nuswing of breaking his kitchen window with a golf ball," Bruce's mother said. Gossip was Gladys Oakleigh's drug of choice.

"And what was it someone was saying about a clitoris?" Bruce's father asked reaching for the peas.

"Clematis, dear," Gladys corrected, shooting a pointed look in Bruce's direction.

Bruce was too busy trying to look innocent of window breaking.

"Bert Nuswing jumped right in and accused the Moodys of being jealous of his Laura Beth's prize clematis. I heard it was ripped out of the ground and shredded into a hundred pieces."

"What about the damage to the fence? That's not going to be cheap to repair," Bruce's dad huffed.

"Well, Laura Beth claims she's never speaking to them again, and Cordelia is horrified that anyone would accuse her of property damage. And the husbands are practically coming to blows on the front porch," Bruce's mom said, breathless with excitement.

"It's the most excitement we've had around here in... well, ever," Bruce's father commented.

"Maybe the window and the fence and the clitoris thing were just an accident," Bruce volunteered. His dinner wasn't sitting well in his stomach. Never having disappointed his parents before, he wasn't familiar with guilt.

"Clamato," his father corrected him.

"Brucifer Oakleigh, I certainly hope you didn't have anything to do with all this," his mother said sternly. She was a shrewd woman who sussed out the truth and then spread it around like raspberry jam.

"No, ma'am," Bruce insisted, a bead of sweat running down his back.

"I'm sure this will all blow over," his father said, turning his attention to the roast on his plate. "This is Blue Moon. No one can stay mad forever."

AUTHOR'S NOTE TO THE READER

Dear Reader,

Welcome back to Blue Moon! I hope you enjoyed your visit. I wasn't sure how everyone would feel about the story expanding beyond the Pierces and Merrills, but I *loved* writing Eden and Davis. And you'll notice we still got to spend quite a bit of time with our old favorites.

It's funny, after seven books in this series (counting the prequel, *Where It All Began*. Are you brave enough to read it?) writing in Blue Moon still makes me feel like I'm coming home. I wasn't sure how I was going to top the insanity of the astrological apocalypse in *Holding on to Chaos*, but I think a stink bombing arson really moved this story along. How many authors can write *THAT* sentence?

Anyway, if you loved *The Fine Art of Faking It*, please feel free to leave a review or email me and tell me how super awesome you think I am. Or terrible and weird. Totally up to you! I've also got a hella awesome newsletter that's not at all annoying. If we're meant to be BFFs, don't forget to come hang out in my reader group, Lucy Score's Binge Readers Anonymous. I can honestly say I've cornered the internet on awesome people in the BRAs.

Thank you so much for joining me on this Blue Moon journey! You're awesome and gorgeous!

Xoxo,
Lucy

ABOUT THE AUTHOR

Lucy Score is a *Wall Street Journal* and #1 Amazon bestselling author. She grew up in a literary family who insisted that the dinner table was for reading and earned a degree in journalism. She writes full-time from the Pennsylvania home she and Mr. Lucy share with their obnoxious cat, Cleo. When not spending hours crafting heartbreaker heroes and kick-ass heroines, Lucy can be found on the couch, in the kitchen, or at the gym. She hopes to someday write from a sailboat, or oceanfront condo, or tropical island with reliable Wi-Fi.

Sign up for her newsletter and stay up on all the latest Lucy book news.
And follow her on:
Website: Lucyscore.com
Facebook at: lucyscorewrites
Instagram at: scorelucy
Readers Group at: Lucy Score's Binge Readers Anonymous

ACKNOWLEDGMENTS

Oh, where to begin?

To Kathryn Nolan, fellow romance novelist, who helped me figure out what was missing in Eden and Davis's story. You saved my sanity when Blue Moon tried to drive me cray-cray(er).

To Joyce and Tammy for reading this book 1,000 times before its release just to make sure it was Blue Moon perfection.

To Dawn and Amanda for your ever-ready eyeballs.

To Mr. Lucy for being a sexy publisher AND mowing the lawn.

To Kari March Designs for the beautiful cover.

To the makers of half-caff coffee, savers of my hummingbird heart.

To Jenny Smith, Andrea Qualls, Annie Dyer, Julie Laszczak, Julie Sadowski, Lee Ann Giangrasso Schwartz, Stacy Dillard Kinman, Kerry Bowman, Bobbi Switlik, Barbara McHenry-Peale, Amy Jackson, Natasha Marie, Meggie Cole, Stephanie Michelle Emma Gow, Katie Mae Dickey, Kandee Snider Engle, Nicolle Walker, Alessandra Williamson, Brianna Evans, Tera

Shideler-Baldridge, and Alyssa Hyde for being incredibly kind and available and willing to help me create characters on the autism spectrum. Thank you for so generously sharing your experiences with me.

To my BRAs for being the best people on the internet. I promise someday we'll meet in person. Maybe I'll show up on your doorstep and demand that you make me tacos.

LUCY'S TITLES

Standalone Titles

Undercover Love

Pretend You're Mine

Finally Mine

Protecting What's Mine

Mr. Fixer Upper

The Christmas Fix

Heart of Hope

The Worst Best Man

Rock Bottom Girl

The Price of Scandal

By a Thread

Forever Never

Riley Thorn

Riley Thorn and the Dead Guy Next Door

Riley Thorn and the Corpse in the Closet

The Blue Moon Small Town Romance Series

No More Secrets

Fall into Temptation

The Last Second Chance

Not Part of the Plan

Holding on to Chaos

The Fine Art of Faking It

Where It All Began

The Mistletoe Kisser

Bootleg Springs Series

Whiskey Chaser

Sidecar Crush

Moonshine Kiss

Bourbon Bliss

Gin Fling

Highball Rush

Sinner and Saint

Crossing the Line

Breaking the Rules

Made in United States
Troutdale, OR
12/06/2024